A KISS OF LITTLE CONSEQUENCE

BC HARTWELL

Indian Prairie Press

Copyright © 2018 by BC Hartwell

Published by Indian Prairie Press

ISBN 978-0-9997482-2-0

Library of Congress Control Number: 2018934084

Acknowledgments

Editing:
Megan McKeever, NY Book Editors
www.nybookeditors.com
Marissa Hepner
Laura Heffernan
Amy Stoller

Cover Design by Jessica Bell
www.jessicabellauthor.com

To Jennifer Anne & Marvelous Marianne

ONE

Riviera Maya

HE WORE RAY-BAN AVIATORS, not because they made him look intriguing - even though they did - but because they were identical to a keepsake pair he treasured, sunglasses that used to belong to his dad. Sliding the specs up the bridge of his nose, the young man rushed from the taxi and hurried through the kitschy hotel lobby, out to an open-air café that sat opposite a vast, vacant blue sea.

There was no one there to meet him, however. The café's only patrons were a handful of uniformed resort workers huddled around a table. They sat there quietly, sipping coffee and munching on foil-wrapped, breakfast burritos. An earnest server called out to him from behind the bar. "Can I help you, señor?"

Stepping beneath the aged palapa, the young man let out an audible sigh and then flipped off his shades. "Jamaica tea, please."

When the barman disappeared he slipped onto a barstool to review the text that brought him there:

"Need help. Meet me @ the solysurf beach bar @ 9 am sharp. I'm in a jam, parker"

Perusing the area for his contact, Parker thumbed a reply:

"I'm here. Where the F are you?"

He could see that the resort workers had used the beach-front as a canvass and he couldn't help but admire their artistry. Volleyball courts were precisely outlined - staked with blue nylon boundary lines - and their nets were strung up tightly, ready for action. Sea kayaks, windsurfers, and catamarans were staged enticingly near the water's edge and wiped so clean they sparkled like new. A dozen blue umbrellas were planted neatly across the center of the beach. Beneath them, a pair of wooden lounge chairs reclined, each one supporting two thick, neatly rolled white towels.

The server reappeared and delivered the tea. After tucking in his white, short-sleeved shirt, the man grinned broadly. "Welcome to the Sol y Surf."

Parker nodded toward the beachfront. "It looks like paradise is open for business."

"And what is your business, señor?" the barman asked.

"Same as yours." Parker raised the cup to his lips just as his leg began to bounce nervously on the bar rail. The surface of his tea rippled from the quake. A knot formed in the pit of his stomach and a shiver raced up the back of his neck. Neither sensation, however, was due to concern for his friend's late arrival. Parker was getting the *vibe*, a sense of meaningful attraction. Then a woman appeared in his peripheral vision and the knot unraveled, releasing a rush of endorphins that caused his heart to race.

She looked to be Mayan, with dark skin and long black hair that dangled loosely across her shoulders, shimmering in the sun. A comfortable, cotton dress accentuated her curves as she sauntered along the edge of the cabana, moving cautiously, as if picking out a prospect. Parker was puzzled by the allure he felt for her; he'd never gotten the vibe for a prostitute before. Avoiding eye contact, Parker felt her step closer, into the shade. "Excuse me," she said. "Are you waiting for someone?"

Parker's hair twirled like the head of a mop when he turned around quickly. "Sorry, but you've got the wrong guy."

The girl giggled. "You don't look like an Indian." His physical features did not belie any distinct heritage: tawny skin tone, heart-shaped face, symmetrical chin and black hair parted off center, brushing against his ears. He had an average build, too, with firm shoulders and limber arms well suited for hoisting hefty suitcases.

His reply was still guarded. "And you don't look like the person I'm here to meet."

She blushed. "You are the tour leader, Parker, no?" An honest smile covered her soft face, projecting a beautiful innocence. "I've come for you."

Apparently, he'd misjudged her intentions. "Yeah, ah, you've come for me?"

"Your friend, the Hawaiian, paid me." She held up a twenty-dollar bill.

"Hawaiian?" Parker choked. "You mean Mako?"

She nodded, still smiling. "Yes. Yes. Come." She waved to follow.

Parker sighed. If bullshit were bloodline, then Mako Moreno was a purebred. He tossed some cash on the bar, snatched up his sunglasses and stumbled to his feet. "Where to?" he asked.

She cleared a wind-blown wisp of hair from her face. "Up there. That is where your friend waits." Parker's eyes followed her gesture, way up the shoreline where a canvas tent could barely be discerned, hidden among a thicket of trees. "Come on, come on," she coaxed.

The tour guide did, grateful for the chance to flirt. "So how did you happen to get caught up with Mako?"

"I love to walk this stretch of beach in the morning. It's still so quiet and peaceful." She rolled her eyes and smirked. "Your friend, though, he came up and just made a move on me right away, you know?"

"I know. I mean I'm not surprised. And I apologize if he was rude or inappropriate."

"No, he wasn't rude, not really. He was more the charmer."

"He can be a charmer, that's true."

"But that's what tour guides do. You charm your clients to make more tips."

"Being charming is part of the job. It helps to make people more comfortable and that way they'll have a better time. We don't all work for tips, by the way."

"Well, I have a tip for your friend. Don't try to pick up any woman you see."

"Good advice. Not to imply that you are just any woman." Parker regretted the words as soon as they came out of his mouth. She said nothing more, looking ahead while trudging through the white sand. He followed gloomily, like a kid who just found out he's too short for the thrill ride. After a few minutes, he made another attempt at conversation. "So I assume that you're not a tourist?"

"No, I am from here." She stopped abruptly. "And your friend is supposed to be there." She pointed to the tent about fifty yards away.

"Great," Parker stepped forward, but the girl didn't move. "Aren't you coming?"

She shook her head. "I have to go back."

"Really? Come on. It's okay." He gestured for her to follow but she was resolute.

"Sorry. Your friend is waiting."

Raising her hand, she waved goodbye. Parker watched her walk away, seduced by the sway of her hips and the lingering vibe that pulsed through his veins. Then reality rang in his ears: a loud laugh, Mako's voice, and the strain of a guitar riff. A drumbeat followed, and the music began in earnest. Parker recognized the unusual Tex-Mex tune. Its rollicking organ intro drew him to that isolated tent like some rock n' roll Pied Piper.

Pulling back the flap, Parker saw his friend dancing with a lanky sun-streaked redhead. All Mako wore were a pair of baggy, khaki shorts and black underwear, the exposed elastic band clinging to his hips. Perspiration glistened off his chest. Mako's dancing companion looked as frayed as her old denim cutoffs. Parker sensed that she was someone stuck between bum luck and bad choices. The pair continued to jump around, oblivious to their audience of one. When the music faded to a hiss, Parker's lone applause startled them.

"Parks," Mako shouted excitedly. "You made it." The next song began, and Mako called out. "It's Joe King."

The dancing duet revved it up again. Mako waved for Parker to join in, knowing that the funky musician was special to his friend. After all, a love of obscure music was something the two tour guides shared; a desire to find tunes long forgotten or perhaps never fully appreciated. Parker had been the one to turn Mako on to this tune, to Joe King Carrasco and the Crowns, and Mako relished the coup.

"It's our jam," Mako cried out. Again he waved for Parker to join them, confident his friend couldn't resist the primal instinct to cut loose, but resist he did.

"What the hell's this?" Parker yelled. "I thought you had a problem?"

Dismissing Parker with a shrug, Mako reared his head back to pick up the beat and explode into dance.

Although disgusted by Mako's cavalier attitude, Parker

wasn't surprised. Flying by the seat of his pants was Mako's modus operandi. He always got away with it too, because of a naughty little schoolboy appeal that seemed to cast a spell over his tourists. Mako was reactive on tour, providing wickedly funny standup one minute and then working the room, pouring coffee like a classy maître d', the next.

Parker was a boy scout in comparison, organized and always prepared. He was completely dedicated to his craft. Capable of charming even the most troublesome tourists, Parker built his reputation on a passion for people and places, and an honest, fun-loving persona. His blind commitment, however, made him an easy mark for Mako. "What's going on?" Parker shouted over the music. "You said you needed help?"

Mako danced to the far end of the sticky-hot tent to turn down the tunes. "This is true. I do need help, but let's be polite here." Wrapping an arm around the woman's neck, Mako led her to Parker for an introduction. "This is my associate."

Obviously stoned, the odd bird addressed Parker with a distinct, Texas twang. "Mako said that you were named after Quanah Parker the famous Comanche chief. You know, he turned the world onto peyote, man. Meeting you is truly an outstanding experience."

"Yeah, well, my name is Parker, just Parker."

Her confused smile exposed a disproportionately large cap that had replaced a front tooth. Mako quickly slipped between them, pulling a bandana out of his pocket to dab his forehead. "This is Laurel Ann."

She held out her hand. "So you're like Mako, you dig old music?"

Parker shook it gently. "I'm not like Mako, but yeah, I love all kinds of music."

Laurel Ann stepped back and spread out her arms. "Well, welcome to my hacienda. It's an amazin' space isn't it?"

Reed mats and a tattered woven rug covered the floor. In the corner, two thin, dirty throw pillows rested on a stack of blankets opened up to form a bed. Three plastic milk crates sat at the foot of the bed, heaped with clothes. Parker sensed it was a lifeless place, devoid of any spirit. Even the fresh sea breeze turned stale as it blew in through the screen window. After mumbling facetiously, "Very nice," Parker turned to Mako. "I rushed over here to help you out," his voice rose with frustration, "and I still don't know why?"

"Whoa," Mako shot back, gently dabbing his face with the bandana. "No reason to get hostile. I've got everything under control."

"What's under control? What am I doing here?"

"What time is it?"

Parker yanked out his phone. "9:32."

"Perfect."

"Perfect for what?" Parker asked, nearly enraged. "What's the plan here?"

A smile crept onto Mako's face. "The plan is just to relax."

"I would be relaxing if it wasn't for your text," Parker hollered. "Why are you screwing with me?"

"Oh, I'm not giving you the shank," Mako replied. "I'm giving you a gift. You said you were headed to Xel-Há, right?" Parker nodded, confirming that the beautiful lagoon and coastline inlet - a natural aquatic park he'd heard the locals pronounce as "Chel-ha" - was indeed his free day destination. Mako continued. "Well, I snagged a group of passengers on the cruise for a privately guided tour to that very spot. I figured to cut you in on the action, so we can both make some side cash."

Parker was still upset. "Why didn't you text me that last night? I could've made plans, got some things organized. What about transportation and a passenger list?"

Mako spied him pitifully. "Listen to yourself, man. You're

wound too tight, and honestly, I'm full of concern."

Laurel Ann leaped into the conversation. "Sounds like you could use a smoke. I have exactly what you need."

"No thanks," Parker snapped.

"How 'bout a drink? I got Cuervo somewhere."

"No booze," Mako interrupted. "My man can't handle the hard stuff."

"Don't stereotype him," Laurel Ann screeched.

"Relax, it's no slight," Mako countered. "Hell, my lineage is rife with drunks." A discussion on genetic predisposition wasn't necessary. Mako needed Parker sober, period.

Laurel Ann took a different tact. "Ya'll just need somethin' to calm your nerves." She pulled off her sweat-dampened T-shirt to reveal her naked upper body. Skimpy breasts sagged low like a cow's udder as she bent down and reached into one of the crates, then pulled out a cigar box.

Mako kept a keen eye on the box. "You got hash oil?"

"No," she said pointedly, then offered them a peek. "They're dried roots. Go on, have a chew."

Parker waved her off, but Mako reached in, took out a small dried fragment and slipped it in his mouth. Laurel Ann picked one out that looked like a gnarled toothpick and held it up in admiration. "I'm sure these things have some amazin' health properties, like dark chocolate."

Parker spied the cigar box wistfully. "But you don't have chocolate?"

Laurel Ann ignored him. Popping the twig in her mouth, she chewed, sucked and swallowed the juice, settling into a wry smile like a junkie after an injection. In half a minute, her shorts fell to her ankles. Stepping out of one leg, she flicked her other foot and tossed them away. "It's too damn hot for clothes. I'm goin' for a swim." She cruised out of the tent. Peeking out of the screen window, Parker watched her wiry, naked body run full speed into the lazy surf.

Turning back, he saw Mako standing outside the open tent flap, "Au natural," his ruddy buns dangerously exposed to the sun.

"Time for a dip," Mako said scratching his neck.

"What?" Parker shouted. "You dumbass. What the hell is wrong with you? Why are you hanging out with her?"

"Muy loco, eh?" He let out a laugh.

"Like you know from crazy? Look at you, chewing that stick."

Mako smiled foolishly before leaning over to spit out the nub. "Tastes like dirt anyway."

"Sweet lord," Parker continued, "I can't believe I let you drag me here for some bogus tour to Xel-Há."

Mako shrugged. "Just looking out for you."

"How'd ya figure?"

"I know you've had more than your share of rough runs this past season."

"So what?"

"So we'll be jumping back into the deep freeze real soon, working our asses off in the cold for a couple of weeks. And you know the boss has great expectations for those Austrian ski tours."

Parker wasn't amused. "But what does that have to do with Xel-Há?"

"Like I said, it's my gift to you, bro. The last respite in paradise before the busy spring season begins."

"But I had time to myself today. How is this in any way, looking out for me?"

Mako firmed his chin and raised his eyebrows. "It's not a real tour, just a bunch of chicks and dicks I met on the cruise. I scored Xel-Há comp tickets to pull this excursion together for half the price of anyone else. Cheap transportation is lined up too. If we get a dozen, maybe fifteen, we make a tidy profit."

"There's always a scheme, right? Had to be a scheme."

"Ah my friend, that is just the half of it. You see, I've got a pretty little package getting the group together. She's also lookin' to fulfill a fantasy, which is where you come in. You see, I set you up real good."

"What? She's not good enough for you?" Parker asked.

Mako smirked. "I'm more interested in her friend." He then sauntered out onto the deserted beach still wearing only the skin he was born in.

"Wait a minute." Parker followed him. "When are these people going to show up? When do we meet them?"

Mako stopped dead in his tracks and gestured back down the beach, off on the horizon. "They'll be on the ten a.m. ferry. She'll have them gathered and waiting at the taxi stand. And we are not meeting them. You are."

"Me? Why me?"

"Because," he paused for added drama, "you have swallowed the bitter pill, baby. You are a mere shell of your former self in desperate need of real pleasure. Besides, I can't go. I've got business right here." Mako looked to the shallow sea where Laurel Ann stood amid the crashing white-capped waves, motioning for him to join her.

Parker shook his head. "You have no conscience, pal."

"Neither does she."

Mako strode away smugly. Parker couldn't let him get away with it, though. "I suppose you get what you pay for."

Mako stopped and sighed. "I will remind you, once again, that you too are just a weekend warrior in the battle of love."

"Don't make this about me."

"But it is about you, Parks," he stated. "It's all about you doin' things the right way." Mako emphasized the word "right" with air quotes. "And don't think I don't know what's already going on in your head. You're wondering about the girl I lined up for you. What did Mako say about me? What if she's like all the others, or what if she's the one?"

"That has nothing to do with this."

"It has everything to do with it. Dude, you live an exciting, exotic, transient lifestyle, just like me. That's our allure. The girls we meet on tour don't want to take us home to meet their daddies. They don't want to marry us and live happily ever after. All they want is a memory, a delicious tale of breathtaking sex that they can brag about when they get back home. The women we meet want all the romance you can muster, my man, and all the sexual pleasure you can provide. But believe me, no matter what they say, they don't want to fall in love with guys like us."

Parker couldn't deny the very nature of vacation relationships. He understood that the odds were against him finding someone to share his life with while working a tour. Even if he did find that special someone, he knew it would be a real challenge to make it stick. Still, true love was his quest.

He had one thing going for him. It was that vibe, a unique sense of a woman's aura. The vibe was a tangible feeling that came over Parker, sometimes from someone he had yet to see, but always from someone with whom he shared an attraction. It began with a flutter in the gut that caused his nerves to jangle, creating a warm, intense tingle to spread throughout his body like an infusion of bliss.

The vibe wasn't salacious or covetous. It wasn't the electric allure he felt for round-faced girls with bright eyes and freckles, or the throbbing desire brought on by a short skirt, long legs or a curvy figure. Parker believed the vibe was a spiritual connection, the spark of love. It was one of his gifts. So it was his edge; the vibe would help him overcome the odds and find his one true love.

It wasn't something Mako could ever understand. Parker's friend was committed to satisfying only his physical needs. Leather boots, thick makeup, exposed cleavage or open-toe pumps were what lit Mako's fire. And the liaison they'd spark would be an all-consuming conflagration for Mako and mate: quick sex in a bathroom or head in the back of the plane. Those were fulfilling relationships to Mako; no cherished feelings to be warmed by or re-kindled, just immediate gratification that was quick to ember and turn to ash.

And those were things that Parker could never understand about Mako. Still, the tour guides were bound by a strong sense of simpatico. It was true friendship. The handsome "Hawaiian" grabbed Parker by the shoulders and spoke with genuine concern. "Listen, I just can't stand to see you be the King of Pain." Parker brushed away his hands. Mako Immediately raised them as if to surrender. "Trust me. I really would like to go on this little excursion, but I promised a few of the cruise ship workers that I'd score them some smoke."

"And Laurel Ann does the dealing?"

"That's how she pays for such an amazing space. So come on, brother, loosen up and take this trip for me? My messenger bag is in the tent. It has the tickets and cash to pay for Jorge's shuttle. It's the funky blue bus, you know? Joanie's your girl, the one in charge. She's comped. We'll divvy up the profits fifty-fifty."

"Oh, and remember, my ship is docked in Cozumel until midnight," Mako started for the water. "Let's get together for some quality party time tonight." He shook a fist in the air to reaffirm the plan. After accepting Parker's silence as a sign of agreement, he splashed into the sea.

"Wait a second," Parker yelled, "how'll I recognize Joanie?"

Mako flipped over to float on his back, then called out. "She's a sassy little package who'll probably be wearing a pair of baggy UCLA shorts."

Directing his voice through cupped hands, Parker took one last swipe at his friend. "What if I fall in love?"

Mako replied sternly. "Just remember, you're already in love with your job."

TWO

Xel-Há

PARKER APPROACHED the small group of young tourists hanging out near the cab stand. "Sorry for the wait. I'm Parker Moon, Pat Moreno's associate."

A buxom girl rushed up to greet him. "I'm Joanie." She wore a white bikini cover up, unbuttoned, and the UCLA shorts Mako had mentioned.

Another woman called out. "Where's Mako?"

"Something's come up, so it's just me," Parker replied. The slender, freckle-faced girl immediately looked dejected. Parker turned to Joanie, "And you of course."

Flattered, Joanie tucked a strand of highlighted, Auburn hair behind her ear. "Right, yeah, right," she said, showing off a bleached white, toothy grin. The others gathered around as Joanie twittered through the introductions. "So that's my best friend Rachel, and her brother Neil, and his friend Elvin, but we call him Einny 'cause he's brilliant, but it's not like he's a nerd or anything. And this is Carlos and Tim. We met them on the cruise." She shook her head and in a coy voice added, "We're all just friends."

Parker overlooked the comment, focusing instead on the lower than expected headcount. "So this is it?"

"Yep," Joanie said, "we're the only ones who got up. Quite a party last night."

"Must have been but, still, I mean, to miss the chance to visit such an amazing place as Xel-Há?" That was the gist of Parker's disappointment, and he shook his head sadly. The fact that there would be no profit in the venture would only bother Mako. "Anyway, our ride is waiting," Parker said, then he led them past a short queue of taxis to an old, navy blue school bus.

PARKER COULDN'T IGNORE Joanie's sexual appeal while on the transfer to Xel-Há. She looked comfortably hot in the sweltering jungle heat; her cheeks were flushed red and her soft neck glistening with sweat. He was enticed too, by her ample cleavage that jostled in the confines of that bikini top with every bump and bounce. No matter how she looked though, or what she did, Parker just never felt the vibe for her.

The bus arrived at the nature park, pulled in line, and parked in an orderly fashion. Swinging Mako's messenger bag over his shoulder, Parker hopped out first so he could hand an entrance ticket to each passenger as they exited. He then led the group over to a large wooden map to familiarize them with the park layout. "You guys mentioned the zip bikes? Well, they're way over here."

Joanie squirmed in real close to Parker to voice a command. "Rach and I are gonna mellow out at some quiet spot so you guys can just do your own thing." She looked up at Parker. "Can you find us some chairs near the water?"

"I'll try." Before the guys could drift too far away, the tour guide called out a reminder. "The bus leaves at five. I expect everyone back here at four forty-five."

The ladies followed Parker past Hammock Island and along a path that skirted the edge of the lagoon. They cruised along, awed by a variety of colorful birds roosting in the trees above, filling the air with their chirps and screeches. Soon they arrived at the lip of a small peninsula that offered a panoramic view of the lagoon. Parker noticed two vacant lounge chairs perched on a slight rise. They sat just above a rock ledge that jutted out into the water. Joanie and Rachel quickly dropped their large straw bags on the chairs to stake a claim.

Parker's instincts kicked in, once more, when he saw Joanie stripped of her cover-up and shorts, her physique exposed in a tiny red bikini. Watching her stretch up on tiptoes to observe something in the water, he could almost feel Joanie's sensuous curves. She was soft where he liked soft, and firm where firm was preferred. The pink skin on her back was alluring too, contoured by supple sides that broadened at the hips. Despite the lack of a vibe, or feelings of endearment, Parker couldn't help but imagine how good would it feel to take hold of Joanie's hipbones and nestle her from behind.

While Parker adjusted the lounge chairs, Joanie dug into her bag for a bottle of sunscreen. The scent of coconut oil filled Parker's nose. Its exotic bouquet was erotic and inviting, accentuated by the other sensual pleasures: the sound of the wind rustling through the bushes and the squawk of a parrot in the tall palm tree behind him. When Joanie poured a capful of lotion into her hand, it triggered a reaction from Parker.

"Let me check your sunscreen," he demanded.

Looking guilty, Joanie replied. "What? Why?"

"I told everyone on the drive in that your sunscreen must be biodegradable."

"So what? Really?"

Parker sighed. "It's a park rule and a big deal." Grabbing the plastic bottle, he thoroughly examined its ingredients. "Some ingredients in non-biodegradable sunscreen can cause a viral infection in the coral reef and kill it off. It's not good for anything living in the water."

Rachel poked her head up from behind the wooden slate backs of her beach chair. "What, so you have to buy the expensive crap they sell here?"

"No, actually they'll swap it out for free," Parker explained.

"Doesn't matter," Joanie interjected. "I'm not going in the water."

"Seriously? You have to go snorkeling with me."

"I don't have to do anything," she stated flatly.

"But the marine life here is unreal. You'll be amazed at the fish in the lagoon."

"That's the point. I'm not going in any water that's got fish in it." Joanie's sensuous lips disappeared behind a scowl, and she crossed her arms defensively.

Parker finally got her vibe, and it wasn't a good one. "I didn't mean to piss you off." He handed her back the sunscreen.

"I'm not pissed off. I just don't like being harassed to go for a swim, okay?"

"Okay." Parker shrugged and then called over at Rachel. "Are you up for some snorkeling?" She just waved him away, so he got up and headed for the trail.

Before getting too far, Joanie's voice called out, suddenly sweet. "Hey sugar, can you please do us a favor?" Parker turned to see Joanie at her most provocative, one luscious leg draped over the edge of the chair, beguiling eyes peeking over the top of mirrored sunglasses at him. "Bring back something to drink?"

THE SUN WAS high and hot by the time Parker got the gear, picked up a towel and peeled down to his swim shorts. Settling onto the rocky ledge of the lagoon, he strapped on the flippers, fitted on the mask and plopped his legs into the refreshing water.

The truth was that Parker understood Joanie's apprehension. He had it too. Although an excellent swimmer, Parker had always felt a bit creepy when plunging into a lake, the sea or the ocean. It was a fear of what was in the water, the things he couldn't see. Studying the scraggly rock bottom, that eerie sensation came over him again. Shadows flashed by and his eyes pursued. It was a school of tiny fish moving closer before quickly darting out of view. Determined to get past the fear, Parker took a deep breath through the snorkel tube, leaned back and slid cautiously, feet first, into the lagoon.

A few short kicks kept him flat on the surface. Hushed sounds of his rhythmic breathing were haunting, but the remarkable scene that began to unfold before his eyes soothed those fears. Soon he became oblivious to everything except that awesome underwater world.

A large Angelfish shot out from behind a snarl of rocks. It was slender and a solid ten inches long. Parker pulled back instinctively and then the fish stopped, remaining still, undulating in a gentle, soothing manner. Transfixed on the fish, Parker was awed by its vibrancy: transparent blue scales, brilliant yellow stripes and dark blue dots above both eyes, circled by whirls of white.

The fish turned its spear-shaped head upward, and with a swish of its tail, propelled itself closer, within arm's reach. Parker was amazed and excited, but he did not extend a hand. The creature remained fixed on him and he stared right back, the two beings suspended in a surreal engagement. A creeping shadow darkened their confrontation. Parker assumed it was a passing cloud until a soft thud bopped the top of his head. Glancing up, the blur of water on his mask ran clear, revealing a familiar face.

"Making friends with the fishes?" It was Mako's errand girl

from the cabana bar. She sat in a few inches of water, on a rock ledge nearby. Parker slipped off the snorkel and grabbed the rocky outcropping to stay afloat, his heart stirred by the chance encounter.

"So it's you," he said, trying to get his mind around it.

"Yes, it is," she said playfully.

"It's crazy that we meet again," he replied. "I mean, what are the odds of that?"

"It's not that strange. Everyone comes here."

A chain of tourists in inner tubes floated past as if on cue, but Parker ignored them. "I thought that maybe it was kismet."

"Kiss what?" she asked, making a sour face.

"Kismet. You know, fate. Don't you believe in fate?" The girl's face paled, but she said nothing. Parker tried again. "I'm just saying that it's quite a coincidence that we meet again." In a split second, he realized something else. "And you came over to me. I was just swimming here, just doing my own thing and you came over and knocked me on the head." A smile settled on his face. "I don't even know your name."

"I'm Zafrina," she replied timidly.

Parker remained lighthearted. "Well, you know what I do, so let me guess what you do." He put a hand to his chin. "Are you the sunscreen police?"

She giggled. "No, no, I don't work here."

"So where do you work?"

"I live on Cozumel, in San Miguel."

"That's where I'm staying the next couple days," Parker said, recognizing another coincidence. "I've got a tour group at the Sol Caribe."

"I have a shop in town. I make jewelry and sell gifts, among other things." She held out her wrist to show off a shell bracelet. "Perhaps your tourists would like to visit?"

"So you came here to give me a sales pitch?" he joked.

Zafrina laughed heartily. "That's right. You figured it out. I want you to be my sales rep and send all of your tourists to my shop."

"Gladly, and I won't even ask for a commission."

She smiled and shook her head. "I doubt your friend Mako would make such an offer."

"Certainly not," Parker replied, "but I will ask for something in return."

"Hmmm," She replied warily, "so what's that?"

"Have a drink with me later tonight?"

Zafrina blushed and looked away. When she turned back, her playfulness had disappeared. "Sorry but I can't. In fact, I have to get going." She braced her arms on the submerged rocks to aid in getting up.

"No, wait. What's your hurry?"

"I have errands to run before catching the ferry back to San Miguel. There's another cruise ship docking later, and I expect it will be hectic after dinner tonight."

Parker scrambled to keep her from leaving. "All right, well, maybe we could just have a cup of coffee tonight after you close?"

Zafrina stood up. "Nope."

"Too late for coffee? Then we can go for ice cream?"

"I don't want to do that."

"Why not?"

"Because you want to be romantic with me." Her demeanor hardened, just as it did back at the beach when they first met.

Startled by her honesty, Parker could only say, "Aw, come on." Then Zafrina stretched her arms out for balance and sloshed across the submerged rocks toward shore. All Parker could do was beg. "Wait, don't leave yet."

She peered back at him wide-eyed and spoke with rising fear. "But it's not safe here. There's a barracuda in the water."

Parker frantically pulled himself up to scan the surrounding depths. Then the light bulb went on, and he settled back down into the water. Smiling sheepishly, Parker pointed at his chest. Zafrina grinned, nodded and once again, walked away.

NEITHER THE FISH that swam around him nor the spectacular undersea vistas could take Parker's mind off Zafrina. Thrilling thoughts gave way to frustration because of the distinct vibe that they shared. After returning the gear and changing, Parker headed back to Joanie and Rachel. Trudging up the path, he realized he'd forgotten the drinks. Then the faint sound of an a cappella chorus could be heard. The crisp notes rang clearly, coming from the same area where Parker had left the girls. He stepped over there quickly.

"That's good, that's good, but let's try it this way," a male voice instructed. The harmony began again. Walking past the nearby palm trees, Parker saw Joanie get up slowly. She tugged at a section of red bikini, trying to cover her round bottom when walking over to the edge of the lagoon.

"Come on guys," Joanie squealed. "Can't you go somewhere else? We came here for some peace."

Hurrying to her side, Parker looked down to see a young man standing in ankle deep water. He was on a ledge that jutted into the lagoon about five feet below the mound of shoreline where the girls were relaxing. The guy implored Joanie with praying hands poised above his little round belly. "So sorry that you don't like our singing. People usually pay good money to listen to our band." He then held up his index finger, widened his eyes, and grinned broadly. "I respect your need for rest, so this next song we will sing for you just like a lullaby."

A handful of men struggled through the water upon his command, pushing and laughing until finally settling in a

straight line. Parker looked down at Joanie. "Are they sere-
nading you?"

Just offshore, another voice answered. "The boys are
singing for me." A thin, petite young woman strode gracefully
through the shallow water. "These are my boys. Hector is my
man." She rested a willowy arm on a patch of grass by Joanie's
feet and pointed to the pot-bellied leader.

Hector grinned through a sparsely sprouted mustache. "I
fell in love with our manager, and now I'm always working."

"We're always working." A skinny singer countered, immediately embarrassed by his outburst.

The woman exhaled slowly and looked up at Joanie. "I
apologize for bothering you. We're here for fun but the guys,
well, they just like to sing. Most people don't seem to mind."

Parker squeezed Joanie's shoulder to help her relax. "This
is Joanie, and my name is Parker."

"I'm Itzel." Her genuine smile coaxed Joanie to apologize.

"I'm not trying to be a jerk," Joanie stated. "We just partied
late last night and were completely zoned out here."

"I understand," Itzel replied. "It's a very tranquil place."

Parker turned to Hector. "So what do you play?"

"We play it all, even brass. We call ourselves The Beach
Snakes because our harmonies are as smooth as a snake
through the sand. We're playing tonight in Cozumel. Come
check us out."

"I'll try to do that," Parker replied.

Joanie leaned over to look at Itzel's wrist. "That bracelet is
the shit. Can I get a closer peek?"

Smiling warmly, Itzel extended her arm so Joanie could
examine the piece, adorned with polished black stones and tiny
shells of varying colors.

"Where did you get it?" Joanie asked Itzel.

"My friend made it. She is very talented."

"Where does she work?"

"She has a shop in San Miguel."

Now Parker was intrigued. "Your friend, the artist, what's her name?"

Zafrina. Zafrina Aguilar."

THE HOTEL SOLE Caribe was one of the newer properties in San Miguel, situated on a slight bend in the coastline out on the far edge of town. That was where Parker's group of ortho-dontists was holding their five-day conference. A pre-dinner meeting soirée was being held outside in the elegant sunken courtyard centering the hotel. All Parker had to do was make an appearance before their meeting, and when he walked onto the verandah through the pastel-colored patio, it was like some grand entrance. Sheila Thompson, the group leader, started the fuss. "Here comes our boy."

Parker dutifully greeted each guest and confirmed that they all had enjoyed their free time. He accepted a mojito from a passing server then settled into a conversation with Sheila and her husband, Paul, beside the softly lit fountain.

"I wish you could join us for dinner," she said. "But it's an official meeting, you know."

"Not to worry," Parker replied. "I'll be with you all day tomorrow, starting with breakfast in the morning. In fact, I persuaded the hotel to move it out here to the courtyard."

"Excellent. Breakfast al fresco," Sheila said happily.

"So how was your free time today?" Parker asked.

Paul answered. "Palancar Reef was awesome."

They relived fun times during their leisure hours, and Parker listened happily. A muffled buzz in the left breast pocket of his blue blazer, however, interrupted the pleasantries. It was his phone, and its rare vibration jolted him like a fire alarm. Turning away, he whipped it out and answered. "Parker."

"Well, thank God I've got someone down there." The

panicked voice on the other end of the line belonged to his boss Don Tourcey. "I suppose it's too much to ask you people to answer your goddamn phone?"

"Let me get somewhere private," Parker barked back. He then turned to Sheila and the others. "Please excuse me."

Unlike everyone else at Tourcey Travel Company, Parker didn't cower at Don's rage. He understood that the boss lived in constant crisis mode: personally, financially, physically, and emotionally. So after finding a secluded spot just off the lobby, Parker calmly prepared himself to be the eye of Don's storm.

"It's all right now, Don. You've got me. Everything's okay."

Don's voice brimmed with anger. "If everything were okay I wouldn't be calling."

Don had a good point, to a point. Delegating responsibilities was one of his talents, so he seldom got involved with the day-to-day tour operations. That was Lorrie's job, the Tour Operations Director. "So where's Lorrie?" Parker asked.

"I'm only calling because she can't," Don huffed. "She got sick or something. I don't know, PTO time. Regardless, I'm calling *you* because I can't reach Mako. That son of a bitch is AWOL again. I've left three messages."

"Don't worry, Don. He's here, I'm sure." Parker tried to reassure the boss, confident that Mako was at least alive, somewhere nearby.

"This is serious. We have an issue with the first ski group in Austria."

"What's the problem?"

"Aw crap," Don hesitated. "It's Jack. He quit."

Parker was stunned. "What? When? Where is he at?"

"In Innsbruck I imagine. He just quit today, tonight, whatever the hell time it is there."

The ski tour itinerary flashed through Parker's brain, but he couldn't grasp it entirely. The shock of what Don said had him reeling. His mind finally focused on Lorrie. Among her many duties was to supervise all of the tour guides, so Jack was ultimately her responsibility. More worrisome though, was the fact that Lorrie was Jack's girlfriend, an extended office liaison of which Don was utterly unaware. It was a relationship Don couldn't be aware of because of a company policy that forbids personal relationships between supervisors and subordinates.

"What does Lorrie know?" Parker asked.

"Not much. She only had a few minutes on the phone with Sally before she had to leave."

"What did Sally tell her?"

"That Jack was acting strange last week, not like himself, and that he was shirking his responsibilities. Apparently, when she called him out on it, he jumped all over her. Said he'd had enough, that he quit, that's all. Sally said he just freaked out."

"Has Lorrie spoken with Jack?"

"Not that I know of," Don concluded, "but I doubt it since she had to bug out of here. I'm sure she'll get it all straightened out tomorrow."

Parker shook his head in disgust. "So why did he just take off like that?"

"I don't give a damn why. I'm just worried about handling the trips. It's the very first tour, and there'll be another large group coming in on Saturday."

"You know I'm scheduled to be out there to manage the last three tours?"

"I know your schedule," Don replied sarcastically, "but that doesn't help me right now, does it? Jack was supposed to be our anchor out there. He knows the place better than anyone and speaks the language like a local. More to the point, we're contracted to have two guides out there right now, so Lorrie's going to send Mako ASAP."

"Not Mako."

"Who else?"

Who else indeed? Parker thought, anyone but Sally's nemesis. In her early thirties, the Asian-born guide was an eternal teenager: cheerleader pretty with unusual, flashing brown eyes, athletic build, and a spirited smile. A stinging divorce, however, had ruined her on relationships. So she focused on work, and a firm Christian conviction. Mako had a conviction of his own, however, pursuing Sally with the zeal of a perverse knight seeking his holy grail.

"Don, I can deal with this. I can easily get there by Friday."

"Forget it, Parker. You've done enough shit details this year. Mako gets back Friday night, and we'll have him on a flight Saturday, as early as possible. Now can't get him there in time, so Sally will just have to handle the Saturday turnaround herself."

Parker was worried. "How tough is it?"

"We've got eighty-eight going out and ninety-six coming in, with a few hours between the arrivals and departure."

"That's pretty hairy."

"She can handle it. She'll have to handle."

"I thought you were trying to build momentum with these trips, and at least double our space out there next year?"

"That's right. I can probably get the tour sponsor to sign a deal right after these trips if we prove our expertise and get the space."

"So we can't afford any miscues, right?"

"Okay, I know where you're going with this," Don said calmly, "but I can't afford to have you burned out either. Lorrie has scheduled a few days downtime for you so take advantage of it. You'll be in Innsbruck in ten days regardless, and we'll need you to be at your best."

"That's all you'll ever get from me, Don."

"I know. Now go find Mako and have him call me, pronto."

Parker hung up and took a deep breath. Peering out of the sprawling hotel window, he saw the taillights of the cars as they zipped along the main coastal road and into the village of San

Miguel. Just offshore, the cruise ship's silhouette rested beneath a flood of lights. Beyond the ship, far off in the watery darkness, was the mainland, the last place he'd seen his wayward friend.

Mako could be anywhere, he thought. Still, he was out there somewhere, and Parker knew he would find him soon enough. That search would have to wait, however. Something much more important beckoned him.

THREE

Cozumel

THE TAXI ZOOMED along the boulevard, hugging the median's white concrete curb to pass a whining motor scooter. Centered on the median were palm trees - their trunks also painted white - and they zipped by the car so closely, so often, that it made Parker dizzy. The cab stopped at Calle 7 Sur, and Parker paid the fare. Strolling up the brick walkway, he passed empty benches, a string of black street lamps and a handful of shops. Soon he arrived at a tiny storefront where a dim light shone through a square picture window. A wooden sign carved in the shape of a small, colorful bird hung above the entrance. It read, *El Periquito Místico*.

Pushing through the full-length screen door, Parker noticed a single customer: a tall, bald man standing at a glass counter. Then Zafrina stepped into view, entering through an opening behind the display case. The shopkeeper looked sharp in a strapless, black and white patterned dress that hung just above the knee. She smiled pleasantly and honed in on the prospective sale. It appeared that she was unaware of Parker's presence.

"Is this what you're looking for?" She set a small white box on top of the glass top, gracefully posing her hand next to it.

When the man leaned in for a closer look, Zafrina glanced up and quickly gave Parker an unwelcoming glare. He grabbed a carved-wood Mayan ceremonial mask displayed nearby and held it over his face, pretending to hide from her wrath.

"These are nice," the man finally stated, squinting to get a closer look at the earrings. "What do these crescent moon symbols represent?"

"That's a Mandorla," she explained. "They face each other, forming an almond shape that is the ancient symbol of wholeness." The man nodded as if he understood. The shop-keeper continued, "You do have excellent taste. And you won't find a better value for custom silver-work, see?" She showed him the tiny price tag. "Certainly you noticed that they match the necklace you've been admiring?"

"I didn't notice that," the man said, happily surprised. Zafrina reached into the bright jewelry case and selected a sparkling silver necklace nestled between two rows of sleek rings.

"My shop has only set prices, but I will offer you a discount of ten percent if you buy the necklace with the earrings."

"That sounds like a good deal," he agreed.

"When you get home and have them appraised you'll see what a good deal it is."

While Zafrina flowed seamlessly through the sales process, Parker set the mask down to check out the other collectibles on display. There were expertly carved decorative plates, and cere-monial bowls resting on legs shaped to resemble those of a jaguar. He also saw a collection of ruddy, etched vases deco-rated with line-drawn hieroglyphics and animal symbols: a croc's head, an arching crane, a smiling frog and a squawking monkey.

One piece, in particular, held his interest. It was a stone

statue of a human head resting on an ornate square base. It looked to be a prominent male, perhaps a king, with narrow, oval eyes and a broad flat nose that ran flush to his forehead. A chiseled headdress rested on him like a crown, extending with furrowed lines above his head and then flopping forward like a rooster's tale.

Tempted by its tactile surface, Parker ran a finger delicately along the statue's nose and then felt the crevasses in the head-dress. "Please don't touch that," Zafrina cautioned.

Parker pulled his hand away. "I'm sorry."

Zafrina stood nearby with crossed her arms. "How did you find me?"

"Well, it was just another one of those strange coincidences, really," he replied. "I met a friend of yours, Itzel, back at Xel-Há, after you left."

"You shouldn't have come," she stated coldly. "I'm going to be very busy tonight." Glancing around, Parker noticed that the customer she was helping was gone. The shop was empty. His puzzled expression challenged her statement, so she explained. "The rush always comes right after dinner, in about an hour. I'm sure it will be hectic then."

"I'm sure it will." He eyed a wooden parrot and a colorful toucan sitting on perches dangling from the ceiling. "You certainly have some fascinating things to sell." A curtain of green beads that hung in a rear doorway caught his attention. A faint light seeped from behind them. "What's back there?"

Zafrina squeezed herself tightly. "I told you, I make jewelry, among other things." Her full lips thinned noticeably, and her last three words smacked out of a dry mouth. Parker saw tumultuous emotions reflected in her eyes, a mysterious mix of feelings that fascinated him. Just like the Angelfish encounter in the lagoon, he felt compelled to reach out, to cradle her soft brown cheek in his hand. But she moved away and walked behind her display case to retrieve a business card from a stack by the register. Stepping back, she presented it to him.

"What's this?"

"Other things."

Centered on the white card, Parker saw a colorful image of an ancient Mayan "Tree of Life" glyph. He read the raised lettering printed to the left of the figure.

Zafrina Aguilar
Spiritualist

"Are you a shaman?"

She straightened up defensively. "What do you know about shamans?"

"I know the history of shamanism in the Mayan culture, the daykeepers, and their role in the sacred calendar. I also know that shamans still play an active role in the daily life of indigenous communities in southeastern Mexico, as well as in Guatemala and Belize."

Zafrina's angst receded. "I grew up in the state of Chiapas," she rubbed her chin apprehensively before sharing more details of her personal life. "I was born to the calling, but so little has changed back home."

"I don't think home is supposed to change," Parker theorized. "We are, though."

His words seemed to comfort her, and she continued. "I left home to study in Vera Cruz."

"What did you learn?"

Her eyes roamed around the room slowly, taking stock of everything in that shop, until finally settling on the tour guide. "I learned that science has yet to prove that the ability I have is real. But it is real. So you understand? I see things about people."

Glancing back at the green beaded curtain, Parker was

intrigued more than ever. "You don't make jewelry back there then?"

"No." Zafrina snickered before growing somber. "Some people say what I do in that room changes their lives."

"A very perceptive psychic once told me," Parker said, "that she was blind to matters of her own heart. Is that true for you?"

"I had no idea that when I left my village, I would end up here, still so deeply connected to it. But I love this place. A woman can make a life of her own here. This place is the best of both worlds for me. It is what I was, and who I am." Although thrilled by her sense of pride and independence, Parker was dismayed that she didn't answer his question. That worry, however, was misplaced. "I know this, Parker Moon," she said, carefully lifting her business card from his fingers. "You are a dangerous man."

"Really?" Parker was incredulous. "I'm harmless."

"Oh, no," she shook her head. "You are the most dangerous kind. You are handsome and full of life. You are nice and sincere, and I am very attracted to you. But I also know that someday you'll be gone, and I will be left alone."

The certainty in her voice pained him. "That sounds like something Mako would pay you to say."

"I told you, I see things about people, even things that they may not like to hear."

"That's got to be tough on repeat business." Like sunshine through the clouds, a smile burst across her face as she held back a laugh. Parker took advantage of it. "Is that it? Is that all you see for me?"

Zafrina didn't reply. Instead, she looked out the front window at the quiet street. Slowly, she moved to the shop door and turned around the "Open" sign. Then she took Parker's hand, and they passed through the green beads together.

Much like its designer, the room they entered was an

eclectic mix of old and new. There was a high back leather chair sitting in front of a massive wooden desk. Two sleek framed university degrees hung alongside an embroidered image of two green parrots surrounded by colorful flowers. A MacBook Pro was flipped open, sitting under the soft light from of table lamp made out of vintage pottery, showing off a painted image of green-stemmed, white lilies blossoming on a dark blue background.

A sprawling, built-in bookcase covered the opposite wall. Jammed with books, Parker tilted his head to read a few of the vertical spines: *The Ancient Maya: New Perspectives*, by Heather McKillop; *An Introduction to the Study of the Maya Hieroglyphs*, by Sylvanus Griswold Morley; Barbara Tedlock's *The Woman in the Shaman's Body: Reclaiming the Feminine in Religion and Medicine*.

A distressed, ladder-back wooden rocking chair sat like a throne in the middle of the room. It rested on a striped, woven rug. Zafrina gestured for Parker to sit in it. Walking across creaking wooden floorboards, he slid into the oversized chair and rocked nervously. Zafrina sat in the leather chair and tapped a few keys to bring the computer to life. She then pulled out a notebook and a sharp pencil.

"What is your sign in the western zodiac?"

"I'm a Pisces, but I don't believe that a person's life is pre-determined."

"Astrology doesn't tell me what's going to happen. It only tells me about your place in the universe. That knowledge helps me understand the opportunities and challenges that I will see for you. I don't envision outcomes. Those are left to choice." Squinting at him, she asked, "I assume you believe in free will?"

"I believe in freedom, mostly. My grandpa taught me that no two people are alike and that no one has the right to tell another person how to live. The gift of life is an opportunity for us to become our own unique, independent beings. He also told me about the Medicine Wheel. He said it was my path, the course of my evolution."

"I know of that. Some call it the Sacred Hoop," Zafrina stated assuredly. "And there are numerous interpretations of its healing powers."

"Grandpa says that where we are born on the wheel determines our natural perspective. If we travel the wheel, we'll learn about other ways, and understand other perspectives."

"You are very in tune with your roots."

"I'm just like everyone else really, a mix of different of ethnicities. I enjoy learning about my ancestors, but cultures evolve. They come and they go. It's the values that we learn from them, that's what matters. I trust those values to guide my life. The rest is up to me."

Zafrina shook a finger at Parker. "That's what I tell my family. You've taught me well, now trust me to find my way, and to use my gifts wisely." With a loud smack of her lips, the spiritualist sat back down to focus on the business at hand. "Where, on the Medicine Wheel, were you born?"

"To the South. Grandpa says it's the way of truth and innocence."

"When is your birthday? It would help too if you knew the exact time."

Parker shared as much information as he could while Zairian pounded away on the keyboard. A printer jumped to life as she turned to face him. "In the western zodiac, you are Pisces. It looks like you are true to that sign. You are a person immersed in the water. The water makes you complete."

She was dead wrong, he thought, and considered how to tell her that politely. Zairian, however, beat him to it. "The fear you have is not with the water itself, but what lies beneath it. You fear having to face those emotions hidden deep inside of you. But the water ... the water is where you belong."

There was power in her words, but Parker didn't tell her

that. Zairian reached for the printed page. "I've completed a chart of the predominate astronomical forces and other aspects of influence." She took a minute to jot some notes on the paper before handing it to him, and then she stepped away, allowing time for him to study the strange circular diagram.

It was complicated, with various sections, scribbled numbers, circled letters, and glyphs. Parker couldn't discern anything from it, but when Zafrina settled back in her seat, she shared a detailed explanation of its meaning. Then she reached over, flicked off the lamp, and rolled the leather chair up to the edge of the rug in front of him.

Light still shone in the room. It was the flickering of candles from somewhere behind him, candles that Zafrina must have lit. "Close your eyes," she commanded. Parker obeyed. Sinking back into the chair, he began to rock gently. The motion was relaxing, and he felt strangely at ease, like a child swaying on a playground swing.

"There are five directions in Mayan spiritualism," Zafrina stated in a soothing voice. "The East is our future. We face the rising sun each morning as we face our goals and the challenges to our aspirations. Our backs are to the West. That is the way of the past, and it is full of the things that help make up who we are, and who we can be. North, on your left, represents our feminine way, while the South, the right, is much more masculine. The ancients perceived this to be the source of prosperity and the richness of life. The fifth direction is our center. It is the place where we take root, our core. It is the center of ourselves in the world."

Parker's eyelids grew so heavy that he couldn't open them if he wanted to, but he didn't want to, even when Zafrina got up and moved alongside him to speak.

"I feel great emotion and energy at your core. Your heart is exposed for all to see, and so you are easily approached, easy to speak with and easy to love. You are a giving person, even to a fault. Still, emotions are complex. You are funny, pleasant and positive, but like many people, humor is also a mask for you to hide behind." She stopped there for half-a-minute. When she spoke again, it was with a firm voice. "Your grandfather is wise. Innocence is your very nature, and innocence is truth. Remain faithful to that innocence. It will never lead you astray."

The words dripped out of her mouth and into his head, sweetened by hope and soured by fear. Parker turned them over in his mind while Zafrina moved behind and rested her hands on the back of the chair.

"Your desire to be the hero is rooted in your southern energies, your masculine side. However, there are strong maternal instincts inside of you too, driven by northern energies and enhanced by learned experiences. Those are every fulfilling traits but left unrestrained they can be very unhealthy. You must learn to find a balance. Recognize that you can't always be everything to everyone. Learn to say no, and trust that if you are true to your nature, you'll find fulfillment."

Zafrina's next utterances began like a pulled thread: slowly, carefully, and her words began to flow as they unraveled from her mind. "Looking back on your western energies, I feel the presence of a father figure. He tells me that despite the pain of his loss, there is no emptiness inside of you. His spirit fills that void. He has healed you so now you have the gift to heal others. You lead many people on their vacation journey, but there are many others who you guide on a path to healing. That is a great power, a wonderful gift to have."

Zafrina paused while she stepped around to the other side of the rocker, circling him like a graceful bird. "In the future," she continued, "I see a lot of movement, of course, because of your business." A few more seconds passed in quiet so she could grasp more premonitions. "I see that your next trip will be cold with lots of snow. I'm just shivering to think of being in such a place. But you will want to go there very soon, to help with a problem. You will go to help out a friend who is in need."

Another long stretch of silence prevailed, creating an eerie calmness that hung in the air. Parker sucked in a full breath of it, then peeked to see Zafrina back in her chair, right in front of him, eye to eye. Her demeanor was warm as if comforted by the vision she was about to share. "I also see a woman there."

Although the attraction Parker felt for the spiritualist still tugged at his heart, a sense of intrigue began to excite his inner being. The emotional force compelled him to lean closer to her as she continued. "She is dealing with a troubled relationship. In you, she will find renewal and a new way of seeing." Zafrina paused, and a smile spread across her face. "You will ignite her heart and her brilliant aura will shimmer like a golden star."

There was something else too, and the spiritualist ruffled her brow, taking some more time to sort things out in her mind. "I also see her connected to Belgium somehow. I'm sorry. It's a bit confusing, and not much clearer to me than that. Perhaps that is the place of her birth or where you will meet her."

Zafrina's chest heaved, and the expended air seemed to settle her body and focus her mind. Shifting in her seat, she eased forward to squint at Parker, as if estimating his value through jeweler's glasses. "I feel strongly that you and she will be very much in love."

Easing back in the chair, Zafrina closed her eyes. She ran her fingers through her hair and then weaved them together to cradle her head. It was a short rest. She soon sprang to life, reaching over to turn on the desk lamp.

The sharp luminosity was like a splash of cold water in Parker's face, shocking him back to the physical realm. Immediately he was drawn to Zafrina's physical beauty: one exposed bare shoulder and the other, supporting thick strands of her jet black hair; her enticing thigh, the smoky-dark skin narrowing to a cute little knee.

But her words, her psychic perceptions, were just too hopeful to ignore. Again, Parker inspected the room: her degrees and the artwork, the wall of books. Slowly he started to rock. His thoughts mimicked the motion, back and forth, from a promising love waiting to be discovered somewhere, to the deep-seated attraction he felt for the curvaceous shopkeeper and enigmatic spiritualist.

Parker found the silence between them uncomfortable, so he was compelled to say something. "Is that it?"

"Yes," Zafrina responded swinging around in her seat. "I hope it will help you in some way." She smiled faintly. "I'm sorry to rush you out, but it is for the best. I should get back to other business."

"Ah, yeah," was all he could say. And then, "I'm sure you don't do this sort of thing for free. How much do I owe you?"

"For you it's free. Consider it a going away present." She peered at him playfully.

Parker looked playfully annoyed. "Ouch," was all he said.

Zafrina blushed apologetically then looked away, her eyes finding a spot on the wall by her framed degrees. That spot held her stare, but Parker sensed that it was he who occupied her mind. Back and forth she seemed to deliberate, just as he'd done, weighing something serious like a judge pressed for a verdict. Her indecisiveness was palpable, but when a determination was made, it came like a landslide. Parker could see the doubt fall from her face as she hoisted herself out of the chair and held out her hand. "Come. We only have twenty minutes before I must re-open."

THE NARROW STAIRWAY WAS DARK. Parker brushed his fingers along the wall to guide each step. They climbed to a second-floor room where dim light seeped through the thin slats of the shuttered plantation blinds. Zafrina stepped up and threw them open, allowing the moonlight and the smell of the sea to rush in.

Parker moved behind and gathered her waist in his arms. She covered his hands, comforting him with her grip then loosened his fingers and turned around. A neighbor's light came on, lightening the room enough to brighten Zafrina's cotton dress. It also exposed a twin-sized bed that sat beside the window. Casually, she slipped out of her t-strap leather sandals and eased onto the twin mattress. The neighbor's light went out.

Lying on her back with an arm tucked beneath her head, Zafrina invited him to curl up next to her, so he did. A section of sky visible through the window drew her attention. He lay still, watching the whites of her eyes roll from side-to-side. She was searching for something, he thought, some constellation or a celestial alignment of some significance. Hopeful to share in her cosmic search, Parker, too, perused the heavens. He looked around and then pointed to the low horizon. Her eyes followed his finger as it traced the path of a shooting star.

Zafrina didn't bristle when his nose pressed against her neck, trying to discover her scent. She didn't react when his arm fell across her belly and squeezed her hip. But when his lips pressed against the soft skin behind her ear, she faced him with anguish and frustration. "Please, no," she whispered, clutching his chin in her hand. "I can't."

"You can't or won't?"

"I can't, Parker. I just can't."

He sighed. "I respect your decision. It's just—"

"It's not virtue," she interrupted. "And it certainly has nothing to do with a lack of desire. The truth is, I would prefer not to know what I'll be missing." The spiritualist hooked a finger in his hand and gently rubbed the back of it with her thumb.

"I understand," he replied. "I do." Tugging at her hip, Parker coaxed her to switch positions. She did, wrapping herself around him like supple satin fabric, her head nuzzling his chest.

Mako would be full of abuse if he ever discovered that they only cuddled. But Parker had no intention of sharing Zafrina with Mako or anyone else; not one detail. Instead, he selfishly savored every second of those twenty minutes with her; her body warmth and slow, rhythmic breaths; their tender caresses and gentle squeezes. But it was precisely twenty minutes later - Zafrina angled her watch in the moonlight to make sure - when she lifted herself off of the bed and whispered, "I must get back to work."

He followed her down the stairs and into the office. They stepped across the coarse rug where Parker nudged the rocking chair in motion before stepping onto the hardwood floor. Zafrina pulled back the green beads and escorted him to the exit. She then stepped up to unlock and open the big wooden door.

Before flipping on the lights Zafrina turned to face him, her eyes filled with a longing that still throbbed in her heart. She slipped her arms around his neck and they kissed. After a few sensuous seconds, her head fell on his shoulder and they embraced firmly, fully, and with finality. Parker shared her anguish with a deep sigh and then slowly pulled away. They stared at each other until she blinked, and reached to flip the light switch. He spoke just as she pushed open the screen door. "Thank you. It was nice to be with you."

Zafrina acknowledged the thanks with a gentle nod. He hesitated to leave, but then did so and the flimsy screen door slammed when it closed behind him. After taking half-a-dozen steps away, Parker stopped, turned and walked back. Leaning against the screen, Zafrina looked tormented, as if the whole evening had come to ruin.

"What is it?" she demanded.

Parker smiled ever so softly and then held up his phone to show her an image of Itzel's bracelet. "Do you have a pair of earrings to go with this?"

THE BAND WAS in full swing by the time Parker arrived. He perused the crowd: an eclectic mix of cool locals and hip tourists. The musicians were set up on the back of a flatbed truck. Two huge spotlights, one on top of the cab and one on a long pole along the side, drenched the portable stage in white light. Hector strummed a traditional Mexican tune that carried across the sand, past a roaring bonfire and a smattering of dancers and couples engaged in close conversations.

Standing in front of the stage/truck was Itzel. She wore a turquoise blue tie-dyed dress, and she clapped her hands in rhythm all the while staring intently at her man on stage. "Hola," Parker called to Itzel.

The girl turned around, smiled, and waved him over. "Hola. Hello."

"I visited your friend," he yelled above the music, holding out the earrings he bought from Zafrina, "and we agreed that you needed these to complete the set."

Itzel's face disappeared behind an enormous smile, but she hesitated to accept the gift. Parker nodded with assurance. Eventually she agreed, and slipped them into her pocket. Parker felt a tap on the top of his head.

"Hey dude, I suggest you should quit talking and start dancing." It was Hector, standing on the stage above, acknowledging the gift with a warm grin. The musician motioned to the dance area with the neck of his guitar. Parker happily obliged, wrapping an arm around Itzel. She let out a shrill laugh and then clung to his shoulder as they strolled together out into the middle of the mêlée.

The poetic voices of "The Beach Snakes" harmonized perfectly with their wanton, acoustic guitars and the haunting wail of their horns. "I want Hector to see us," Itzel exclaimed. "I want him to be jealous. He doesn't dance with me enough."

Showing off, Parker went into serious swing dance mode. He twirled Itzel around, from a basic step to a tuck turn, from a swingout to a push around. When she snapped her head at the stage to lock eyes with her man, Hector beamed. But the only one jealous was Parker. The mirth-some expression on the tour guide's face hid the envy he felt for the couple. The richness of their love was something he coveted.

Parker looked at Hector again. The musician was still smiling and flirting with Itzel. Someday, Parker thought, that'll be me. Comforted by that notion, Parker was lost in the music, lost in the dance, and lost in the arms of the lithesome young lady who floated like an angel across the sand.

Unfortunately, Joanie found him. "So there you are," she said just as the song ended. Joanie ignored Itzel and, with a determined look in her eye, grabbed Parker's hand. "Come on. We've got a fire going down the beach." She wrapped her other hand around his bicep and nodded to a lone blaze a hundred yards away. "Mako's going to grab some tequila," she explained. "We've already got a bunch of beers."

Glancing at the bar, Parker noticed Rachel flirting with the bartender, holding the boy close with her solicitous smile. The glow of love flickered in his eyes while Mako snuck in behind him and lifted two bottles off of the unguarded table. Annoyed, but resigned to his fate, Parker waved goodbye to Hector before turning to his dance partner. "Muchas gracias, Itzel."

PARKER SAT CROSS-LEGGED, furthest from the fire. Joanie sat right in front of him, her back resting against his knees. Mako got up, stepped over and dangled a bottle of tequila in Joanie's face.

"Oh no," she cackled, "I can't drink anymore, I swear." Grabbing the bottle, she chugged down a mouthful anyway. Then she handed the liquor back to Parker, and he passed it along to the tow-headed Einny.

Kneeling to poke at the flames with a stick, Mako began another story about life on the road. He had been entertaining the group for quite awhile, long enough to put Rachel to sleep. She lay passed out in the sand a few yards away. Meanwhile, Joanie and the guys clung to Mako's every word. Parker's indifference went unnoticed. He had heard every one of Mako's tales far too often to care.

Regardless, Mako's memories couldn't compete with his recent remembrances of Zafrina. Parker still coveted her, infatuated by her confidence and independent spirit, thrilled by the vibe they shared and calmed by the warm weight of her body resting tightly by his side. Although intrigued by her psychic perceptions Parker took no comfort in them. They were still just words to him - wishes really - to be tossed aside like coins lost in a fountain.

Parker's eyes fell on the soft, pink skin that ran along Joanie's spine. Once again he was tempted to reach out and touch something. Once again he held back, not wanting to lead her on in any way. She slowly squirmed as if sensing his quandary. Then she glanced back at him and smiled seductively before returning to Mako's story.

Parker was drunk, and he wondered why Zafrina hadn't foreseen the condition. She hadn't said anything about how he would be feeling just then either; sad, lonely and all alone, completely detached from the group of acquaintances he'd befriended that day. If only it were Zafrina snuggled up to his legs, he thought. If the soft back he longed to caress belonged to *her*, someone he had feelings for, then who knows? Perhaps that acquaintance could become a lover, and that lover may be the *one*.

If it had been Zafrina, then he wouldn't be wasting time listening to Mako's musings. He'd just get up, grab a blanket, and lead her down the darkened beach. They'd walk along, sharing their loving vibe through clasped hands. Their beating hearts would spread that exuberance through every vein and capillary, nourishing every cell in their bodies. Full of each other but not yet satiated, they'd stop to kiss.

He would spread the blanket out across the soft sand and Zafrina would sit down alluringly, as if posing for a photo shoot. She'd lie down on her side, her head resting on her arm, tucking her legs up beneath her. Parker would ease down next to her, sidle up along her side, all the while taking in her loving gaze. A salty breeze would blow a wisp of hair across her face, and Parker would slide his hand across her forehead to move it away, clearing a path to her lips. And they'd both surrender to that next kiss.

Falling back together, wrapped in each other's arms, Parker would peer down at her. He'd kiss her tenderly at first, then openly as their passion began to peak. He'd kiss her mouth and then nibble her ear before brushing his lips across her tender neck. His lips would move down to arouse her nipples, teasing them hard through her cotton dress. A lingering sigh would escape from Zafrina's mouth, and she'd grab hold of his chest. Working her hands deliberately down his belly, she'd find the snap on his shorts.

They would make love half naked, exposed only to the natural light of the moon. They would move together slowly with flashes of passion: gentle, loving strokes interrupted by firm thrusts, punctuated by moans of satisfaction. Their thrills would come from the simplest of sensations, from delicate touches and wet kisses, from the exhilaration of skin on skin, two people making love as one.

It was a beautiful fantasy, but a fantasy none-the-less; one that Parker felt would never come true. Then Joanie abruptly turned around, catching his eye. When she gave her hair a quick flip and blew him a kiss, Parker remembered that she too, had a fantasy to fulfill.

There would be no romantic lovemaking in Joanie's sensuous daydream. It would be more like a roller coaster ride. She'd wrestle him down and smother him with wild, passionate kisses. Then she'd swing on top and straddle his hips, soon to be jerking with violent delight, back, forward, up, and down, boobs flopping while her hands smashed into his chest, pressing him harder and further into the sand. Parker would pray for her to come, to just get it over with. She would gasp and grunt and ride him only for her own satisfaction, selfishly fulfilling her physical needs, one of two people having sex together, completely alone.

"That'll never happen," Parker vowed silently to himself. Just then a streak of terror shot through him. Something important had been forgotten. Parker shook his leg impatiently, as the group let out a hearty laugh. Finally, they grew silent. Mako's story had ended. Parker quickly filled the void.

"So Mako, you said you spoke with Don about Austria. What's the plan?"

The query was unwelcome. "I'm heading out early. That's all."

Parker pressed him. "How soon?"

"Too soon."

"Too bad. I suppose it would do no good to bitch about it. Any way that I can help?"

"No, you can't help. And bitch I did, my friend," Mako countered, "but then Don dangled a carrot, reminding me that it was Sally I was going to rescue. She's out there all by herself.

So you get a break, and I get to go one-on-one with that sweet dish."

"You selfish bastard," Parker said with growing rage. "Aren't you the least bit concerned about the problem out there?" Twisting quickly to get up, Parker forced Joanie to turn away. "Don't you care about the tour? Jack quit. Sally's alone, out on a limb, and all you can think about is getting in her pants."

Mako kept his cool. "You're the one who's always talking about falling in love." He then reached for a stick, eased up toward the fire, and poked at the glowing embers. "What if she's the one for me, Parker? Maybe Sally can lead me to redemption?"

Parker dismissed his sarcasm, reacting instead to the leer that slowly settled on Mako's face. "This isn't a game Mako. It's a real problem in need of a serious solution. I know Sally. I know she's got to be struggling with this. She needs you to be in charge of the business. You can't be fuckin' around and flirtin' and shit. She needs to be supported, not seduced."

Mako's eyes remained fixed on the fire. "If you're that worried about her then maybe you should take the fuckin' trip yourself?"

Parker chugged his last mouthful of beer and then dropped it in a pile of empties. Without uttering another word, he headed down the beach. Joanie reached for a blanket. "Do you want me to come with?"

"No."

Startled, Joanie turned to Mako. "What the hell's he so worried about?"

After watching Parker become a mere shadow in the moonlight, Mako tossed the stick aside. "Everyone but himself."

THE FIRE WAS JUST a faraway flair, but Parker kept walking,

alone in the dark on that deserted beach. The group's chitchat had faded away too, like the repeated refrain at the end of an old song. Parker was glad. He no longer wanted to hear them. A humid breeze kicked up, ruffling his hair, but it did little else to distract his mind from contemplating the dilemma at hand.

Mako was right about one thing: he was wound too tight. Troublesome tours had been the norm since September, beginning with miserable weather and flight delays out of O'Hare. Then there was the mechanical problem in Nova Scotia, stranding his group in the middle of nowhere. Next, an older woman took a severe fall while wandering Madrid. The annual ski weeks in Colorado didn't go so well either. Besides the usual flight delays, whiteout road conditions, and midnight rowdies roaming the hotel halls, there was also that girl who smacked a tree when skiing out of bounds.

Although he handled it all like the pro he was, Lorrie helped. She kept him calm, calling often until every delayed flight took off. For the Nova Scotia trip, Lorrie scrounged up a replacement coach somehow and got the group to Halifax in time for their fresh lobster dinner. While Parker got the old gal in Spain bandaged up, Lorrie rented them a wheelchair so she could finish the rest of the trip without missing an attraction.

As for the injured skier, well, Parker was there to provide some comfort for her when they placed her in the ambulance. He shuttled her friends to the hospital too. And Lorrie let him stick around until learning that her prognosis was good.

Now Lorrie was the problem, not the solution. Parker contemplated that on his beach walk. He remembered the first time he met her a few years earlier, a geeky, clip-board hugging blonde who organized one of the biggest, best College Ski Week they ever had. Right from the beginning, Lorrie made doing your job feel like you were doing her a personal favor. She always said please and thank you. It didn't take long for her to become everyone's little big sister. More than that, she proved to be a rock, the real person in charge of Tourcey Travel Company.

Her relationship with Jack had always bothered Parker. Sure, Jack was handsome, sporting a casual, sophisticated, prep boy look. But beneath that tussle of light brown hair was a head full of who-knows-what. Jack was at his best on tour: in-charge, organized, personable, and caring. When he took off that name badge, however, his self-confidence seemed to go with it. It was hard to engage Jack in a serious conversation because his eyes always strayed away as if compelled by some strange, opposite polarity.

That inaccessibility helped to keep their relationship an office secret. Lorrie also leveraged her position to keep people off track. "Jack is my protégé," she'd say. "I'm grooming him for a job in Tour Ops." Parker was the only one who knew the truth about them because when she took off her name badge - when she wasn't the boss - Lorrie was one of Parker's best friends.

Parker's thoughts turned to Zafrina again as he plodded through the sand. He relived the twenty-minute respite they shared. How good would it be to spend a lifetime feeling like that? His mind drifted further back to childhood pals who had chosen different careers, their lives diverting drastically from his. He thought about Jeremy and Erin, friends who had gotten married right after college. What would they be doing just then, he wondered, while he shuffled drunk and alone down a dark stretch of beach?

They were probably getting ready for bed, with the children fast asleep. Jeremy would fill the coffee maker and set the timer while Erin would loosen the covers and fluff up their pillows. They'd meet in the bathroom where she'd brush her long brown hair. He'd floss and then she'd groom his face, searching out an errant eyebrow hair or a blemish, smoothing his skin for a closer look. Settling into bed, they'd lean over to share a goodnight kiss. It would be an ordinary kiss too, a simple expression of their commitment, and the wonderfully complex feelings that they shared.

Those thoughts made Parker long for a true love of his own, someone to gift shop for in Hong Kong, and share Face-Time with on a Caribbean cruise. When would he have someone to hide a love note in his travel kit and eat his left-overs when he was gone? How long would it be before he would share a kiss of little consequence with his true love and be so thoroughly comforted by it? Would anyone ever love him that much?

Dropping to his knees in the sand, Parker gazed at the two opposite expanses of darkness before him. The one above the horizon was endless, speckled with an infinite number of stars. The one below the horizon was the sea itself. It was equally vast as it rolled toward him, glowing from the reflected light of a half-moon. After a long, deep breath, Parker slipped off his shirt. Then he dropped his shorts, stepped out of his boxers and walked into the sea.

There was no fear, no hesitation. Parker strolled into the black water as if a welcomed guest. A sudden exhilaration came over him, and he pushed through the water until his toes couldn't touch bottom. Leaping up and diving forward, he surfaced to plunge further into the depths. His arms shot out in front, and his hands cut through the water like a boat's keel. Pulling back mightily, Parker propelled himself forward, aided by a few strong kicks. He laughed out loud underwater, finally comfortable beneath the waves.

Surfacing once more, he peered down the shore at Mako and the others gathered around the fire. Their voices rang out clearly from that distance. Parker swam closer, lurking in the shallows like a wily predator. His head broke the surface just enough to catch a mouthful of air. He listened as Mako spoke.

"I don't mean to be a dick or anything, but sometimes

Parker just pisses me off. I know we think differently, him and me. We're opposites in a lot of ways. I'll tell you one thing, though, he's a great friend, and without question, the best goddamn tour guide in this whole fucked up business. Groups always request him because he gives it his all. He'll do anything for his people. He drives me crazy because, I swear to God, he always does the right fucking thing."

Parker flipped over and floated on his back, comfortably adrift in the calm sea. Above, the vast cosmos filled his vision while Zafrina's psychic perceptions filled his head again. Slowly the emotional bumps and bruises he had earned the past few months began to ease as if healed by the power of her words.

Pleasant memories from those challenging tours came sweeping back to him: low tide on the Bay of Fundy and that flavorful seafood chowder. He smiled too, thinking about the free day in Barcelona, and the pleasure he took from wheeling the injured woman through the fantastic Monastery of Pedralbes. Next, he was back in Steamboat, taking some time off to snowshoe through the virgin snow that settled among the Aspen trees in Pleasant Valley, moments just as religious to Parker as a Sunday morning mass.

For the first time in a long while, Parker felt whole. Meeting Zafrina, he realized, wasn't just good fortune. It was good medicine. The twenty minutes they shared had soothed his spirit. Her perceptions healed his soul. Most importantly, she had rekindled his hope.

A sense of conviction built with each breath as Parker rose and sank with the surge of the sea. He would go to Austria no matter what Don said. He would spare Sally from Mako, find out what happened to Jack, protect Lorrie's secret relationship and save her job. He would take over full responsibility of the Austrian ski program, not because he was one of the best damn guides in the business, but because it was the right thing to do for the tours.

49

There was another reason, of course, one much more compelling than all the others. It was the woman of Zafrina's vision, the shining, golden star, the one connected to Belgium. She offered him a chance at love and the opportunity to do something right for himself.

FOUR

Welcome to the Tirol

PARKER ARRIVED in Frankfurt just ahead of a massive snowstorm. Still, he wasn't concerned that the connecting flight to Innsbruck would be delayed or canceled. He was flying on a workhorse: the Canadian built De Havilland Dash 8, an aircraft renowned by pilots for its ability to buck through nature's nastiest elements. It would be a safe flight, he knew, although perhaps a bit bumpy.

After taxiing into a stiff crosswind, the 76-seat turboprop took off into an ominous sky, colored black and blue like a bruise. The cabin shook, the engines whined as the plane pushed through the murky gloom. In minutes they broke into brilliant sunlight and leveled off. Parker welcomed the peaceful ride. Unfortunately, the thick slab of clouds below kept him from viewing the German countryside below.

Seated comfortably alone in the last row, Parker pulled his backpack from under the seat in front of him and retrieved his iPhone. Slipping in earbuds, he tapped the music app and selected his "Equilibrium" playlist. It was the perfect mix of jazz and classical music to relieve his pre-tour tension and allow him to prepare for the job at hand. Opening up copies of the tour documentation, Parker held the phone up to review tomorrow's transition itinerary:

SATURDAY, JANUARY 27th
7:30 a.m
- *Group A departs hotel for Innsbruck Airport*
- *Approximate travel time is 15-20 minutes*
- *Contact Lutz Travel to confirm transfer*
8:00 a.m.
- *Group A check-in: Austrian Airways #285*
11:30 a.m.
- *Group B arrival: Austrian Airways #278*
12:30 p.m.
- *Group B Approximate arrival time at hotel*

The contact list followed. Parker studied the names and positions of his key contacts to commit them to memory. He then keyed them into his phone along with their contact numbers as the mellow music streamed through his subconscious. Opening up an Innsbruck city map, Parker identified the hotel's location. Then he began to connect it with the primary tourist sites, following the shortest routes and cross-streets as if playing a maze game.

The next shuffle landed on the song, "Evening in Paris," and Stan Getz's saxophone oozed into his ears. Giving into the melody, Parker leaned back, allowing his eyes the luxury of following the flight's lone attendant. She sauntered past, heading to the front of the cabin to take drink orders. Graceful, like a Parisian runway model, her desirable figure swayed up the aisle in perfect rhythm to the music in his ears.

Her physical beauty was irresistible. Flat, broad cheekbones gave her face a smooth symmetrical shape, which was framed by chestnut blonde hair, tapered to shoulder length. Her personality, however, was the hook for Parker. It manifested itself in a fantastic smile. While flight attendants are expected to smile, they don't have to mean it. This one did.

Parker contemplated whether or not this stunning woman in the red Austrian Airlines uniform was the woman of his dreams, the one in Zafrina's vision. Sure, he was genuinely attracted to her, but so was everyone else on the flight. Heads snapped to attention when greeted by her captivating smile. Her voice, too, was irresistible, asking each passenger if they wanted something to drink with so much sincerity that it sounded like a marriage proposal, "Möchten Sie etwas trinken?"

Unfortunately, Parker had yet to get a vibe from her. His nerves did tingle while watching her happily adjust a seat back and gently pat a passenger's shoulder. His throat also slackened when she nodded reassuringly before reaching up to twist open an air vent. His heart even thumped a bit when she stooped to speak warmly, eye-to-eye, with a child seated along the aisle.

Parker found himself leaning forward as she drew nearer, pulled by the force of her beauty. The only person resistant to the flight attendant's magnetism was a dour-looking middle-aged woman seated across the aisle from Parker. Head buried in her laptop, the woman reminded him that there was work to be done. He sighed, shut off the music, and opened up his German language app. He then hunkered down to review the language lessons and practice mouthing the pronunciations in a low voice.

"Ich bin geschäftlich hier - I am here on business."

Outside the small window, the sky below was now a roiling sea of milk-white clouds, Mother Nature's apology for the angry thunderheads they had flown through on takeoff. The thick tufts of white merged with a steel blue sky. While it was a typical view from 35,000 feet, it was something Parker still found beguiling; one of those things that he would never take for granted. Smitten by the vista, he didn't notice the flight attendant looming over him. "Möchten Sie etwas trinken?" Her silky voice was barely audible through his earphones. "Möchten Sie etwas trinken?" she repeated.

Parker looked up, pleasantly startled. Returning a smile, he shrugged. "Nien."

The woman then noticed his language app. "Versuchen Sie, Deutsch zu lernen?"

Parker blurted out a loud, "Ya."

After covering her mouth to stifle a laugh, she replied with an accent just as provocative as her looks. "Oh, you are already fluent."

Parker nodded uncomfortably, and she scooted away, leaving his stomach a flutter. Trying to be discreet, he watched her distribute the beverages. She engaged with every passenger as if they were family. No question seemed trivial. Every reply, whether in German, French or English, was stated with genuine sincerity. Even her fluency was admirable. Determined to avoid any further embarrassment, and perhaps even impress her, Parker returned to the language app.

"Ich komme aus den Vereinigten Staaten - I am from the United States."

Using the loud drone of the engines to mask his mutterings, Parker raised his voice a bit and imagined he was speaking to the flight attendant.

"Tanzen Sie gern - can you dance?"

"Möchten Sie mit mir tanzen gehen - would you like to go dancing?"

The prop engines roar lulled him into near delirium. He closed his eyes and began to fantasize a romantic scene with the flight attendant.

"Möchten Sie mit mir ausgehen - do you want to go out with me?"

"Sie haben schöne Augen - you have beautiful eyes."

"Ich liebe dich - I love you."

Without warning, the flight attendant slipped into the

54

vacant seat next to him. Parker grabbed his waist belt to keep from jumping out of his seat.

"I startled you, ja?"

"No, no I'm fine."

She pointed to the iPhone. "So, what did you learn?"

He exhaled deeply, trying to calm the butterflies. "That I'd much rather speak English."

"You're better off. Austrians speak English."

"So, are you Austrian?" he asked awkwardly.

"Ja. I live in Innsbruck, whenever I'm around." She blithely rolled her eyes.

"I know how that is," Parker replied. "I'm a travel guide, always on the go."

"Have you business in Innsbruck?"

"Ski tours. One group is there now, and a new one comes in tomorrow. We've got groups coming and going for the next three weeks."

"Where do you stay?"

"We've booked the Austropa Hotel on Maximilian Street."

"I love the Austropa." She sat upright and faced him, bearing the depth of her beauty, from skin to soul. "The Bistro there has such good food, and they have the most delicious Black Forest cake."

"Good to know. I'll be having breakfast and dinner there just about every day."

"So you are handling this all?" She peered at him quizzically.

"I have an associate waiting for me. Next week there'll be three of us, so I expect to get some free time then. I've never been to Innsbruck before, and since I'm a history nerd, I'm looking forward to checking out the historic sites around Old Town."

"My friend owns a shop in Old Town. She has the best gelato."

"Sounds like I'll be eating a lot of desserts," he said with a chuckle.

The flight attendant laughed defensively. "No, no, no. There are other things besides great food. And your hotel is so close to everything. It's just a short walk to the Altstadt ..."

She began a detailed description of her favorite landmarks. Parker struggled to listen. Not because he wasn't interested or that her accent and dialect were hard to understand, but because he was just more interested in *watching* her speak; to see those shapely red lips form every syllable. The pride that flashed in her burnished brown eyes was also enchanting. Even her gestures fascinated him; her lithe hands that punctuated the emotional connection she had with her hometown sites. Her words had no chance to take hold on Parker. They could only evaporate like wisps of warm breath in cold air, sacrificed to her charismatic charm.

"So when you stand around with other tourists," she continued, "staring at the famous Goldenes Dachl, you'll say, okay, I've seen the golden roof, now how about some gelato?"

Her mouth gaped wide with a self-inflicted laugh. Parker laughed too, but only to buy time while figuring out the best way to angle for a date. But a crackle of static came from the overhead speakers, foiling the chance. The plane pitched forward and began its descent. The captain's voice bellowed out loud and clear in German:

"Meine Damen und Herren, wir bitten Sie sich anzuschnallen, Ihren Sitz senkrecht zu stellen und Ihre Tischlehne aufzuklappen. Wir muessen una auf einige Turbulenzen gefasst machen."

"Excuse me." In one swift motion, the flight attendant shot out of the seat to snag a white plastic garbage bag from the service area behind Parker. His heart raced as she scurried past. Sensing that there was a potential attraction between them, Parker struggled to understand why he hadn't felt a vibe.

The announcement was repeated in French. Parker didn't

understand that either, but he pulled his seat belt tighter knowing that at least, they were making their final approach. The captain then gave the announcement in English, but Parker was distracted by the view below, as the plane finally emerged beneath the cloud cover.

"Ladies and gentlemen, please fasten your seatbelt and return your trays and seat backs to their upright position."

A massive panorama of mountains, capped by jagged, snow-covered peaks, surrounded the plane. Below the tree line, swatches of evergreen and bark-gray layered the mountainsides, cut by meandering streaks of white snow. The city of Innsbruck rested quaintly in the center of the scene, a broad, snow-splashed valley, the Inns River running through it like a thick vein.

"We are expecting severe turbulence ahead."

Parker had heard the words "severe turbulence" uttered over an airplane intercom system before, and it was always frightfully accurate. Up the aisle, the flight attendant was frantically collecting the trash. Her eyes were wide with concern, and Parker realized that either the turbulence was unexpected or her timing was off.

She moved as if mired in muck while the plane shook, plowing through rough air. Passengers squirmed to fasten themselves in. The bleak lady across the aisle was as pale as milk glass. Parker watched the flight attendant who was just a few rows ahead. Her calm countenance was unable to hide nervousness eyes. Suddenly the small plane rocked to the left as if it had been punched in the side.

Catching her view, Parker motioned with his head to the vacant seat. She peered back with determination. Although a short drop buckled her knees, the flight attendant straightened up and lurched forward. When she was close enough, Parker reached out, grabbed her hand and pulled her next to him. She squeezed the garbage bag between her knees while Parker yanked the seatbelt free from beneath her. Strapping in, she snugged the belt up just before the plane caught heavy air, slamming down with a spine-numbing jolt.

The small plane shook violently as it rolled over bumpy air. Then it suddenly stabilized. Level and steady, the plane cruised smoothly, descending lower and closer to the runway. Upon landing, the flight attendant hopped out of the seat and offered Parker her hand.

"Thank you. Thank you so much."

There was a flicker of light in her eye, a small reflection of bright sunlight. It glistened off her pure white teeth before dancing onto the ceiling. Bewildered, Parker tried to wrap his head around the phenomenon. Then he noticed that the source of the light was an engagement ring on her left finger. It was a big chunk of a diamond.

That was why he hadn't gotten the vibe: she was unavailable, already spoken for. Relived that he hadn't asked her out, Parker accepted her handshake. "You're welcome. The pleasure's all mine."

Seconds later they were on the ground and secured at the gate. The captain's voice crackled pleasantly over the speakers:

"Welcome to the Tirol!"

Parker swung his backpack over his shoulder, tugged his duffel out of the overhead and stepped toward the rear exit while the other passengers still fumbled for their luggage. Waiting dutifully, the flight attendant stood just inside the open door. Parker winced as he approached her, knowing that if she had been available, this would've been his last best chance to make a date.

"Thanks for the tips on Innsbruck," he said, being polite. Then he realized that they hadn't ever introduced themselves. "I'm Parker Moon." He pulled a business card from his front pocket and handed it to her.

She accepted it. "I'm Kara. Kara Hetzler." Glancing

anxiously at the line of passengers filling the aisle, she shook his hand again. "It was good to meet you."

Parker fixed his vision on her face to capture the memory of her in his mind. After entering the main terminal, he closed his eyes and conjured up that image just to make sure it took. It was an image to savor, a likeness of someone whose glamorous features were the physical manifestation of her inner beauty, of her goodness. Kara Hetzler, he surmised, was living proof of something his grandfather had told him long ago. The old man's wisdom was always matter-of-fact, conveyed in simple terms. "You want to make a better world? Be a better person."

SALLY MADE WORRYING AN ART. Straining her eyes and ringing her hands as Parker came into view, she ran up and gave him a bear hug, then clung to his arm all the way to baggage claim. Even as he wrestled his duffel bag into the hotel van's rear door, her neck stretched beyond the upright collar of her gray, company-issued ski jacket to keep him in sight. Ignoring the annoyance, Parker crawled into the van, and they departed.

There was no neon sign to greet them, just a quaint, brick building, the cornerstone of two streets lined with tightly packed structures. A slim man in baggy slacks and a navy blue, wool commando-style sweater, waited for them at the hotel entrance. He wasn't the bellman. "This is Oliver Hauptmann," Sally said, "the owner and manager of the Austropa Hotel."

A closely cropped beard couldn't cover the grave countenance on his face. Parker shook his hand vigorously. "Great to meet you," he said.

"Please call me Ollie. And the pleasure is all mine." There was nothing pleasant in the stoic tone of his voice, however. Projecting that earnest persona, Ollie led Parker and Sally through the elegant, wood-paneled lobby and up to the front desk. "This is Günter," Ollie gestured to a large man wearing a caramel-colored vest, white shirt, and gold tie. Parker reached out but the man was busy, so he offered Parker a grin and a nod.

"Günter is our front desk manager. He takes care of everything," Ollie said with assurance. "He's also my brother-in-law, and he keeps me out of trouble with the wife."

Like a gentle giant, Günter smiled bashfully, forcing his thick neck to strain around the collar of his white shirt. Rolling back his broad shoulders, the front desk manager stretched to retrieve one of many key fobs dangling from the wall behind the desk. Ollie accepted the key and passed it to Parker. "You will stay on the first floor. There's an enclosed balcony with a small table. It's a good place to work."

"You'll need this too," Sally interrupted, handing him the company-issued iPad. "All of our numbers should be up to date. I've printed off manifests for each day trip we're running this week. Our local tour partner, Lutz Travel, will email you every day right before dinner, noting any availability for the next day's drip. That way we can push for some last minute sign ups."

Parker unlocked the iPad and began to scroll through the tour documentation until Ollie Hauptmann spoke up. "Günter can see to your bags."

Parker tugged on the shoulder strap of the pack on his back. "He can handle the duffel bag, but I've got this one."

"That's fine," said Ollie, "then I will familiarize you with the hotel."

Sally finally looked relaxed. "If you two are okay then I'm going to run up to my room. Catch up with you a little bit later, Parker?"

"Sure thing," Parker said closing the iPad cover.

He followed Ollie into the Austropa Bistro. The chic décor included marble-topped tables and ornately scrolled wrought iron chairs. Remembering Kara's review of the food, Parker quickly perused the menu posted on the wall when they exited. Stepping back through the lobby, they walked down the main hallway, past a classic, wood-framed elevator and a set of broad black metal stairs set into the aged, brick walls. Parker and Ollie continued into the main dining room; a spacious area divided in two by a narrow half-wall, covered with horizontal wood planks and topped with various, small plants. Parker's room was tucked away down a short hallway behind a dining room wall.

"Okay if I drop my backpack?"

Ollie nodded. Parker hiked down to the room, slid the key in and opened the door. It was Spartan compared to most of the American-style hotels that Tourcey Travel booked world-wide. White trim and pale green painted walls gave depth to the space, while colorful alpine prints hanging around the room gave it some character. The bed seemed oddly sized, somewhere between a twin and full, but it rested on a solid oak frame that was built right into the wall.

Parker tossed his backpack on the bed and stepped over to peek into the bathroom. There was only space for shower, no bath, which was disappointing. A hot bath was often his refuge on tour, whenever he needed some "me" time, and intro-spection.

Ollie stuck his head in the room and startled Parker with his deep voice and thick accent. "How about a bier?" It was the first time Ollie smiled.

Parker smiled back. "Please."

The small Austropa bar was tucked in a corner across from the dining room. The wooden bar top was only six stools wide. Walking past a couple of bar-height tables and chairs, Ollie moved behind the bar to grab two tall beer glasses. Parker claimed a stool, eager to bond with the main man at the Austropa, a key player in the tour's success.

"Here you go." Ollie handed over a freshly poured brew and then tapped himself one. "I'm the second generation to own the hotel." The proprietor smiled again, this time, proudly. "My whole family works here."

"You've got to be dedicated to succeed as an independent in this business."

"I am dedicated to the happiness of my patrons. Running this hotel properly makes them happy."

Parker grinned. "I can appreciate that. So let's talk about those patrons." He pulled out the iPad and tapped open a list of files. "We have groups coming the next three weeks, Saturday to Saturday. The last two weeks are solid, with fifty-four rooms each week."

"You have almost every room."

"Did Lorrie send you the final rooming lists?"

"We have them," Ollie replied. "Are you aware of our annual Fasching dinner buffet?"

Fasching is Carnival in Austria, and Lorrie had discussed it in detail with Parker at the pre-tour briefing. The only thing that stuck in his mind about the tour briefing though was just how scattered she was; how she still hadn't heard from Jack and how she refused to discuss their situation "on company time."

"Yes," Parker told Ollie. "It's the last Tuesday of our tour, so it'll only impact the final group," he answered. "Apparently it's a big to-do around here."

"The Shrove Tuesday festival is a huge event for us at the Austropa," Ollie reiterated. "Our kitchen, lobby, dining room and Bistro will be closed on Monday evening so we can make preparations. We will provide vouchers for Monday night's dinner, of course. Our guests can eat at some of Innsbruck's best restaurants, all very close by."

Parker nodded. "The office already notified each customer who'll be impacted, but Sally and I will reaffirm that info so there'll be no surprises."

"They will be pleased," Ollie concluded. "I apologize that we cannot provide the tour guides with a ticket for Tuesday's Fasching buffet."

"No big deal. We spend enough time with our clients so we can appreciate a night away, on our own."

"I understand. So now that you are here to replace Jack, is there anything else I need to know?"

"Not really. Lutz Travel will handle all transfers and day trips. We have a lot of pre-tour sales, so we'll assign one guide to the day tour. Our contract with the tour sponsor is to have a guide here in town every day to keep an eye on everything and be available in case of an emergency. Since our largest groups are coming the last two weeks, Sally will be staying on, and we'll have another guide join us."

"So are you a skier?"

Parker shrugged. "Sure, I like to ski."

"Like to ski?" Ollie shook his head slowly and then let out a sweet smile.

"And you?" Parker asked knowingly.

"There are only three things I live for," Ollie explained, "my family, my hotel and my skiing."

Ollie was ready to tap a third beer when Sally appeared to break things up. "The morning transport coaches arrive at seven o'clock to load up. We have to leave right at seven-thirty. I need you to make sure room charges are cleared, and you can help the drivers load up. Then I'd suggest a short nap before I get back with the group."

Pointing to a small black notebook that Sally clutched close to her chest, Parker asked, "What's that?"

"These are my notes to share with the incoming group."

Parker quickly pulled the notebook out of Sally's hands. "Thanks. These'll be very helpful. I was just going to wing it."

"Parker?" Sally cried as if appalled. "You can't do the transfers. You just got here."

Deep down he sensed that Sally was more than happy to concede the transfers to him. "Relax, Sal. I'll be awake half the night anyway and useless here. I'm sure Ollie will appreciate having you around to help the staff with room assignments and everything else, especially with such short turn around times." Ollie nodded. Parker waved the notebook in the air. "Is there anything else I need to know?"

Sally shook her head. Ollie Hauptmann hoisted his beer glass. "They are expecting heavy snow tonight," he deadpanned. "Hopefully the flights aren't delayed."

FIVE

Innsbruck

TINY PELLETS of snow fell straight out of the early morning sky Saturday, tinkling off of the transport coaches like kosher salt. Warm in his company-issued gray ski jacket and black, Stormy Kromer cap, Parker greeted each passenger as they exited the hotel. The drivers worked methodically, staging bags based on size before stowing them below. When the bay doors were closed, Parker jumped on board to get a head count and review names. Returning to the lead coach, he confirmed all was good and then nodded to the driver who put it in gear.

Sunrise stained the pale clouds pink, revealing a broken sky and reassuring Parker that the flights were on time. Soon the vehicles arrived at curbside. Leaving the tourists on board, he met with both of the drivers. "I'll lead everyone inside and wait there for the new arrivals. When I have them all together, I'll give you a call." After agreeing, the drivers began to unload the luggage.

Although Tourcey Travel operated the Austrian ski tour program, it was sold through SojournSports, an independently owned retail sporting goods chain. Highly regarded as adventure sports specialists, SojournSports drove tour participation through their "Adventure Travel Club." Customers earned membership automatically by purchasing any of their high-quality sports equipment. The members earned reward points that could be redeemed for other purchases as well as sponsored travel tours.

Adventure Travel Club meetings were held quarterly at the major market stores. They were classy wine and cheese events, featuring reps from equipment manufacturers who would show off their products, provide tips and insights as well as giveaways. The September meeting was when Tourcey Travel began taking reservations for the "Austrian Ski Adventures," a series of four, seven-night tours.

Parker knew that there would be no snowboarders on these trips. SojournSports' target market were ski purists, experienced and well traveled. They'd be wearing traditional ski apparel brands, most likely; colorful parkas, ski jackets, microfleece. No doubt they'd be burdened by huge rolling duffel bags, gusset-sided suitcases on spinner wheels and more than a few elongated ski bags.

Settling into a cozy seat, Parker sipped on a decaf coffee and waited. Eventually, a small group of new arrivals filtered in looking just as he had imagined. Once he recognized the familiar, acrylic, silver Tourcey Travel bag tags, he got up and hurried over.

"Hi, I'm Parker," he announced, "one of your tour guides from Tourcey Travel. As soon as everyone is together, I'll call up the transfer coaches and get you right to the hotel." He directed them to a location off to the side. The bedraggled tourists dutifully obeyed.

Once all of the tourists had gathered, Parker texted the drivers and led the group outside. The coaches pulled up in minutes and Parker led the large group of tourists outside. "Please leave your luggage here," he, pointing pointed alongside the vehicle. "And I'll have to ask you not to load the luggage yourselves. That's the driver's job. It can be a tight fit, and they've got a system."

One by one the people did as instructed. After eyeing the sea of bags, the drivers began a methodical process of selecting specific pieces, lining them near the vehicle, and then placing them into the bottom luggage bay. Parker loaded the people on board the second coach first, standing by the open door and counting each passenger who boarded. Once full, he ran up to the lead vehicle where he saw two tourists tossing luggage into the open bay.

"Thanks, guys," Parker hollered politely. "But the drivers will load 'em up." One of the men pushed a ski bag into the bay before turning around.

"We can handle it." The man shouted back, sounding agitated. He then waded through the pile to grab another one. "I'm not going to wait around here all morning."

He was a big man, with wavy brown hair that stuck out haphazardly, from under a red, tattered, "Ski Mauna Kea Hawaii" baseball cap. "Well, if you're going to do it," Parker countered, "please pack them in well, so everything fits. Otherwise, we'll have to repack it. Oh, and you'll have to keep a count. I need to know precisely how many bags we have."

The burly tourist didn't respond. He only directed his helper to hand him another bag. Parker swallowed hard. Then he hustled back to the second coach with the official rooming list document opened up the iPad.

"Okay, it'll only be another few minutes for me to confirm we have everyone on the other coach," he announced. "Then we have a short ride from our hotel. Once there, please go right to the dining room to check in and get your room assignments. There'll be a buffet lunch ready for you, too."

Parker left quickly, ran up to the first vehicle, and hopped on board. A surly attitude greeted him.

"Let's get the show on the road already." Came a shout.

Cradling the microphone in his hands, Parker studied their weary faces and repeated his spiel. "We'll be off in a couple of minutes, I promise. I've just got to make sure that everyone's on board."

A few moans erupted, but Parker worked right past them. "All right," he said while reviewing the list on his iPad, "are Ralph Stantz and Sherry Redant here?"

Working quickly, Parker soon came to the very last couple. There was an asterisk by the names and Parker understood its meaning. "Last but not least I have the group leaders, Steve Severin and Veronica Andrus."

A slight woman seated up front raised her hand. She had a round face and a dove grey scarf around her neck. "Everyone calls me Ronni." She offered him a coy, restrained smile.

Parker couldn't admire her beauty - the smoldering eyes, dark brown hair and glowing, olive-skinned complexion - because the overbearing male presence seated beside her would not allow it. "I'm the only group leader on this trip," the man growled. He then slicked back his thick hair and tugged on that familiar "Ski Mauna Kea" cap.

Parker summoned up some grit. "Great," he announced while closing the cover of the iPad. "It looks like we've got everyone on board."

"Great," the towheaded group leader mocked derisively. "So we can finally get the fuck outta here?"

A despotic group leader was a tour guide's worse nightmare. Parker had his share of horror stories, but he learned from those experiences. He understood the necessity of appealing to their ego, sharing behind-the-scenes insights with them, and keeping them in the know without compromising his authority. So when that motor coach did get the fuck out of there, exiting the airport and heading toward the heart of the city, Parker made every effort to bridge a connection.

"I've been with SojournSports for thirteen years," Steve

replied to Parker's query. "Worked my way up to a corporate position because I know how to ski. I know what the customer wants, and I give it to them."

Parker listened intently, squatting low on the front steps. Before he could engage Steve any further, the second dilemma of the tour raised its ugly head. It started with some unintelligible grumbling in back. Finally, a voice called out clearly, "Hey, how 'bout some heat back here?"

Reaching over to the front windshield, Parker felt warm air spewing from the vent. "We have heat here," the Austrian driver matter-of-factly.

Parker walked down the aisle toward the back and quickly realized that the temperature had dropped. The windows were frosting over. Once more he plied the driver, but it was useless. "I don't know," came the man's reply.

"What?" Steve shouted. "We've got no heat?"

Parker decided to use the problem as leverage with Steve. Once again he knelt by the group leader's side. "Okay, Steve, we're only fifteen minutes to the hotel. I don't know how long it'll take to get another transfer coach out here but we can stop right now and I'll call for a replacement or we can bundle up and tough it out. Since you're the group leader, I'll defer to you."

Steve's right to bitch had been revoked. "Well, that's crazy, we're so close. Just keep going, goddammit."

Parker grabbed the mic and relayed Steve's decision. After more grumbling, he added, "I've got some info to share to help keep your minds off the cold." Parker pulled out Sally's notebook. "First off, all of your rooms will be ready right after an early lunch buffet which will be waiting for you upon arrival. Once you exit the coaches, you'll be taken past the front desk and into the dining room. While you enjoy lunch, my associate and I will go around and pass out room assignments and keys."

"You are already aware that we're staying at a privately

owned hotel. It is a classic European property where they still require their guests to turn in and retrieve their key fobs from the front desk every day. It may seem like a bit of a hassle but believe me, it's not. There's always someone at the front desk, and they have this system down so you won't be waiting around. The oval, wooden key fobs also have the hotel logo on them and make a great souvenir, but please don't accidentally forget to turn yours in and keep it as a souvenir. We'll be providing everyone with a souvenir fob, imprinted with the SojournSports logo, as a gift after the tour."

Tired eyes stared back at him blankly, but Parker continued. "A key to the storage room and one personal ski locker key will be given out to each room. Please hold onto those keys and don't lose them. Anyone who brought their own equipment can go and store it right away. The locker room is just inside the front lobby. After lunch, those of you renting equipment will be shuttled to Ski School Innsbruck to get fitted for your gear."

A male voice shouted out the back. "How's the skiing in St. Anton?"

Parker was surprised by the question. St. Anton was in the Arlberg region, a ski area an hour away from Innsbruck and not included in the tour package. Before Parker could respond, Steve cleared his throat and twisted back in his seat. "It's amazing. They don't call it the cradle of Alpine skiing for nothing." He then motioned impatiently for the microphone. Parker handed it over.

"In fact, Ralph and I are looking to take a day trip to ski St. Anton," he cackled. "We're gonna hire a local guide and go backcountry or maybe even heli-skiing if we can get enough people to share in the cost. So, a show of hands," he continued, "who's interested in skiing St. Anton?"

The same worn-out indifference that Parker faced, now greeted Steve. Eventually, a woman seated in the middle of the coach called out. "We've got nine areas to ski in Innsbruck, Steve. That's enough for me."

Then the man who first asked about the weather in St. Anton, spoke up again. "Before I commit, I need to know how much this excursion's going to cost. We've already paid for plenty of skiing in Innsbruck."

"The cost depends on how many people go." Steve barked. "How 'bout it, any interest?"

"How far away is it?" Came another query.

Frustrated by the questions, Steve sighed before responding. "It's probably an hour drive or so. If we don't want to rent a vehicle or hire a shuttle we can take the train."

Loud grumbling erupted followed by the inevitable question. "How much will that cost?"

Steve had had enough. "Hey, no one's saying you have to go. It's just an opportunity to ski the place where skiing was invented." Realizing that there'd be no immediate commitments, Steve waved the black plastic mic at Parker and the guide quickly retrieved it.

"Okay," Parker said over the loudspeakers, "I'll check on some ballpark pricing for a day trip to St. Anton and get that to Steve so you'll have the option. But for now, let's focus on skiing right here in Innsbruck. After dinner tonight we'll be passing out your OlympiaWorld ski pass. Just to remind you, that pass gives you access to nine different ski resorts. You'll be able to utilize ninety cable cars and lifts and ski over two hundred and sixty kilometers of trails. That's about a hundred and sixty miles."

"The pass also includes round-trip transportation to each area, discounts on ski lessons and more. We'll also have a representative from Ski School Innsbruck talk to us tonight. He'll tell you everything you need to know to have a great ski week, including access to ski guides and lessons. And I'm sure he can answer all of your questions."

The vehicle erupted in friendly chatter, so Parker turned around and stepped beside the driver. The Austropa hotel was just ahead. Reaching to slide the microphone back on its clip, Parker felt the cord get stuck. Looking back, he saw it twisted around Steve's armrest. The group leader glared back at him, and then slowly looped it free. Parker sensed that somehow, he had made an enemy of the one person he most needed to befriend.

SALLY AND PARKER split up at dinner that night so they could share a table with different guests. Although he made small talk with his tablemates, Parker's mind focused on how to win over Steve. Right before dessert, the guides met at the small bar. Wrestling with a metal delivery cart, Parker examined the thick envelopes set in a cardboard box on top of it, making sure that they were arranged alphabetically.

"You wheel it, and I'll pass them out," Sally said.

Parker identified two packets belonging to Steve and Ronni from the stack. "Okay, but these two are mine."

The guides stood in the center of the dining room. Parker called for attention. Next to him, Sally started to bounce on the tips of her toes as if in mid-cheer. "Hey everyone," she called out. "My name is Sally Hyong, one of your US guides. Parker and I are here to ensure that your vacation is everything you expect it to be." Bottling up her enthusiasm, Sally addressed the crowd with poise, speaking precisely, and turning around occasionally to make eye contact with each member. "We'll be passing out your tour packets now," she concluded. "Please identify your ski pass first. Then check to see that your day tour tickets are for those trips that you pre-ordered. On the off-chance there's a mix-up, we want to correct that immediately."

Moving from table to table the guides systematically delivered the individual packets, working swiftly, in tandem. "Please,

please, please do not lose those passes." Sally reiterated, shaking her head, her shoulder length hair swaying back and forth like a shimmering, black silk curtain.

"Yeah," Parker added. "Think of them as cash. I suggest you secure it inside the grey lanyard we've included in the packet and slip it around your neck right away."

Everyone did as directed, searching through the envelope, perusing its contents and securing their passes. The two guides visited Steve's table last. Parker dished out the envelopes and then spoke directly to Steve.

"If you have any questions or concerns, please give me a call anytime." He offered Steve a business card. "My room is here on the first floor, right around the corner, number two. My mobile number is on the card." Steve didn't reach to accept the card, so Parker set it down on the table.

"I don't want to have to call you," Steve said ominously while easing back in his chair. Parker didn't respond. His attention was drawn to a ruggedly handsome man in a green fleece pullover, who marched right into the middle of the dining room.

"Marc," Sally said with a shriek. Rushing over to hug him, she held his hand and introduced him to Parker. "This is Marc. He runs the Innsbruck Ski School."

Small in stature but with a firm build that manifested itself in a thick, muscular neck, the earnest man didn't say anything beyond a curt hello. He did manage to crack a reasonable grin while shaking Parker's hand.

Looking around the room, Marc suddenly waved an arm to get everyone's attention. "Good evening everybody," he hollered, with a firm, deep voice that reverberated throughout the dining room, startling some of the tourists. "I am so glad to have you all here in Innsbruck, my hometown. My name is Marc Hilscher, and I'm with Ski School Innsbruck. I apologize for interrupting your scrumptious dessert, but I'm here to give you a little taste of what skiing is like here in the heart of the Austrian Alps."

Marc paused to clear his throat, then continued. "Your tour provider, Tourcey Travel, has contracted with us to furnish you with the best ski rental gear, guides, and lessons. Those of you who have already made arrangements, please review the schedules and make sure your name appears on the appropriate list. Those of you who are renting should have been fitted for your equipment earlier this afternoon. If for some reason you did not get your gear today, not to worry. We'll shuttle you to Ski School to get that done anytime."

Guests who pre-paid for a lesson or guided ski excursion studied the schedules intently. The two guides meandered through the room checking with everyone to make sure they were satisfied. Marc then began to detail each ski area amid the ruffling of open trail maps and the low chatter of excited tourists. When he mentioned their ski guide services, Steve raised a hand.

"What's the cost to go off trail with a guide at the Arlberg?"

Marc shrugged. "We work the Innsbruck ski area. There is a ski school in St. Anton. I can get that contact info to you if you're interested."

Annoyed, Steve just shook his head. Parker intervened. "You can get that info to me Marc, and I'll make sure Steve gets it."

Marc concluded his talk with an invitation to the Innsbruck Ski Club meeting on Monday night, held at the Grosse Gabel Brewpub. "So can I expect to see you both at the Grosse Gabel?" he questioned Parker and Sally before departing.

His snarling pronunciation, "Grrrosse Gabel," made it seem like an order more than a request. Intrigued by Marc's gregarious persona, Parker confirmed that they would attend the meeting.

AN EARLY BEDTIME would've been ideal for the hard working guides. Sally, however, had other plans. "Can I buy you a nightcap?" she asked Parker as he strolled around the corner.

He nodded and then stepped behind the bar, taking advantage of Ollie's offer to help himself anytime. Pouring two cordials of Grand Marnier, Parker stepped around and took a seat on the wooden stool next to Sally.

"I prayed that everything would work out fine," she said, confident that Parker's arrival was the answer to at least some of those prayers. Raising her round-bottomed snifter to toast deliverance, Parker genially hoisted his drink, and they clinked.

"It'll all work out once I win Steve over," he said assuredly.

"He's a real package, isn't he?" Sally queried. "At least his fiancée Ronni is nice."

"Fiancée?" Parker paused to wonder how such an adorable woman could date a guy like Steve, much less agree to marry him. Sally shared some more bad news.

"Lorrie told me that Steve manages the Midwest region for SojournSports. He's number one in sales."

"Well, she didn't say anything to me at the briefing. Regardless, that guy must carry some clout."

"I suppose."

"Sounds like I'll need to do some strategic schmoozing."

"It'll take more than that old Parker charm."

"The charm will work, it always does," he countered. "I'll just have to stay on top of things and minimize the surprises."

Sally scowled. "Well, it probably won't surprise you that Steve and Ronni are staying over with the next group. We have them here for two weeks, so there'll be plenty of time to schmooze."

"Great," Parker said, grabbing hold of his head, "where can I hide?"

"There's nowhere to hide," Sally stated cheerlessly, "not with this job. It's nothing but surprises. None of which are any good. It's just one dilemma after another."

She bore the countenance of someone overwhelmed by the pressure of her job. Seeing her typically bright eyes barely alight, Parker worried that he had coddled her too often; softening the blows so much that she couldn't handle it now that the going was tough. No doubt Don and the operations team hadn't helped either, treating her like a diva as much as they did.

"What do you think?" she asked. "Am I burned out? Am I beyond the point of no return now that Don and Lorrie have lost faith in me?"

Parker spoke honestly. "No one's lost faith in you. It's a big group and an important ski program. Someone had to come out here. Here's the real question, though. Are you sick of the people? Does the thought of eating another meal with a bunch of strangers completely turn you off?"

"No, no, I love my people. They're what keeps me going."

"Then you'll be fine. And if anyone at the office had lost faith in you, if they didn't feel you were up to the job, you'd be home already."

Sally looked relieved, even comforted, by Parker's words. She let them sink in, holding back any response while sipping the orange-flavored liquor. A hint of her energy returned as a warm recollection stirred in her head. "Remember the Canadian Rockies trip, when we first worked together?" A sly grin flashed across her face.

"Absolutely," Parker confirmed. "That was my first two-group move."

"And you had Jack. It was his very first training trip," she giggled.

"Yeah, and to be honest, I was a bit worried about him, so somber and cerebral. But he loosened up enough for the folks to love him. I figured right away that he'd be great one-on-one with customers, working the smaller group tours."

"Jack was lucky to have you. He would never have survived with Mako as a trainer."

"Jack's too intelligent for Mako. Smart, serious people like Jack scare the crap out of him."

She agreed. "Mako is only comfortable working with certain people."

"Yep, those he can fuck with and those he can fight."

Dropping her head, Sally eked out a confession. "You know, Jack scared the crap out of me over here."

"What?"

"I'm serious," she confirmed. "He was just unpredictable. You know how Jack could be kinda uncomfortable around others sometimes?"

"Yeah, he can get a little weird in social settings. But he's just a loner, Sal. Some people are like that. The important thing is that he was always fine on tour. He always treated his people well."

Sally shook her head. "Not on this trip. He started out fine but all of a sudden he got this attitude. He was kind of short with some of the folks too, Parker. There was an edge to him. It felt like he could just snap at any time, and then he did."

"What do you mean?" Parker asked anxiously.

"I mean he snapped." She snapped her fingers.

"Did he get violent? Did he hurt you?"

"No, nothing like that."

"Like what then?"

"He just lost it. He was supposed to go on the Castles Tour. We had a ton of folks signed up, too, but when they returned he wasn't on the coach. I was so worried, and so I asked the driver, and he told me that Jack never got on board that morning. About an hour later, I caught him sneaking back into the hotel."

Sally paused to take a sip of her drink. Parker clenched his jaw, anxious for her to continue. After another sip, she did. "I didn't speak to him until after dinner. We came here to the bar, right here, and had a glass of wine. And then I asked him where he went."

"What did he say?"

Suddenly animated, Sally's hands shot out in the air, her fingers fully extended and her eyes opened wide. "He got all crazy. His whole body shook, and he yelled at me. 'It's none of your business,' he said, and 'I'm sick of being everybody's babysitter.' I said I was sorry and that I only wanted to understand what had happened. It wasn't like him to leave the tour group alone like that."

Calming to the point of sadness, Sally withdrew, wrapping her hands around the small aperitif glass as if it were her most prized possession. She sighed before continuing the story. "After the outburst, he just stood there and stared off into space. I've never seen a person so torn apart. Then he just walked up those stairs to his room," she nodded at the staircase behind them.

"I said goodnight, but he didn't respond. The next morning, Günter told me that he checked out. All he left was his name badge and the company iPad in his room. I haven't heard a word from him since."

Contemplating the whole scene, Parker wondered what could have possibly triggered it. Then he thought genuinely about his relationship with Jack and realized that, although they had been good friends, he really didn't know Jack that well. Not enough, anyway, to understand why all of this was happening.

Sally sulked quietly until finally muttering, "I don't want to go out like that."

"Don't say that, Sal." Parker's voice swooned with empathy. "Please, don't even think that way. Besides, we don't know how this is going to end for Jack. He may be okay. For all we know, he could walk right through that front door any second now."

"You're right." Her agreement was half-hearted. "But honestly, Parker, right now I feel that I could walk away just like Jack. As much as I love being with my people, I could give it all up tomorrow and go home. But why would I do that? There's nothing to go home to."

Despite the years, Sally's divorce still pained her. Adrift in an exotic lifestyle of adventure and excitement, she vested all of her pleasure in managing her clients - her people. She seldom mingled with her co-workers. Parker was one of only a few men she'd ever visit with alone because he respected her space and her feelings.

Still, Parker worried that she'd never find happiness until she made an effort to move on. He measured a thoughtful response. "It'd be great to have someone to come home to, but you've got to be open to meeting that someone."

"I'm open." She spoke defensively before softening. "You just don't know it."

"I know you let a lot of opportunities pass by, that's all." Parker took another sip of his Grand Marnier before concluding. "I just wish that, sometime, you'll give yourself a chance."

Once again Parker's words affected her physically. A glow of understanding poured over her like a shower of rain. Then her lips parted, and her mouth hung open as if astonished. Then she spoke. "That's the last thing that Jack said the night he left."

"What?"

"He said, 'I have to give myself a chance.'"

"A chance at what?"

"I don't know. That's all he said. It was such a surprise that he just left like that. Looking back on it though, I shouldn't have been so shocked. I doubt if anyone understands what's going on up there." She pointed to her head.

"But what else did Jack say? What else did he do?"

"Well, he did say something else, like, you'd understand."

"*You'd* understand?"

"No, he said, '*Parker* would understand.' That was it."

"Understand what?"

"I don't know. I really don't know."

SIX

Monday Night Ski Club

THE ALPINE-STYLE PUB reeked of tradition: dark, rough-hewn wood-beamed ceilings, a wooden plank floor, and a massive stone fireplace that took up half a wall. Marc stood at the bar, surrounded by tall cocktail tables full of drinkers. Wading through the thick crowd, Parker and Sally led a handful of their tourists toward the affable Ski School Manager, including Steve and Ralph, following closely behind.

"You've finally made it," Marc announced happily. He huddled them together to introduce his companions, beginning with two young women seated at the tall table behind him. "This is Marie and Alyssa, two of my best ski instructors." Parker smiled and waved. The girls nodded back. "And this is Dante."

A debonair man skirted around Marc to greet everyone. "Yes, I'm Dante Santos." He shook hands with Parker before speaking with a brash glint in his eye. "I'm with Euro Journey Tours."

Parker didn't recognize the name, but he knew the face, having seen Dante stroll out of the Austropa Hotel just as he was checking in. "We're with Tourcey Travel," Parker replied. "This is my associate Sally, and this is Steve Severin and Ralph Stantz."

Steve shouldered his way in between everyone to shake Dante's hand. "I'm in charge of the group ski tour program my company, SojournSports, is sponsoring."

Marc intervened. "So, Steve, did you make plans to ski St. Anton?"

Steve couldn't hide his disappointment. "I'm having trouble getting commitments."

Dante eyeballed Steve like a starving man sizing up a steak. It was Marc, however, who kept up the conversation. "So where have you skied so far?"

"We did Axamer Lizum yesterday. One of my friends back home told me that Stubai Glacier was the best. We did it today."

"And how was it?"

He nodded. "We had a really good day."

"Ah, ha!" Marc bellowed, and he slapped Steve on the back. "Good is not good enough. Your friend back home is where he should be, back home. In Innsbruck, Marc is your friend. I'll take you out to the backcountry where there is powder up to your ass."

Laughing heartily, Marc fastened his arm around Steve's shoulder like a pipe wrench. "Ralph can come along, and Sally and Parker. Tomorrow I take you all."

Dante leaped at the chance. "I can ski tomorrow."

Sally was apologetic. "I can't go. I'll be on the Castles Tour with our group. Besides, I'm not much of a skier." Marc looked bummed as Sally concluded, "Parker can't go either. He has to stay in Innsbruck. He has to be accessible in case there are any problems or if there's an emergency."

Her reasoning was sound. Parker knew it was proper protocol. Still, leaving Steve at the mercy of a competitor wasn't a good idea. "I'm sure Ollie would be available for the group in case of emergency," Parker suggested.

Sally shook it off. "I know his schedule. He can't support us tomorrow. You'll have time to ski, Parker, but tomorrow is not that day."

Insecurity had forged the resolution in Sally's voice. Parker knew that the right thing to do for the business was to go on that ski trip. The right thing to do for Sally, however, was to forget it. Challenging her in front of everyone wasn't going to help rebuild her confidence. At least Marc was reassuring. "Trust me to take good care of them." Parker and Sally nodded in agreement. Dante smirked with delight.

SKI CLUB INNSBRUCK wasn't much more than an excuse to party: a whole lot of skiers packed into a big beer hall to drink, mingle, and watch ski videos on big screen TVs. Parker enjoyed the room's energy. With beer stein in hand, he grabbed an open seat at the tall table with ski school instructors Alyssa and Marie.

Although he didn't get a vibe from either girl, Parker accepted their warm greeting. "So Mister Parker," Alyssa asked. "Are you a skier or just here to work?"

Parker sensed trouble lurking behind those intriguing brown eyes. "Sally and I handle all logistics for the tour group. We're pretty much everything to everybody all the time."

"No time for fun?" She pondered him suspiciously, raising two fingers to her lips as if smoking a cigarette.

"We manage to squeeze in some fun now and again."

Alyssa took a sip of wine. Her associate Marie seemed to be ignoring Parker, looking off into the crowd. Nonetheless, her cherubic face drew him to her. Although a sense of adolescence danced in her eyes, Parker was confident that there was a woman in there somewhere. Alyssa interrupted his search, speaking with an air of sophistication. "So how are you finding Innsbruck thus far?"

"Not bad," Parker said, "if you're into magnificent scenery, engaging architecture, amiable people and that comfy, European charm."

Alyssa frowned. "I know, how boring, right?"

Parker didn't know how to respond to that. Instead, he changed the subject. "Are you from Innsbruck?"

"I was born in Vienna, but we moved here when I was ten. I lived in Vancouver for a few years too."

"Been to the States?"

"Oh yes, I've skied Squaw Valley, Snowmass, Vail. But Canada is my favorite place in the whole world. I studied in Vancouver and skied the Bugaboos and Banff."

"I've taken a lot of group tours to Canada," Parker replied, "but I've only been to Banff in the summertime. When I think of Canada, though, the first thing that comes to mind is a fishing trip I took with my buddies to Ontario. I remember lying on a huge rock by the water, watching the northern lights play all night in the sky." Waving his hands in the air from left to right, Parker swirled his fingers in an attempt to bring the memory back to life. Marie's eyelids spread wide with astonishment, and she giggled.

"Have you ever seen the northern lights?" he asked her. Flustered, Marie shook her head emphatically before retreating behind an unapproachable pout.

Alyssa laughed. "Forgive Marie. She's a just a shy farm girl at heart."

Marie's general demeanor seemed to confirm her friend's description. Hiding amid voluptuous waves of auburn hair that cascaded beyond her shoulders, Marie's plain beige sweater also kept her from standing out in the crowd. Her lipstick, however, was oddly vibrant, a plum-colored shade that seemed utterly out of place on her thin lips.

Alyssa's appearance brought no such ambiguity. Sporting a tight, cranberry-colored hoodie over a lacy black tank, she sat upright, with her shoulders pushed back regally. Short, black hair was set fashionably askew, perfectly imperfect, with short spiky bangs. Parker recognized the same purple-shade of gloss on Alyssa's plump lips, glistening in the dull overhead lighting. Apparently, she had shared her lipstick with Marie. It fit Alyssa's style and accentuating her tawny cheeks.

Alyssa's sensual energy attracted every male nearby, including Dante who slipped between the two ladies, breaking up Parker's monopoly. "Excuse me, Seid Ihr beide von Innsbruck?"

Alyssa peeled his fingers off of her shoulder and replied in English. "Yes, we are both from here."

Dante remained undaunted, asking the girls if they were able to go skiing the next day with the group, in German. Finding him rude, Alyssa looked directly at Parker when she replied in English. "We're both busy with ski lessons all morning."

Dante didn't shirk from the admonishment, so Parker rejoined the chat. "Dante, I've seen you at the Austropa Hotel earlier. Are you staying there?"

An impudent glare fell across his face. "I'm staying at the Hotel Franz Mair. We overbooked a couple of our trips and had to stick a few people at the Austropa. I'm only there to check on them."

"That's the problem with overbooking," Parker countered, infected by Dante's snootiness. "You just can't give everyone the same quality trip."

Dante's nostrils flared. The jousting match would've

continued if Marie hadn't surprised everyone by reaching out to tug at Parker's sleeve. "You talk more, please?"

Parker looked baffled. Alyssa explained. "Marie and I enjoy listening to you speak. Your accent and the way you tell a story is quite entertaining."

Mako would have leaped through the window of opportunity that Alyssa left opened. But Parker didn't feel like taking that plunge. "I'd rather learn more about you girls."

"Sorry," Alyssa responded, "you are the guest here, so you must tell us all about yourself." She paused to gesture once again with fingers raised to her lips before pressing him further. "So where are you from? Where do you live?"

Marie scooted up in her seat as if preparing to hear some juicy gossip.

"Okay, well, I'm from the Chicago area, growing up in a small town just outside of the city. I still live there, too."

Alyssa continued the interrogation. "But you travel a lot, right?"

"All the time. I'm here for the next three weeks."

"And it doesn't bother you to always be away, to travel all the time?"

"Traveling is easy for me because I have a great family and lots of close friends. They give me a good reason to come home so I guess you could say that I have the best of both worlds."

Parker was surprised by the silence that followed his answer. It made him uncomfortable. So he took a sip of beer and observed the various reactions. Dante just stood there, unaware or at least uninterested. Marie seemed warmed by Parker's heartfelt sentiments, and she gazed at him wistfully. Alyssa, however, seemed unnerved. She leaned back stiffly and announced, "Let's have some shots."

"Schnapps?" Marie asked.

"She said shots," Parker explained.

"Yes," Alyssa concluded, climbing out of her seat to go to the bar. "Shots of Schnapps. Lots of shots of schnapps."

The classic fruit brandy helped coax a good mood back into the conversation. Parker's ego flourished. He had won over the women, forcing Dante to creep away. Rather than accept defeat though, the rascal merely engaged Parker on another front. "Every time I am at the Austropa Hotel," he said to Sally, standing behind Parker near the bar, "I ask myself, who is that girl?"

Parker was surprised to hear Sally defended herself so adroitly. "The one who's going to ignore you because of that ridiculous line."

Trotting a stool out to the middle of the room, Marc parted the crowd. He stepped on the lower rung, placed a hand on Steve's shoulder and hoisted himself onto the round, wooden seat. Standing over the bustling group, Marc funneled his voice with his hands to shout. "Quiet now. Quiet please." The crowd hushed. Marc grinned like a jolly king reviewing his subjects. "Ski Club will come to order."

Silence reigned. Those needing to quench their thirst raised their drinks quietly. Those needing to speak did so only in quick whispers. After summarizing much of what he stated at the hotel earlier, Marc then announced a series of free ski races they'd be sponsoring. He went into detail explaining the event process: the date, the time and the place; how each skier would be timed; how those times would be recorded and confirmed. The final rankings would be sent via email to everyone who signed up. Cash, trophies, and bragging rights went to the first five finishers in various divisions.

Concluding with a bit of theatrics, Marc waved his hand toward a banquet table at the opposite side of the room. There, three ski school instructors sat, ready to take sign-ups.

"Space is limited," he finished, "and the last person to sign up will have to buy me a bier."

Steve pushed through the crowd like a Black Friday shopper, with Ralph nipping at his heels. Parker got up to help Marc climb down from his barstool perch, but Alyssa's voice stopped him. "Parker, I have a question."

He turned quickly, catching her staring at her phone. Raising her eyes, Alyssa's beguiling look immediately stimulated Parker's imagination. He took a few long seconds to imagine her lying in bed next to him, reposed on a white pillowcase, beckoning him with that same, furtive gaze. "What is it?" he finally replied.

She cast a sly smile. "Are you skiing with Marc tomorrow?"

"Oh no, I can't. I've got stay in town."

Again she took a quick glance at her phone. "Good, then you must have lunch with Marie and I. It will be so fun, and well worth your time, I promise." A naughty grin accompanied Alyssa's insistence.

"Sure," he said without a hitch. "I'll be scouting out the local sites for my people in the morning, but open after that. What time and where should we meet?"

"Come to ski school at noon. We'll be free for lunch then." Alyssa turned to Marie and motioned for them to leave. "Now I'm sorry to say, but you must excuse us," she continued, "our day starts very early tomorrow."

Parker couldn't think of anything witty to say that might entice them to stay. So they slipped out of their chairs and tugged on their hats and gloves. "We'll see you for lunch tomorrow?" Alyssa confirmed.

Parker smiled. "Yes, you will."

Watching them walk away, Parker brooded over the lunch invitation. Despite Alyssa's pretenses, Marie's timidity, and the lack of a vibe, there was still a chance for romance to blossom. That, however, was proving more elusive for Dante. "I've always been turned on by Asian women," Parker overheard him confess to Sally.

The rude remark went unheeded. Seeing Parker alone, Sally called out. "What are you doing there all by yourself?" Using her half-filled beer glass, she waved for him just as Marc surprised Dante and squeezed in next to Sally.

"Come on, Parker," Marc added, "join the party."

Agreeing with a nod, Parker gave up the table to some fellows who were eager to sit. Happy that it was Marc, not Dante, commanding Sally's attention, Parker stepped over and let Sally slip an arm around his waist. "Do you know how nice of a guy Marc is?" she asked Parker. "He just offered me free ski lessons. How am I going to tell him that I'm afraid to ski?"

Parker shrugged. "You just did."

Sally froze, wide-eyed as if caught in a prank. Breaking into a smile, though, she suddenly burst out with a bellowing laugh. It was a giveaway - Parker knew she was drunk. Her silliness confused Marc. He tried once again to negotiate a ski date with her. "All you need to do is get out there once. You don't know what you're missing."

Dante stepped in to renew the competition. "I'm sure she does, Marc. I'm also confident that what interests Sally most is Innsbruck itself, the sites of this historic locale. Dedicated guides like Sally prefer to experience the local culture. They want the services of a seasoned professional who can help them focus on primary points of interest, those things that she can, in turn, share with her clientele. Am I right?"

Sally replied sarcastically, "You make it sound so fun."

Marc wasn't ready to concede. "Then she should have a native Austrian, a local to show her around, someone who has strong, ethnic roots in the city."

Sally's dull eyes bounced back and forth, from Dante to Marc and back again. While the two rivals sparred for her affection, Parker worried that the liquor had only given Sally a false bravado, and his big brother instincts took hold. When Marc set his empty beer glass down and called to the others, "Who's ready for another?" Parker prepared to intervene. Sally, however, spoke up first.

"None for me." She looked at the mouthful of beer left in her glass and made a sour face. "I think it's time for me to go." She set the glass down. "Dante said he'd walk me back."

Although startled, Parker said nothing, but Marc protested vehemently. "But you aren't going skiing tomorrow. Surely you can give us the pleasure of your company for a little while longer?"

His plea fell flat. "Sorry, but I really can't. Parker can tell you. I am not much of a night owl. I can't believe I lasted this long." Suddenly charming, Sally leaned in to kiss Parker on the cheek. Tossing him a clandestine leer, she whispered, "I'll try to get some intel on Euro Journey." Pulling away, she then slipped an arm around Marc's waist for a goodbye hug.

"So you'll be all right?" Parker questioned.

Sally scrunched up her face. "Aw Parker, don't worry about me." Breaking into a grin, she pulled her ski jacket off of a hook that dangled beneath the bar and put it on. Dante slid into a long, black wool coat. He turned up the collar, shook back his head and led her away.

Parker and Marc watched them sift through the crowd and out the door. "Don't trust him," Marc warned, "whatever you do. He's a snaky guy. I wouldn't let him alone with any of my sisters."

"My sisters would bury that guy," Parker stated. "But I'm more worried about my group leader."

"Steve?"

"Yep. He's a key stakeholder at SojournSports. I expect he'll have some influence on which tour operator they contract with next year. And he'll be skiing with my biggest competitor all day tomorrow. It makes me sick."

Marc gritted his teeth, upset that he hadn't thought of that sooner. "I can't stop Dante from going along. It's bad for business. But I won't let him have a minute alone with Steve, I promise." Rubbing his chin, Marc concluded, "That would be bad for business, too."

"Yeah," Parker remembered, "and business does start early tomorrow, right?"

Marc nodded. They downed the last of their beers and readied to leave. Then Parker noticed a classic burnt orange mountaineer's hat sticking out of the crowd. It topped the head of a woman standing in a small group nearby. The short pheasant plume stuck in the black headband wiggled every time she laughed. "Go ahead, Marc," Parker said. "I've got to say hi to someone."

As soon as Marc left, Parker shouted out. "Kara!"

She turned around, smiled, waved hello, and then turned back to her friends. Parker felt foolish for yelling. But after shaking a few hands and nodding to others, Kara joined Parker at the bar. "Thank you for saving me," the beautiful flight attendant said settling into the stool. "The ladies are nice, but the men are boring." She rolled her eyes. "They are so arrogant."

Her fresh-faced countenance suggested anything but boredom. She shone like sculptured porcelain, with an enchanting smile and an erotic aura. It was a thrill just to be near her. Parker said the first thing that popped into his head. "How long are you in town?"

"I don't have to leave until tomorrow afternoon."

"So are you up for a drink?"

Her nose wrinkled as she smiled. "Sure, I'll have a bier."

Parker leaned on the bar and waved for the barkeep. Despite his feelings, Parker wasn't going to flirt with her. Messing around with a woman in a committed relationship was something he never wanted to do. There were consequences to that: bad vibes, bad karma, and inevitable retribution. Mostly though, there was the guilt he'd carry for crossing that line, knowing the pain he'd feel if the person he loved ever did something like that to him.

"So you must tell me," she said excitedly, "how was it?"

"How was what?"

"The gelato. On Herzog-Friedrich-Strasse? Don't tell me you didn't tour the Altstadt yet?"

"Oh, no, not yet anyway. I've been too busy, but I've got tomorrow morning free to walk around town and get acquainted with all of the sites. I'll check out the gelato then."

He wasn't interested in making small talk either. Something was pressing on his mind; a personal observation, a truth that he felt obligated to share. The only challenge was how to broach the subject without alienating Kara. The bartender delivered their beer and Parker handed a full pilsner glass to her. After taking a quick sip, Parker set down his drink and ventured prudently down that path.

"I have a friend back home who's a flight attendant," Parker said. "She loves the gig and her work schedule. How does the airline treat you?"

"Wonderful. I have a very comfortable routine. Of course, I've been doing this for a long time."

"I can tell you're a pro."

She blushed. "Well, it's just something I wanted to do since being a little girl."

"That's cool. I knew I wanted to be a tour guide when I was a little too."

"So whom do you work for?"

"I pretty much work for one company, Tourcey Travel. Our headquarters are in Chicago. We run all kinds of trips."

"Do you have a regular schedule?"

"Not really, although a lot of our trips run seasonally. Every fall I can count on a few foliage trips, and during the winter there's always skiing. But spring and summer, anything goes."

"So you are gone a lot from home. No time for a family?"

Parker shook his head slowly. "Not yet, my job keeps me busy. Even though we're supposed to be gone no more than twenty days a month on tour, it doesn't always work out that way. You can take a ten-day trip, be off for two days, then go again for a week, and have three days off before you're on another long one. Sometimes I come home and my head's spinning. But the boss is cool. She's good with downtime when you need it. I'm here for three weeks straight, but that'll earn me about a week off."

Daintily, Kara took a sip of beer, creating a lull in the conversation. A coy look covered her face when she finally asked, "So what do you do when you're off?"

"Well, this time of year I'd be ice fishing or snowshoeing in the Northwoods. Then again, I might be sick of the cold and just spend the week relaxing at home, maybe hop in the tub and enjoy a good book."

Kara smiled at the thought. "So you like to read?"

"I love to read."

"Me too. My fiancé Thomas only likes to see the movies."

Parker pretended to be annoyed. "Doesn't he know that the book is always better than the movie?"

Kara grinned good-naturedly. "That's what I tell him. I read the book. I don't want to see the movie."

Parker chuckled and held up his hands in protest. "Honestly though, I love movies too, especially the old ones. Watching old movies or listening to old music is a hobby of mine. It's like finding buried treasure. There's an awesome sense of adventure in it."

"And you like the action movies? Like Thomas, you want the guns and the cars and all the hot women, right?"

"A mindless action flick is okay," Parker replied. "But I

prefer something more suspenseful with good dialogue and great characters. When I was a kid I got hooked on the old James Bond movies, the ones with Sean Connery, you know?" Kara nodded, and he continued. "My favorite one was 'From Russia With Love.' There's an actress in that movie who plays a Russian intelligence agent, and I remember thinking at the time that she was the most beautiful woman I had ever seen."

"I don't remember that movie."

"Well, to me, she was the epitome of European beauty, the kind of exotic, foreign woman that I suppose, a lot of guys would dream about." The memory made Parker smile. He then dropped an elbow on the bar to support his head, cradled in his hand and spoke candidly. "Please don't think that I'm throwing you a line, but the truth is, you remind me of that actress. You have her face and her smile."

Kara laughed from embarrassment, a rosy hue settling on her white cheeks. "I don't think of myself as beautiful as the celebrities. I don't wear much make-up. My fiancé thinks my hair-style is old-fashioned, too plain."

Glad that he hadn't frightened her, Parker asked, "Did you meet him on a flight?"

She smiled. "Yes, I did."

Parker softened his voice and spoke slowly. "I can see how that'd happen. You were amazing on our flight. It was clear to me that you love your job, and that you genuinely care about your customers."

Kara rolled her eyes. "There were no jerks on the flight, so it went well. Those are the times when I love my job the most."

"Don't I know it. I live for those kinds of trips. I love my job too, not that it isn't a real bitch sometimes."

"The traveling is not glamorous. Sometimes it's hard to leave. Thomas is in sales, and he travels for work, too. Even when he's gone for a few days, he always complains about it."

"Well, selling is his profession. When he jumps on a plane

it's so he can get where he needs to go to do his job. But travel is our profession. Guys like Thomas are our customers. It's our job to make their travel the best experience possible. Travel is what we do, and how well we do it matters to people. Watching you work my flight was like watching a master."

Kara glowed with pride at Parker's observation. "Most customers don't notice when we do a good job," she countered. "They only notice when we don't do so well. It makes me sometimes think that I'm selfish to try for the perfect flight all the time. If customers don't care why should I? But I care because it makes me feel good to do my best. How well I do my job is an expression of who I am as a person."

Her narrow-mouthed smirk reminded Parker, once again, of that movie actress. He stared back in awe as if he were still that young boy gazing up at the big screen star. "I couldn't agree more," he said. "To me, art is an expression of something beautiful inside a person. No matter what you do for a living, I believe you can be an artist at it. That's what I strive for when I'm on tour anyway, and that's what I saw watching you on that flight. I saw an artist at work. It was beautiful."

A soft buzz sounded from Kara's leather handbag. Anxiously she scooped it off the bar and pulled out her phone. Reading a text, her brow lightened. "It's Thomas. He wants to know when I'm coming home."

Parker smiled. "He misses you."

Kara lowered her eyes and glared playfully at Parker. "He wants me to bring him something to eat." They both laughed.

"Just as well," Parker said, swirling the remaining beer in his glass and downing it with one big drink. "I have an early day tomorrow, so I better go too. I'm still searching for an artistic moment of my own on this tour and tomorrow might be the day."

"I like your chances for that," Kara stated, smiling broadly.

Sliding off the bar stool, Parker took her hand. "It was great to see you, Kara."

She squeezed his grip politely. "The pleasure was all mine, Parker Moon."

He turned away and walked out the door, shuffling off alone into the cold Innsbruck night.

SEVEN

Ski School Innsbruck

THE CITY HAD BEEN BLANKETED in a powdery snow that roiled in the air with the slightest gust of wind. Up early, Parker stood in the lobby sipping tea and watching an industrious hotel worker shovel the sidewalk clear. Sally jogged into view from around the corner sporting a cobalt blue running suit. She waited for the shovel to pass before scurrying inside.

Parker greeted her. "Good morning."

Sally peeked up at him, her eyes nearly covered by a tight, pink, running cap. "How'd you sleep?"

"I slept great," he replied, "but then I wasn't the one who went home with Dante."

"Stop it." Sally's hair crackled from the static as she pulled off the cap.

"All right, I won't bug you ... what did he do? Is he as bad as Mako?"

"No one is as bad as Mako, although Dante might be a very close second. Geez, Parker, what was I thinking? How could I let him walk me home?"

"I assumed it was the alcohol."

"I wasn't that drunk, was I? But oh my goodness, he

97

wanted to walk me to my room. No way was I going to let that happen. He wanted to give me a massage, too. Really?" She shook her head, completely dejected. "I am so worried about Steve spending the day with him. Don would have a fit."

Tempering his frustration, Parker replied, "I did have a remedy for that."

Sally's face fell. "I'm sorry Parker, but you know we have to have someone nearby for emergencies. Anyway, what if you got injured? The last thing we need is for you to be chasing Steve down the slopes and breaking a leg or something."

He understood her concern. Besides, it was too early to argue and too late to try to join Marc's ski trip, so he eased her guilt. "It's fine. I'll have plenty of time to schmooze Steve next week when Mako gets here. Who knows, maybe he'll have softened up a bit by then."

If Vegas had a line on that, the odds would've doubled the moment Parker stopped speaking. "Excuse me." Steve's voice bellowed as he stepped to the front desk. "Who do I have to sleep with to get some extra towels in my room?"

PARKER'S WALKING tour had been meticulously planned, with a minimum of time allotted for each key stop: The Golden Roof, The Cathedral of St. James, Museum of Tyrolean Folk Art, The Hofkirche, and the Imperial Palace. He would walk through the quaint Old Town, and past as many sites in the historic city center as he could. Viewing every attraction through tour guide eyes, he'd assess, evaluate, and analyze the sites and their surroundings to gain a first-hand perspective, and valuable information that he, Sally and Mako could share with their clients.

Pacing himself through each attraction, Parker took time to write a detailed review of every stop, including any specific nuance that would be beneficial to their tourists:

Imperial Palace: *Only tour two floors. Palace rooms on second but can be confusing. Not opulent but very interesting. Min. time to tour: 30-45 min. Audio tour included but all placards in German/English.*

Museum of Tyrolean Folk Art: b*ig collection, well organized, focused on arts, crafts, interesting furniture. Funky mannequins. Easy access to bathrooms.*

Hofkirche - Court Church - and Mausoleum: *make the most of this site. Seriously consider extra expense to hire a docent. Must see 15-min. multi-media intro display.*

He finished before noon just as planned. Retracing his steps through Old Town, Parker headed back down Maria-Theresien-Strasse, stopping only to view the tall monument, St. Anne's Column, set in the middle of broad, pedestrian street. Soon he arrived at the storefront school, sandwiched between a computer store and clothing boutique. A bearded, middle-aged gentleman standing behind the counter greeted him. Parker asked for the girls, and the man gestured to an open doorway behind him. Hurrying past a full rack of skis, through the opening and down a hallway, he came to another door that was open just a crack.

Pushing into the room, Parker saw Alyssa bending over, wearing a pair of tight black performance underwear, a black, long-sleeve top and tall white socks with individual, red toes. She stood up and posed when he came in, the elastic and polyester fabric clinging tightly to her form.

"You're early," Alyssa stated. "Take a seat." She nodded toward the table and chairs that centered the room. Parker did as told, while she reached into her locker for a hairbrush. The room reminded Parker of a college dorm, with a small kitchen area and a white, apartment sized refrigerator. A blue milk crate sat on top of a fridge, stuffed with various gloves and knit hats. Parker read the handwritten sign duct-taped to the front: "Gefunden."

Alyssa called out to her friend. "Marie, Parker's here.

Hurry up. I'm hungry." A rustle was heard from behind another doorway and seconds later Marie entered the room dressed in black leggings and a thick, white wool sweater. "Hello," she said in a soft, staccato voice. "I am glad you could come."

Smiling generously, Marie walked over, pulled out the seat across from him, and sat down. Alyssa slammed her locker, refocusing Parker's scrutinizing gaze. Sauntering across the room, she slid a chair away from the table and settled on it lightly, as if being lowering onto a cloud.

"Great socks," Parker said.

"Thanks." She wriggled her red toes. "I love to wear them in my ski boots."

"They look comfy," Parker surmised, "but it must be a pain to get them on."

Alyssa laughed before speaking to Marie. "I thought men only worried about how to get a girl's clothes off?"

"That's not what I meant," Parker protested.

Alyssa pointed toward the kitchen. "Marie," She barked. "Can you grab the lunch? I'll get drinks."

"Aren't we going out for lunch?" Parker asked.

"No, no," Alyssa explained, "we brought lunch, and since we've only had to work half a day, we also have drinks."

Slipping out of her chair, Alyssa strutted to the cupboard. Parker watched her firm cheeks sway beneath the tight shorts. She returned with a paper sack, set it at her feet and pulled out a few dark bottles of beer and a clear bottle of schnapps. Marie hauled a large vinyl tote bag out of the refrigerator, dropped it on the table and dispensed its contents: knives, a cutting board, a stick of dried sausage, a hunk of white cheese, a jar of Dusseldorf mustard, rye bread, a stack of sliced ham, and three giant pickles.

Alyssa rushed back to the counter to grab three juice

glasses, and then returned to her seat where she began to fill them with schnapps.

Parker wasn't planning on midday buzz. "I'll have a beer, but pass on the schnapps."

"Just a little," Alyssa asked, wrinkling her nose, "to celebrate?" She waved the bottle in the air.

"What are we celebrating?"

Alyssa thought for a second. "How about friendship?"

Marie scowled at the suggestion, but then managed a grin when raising her glass. "To friendship then."

Although excited, Parker still hadn't gotten a definitive vibe from either girl. He did feel a weird sense of angst, however. It followed the silence after Marie's last word and lingered from the clink of their glasses through the hush as they drank. But that feeling couldn't compete very long with the scintillating energy the women emitted, a sexual dynamic that intoxicated him.

Marie's was subtle, culled by dark beauty, genuine warmth, and an angelic countenance. Alyssa, on the other hand, came out throwing. It was her best stuff too, challenging Parker to take a swing. The tightly knit top contoured the shape and mounds of her form like some erotic topographic map. Lean, muscular legs were crossed and uncrossed almost incessantly while she sat. Her saucy giggle and edgy personality made every minute seethe with erotic anticipation.

After accepting the schnapps, Parker took a sip of beer. "So what was your favorite place to visit in the US?"

Suddenly exuberant, Alyssa responded, "Vail is my favorite place in the whole world." Parker grimaced, recalling that it was just last night when she said that Canada was her favorite place in the whole world. She continued, "My cousin, who is gorgeous, took me to this upscale bar where we had drinks and met some men from Hollywood, a writer, an executive and an actor on a television show."

The tale she recounted was a struggle of egos: three narcissists flaunting themselves in a competition to pick up the hot foreigners. Alyssa mocked their machismo and arrogance. Marie laughed at the men's petty shallowness. Parker, too, was amused, but only mildly. It was hard for him to ridicule those men. They just deserved pity, he thought, because they had no chance with Alyssa. She was way out of their league.

The air of dignity that swirled around Alyssa was even evident in the simple act of sandwich making. Manipulating the cutlery like a tiny trowel, she slipped it into the mustard jar, swishing the blade deftly in slow, precise movements, her wrist elegantly poised. It was even evident in the way she ate, with her chin protruding nobly as her lips reached for a bite.

Those guys in Vail were too arrogant to understand that Alyssa was above their celebrity. A refined woman, she could never be a trophy to pose on any of their arms. She was someone to be worthy of; the kind of woman who guys aspire to be with, at least regular guys like Parker.

Sure he had an instinctive yearning to feel every square inch of her excellent body, to kiss, lick, suck, and thrust on her as if there were no tomorrow. But just as intense was an ardor to please her. He began to imagine all sorts of ways to appeal to her: challenging her intellect with a meaningful discussion, being witty enough to make her laugh out loud, reading to her from his favorite book of poems.

The clinking of metal on glass interrupted Parker's fantasy. It was Marie, stirring her knife blade in the bottom of the mustard jar. Being careful not to break it, she peered deep into the container while the tip of her tongue peeked out from tightly pressed lips, mimicking the knife's motion.

Their eyes met, and Parker was overcome with a primal desire to tap into that good girl's pent-up passion. Smiling as if she could read his mind, Marie dipped her head to the side. Her auburn curls fell off her shoulder, exposing the tender flesh of her neck as if inviting him to nuzzle. Vibe or not, Parker though to himself, he could be the right guy in the right place at the right time; perhaps he'd even be fulfilling a fantasy of hers.

"I have another jar, Marie," Alyssa interrupted, obviously annoyed. "It's in the bag." Marie looked up at Alyssa, confused by her hostility. Parker peered at the two women, back and forth, alternating between lustful desires for both of them.

Alyssa took a nibble of white, brick cheese and a mouthful of schnapps before beginning another tale. This time it was about an exclusive political fundraiser in Washington DC. She went with another gorgeous woman at the invitation of a wealthy uncle. Her suitors were all prominent politicians. Once again she bolted before things got too steamy and mocked those poor suckers with a derisive laugh.

Parker didn't question his merit while cleaving off a chunk of sausage with the short, sharp knife. He wrapped a thick slice of cheese around it and stuffed it in his mouth, all the while assuring himself that he was a better man than some political hack or a second-rate celebrity. Alyssa ordered more schnapps and Marie obliged. Parker grabbed the bottle. "I shouldn't do this. It's terrible."

"It's like medicine, ja?" Alyssa philosophized. "Even though it tastes bad, it makes you feel good." Her eyes twinkled in the high noon sunlight that leaked into the room from a rear window. "So this is what you came for," she giggled. "To get besoffen with the ski bums."

Parker laughed while in mid-pour, spilling some schnapps.

"See?" She squealed, pointing to prove the point.

"I just don't want either one of you to take advantage of me," he joked.

Alyssa leaned onto the table, cradling her chin in the palm of her hand. "Too late. Marie and I have been taking advantage of you ever since we met."

"Alyssa!" Marie shouted, and slapped at her from across the table.

A heated conversation in German erupted between the two ladies. While sipping his beer, Parker felt his self-control begin to wane. Lusting in his mind, back and forth between the two Austrians, he wondered if given a chance, which one would he choose? Then again, maybe he didn't have to choose at all?

Group sex had always been a deviation from Parker's norm. It just seemed a bit unseemly to him; too lecherous, like bad porn. Still, it could be an opportunity to experience another way of seeing, a new perspective. No doubt there would be a lesson in it and some powerful medicine. He could easily imagine an exploratory threesome of sensuality with the girls, played out on a comfy canopy bed, laden with luxurious white bedding, lace and sheer fabrics. There would be romantic moments of tender sex, soft moans, gentle kisses, as they all came together as one.

The booze was like pastels to Parker's fantasy, coloring in the details of that illusion. But the alcohol only sharpened Alyssa's thoughts so that her words came out pointed, in black and white, shaking him back to reality.

"All of this time I am wondering, why did you really come here, Mr. Parker?" She bent over, reached into the bag, pulled out a pack of smokes and a lighter before continuing. "What did you think would happen?"

"I came here for lunch," he said. "I guess I didn't count on getting drunk."

Alyssa was no longer the seductress. "Getting drunk has nothing to do with it. So we shouldn't assume that you are not just another horny man who wants to work himself into one of our hearts, and maybe into one of our beds?"

"That's enough, Alyssa." Marie protested.

Parker leaned forward and tapped his pointed index finger

on the tabletop. "You invited me here, Alyssa. I could question your motives, too."

There was no reason to do so. Parker had already figured that out. Guys like him were just sport for Alyssa, small peaks to hone her skills on. The first night at ski club she had only been searching him out, looking for the right route to climb. That day, the moment he entered the locker room, she began the ascent, wiring her movements to get to the top, to conquer his ego and make him want her more than anything else in the world. After all, Alyssa breathed rare air. She could only be with someone who shared her sense of self-worth. She could only love a blue blood, her Everest.

Alyssa's phone dinged loudly. She snatched it from the table and perused the incoming text. Parker turned to Marie. "I just thought it'd be fun to hang out, have lunch and get to know you both," he said less than honestly. "Besides, you girls invited me."

Marie glanced down, hiding a strange, sympathetic frown. Alyssa set the phone back on the table and looked up. "Parker," she confessed, "we didn't invite you."

The wooden floorboards creaked loudly, pressed by the weight of the heavy boots of someone entering the room. That same harrowing sense of apprehension that Parker felt previously, returned. Looking back at the door, Parker saw a grim, unshaven young man.

"Hey, Parker."

"Hey, Jack."

The ladies quickly escaped to their lockers. Alyssa struggled into a pair of tight blue jeans while trying to explain. "I'm sorry, but it was Jack who asked us to bring you here, Parker." She forced a grin. "I know you'll be glad that you came."

She pulled on a crew neck sweater followed by a light nylon shell and hiking boots. Marie stood by, holding her ski jacket and purse. The two girls slammed their lockers shut at the same time, and walked past the two guys, stopping by the door.

"We'll be at Club Pasha tonight," Alyssa said. "If you'd like to join us it would be fun." Although she sounded sincere, Parker knew she was just being nice.

"Maybe," he replied.

Marie never made eye contact. She just glanced at the floor and followed Alyssa out. The door closed and Parker's stomach soured. Jack settled uncomfortably into a chair. A new hairstyle and color punctuated his disheveled appearance: closely shaved along the sides, white-blonde strands of slackened curls waving atop of his head, resting on a bed of dark roots. It was the inside of Jack's head, however, that concerned Parker the most.

"Good to see you, Jack."

"Yeah, ah, I want to apologize to you first of all, Parker," Jack said robotically. "I'm sorry you had to rush out to Austria. You were probably enjoying a nice beach somewhere."

"Yeah, well, that's the nature of the beast."

"I'm also sorry about this." He pointed to the table, the room and the doorway behind them. "I did ask them to arrange the meeting."

Jack attempted to grin, but Parker's glare wiped it away. "Everyone is worried about you, Jack."

"I know. I know." Once again he waved a hand in the air, at himself, and at the table. "You're the only one I could talk to."

"That's what Sally said."

"Sally," he shook his head. "Yeah, please tell her I'm sorry?" Parker understood that this conversation wasn't going to be easy for Jack. He had always been a private person; that was his nature. He had stepped uneasily into the tour guide role but brought an excellent pedigree to the job, being well traveled and fluent in multiple languages. Still, Jack eschewed being the center of attention.

The traits that kept Jack from being a stellar travel guide, a "star" in Don's eyes, were the same things that Lorrie found attractive in him. She'd often brag about Jack, stressing how it was his intellect that solved a logistics problem she was having with a new tour, or how his quiet authority endeared him to a particular group. Concern for Lorrie was on the forefront of Parker's mind.

Apparently, she was on Jack's mind too. "What about Lorrie?" he asked. "How's she dealing with this?"

"We've only talked business," Parker said. "How did she react when you spoke with her?" Wild-eyed, Jack raised his hand to his mouth. It quivered as if clutching a live wire. Parker reacted quickly to ease Jack's despair. Taking a deep breath, he sunk back in his seat, lowered his voice and spoke with a caring disposition. "So Jack, let me understand this. You haven't spoken with Lorrie yet?"

Jack's lips puckered as his head shook.

"Why not?"

"I don't know."

Irked by his weak response, Parker almost lost his cool. "She hasn't tried to call you either? Did she leave you a message or send you a text?"

Jack's head lolled. "I haven't checked."

After another deep breath, Parker continued. "Okay, well, it's your move, Jack. You owe her an explanation. I suggest you get on that fucking phone and give her a call. I'm sure she's worried about you." Parker's anger grew with each syllable he spoke. Through clenched teeth, he concluded, "Not only do you have a personal obligation to tell her what the hell you're up to, but you have a professional obligation, too."

Jack sagged further in his seat and rubbed his eyes. He stammered, trying to explain. "This has, this has been rough, really rough on me, Parker."

His presence was pitiful, so Parker mellowed. "Jack, I know

how this business can be. It's a ball-breaker sometimes, a real strain. I also know that it's a hard job to walk away from. We can't all leave under the best of circumstances. I understand if something pushed you over the edge. I've been there myself. Just please, let me know if there's anything I can do to help you."

He eyed Parker suspiciously and then softly replied. "Tell her."

"What?"

"Tell her for me, Parker."

"You want *me* to talk to Lorrie?"

Suddenly animated, Jack begged his friend. "Please, Parker. Please? You can talk to her." He gazed at the table for a second before continuing, "Promise me you'll do it? You're like her best friend, and you'll know what to say. It'll be easier for her, coming from you."

"All right Jack, I promise," Parker said. "If that's what you want. But what do I tell her? What's going on?"

The weary young man rubbed his chin nervously. Then he sat up and folded his hands on the table. "I'm not going back. I'm staying here in Innsbruck. I've got a job with the ski school."

Trying to appease Jack, Parker was supportive. "That's cool. I know you love to ski. Besides, you're an army brat, right? Weren't you born close to here?"

"Close, yeah, in Germany. I still have relatives on my mom's side in Munich."

"Hey, it makes sense to take advantage of that. For whatever reason, if you think it's right for you, then it's the right thing to do."

"It is the right thing to do." Jack firmed his jaw, trying to sound confident. "I know it is. I've thought about it a lot, you know."

"I'm sure you have."

"I have," he repeated, nodding his head, "and I knew you'd understand."

"Understand what, Jack?"

Jack's eyes widened. "Why I'm doing this. What has happened to me." Parker gawked as Jack tried to explain. "You know how you talk about your vibe, right? Well, something like that has happened to me, Parker. And for the first time in my life, I'm in love. I'm really in love."

A friendly grin creased Jack's face. Parker leaned up on his haunches, reached for his friend's shoulder, and squeezed it. "That's excellent. I'm happy for you, man." They both finally smiled, and Parker would've laughed out loud if he hadn't thought of its impact on Lorrie. "I understand it's a delicate situation with Lorrie, though," Parker explained. "It's got to be tough. I know you don't like having to hurt her."

It was tougher than Parker would ever know. Jack grew quiet, and then he started to speak, but stopped, then started again. "His name is Franz ..."

IT WAS early afternoon when Parker left the ski school. He wandered along the river until the sun sank low over his shoulder, darkening the water but brightening the tall, colorful row houses lining the embankment. Walking past a cluster of leafless trees, Parker strolled across their finger-like shadows as they stretched along the ground. It was the long way, but Parker needed the time to sort out his feelings.

Parker finally understood Jack's torment. He was sad to learn his friend had been trying to be someone he wasn't. Still, Parker was angry because of the way Jack ran out on Lorrie, Sally, the tour, and the company. He had every right to quit and make a better life for himself, but he didn't have to do it the way he did. He didn't have to risk putting the tour in jeopardy.

Happy that Jack may have found real love, Parker was still concerned for him. It was a significant move he made, a massive change. Falling in love and navigating through a new lifestyle could be a real challenge. Especially since Jack wasn't going to have his immediate family nearby to give him the support he deserved.

So Parker promised to be there for him. He'd call Lorrie when he could, and reassure her that Jack was all right, but he wouldn't share anything at all about Franz, Jack's new love. The right time to share that with her was after the tour. He would speak with her in person, face-to-face when he got back home. While Parker had promised to do that for Jack, the truth was that he would do it mostly for Lorrie.

THAT EVENING, while they sat in the dining room waiting for dessert, Parker told Sally that he met with Jack. Sally was too furious to be discreet, so Parker grabbed two slices of apple strudel and two forks, then led her to the bar for a private conversation.

"How could he be so sneaky?" she cried. "Why can't he come over here and meet with both of us?" Sally would've been more understanding if she knew the reason for why Jack's behavior. Parker couldn't tell her any of that, of course. So he just tried to assuage her anger. "He's embarrassed, Sal. He feels terrible about what he did."

Although her animosity subsided, Sally was still upset. "That's good to know. I feel bad too, but Jack and I have become close friends these past few years. I can't help feeling betrayed."

"I'm sure you do, but if he is a good friend, which I'm sure he is, then you have to trust him. He'll explain everything when he's ready."

Sally shrugged as if she understood. Then she gave Parker a questioning gaze. "So have you said anything to Lorrie yet?"

"Not yet."

After pondering his answer, Sally had a thought. "Why don't we try her now? Just give her a call. It's almost lunchtime at home."

Initially nervous at the suggestion, Parker quickly realized that call was a good idea. Sally's presence would keep the conversation short and impersonal. Putting his phone on speaker and holding it flat so Sally could hear, Parker dialed up their manager's direct line at the office.

"This is Lorrie."

"It's Parker. I'm here with Sal."

"Hi, Sal."

"Hey, Lorrie."

"So what's the problem?"

"Nothing. Nothing's wrong. It's all good."

"Okay."

Her voice was impatient. Parker went right into it. "Listen, Lorrie. I met with Jack today."

She replied coldly. "And?"

"He's all right, I mean, he's obviously burned out. He didn't want to go out like this, but these things happen. He's staying here in Innsbruck for a while, working for the ski school. He has a relative nearby in Munich, you know."

"Good," Lorrie replied. There was a long stretch of dead air before she spoke again. "So did we get his company jacket?" The sound of fingers flying across a keyboard filled the background.

"Yeah, we have it," Parker replied.

Sally leaned into Parker's ear to whisper. "Already told her that." Parker shushed her.

Lorrie continued, "I contacted the bank and had his name

and signature removed from our tour account. What about the iPad?"

"Yeah, we have that too." Another few seconds of silence occurred. Parker spoke up as Lorrie continued to flail away at her computer. "Listen, Lorrie. You should know that Jack is seriously shaken up. There's no doubt that he's hit the wall. Some of us have come pretty close to that too, so we know how it feels." He glanced at Sally who frowned. "But when I left him he was in good spirits. At least he was good with the decision. I can't explain it all now, but I feel like he's on the right path. I'll try to stay connected with him as long as I'm here."

This time there was no lull between replies. "You can do whatever you want, Parker. My only concern is the ski program. That's why we sent you there. You said you'd handle it and we have faith in that. Whatever Jack decides to do is no longer the concern of Tourcey Travel."

"I understand," Parker said.

"Good. So what else?"

Parker thought about his challenge with Steve, but decide not to mention it. "Nothing, we're all right now."

"Excellent. Well, take good care of these people. Although I feel some loyalty there, SojournSports wasn't willing to sign a multi-year deal. I'm confident they will if we prove our worth. Call if you need me."

After hanging up, Parker noticed Sally peering at him knowingly. "Lorrie's upset."

Parker was defensive. "Of course she's upset, with all that's going on. This whole series of tours has her on edge."

Sally smirked. "No, this is personal for her."

Parker's face paled. "How do you mean?"

Sally peered at him suspiciously. "Come on, Parker. Everyone knows that Jack was her favorite. The way she bragged about him and always comparing us to him on tour."

Parker played it cool. "You're right. There's no denying that he was the teacher's pet. But to tell you the truth, I always thought he was a loose cannon."

"Speaking of loose cannons," Sally said, "apparently Steve had an amazing day on the slopes with Marc."

"And Dante?"

"He worked it hard, according to Marc."

"That's unfortunate."

Sally took the last bite of her pastry before patting her tummy. "That's it. I'm going to bed."

Parker got up and gathered the dishes. "I'll run these in the kitchen." Sally had left by the time he swung through the kitchen door. Turning the corner to go to his room, Parker almost ran into Günter. "Dude, you freaked me out."

The dreary looking man shrugged and muttered, "A message for you." He handed Parker a small envelope then left. Ripping it open, Parker read the note.

Please come see me. I am in the Bistro.

There was nothing more, not even a name. Intrigued, Parker walked to the lobby and then cruised through the glass door that led to the quaint restaurant. There, in a booth along the window, sat Kara. A perplexed gaze rested on her face, reminding Parker of Jack.

When their eyes met her cheeks blushed, and she broke into a full smile. She pointed to her glass of red wine. Parker shook his head no and settled into the elegant wrought iron chair opposite her. "So how are you?" he asked, not knowing what else to say.

She didn't answer his query. "I needed to see you."

The soft light overhead reflected off the rim of her wine-glass. There was also a glimmer in her eyes, but it wasn't a reflection of the light. It was the clash of conflicting emotions. Parker tried to make a joke. "If it's about the gelato, well, I haven't had a chance to try it. Got there a bit too early today."

Kara ignored the comment. "Remember my friends at the Grosse Gabel the other night?"

"Yeah."

"I've known them for a long time."

He shrugged. "They're your friends."

"Yes, but here you are, a stranger, and we just met. Then you see me for just a short time, and then we talk, and I feel like you know me better than any one of them."

"Maybe because we have similar jobs. I understand what it takes to do what you do. And, as I said, you do it so well."

"I wish my friends could see me like that when I am at work and taking care of my people."

"You've never had any of your friends on a flight?"

"Oh yes, many times, but they don't see me like that. They aren't capable of seeing me the way you do."

Parker smirked. "Yeah, I get it I suppose."

Kara finished her wine and stared at the empty glass. "My friends tease me that all I care about is my job. They don't understand. They don't believe that if I had a choice between a great career and a great marriage, I'd rather have the great marriage."

"I would too. As much as I love this job, and it is a great job, I'm not defined by it. It's what I do, not who I am. But people like you and me; we don't have to make that choice. We've already achieved one of those goals. I'm sure you'll have a great marriage, too."

Kara smiled and patted his hand. "If you find the right job you make it great. It's the same thing with love."

"Don't your female friends ever talk about that?"

She shook her head. "They talk about their great house or their amazing car, the fancy clothes or the newest styles. It's always about eating at the chic restaurant but never about the food. It's first to see the popular movie but never about what that movie means to them."

Parker pointed his finger and Kara, then back at himself. "We talked about a great movie."

Kara brightened. "Yes, we did, and I watched it last night. At least I tried to watch it, but honestly, I was so tired I fell asleep." She let out a self-effacing laugh before speaking seriously again. "We didn't just talk about the movie. You spoke to me about how it made you feel, and the impact it had on you."

"Mostly I talked about the crush I had on the female lead."

"You said I look like her too, and you were right. I couldn't believe it myself. Even with that, you never hit on me like so many men do."

"Yeah, well it's just not right to hit on a woman who's already committed."

"You should tell that to my friends."

"Seriously?"

She shook her head. "Yes. All of those boys last night? They've hit on me at one time or another."

Parker shrugged. "Does Thomas know?" A stern look crossed her face as she shook her head. Parker shook his head too. "I wonder how they'd like it if someone did that to them?"

"They're too arrogant to think that anyone would do that to them."

Kara reached down and pulled her handbag up from the floor. "So that is why I came here. I came to thank you for our conversation last night. I wanted you to know just how much I appreciate your kind words and the way you spoke to the beauty inside of me. It's so nice to know that there are people in this world who understand and respect the importance of a person's character." Reaching into her bag, she pulled out a white envelope. "This is for you." Standing up, Kara held out her hand. "Goodbye, for now, Parker Moon. Please be careful in your travels, and friend me on Facebook so we can stay in touch."

Parker grasped her fingers and gave them a gentle squeeze. "I'll do that, Kara. Goodbye."

After she walked away, Parker ripped into the envelope to find an Austrian Airlines trifold brochure. Opening it up, he saw an image of Kara serving a passenger on board a flight. It was a lovely image, one that reflected her physical beauty, as well as the goodness that projected from her soul. On the bottom of the page the following words were written in black marker, just below her image: "From Austria, With Love."

James Bond never had it so good.

EIGHT

The Grosse Gabel Brewpub

PARKER HELPED the drivers unload the jam-packed luggage bays. He then worked his way through handshakes and hugs to say goodbye to everyone in that first group. Following the last few passengers into the terminal, Parker settled into a metal lounge chair at a familiar, strategic spot. He played on his phone while keeping an eye out for that recognizable, silver Tourcey Travel bag tag. The first one he saw was dangling from an upright, wheeled suitcase. It belonged to an ashen-haired guy wearing metal-framed specs. Parker waved at him.

"You must be one of us," the middle-aged man exclaimed with an enthusiastic shake of the hand.

"Yep, I'm Parker Moon, one of your US-based, Tourcey Travel guides."

"Great to meet you."

A hand full of tourists swarmed around the pair. A bearded fellow interrupted any further introduction, ignoring Parker to direct a question at the older guy. "Hey Mr. Dee, did you bring your own equipment or are you renting?"

"Renting, Tom. I decided to avoid being burdened by a lot of heavy luggage. I'm sure they'll have plenty of quality rental gear for me to choose from." A youthful, thrilled-to-be-here exuberance colored his words. Turning back, Mr. Dee grabbed Parker's shoulder and gave it tug as if they were old chums. "Mako's bringing up the rear," he told Parker. "Flights went well, very well. I doubt if anyone is as eager to get on a mountain as I am. How's the skiing been?"

"To be honest," Parker explained, "I haven't had a chance to get out on the slopes yet. But I hear everything's great. The weather's been perfect throughout the area. Every ski area is reporting lots of fresh snow and yesterday. It was bright and sunny everywhere."

The man's grin grew larger with every word Parker spoke. "Oh, you must be chomping at the bit." He touched the corner of his eyeglasses to make sure they sat straight on his face. "But don't worry, I'm sure you'll find time to ski."

Until that moment, Parker had had very little desire to ski, but something about this man brought it out of him. "I'm sure I will, and I'm looking forward to it. But the job comes first. I'm here to make sure everyone has a great time, whether they're skiing or taking in the sites."

The surrounding group had grown in number, filling up a large chunk of the walkway. So Parker delved into his "Welcome to Innsbruck" spiel. As soon as he finished, Mr. Dee introduced him to another middle-aged man. "Parker, this is my good friend Doctor Franklin Manning."

The oval-faced physician leaned over rigidly as if cranked into place. "I've always gone by Doctor Frank. I hope you don't mind." His stiff demeanor wavered as a vivacious woman slipped in-between the three men, forcing Doctor Frank to introduce her. "Oh, and this is my honey."

"Nice to meet you," Parker said.

She had an older woman's face, a younger woman's short, frilly hairstyle, and a caustic personality. "It's just nice to meet someone on the ground," she cracked. "We've been on a goddamn plane for so long I feel like a caged animal." Parker could appreciate the appropriateness of her comment after glancing at her leopard print coat. "I suppose we're staying with this whole group?" She reached up to primp of her hair, forcing a set of gaudy, thick, silver bracelets to clank down her forearm.

Parker put a spin on his reply. "Yeah, but we'll pretty much have the hotel to ourselves. We've booked almost every room. I think Mako's gonna have to find a closet somewhere."

Ripples of laughter went through the group, assuring Parker that the long flights had afforded them plenty of time to get to know his pal. Doctor Frank's lady friend confirmed as much. "Don't worry, sweetheart, I'm sure Mako will find a very comfortable place to spend his evenings."

Seconds later, Mako's commanding voice boomed down the corridor. "What's going on up there?" The crowd parted and up stepped Mako wearing a skinny black tie and navy blue sports coat. His white shirt was a bit wrinkled, and Parker assumed it had started the journey that way. "So what's up with our transportation?" he asked Parker. "Is it ready and waiting?"

"Yep," Parker replied, holding up two fingers.

Mako nodded his approval then stepped back so the entire group could hear his voice. "All right people, listen up. Most of you have already met my associate, Parker Moon. He's going to make a call right now to queue up our ground transportation so we can get on board and get to the hotel without a hitch. I want everyone to follow us out, and we'll direct you accordingly. It's time to lock and load."

The mass of people obeyed without question, moving deliberately to gather their luggage and file out. Mako wheeled a khaki colored duffel bag, and Parker snatched up his friend's backpack. Soon they were through the double glass doors and out onto the cold concrete. After announcing the boarding protocol, Parker and Mako stopped to watch the tourists deposit their luggage and skis and queue up alongside the waiting vehicles.

"You've got 'em well trained already," Parker said.

"Of course I do," Mako boasted. "How's it going on your end?"

"Sally's fine. Everything else seems to be okay, accept the fact that the group leader hates my guts."

"The group leader?"

"I know, hard to believe huh? Usually, I've got them right in the palm of my hand." As Parker spoke, a spicy, woody fragrance enveloped him. Another whiff sent his head spinning, as it triggered the vibe. Glancing around, he realized the source of his immediate attraction was a woman in an insulated, red bomber jacket.

She had a slight crook in her nose and a Dodger blue baseball cap on her head. Sandy blonde hair was scrunched up between her ball cap and the jacket's faux fur hood ruff. Cruising past them, she left quite a lovely wake. Parker's eyes followed her.

Mako grabbed his shoulder and gave it a yank. "What group leader?"

Parker glanced at Mako to reply. "Steve, Steve Severin."

Returning to the woman, Parker watched her spirited walk, focusing on shapely, jean-covered legs. She traipsed along the pavement in well-worn, leather hiking boots, finally stopping to join the queue that waited to board the second vehicle in line.

"Steve Severin?" Mako badgered, regaining Parker's attention.

"Yeah. Why?"

"Steve's second in command," Mako explained. "He's the top sales guy, but he's not Mr. Big."

"The itinerary has him listed as a group leader?"

"Okay, so he's *a* group leader, not *the* group leader."

"So who?"

"You just met the man, a-hole," Mako jeered. "Mr. Dee? Max Dittmar. He's el jefe, the owner of SojournSports."

Peeking discreetly over Mako's shoulder, Parker watched the blonde board the last coach. "Oh, okay," he replied.

Mako noticed the drivers slowly loading the baggage onto the coaches. "Come on. We'd better help."

They waded into a sea of luggage and ski bags, selecting them by size and lining them up beside the rear coach. Working as a team, Parker and Mako then moved on to the lead vehicle. As soon as the last bag slid into the luggage bay, Parker hurried back to last motor coach.

"Where are you going?" Mako asked, forcing his friend to stop.

"You take the lead coach," Parker said, raising his eyebrows up and down. "And I'll take the one in the bomber jacket."

Mako got into Parker's face. "What the fuck, chief? You're kidding, right?"

Parker pulled his head back. "Not at all. You have no idea how strong of a vibe I'm getting from her."

Mako let out a devious laugh. "Forget that right now, pal. Just write her off."

"What, like you have?"

"Abso-fucking-lutely." Mako's jaw slackened. "I mean, she's cute, but no cover girl."

"Not for any magazine you'd read."

"Regardless, she's taboo."

"For who?"

"For you, dude, especially for you. I know you, man, and I can see how this girl may fit your build. But you've got to listen to me. Don't even think about that girl. She'll only bring you trouble and pain."

"You're my only pain," Parker quietly raged. "I'm getting the vibe. There's something special about her."

"Oh yeah, there's something special about her, but not your kinda special."

Parker was exasperated. "What's with you lately? Why are you so compelled to protect my emotions?"

"Parks, trust me. I'm telling you that this one's verboten, and for a good reason."

"Which is?"

Mako sighed. "She's Max's babe, bro."

His words were like a pin in Parker's balloon. "Can't be."

"Yes, she's already someone's special lady."

"No way."

"Brooke and Max are a couple, sure as shit. They've got the only suite in the hotel, aka, the honeymoon suite." He pulled up a copy of the rooming list on his iPhone and shoved it in Parker's face. Typed together in the last space it read:

Max Dittmar
Brooke McCaslin *Group Leader*

It was a cruel twist of fate. Mako understood and immediately tried to bolster his friend's spirits with a one-armed hug. "All right, all right, I can feel your heart melting all over the cold ground. So I'll make you a promise. If you can steer clear of her, then I'll be cool with you-know-who."

It wasn't much of a bargain. Protecting Sally from Mako was merely a hassle. Parker's real conflict was with his recent commitment to self, the resolve that burned in his belly to give love a fair shake the next time it came his way. Still, it was only an initial vibe. Parker didn't know for sure if those feelings were mutual or genuine. How could Brooke McCaslin be the right one if she was already with Max, the big boss at SojournSports? A relationship with her could ruin his career.

Parker had no choice but to avoid her, so he shook Mako's

hand. "It's a deal." He then ran back and jumped aboard the lead transfer coach.

IT WAS APPARENT, as some of the group gathered at the bar before dinner that evening that, Max's presence diminished Steve's notoriety. Steve didn't do himself proud either by fawning over his superior. "Can I freshen that drink, Max? How about a shot?" But it wasn't "Max the Money Man" or "Mr. Big" who took center stage. It was just Max, a charming, unambiguous fellow. He was an amiable man, too, speaking proper English in a soothing voice. Parker thought that Steve could learn a lot from a guy like Max.

Something else was quickly evident to Parker that early evening: the beautiful essence of Brooke. He stepped into the small, crowded bar only to be consumed by that sense. She stood at a tall table talking to Ronni, and when Parker slipped past her to grab a beer, his heart twitched like a meter.

She glanced at him when he stepped up to the bar, smiled warmly, and then turned back to Ronni. Parker couldn't look away from her, however. Her face was too hypnotic, holding his stare like a silver charm swinging right before his eyes. Ollie's voice was the only thing to break the spell.

"Parker, can you give me a hand?" The flurry of pre-dinner drink orders swamped the erstwhile hotelier and his bartender. Parker did as asked, slipping behind the bar, reaching for a glass, topping it off and passing it over to a waiting hand. After a few more pours, the orders subsided, and everyone made their way to the dining room.

Ollie motioned for Parker to leave but the guide stuck to his chore, wiping down every inch of the bar. That's because he was reluctant to go. The force of Brooke's attraction had such an impact on him that he was sure the other tourists would sense his feelings for her. Still, he was obliged to join his guests.

So after another few minutes' delay, Parker set down the towel and walked into the dining room.

Swiveling his head, Parker sought out her location so he could take a safe seat far away. That one glance, though, betrayed his plan. It was all he could do after that to let her out of his sight. Seeking a place to hide, Parker meandered the room, bumping into a chair here and squeezing between two dinner guests there. Stopping to survey the room, again, he looking despondent, like the last one left standing at musical chairs.

The only empty seat he could see was at a table for five. However, it sat at the end of Max's long table, where Brooke also sat. Sensing that everyone was watching, Parker pried the chair away and awkwardly plopped down. A slow, solo clap began. It was Mako, seated beside Max. "Looks like you got a winner there, Parks."

It was classic Mako, drawing huge laughs. Parker acknowledged his friend's joke, smiling and waving. He then introduced himself to the guy in the blue hoodie seated next to him. "I'm Roberto," the man said. Roberto, in turn, introduced Parker to his three friends, Anish, Jason, and Zack. They all began to badger Parker about the ski conditions.

"You can ask the local guy, Marc. He'll be here right after dinner," Parker answered. "Trust me. No one knows more about skiing Innsbruck than him."

Roberto wiped his thumb across his nose. "I can't believe we're here."

"Yeah," Jason explained while scratching at the short growth of beard on his neck. "We've been planning this trip forever."

"You guys ski together often?" Parker asked, glad for a conversation to distract him from Brooke.

"Every year since college," Roberto explained.

"This is year seven for us," Jake said.

"Yeah, but it's probably the last one for Zach." Roberto cast a glare at his friend across the table.

"Cut it out," Zach replied.

Roberto laughed and then explained to Parker. "Our boy here is getting hitched in June, and his lady's not gonna be keen on him taking a full week away from her."

Anish interrupted. "Our first trip was to Stowe. We were very tight for cash, so we slept in our car the first night."

"Yeah, that trip was crazy," Jason nodded at Roberto. "And you skied the whole time in those old bibs with duct tape holding the crotch together."

"Dude, I had a blowout," Roberto explained. "Those were my lucky bibs, too."

Leaning back to laugh, Parker noticed that he had a clear view of Brooke. She hovered just beyond Jason's ear. Better still, Roberto's sizable head completely hid Parker from Mako's suspicious eye. Throughout their conversation and delicious dinner - braised beef tips, roasted root vegetables, and garlic-mashed potatoes - Parker took advantage of that view. He couldn't have chosen a better seat if he tried.

Regardless of Mako's perspective, Brooke was beautiful. He relished her visage with every single peek he sneaked: her modest smile; her smooth skin, clear like fine sand that rests beneath clean, shallow water. Even the imperfections of life lent themselves to her beauty: the tiny birthmark on the left side of her neck, the uneven brow, and the slight twist in the middle of her nose.

Her aura thrilled Parker the most. It enveloped him in a rare, radiant vibe; comforting and yet coercive, driving his desire, like the smell of fresh cinnamon rolls in the morning or bacon sizzling in a cast iron skillet. Closing his eyes, Parker called on his inner voice to help fight off the craving he felt for her. It was Sally's voice, though, that rang in his ear.

"Hey, Parker?"

"Yeah?"

She knelt down by his side. "Max wants to take the group out for a drink."

"Seriously?"

"Yes."

"Everyone? Tonight?"

"Right after Marc leaves. I was thinking about the pub where we went to the ski club meeting."

"Yeah that's a great place, and an easy walk from here but dropping in on them with a ton of folks last minute? He does know that we have over a hundred people in this group?"

"I've already asked a few of the tables, and there's not much interest. Most everyone's tired from the long travel day. He just wants us to offer it, that's all."

Parker looked at his four tablemates. "You guys up for a pub crawl?"

Roberto shook his head. "No way, man. We got beer right here. The plan is to play some cards and cash in early so we can hit the slopes tomorrow."

Jason spoke up. "Why go anywhere? I'm already sitting at a table full of suckers with money to burn."

He pulled out a deck of cards. Still eating, Roberto cast Jason a glare. "Put those away and let me finish my food first."

Parker turned to Sally. "Okay, I'll make an announcement, but Max has to understand that we'll only be able to accommodate twenty people or so, last minute like this. Any more than that and it's off."

Sally looked hopeful. "Maybe no one will go, and we can call it a day?"

UNFORTUNATELY FOR THE TOUR GUIDES, a handful of tourists did elect to go. A cold wind ushered them inside the Gross Gabel Brewpub. A burly hostess led them upstairs and into a cozy, private room that Günter was able to reserve for them. The timbered, open room gave the space a cavernous feel. Brooke was there with Max, of course. Parker was glad when she filed down the long banquet table first. Max, Ronni, Steve, Doctor Frank and his honey as well as the Donovans, followed. Three other couples moved in on the opposite side, followed by Sally and Mako.

Parker took the last seat by the entrance. A server stepped in and detailed their beer choices. Steve quickly ordered a liter of the local brew. Everyone followed his lead.

Although Brooke sat far away from Parker, she still gave off one hell of a vibe. It shimmered from her body like burnished waves of radiating heat. Fortunately, a conversation with Alice Donovan diverted Parker's attention.

"Thank you so much for bringing us here." The petite, older woman's grin seemed to float just above the collar of her cream-colored turtleneck sweater.

"Just so it doesn't keep you from the slopes tomorrow."

"Oh, we're not skiers, dear."

Parker joked. "So you two must be snowboarders?"

Alice took his facetious query to heart. "Oh no," she responded. "Bill visited Austria when he was in the service. He wrote and told me how beautiful it was here. He wrote often." Bill Donovan wore timidity like a cheap mask. His square chin hardened, cheeks reddened, and his narrow mouth barely managed to smile. Alice blushed and continued. "He promised to bring me here someday. It only took forty-five years, but he kept that promise." Apparently pleased by that kept promise, Alice leaned into Bill and hugged him with such affection that Parker felt a bit embarrassed for watching.

The conversation halted when the large, liter-sized mugs of beer arrived. Steve cried out before anyone could take a sip. "Don't drink yet." One by one the heavy glass mugs thudded back onto the tabletop. Everyone gazed at Steve curiously.

"Have any of our tour guides been to Oktoberfest in Munich?" He asked. Mako shook his head. Steve looked at Parker, then Sally. "Either of you?"

"No," Parker answered for them both.

"Huh? I thought you were all world travelers?" He asked with a smirk. "And you haven't been to Munich?"

"Been to Munich," Mako responded, "just not for Okto-berfest."

Steve ignored him. "Okay, well they play a little game there called masskrugstemmen. It's a challenge of strength. You hold your full beer mug out in front of you, arm straight. Whoever holds it the longest, wins."

"What do you win?" Parker asked playfully.

After an odd gaze, Steve replied. "You mean at Oktoberfest?"

"Whenever."

"Well, we always played for the beer." Steve held out his beer, just as Parker raised his for a sip. Steve assumed it was a challenge. "So it's you and me."

"You and me what?"

"Competing. Let's go. We'll play for the beer."

Max interrupted. "I'm buying all of the beer tonight, Steve."

"Okay, well, we'll play for cash. Twenty bucks." Reaching awkwardly into his pocket with one hand, Steve threw a folded bill on the tabletop.

The schoolyard competition caught everyone by surprise. Max protested meekly. "Steve, this isn't necessary."

"No, no big deal. It's just for fun."

Parker looked like the guy at the carnival stuck sitting over the dunk tank. Then he shrugged, accepting his fate. "Yeah, all right." He pulled out two tens to cover the bet.

"Just so you know a liter of beer weighs about five pounds," Steve said, laughing. "On the count of three, you have to stick your arm out straight. You can't bend your elbow, not even a little bit, or you lose."

Steve counted down, and they both extended their arms. Parker stretched the beer mug out so far that Alice only had to lean forward to take a sip. Then Steve started trash talking.

"Oh I bet that feels good, doesn't it? I can hold it here all day. How's your shoulder feel? Starting to strain yet?"

Mako tried to support his friend. "Come on Parks. You can do it." Parker closed his eye to focus. He held strong for a long minute before his arm began to quiver. "Hang in there." Mako exhorted.

Parker's arm and shoulder muscles burned. Firming his wrist, he squeezed his eyes closed to psyche himself through that second minute. When he opened them to check on Steve, however, Parker saw that his competitor's strength hadn't wavered. The glass mug stuck out straight at the end of Steve's rigid arm. His confidence shattered, Parker set the cumbersome glass down, bouncing the edge firmly on the table and sloshing some ale down its side.

"Yes." Steve hollered. "I knew you couldn't do it." Smiling proudly, Steve leaned forward and swiped up the bills. "You know, we're offering discounts on training classes with a health club partner. They have a few clubs in the Chicago area, so maybe you should take advantage of that promo and sign up for some strength training? I think the women's class is on Tuesdays and Thursdays."

Although Parker grinned good-naturedly at Steve's taunts, he was seething inside. After all, what did Steve know about his strength? He'd never seen Parker on the job, under duress. Steve had never witnessed Parker at his best, dealing with a dilemma. Not some lost piece of luggage either, but an actual crisis: a sick driver, broken down transportation, a missed ferry-boat or an injured passenger. Parker solved every problem that came his way, making sure his people were dealt with calmly, respectfully, and taken to where they had to be safe, as soon as he could get them there.

Parker had the kind of strength that really matters, strength of character. Steve wasn't capable of understanding that. His loud prodding was irritating, and Parker wanted nothing more than to sock him on the chin. As it turned out though, Parker didn't have to defend himself.

"My turn, Steve," Brooke said. "Double or nothing." She tossed forty dollars on the table and cocked her head. Only stone cold seriousness shone in her eyes.

The silence that had allowed Steve's cajoling now turned on him. Waving a hand, Steve tried to dismiss her. Then he squinted his eyes to play dumb. "What?"

Brooke pointed to her beer. "I haven't taken a sip yet if you're worried that I'll cheat."

Steve's eyes remained fixed on her beer glass. Then his face contorted. He twitched and huffed and looked to Max for an out, but Max would have nothing to do with it.

"What's the matter?" Brooke challenged. "Are you afraid that I'll show you up?"

"Cut it out," Steve said, chuckling through clenched teeth.

Brooke eased back on the bench seat and then leaned into him. "You know, Steve, this is our vacation too." She glanced around the room. "We're here to enjoy ourselves, to have fun. We don't need this kind of macho crap. So can you please just let it go?"

Steve cowered. "All right, I'm cool." He held up his hands to surrender. "Like I said, it was just for fun. No big deal." Again he chuckled uneasily and then tossed the money back to Parker. Relieved, everyone enjoyed a drink.

Brooke leaned forward and turned to Doctor Frank's lady. "I'm sorry, but that was just too much testosterone in the room for me, right, Honey?"

Parker smirked to discover that Honey was Harriet

Manning's legitimate nickname. "I can't even lift this thing to drink it." She barked before looking at Doctor Frank. "Why the hell didn't I order a Manhattan?"

Laughter erupted at her blunt honesty. Alice Donovan pondered the statement, and as soon as the outburst receded, she agreed. "That sounds so good, Honey. I've not had a Manhattan in ages."

Her remark triggered a conversation about memorable cocktails, drawing everyone's attention. Parker took advantage of that and glanced at Brooke. She turned her head, met his gaze, and smiled. He returned the smile. After she looked away, he lingered over her for a while, at least until he felt a sharp pinch to the thigh.

"Off limits," Mako whispered, leaning close to Parker's ear.

Parker twisted in his seat to get closer and mumble a reply. "I know. I know. I'm cool."

"You're far from cool." Mako's breath warmed Parker's ear. "I can see behind those big brown eyes that she's already got a hook in you."

Honey's booming voice disrupted their liaison. "So what are you doing tomorrow, Parker?"

Surprised, Parker replied, "I'm scheduled to stick around the hotel to troubleshoot."

"I know that. I've already checked with her," Honey pointed to Sally. "What I want to know is, can you get away in the morning? Brooke and I want to walk around and see some of the local sites. We'll need you to take us if you don't have anything important to do?"

Ambushed by her request, Parker reeled. He looked to Sally for an out, but she only made it worse. "Of course he can do it. One of the reasons why we keep a guide in town is to provide services, like local tours, for our guests. He just has to have his phone to be accessible in case of an emergency."

"Good, then we're set," Honey confirmed.

Parker hid his dread well. "All right, then let's meet in the hotel lobby at nine in the morning."

Honey winced. "That's a bit early isn't it?"

Brooke intervened. "Nine o'clock is perfect. We just want to go for a couple of hours then you can leave us where we can shop and have a nice lunch."

Parker firmed his lips. "I'll have some restaurant suggestions for you in the morning. If you decide where you'd like to eat before we leave, Günter can make the reservations."

Honey waved him off. "We'll do our own thing."

Sally leaned up on her forearms and cleared her throat loudly before speaking. "Hey everyone, earlier today we were in contact with Mr. Reinhold Lutz from Lutz Travel. They're our tour partners here in Innsbruck. We've hired them to provide all of our ground operations, the tours, and transportation.

"He's offering our group an opportunity to test run a potential new excursion. It's an evening toboggan trip. They'll provide round-trip transportation and sleds. They'll run shuttles back to the top of the run as long as anyone wants to go. Afterward, they'll have a bonfire at an old barn so we can enjoy hot grog, along with some fine Austrian music."

"Ah yes," Mako joked, "Mozart and manure."

Honey burst out laughing. Sally paid no mind. "This is just a test run, the first trip he's done with this vendor so he'd like us to critique it. Best of all, the trip is free for our Sojourn-Sports guests to compensate for any inconvenience caused by the transfer problem last week."

Max looked at Steve. Steve responded, "We had a bad heater. Froze our butts off."

"That was on your airport shuttle?"

"Correct."

"The Innsbruck airport shuttle?" Max shrugged. "Okay, I suppose."

Parker could have sat back smugly. After all, he was the one who had worked out the deal with Reinhold. Parker's feelings for Brooke, however, left no room for complacency. He couldn't avoid her tomorrow, of course, and Honey's presence made the walking tour much more vexing. No doubt she'd be sensitive to any hint of feeling that Parker may show for Brooke.

He mulled that over while Sally concluded. "The event takes place on Tuesday night. Transportation will arrive precisely at nineteen hundred hours. We'll pass out flyers tomorrow night at dinner and take reservations. I'll need a final count right after breakfast Monday morning so that I can call it in at noon. Just to get an idea, how many here think they want to take the trip?"

A few hands shot up in the air. After taking a count, Sally turned to her associates. "You guys can go. I'll hold down the fort."

Both Mako and Parker nodded, and then Parker shot a glance toward Brooke to confirm that her hands were still resting on the table. He also noticed that Steve looked noncommittal.

"How about it Steve?" Parker asked. "Are you in?"

The big guy peered sheepishly at Max. "I'll go if you go Max?"

Max shook his head. "It's not for me. But you should go, Steve, and represent SojournSports." Encouraged, Steve nodded his head and raised his hand.

Parker took a sip of beer while mulling over tomorrow's dilemma. At least he'd be able to work the toboggan trip without the pressure of Brooke's presence, he surmised. That relief lasted only a few seconds, however. Lowering the stein from his face, Parker saw Brooke smile and slowly raised her hand.

"I've changed my mind, Sally," she said. "The toboggan trip sounds like fun."

NINE

Old Town Innsbruck

PARKER PACED BACK and forth in the Austropa lobby, occasionally stopping to watch the pedestrians pass by the window on their way to work. He glanced at the time on his phone. The women were late. A voice called out from down the hall. "Sorry!" Parker turned to see Brooke looking adorable in a multi-colored beanie and a long, black down coat. "So sorry I'm late."

"Where's Honey?"

Brooke's face soured. "It's no use trying to drag her out of bed. She says it's jet lag but the only thing Honey likes better than shopping is sleeping."

Parker mustered up a nervous grin. "That's fine. We can still go."

"That's good to know." Her sarcasm was calming.

"What time do you need to get back for lunch?" he asked.

Brooke thought for a second. "How about eleven-thirty?"

Parker checked his phone. "Okay, that'll give us enough time to get an overview of the landmarks and key historic sites. If we keep a good pace, we'll still be able to tour at least one main attraction. Do you have any preferences?"

"Whatever you think's best."

"Then I suggest we visit the Hofkirche, Court Church. It was built as a memorial to Emperor Maximilian the first, and it houses his cenotaph along an amazing collection of artwork. I'd bet even Honey would be impressed."

"That's saying a lot," Brooke said cheerily. "Let's go."

Parker tapped his phone to open the scouting trip notes for backup and then led Brooke to Maria-Theresien-Strasse. As they strolled down the wide boulevard, Parker delved deep into a history lesson, detailing Innsbruck's ancient beginnings, strategic location, and its pivotal role in early European development. Despite his lecture, Brooke didn't appear to be bored. She just kept peering up, her eye intent on the white-capped peaks of the Nordkette mountain range that dominated the skyline.

Parker shifted his focus to the early seventeen hundreds, as they closed in on St. Anne's Column that centered the square. He pointed a gloved finger at the statue of the Virgin Mary sitting atop the smooth, pink marble pillar. They stepped to the base of the column so the guide could finish his spiel.

Parker commanded her attention with his gestures, his words and the passion of the subject in his voice. Again he raised a hand toward Mary, denoting the golden stars that formed a halo around the statue's head. Brooke shaded her eyes to fend off the sunlight that glistened off of them. Then she studied the figures of the four saints surrounding the base.

A middle-aged man nearby was also sharing information with someone about the celebrated column. He read out loud from an app on his phone. Parker noticed the woman with him had scrunched up her shoulders. She looked cold and bored. He motioned to Brooke for them to leave.

"Just so you know," Parker said as they hiked away, "you can download some excellent apps that offer self-guided tours of Innsbruck's historic sites. I toured these places on my own, though, and gathered info from more than a few sources. I'm no expert on Innsbruck, but I did my due diligence."

Brooke grinned. "I'm sure you did, and I do appreciate your efforts."

Her honesty made Parker smile. It was her beauty; however, that thrilled him. Her charming face was framed appealingly between the hat that edged down her forehead and the puffy coat collar that squeezed her neck. Sharing his knowledge of history was one of Parker's passions, but he wondered how much of his current enthusiasm was due to Brooke? Buzzed often by her warm vibe, he struggled to control his emotions. He talked a little faster than he would have if she'd been just another tourist. His smile radiated just a bit more often, and his wit was sharper than usual, trying to impress her while strolling up Herzog-Friedrich-Strasse and into Old Town Innsbruck.

The "Goldenes Dachl" was soon upon them. Standing on the street below, Parker and Brooke looked up to admire the landmark. The copper-tiled roof covered an alcove balcony on what once was the Tyrolean sovereign's place of residence. After recounting the Golden Roof's history, Parker offered Brooke the opportunity to visit the museum, housed inside the building, to learn more.

"No, I'm good," she said.

A passing cloud had dulled the roof's luster. Brooke shifted her feet on the frozen cobblestones as if antsy to walk away. "Not impressed?" Parker asked.

"It's interesting."

"You know, if you look at it with a little perspective, it's an amazing work of art."

"How's that?"

"Well, back in the late middle ages, few people would ever see something as lavish as this."

"I suppose."

Parker tried a different approach. "All right, close your eyes."

"What?"

"Close them all the way, real tight." She did as instructed. "Now pretend that you're standing here back in the early fifteen hundreds. There's no sprawling city, just these small, medieval buildings that surround you now. You're standing right in the heart of the old Gothic town."

"Okay." Brooke squeezed her eyes tighter.

"Now imagine that you're a baker and you toil at your trade all day, every day. Your drab life is completely out of your control. Your pay is determined by a local craft guild that also decides how much bread you can bake."

Brooke shook her head slowly. "I don't want to be a baker."

"You have no choice. You come from a family of bakers. You started working at the age of seven."

"Seven?"

"I'm afraid so."

"Boy, I really don't want to be a baker."

"What can I say? Anyway, you've just delivered bread to a local merchant for a big event being held later that day. Above you is the ornate balcony and its golden roof, where the Emperor, the Holy Roman Emperor, Maximilian the first from the famous House of Habsburg, will sit to view the festivities. Now open your eyes and look up."

Brooke did, and as Parker began to detail the numerous artistic aspects of the balcony, she began to admire the unique craftsmanship adorning it: the sculptures, frescoes, paintings, and reliefs depicting Emperor Maximilian's life. When the sun peeked out, the tiles shimmered in its light.

"It's beautiful," Brooke said, surveying the scene. "And to think they created all of that way back then without technology. It is very impressive." Then she turned to Parker. "But I still don't want to be a baker. How about a princess?"

Parker shook his head. "Sorry, but that can't happen. You weren't born to royalty."

"All right, if I'm a baker then I am, without a doubt, the best baker in the city. I make the most delicious pies and hearty loaves of bread."

"Don't forget about the strudel."

"My strudel? Of course, it's luscious." She gestured as she spoke. "In fact, I've built up such a reputation that even the emperor orders from my bakery."

"So you bake for the royal family?"

"I do bake for the royal family."

Parker looked reticent. "I don't know. A baker such as yourself, baking for royalty could be troublesome."

"Why? What do you mean?"

"I mean a baker of your caliber, with your looks, might easily capture the heart of the emperor."

After a quick blush, Brooke looked aghast. "Oh, my, I'll have an affair with the king."

"With the Prince."

"Then it's the Prince."

"Either way, the Queen will be pissed, especially if you are with child."

"Oh my, a bastard."

"Could be a bastard, or worse."

"What's worse than a bastard?"

Parker grinned. "A very punctual tour guide." He bent over and swept his arm in a grand gesture, directing Brooke down the narrow lane. She complied, giggling as if it was the funniest thing she'd ever experienced.

While they meandered up and down the quaint village streets, history wasn't the only subject of discussion. "So you're from Chicago?" Brooke asked.

"The suburbs."

"I've only been to Chicago a couple of times. The neighborhoods there are fascinating. I'd love to live in some awesome old neighborhood."

Remembering her Dodger cap, Parker asked, "I assume you're from LA?"

"Southern California. Our home is out in the middle of nowhere," Brooke shrugged. "I don't know our neighbors. I've only seen them pulling in and out of their private drives. We run the businesses from home, so when we're there, we're mostly working."

Brooke stared straight ahead as she spoke, allowing Parker a chance to admire her profile: the soft slope of her jaw, her flat cheek and the gentle turn in the middle of her nose. Every so often, wisps of blonde hair would blow across her face, and she'd reach out to pull them away. Parker thought to reach out, too. He could quickly solve the problem by tucking those errant hairs back beneath her beanie, but that wouldn't be appropriate. More so, the temptation to kiss her would have been too much to overcome.

Surrounded by quaint shops and antiquated architecture, they enjoyed a pleasant walk up and down the narrow streets. Then they worked their way over to the grand Cathedral of St. James, where they stopped for a while to admire its opulence. Skirting the edge of the sprawling park, Hofgarten, the couple walked past barren limbs of trees frosted over from blowing snow. They saw the columned façade of the Tiroler Landestheater and enjoyed a view of Leopold's Fountain. The couple continued their journey, walking parallel to the Imperial Palace that stretched the length of the avenue.

Somewhere along the hike, Parker realized that he no longer had any personal space. It was as if he and Brooke were in a bubble, isolated from the outside world. He didn't notice other pedestrians as they passed, and soon they weren't interested in ruminating over some rich architecture.

"So, what do you do for work?" Parker asked Brooke.

"I run Max's nonprofit, and manage his investments and real estate. I also run Max. I keep him on schedule."

"What about SojournSports?"

"That's his baby, even though we're lucky to break even at the end of the day."

"I assume he's a good boss?"

"He should be. I'm good to him. You have no idea what I do for that man." A moment of silence allowed Parker to contemplate the meaning of her reply. Then she added, "One thing for sure, they couldn't pay me enough to do your job."

"They don't pay me enough. But I love the job."

"So here you are in such a beautiful place, and you're working. Wouldn't you rather be playing?"

"I can always find time to play when it's important to me. The thing is that I enjoy my job. I love what I do. I mean, come on, how can it not be fun to take people on vacation and show them a good time?"

"How can it not be incredibly stressful sometimes?"

"No lie, the work part can be rough."

"But you do get to travel all over the world."

"The travel part's great," Parker said. "What I appreciate most is the feeling of value that this job gives you. There are a lot of challenging times on tour, but those are the days that leave me with the most amazing sense of satisfaction. At the end of a tough day I can kick back, relieved, but also relaxed, and say to myself, wow, I did that. I solved that problem. I made somebody happy today. I helped someone make a lasting memory."

Brooke peeked over at him as they crossed the street. "If it's a stop-and-smell-the-roses-perspective, you're right. I can't complain. Our lifestyle is very comfortable and exciting."

"And now you're on vacation?"

"We're here for two weeks and then it's off to Vienna for the Spring Stamp Show."

"The what?"

"The Stamp Show. Max is a stamp collector."

"For real?" Parker asked.

She paused mid-step. "Trust me, it's Max. He invests heavily in the things he loves. When Max commits to something like his stamps or his ski program, he takes that investment very seriously." •

Those were ominous words to Parker's ears, portending to the enormous risk it would be to fall in love with Brooke. He countered with a more auspicious perspective. "If it's something you love you should take it seriously. I love my job, so I take it very seriously. That commitment allows me to get more out of it, I think."

Brooke smiled benevolently and replied. "I envy you for that."

HAVING CONCEDED HIS PUNCTUALITY, Parker decided to go with the flow while touring the Folk Art Museum. He and Brooke maintained an even pace through the assortment of Tyrolean artifacts: clothing, woodworking equipment, and furniture. Reminding her that a follow-up visit to the museum was always an option, they made their way to the top floor. Parker directed Brooke to a door that opened automatically, ushering them onto a walkway that overlooked the spectacular interior of the Court Church.

Brooke's reaction was even more than Parker could have expected. Gasping at the scene below, she admired the stunning high altar, massive, wooden organ, the marble covered tomb and the wrought iron grille surrounding it, black with gold highlights and edging. Coming down to enter the church nave, its central aisle, they slowly reviewed the substantial blackened-bronze statues that stood in two opposite rows, like sentinels guarding the tomb. They got as close as they could to examine each figure, one by one and shared their reactions with one another.

Brooke marveled at the detail of the male sculptures, the intricate patterns cast into their armor, their weapons, poses, and posture. Parker was impressed with how the women's dresses flowed to the floor and draped delicately over the statue's base. Many of the figures, they noticed, were crowned, hatted or helmeted. Even their hairstyles were the subject of discussion.

"Check out her braids," Parker said, noting the two long ropes of meshed hair that ran from thick to thin, far down the back of one of the castings. Brooke laughed out loud at the king whose pageboy hairstyle ended in a tightly curled flip. Parker enjoyed comparing the styles of mustaches and beards.

After examining each of the statues individually, Parker and Brooke took one long, last look at them all, standing at the end of one of the rows. The eerily silent moment spooked Brooke. She seized Parker's arm and held it securely. "These things are creeping me out. What is it about them?"

Her grasp and the closeness of her body caused an incredible tingle to run up Parker's spine. He firmed his emotions and theorized. "I think it's their faces. They're expressionless, and that makes them look grim, even haunting. It's the metal, the bronze. It can only reproduce their image. It can't capture their souls."

Affected by his explanation, Brooke squeezed his arm gently. Her tender touch was like an electric shock to Parker though, and he pulled away. Quickly, he tried to cover up that reaction by yanking out his phone. "Well, we'd better head out if you want to make an eleven-thirty lunch." Using his official tour guide voice, Parker hoped to create some emotional distance between them.

"Honey and I never made a firm reservation anywhere,"

Brooke stated. "So nothing is set in stone. I'm sure she'd prefer to sack out a while longer. Why don't we get some coffee?"

Although they had already grown too close for his comfort, Parker was easily swayed. "How about some gelato? I know a great place back in Old Town."

PARKER WANTED to be a travel guide ever since he was seven years old. That was the defining summer of his youth, the summer he lost his father and found his way. "Mom took us to the Wisconsin Dells," he said while dipping a plastic spoon into a cup of chocolate gelato. "I saw a billboard to ride the Ducks and begged her to take us on it."

Stifling heat had welcomed him on board the amphibious craft, but Parker never mentions that when retelling the story. He only talks about being awed by the guide. Seduced by the uniform - khaki shorts, safari shirt and a cool pith helmet - Parker was also captivated by the man's confidence, knowledge, and sense of humor. What fascinated him most of all though, was when the guide hopped on board, leaned over, and invited Parker to ride up front, to sit next to *him*.

Brooke listened with interest while tasting a mouthful of her creamy, hazelnut flavored dessert. She then interrupted Parker's storytelling and asked thoughtfully, "What happened to your father?"

Parker prepared to make a witty reply, something to diffuse the sympathy she was sure to extend him. The seriousness of her query, however, and her discerning look, tempered that urge. "He died of cancer," Parker answered. "He was thirty-two."

"I'm sorry to hear that. Your father was so young. You mustn't have known him very well?"

"I know enough. My family talks about him often. I've heard lots of stories, great stories."

"I bet he was a decent man."

"A lot of people loved him."

That was legacy enough. Brooke didn't need to know any more about his father's suffering and the loss the family still felt. Besides, Parker wasn't comfortable talking about those memories, like the old aunt who'd seek him out for a dance at all of the family weddings and parties. How she'd rest her head on his shoulder, close her eyes and relive a dance that she danced with his dad long ago. He couldn't put into words, anyway, how it felt to hold that dear woman in his arms, slowly swaying to the music while she wiped away her tears.

"We were lucky to have him as long as we did," Parker concluded. "My mother worked hard to make up for him. She's an amazing woman, strong and yet sensitive, who's filled my life with love. So things turned out well for me. All in all, life has been great."

Brooke dropped her eyes to the table. "It's all relative, isn't it? It's not how bad things are. It's how well you handle them. You were given a tough situation, suffering a great loss at such a young age and growing up without a father. And yet, you handled it well. Why is that?" A puzzled gaze etched her face. "And why is it that, despite your situation, your dream came true?"

She wasn't looking for an answer. Besides, there aren't always answers for everything. Sometimes there are only scars. "I grew up without a father, too," Brooke slowly began. "Except mine didn't die, he was just too busy and too selfish to care about my mother or me. My dad left us when I was little. All he could ever do was send us money. I suppose I should be grateful for that."

"As soon as I could, I got married. Yeah, I was married once. My husband was older than me. He was a workaholic. He was abusive, self-centered, petty and insecure. He was probably the biggest asshole I'll ever know. At least I hope so. I married him just to hurt my dad, at least that's what my thera-pist suggested. It turned out though that the only one who got hurt was me."

It just came right out of her, like dumping a bucket. The thought of her heartache was painful for Parker, and he hoped that by talking about it, Brooke would feel better. But talking made it worse. She spoke about how it was better never to experience real happiness, but Parker didn't believe those words because she was just so uncomfortable speaking them. Her whole demeanor had shifted. Her eyes flitted around the room as if searching for a place to hide; wanton eyes that glowed like the light of a candle.

"I know about pain," Parker replied, "I know the harm that it can do to a person. But I also know that pain can be a great teacher. I've learned a lot from it, anyway. It's given me a sense of perspective. It's also taught me tolerance, and respect for the simplest of blessings, like a delicious gelato," he held up his spoon and smiled, "or a great conversation."

Brooke smiled back at him, slowly and tenderly. Her anguish seemed to melt like wax around the wick. "I appreciate your insights and your wisdom. But I'm afraid that I'm one of those people hardened by pain."

"Maybe you're just hard on the outside so you can protect the real you, the person on the inside?" Parker glanced down at his gelato, afraid that he said too much.

Brooke pursed her lips and raised a brow. "Well, I suppose that's a fair analysis."

Parker shrugged. "Sorry for being so presumptuous. The older I get, the more I start to sound like my grandpa."

"Is he a philosopher or something?"

"In some ways, yeah," Parker replied, "I think he's wise. He's also a legend when it comes to fishing, at least up in the Northwoods."

Brooke was intrigued. "I bet he's a fascinating person."

"That he is. He's also a very independent person. He owns a fishing resort, the Arrowhead Resort."

"Oh, so he's a businessman." There was a tinge of contempt in her words.

Parker came to his grandpa's defense. "At least he has an interesting business, and it makes him happy."

"I suppose, as long as he's making money."

Parker shook his head. "No, he doesn't make much money. That's not what's important to him. Self-determination is his driving force. He values liberty above all else. Money is just the means to that end. Owning the business gives him his independence, but it also gives his life purpose. Money can't buy you that."

Brooke's face froze as if he'd touched a nerve, so Parker shifted gears. "Grandpa's a very positive influence on my family, but as I said before, my mom is everything to us. She's always been there, encouraging you to find your way, do your own thing. And if you fall, she'll be there to pick you up. She'll pick you up and dust you off and push you right back out there so you can give it another go. My family has not always been happy with my decisions, my choices or my actions, but as long as I'm true to my values, they'll love me no matter what."

Brooke began to glow like the open door on a cast-iron stove, warmed by his words from the inside out. "That's it," she said, "that's why you are who you are. Your whole life, you've been surrounded by people who support you, by a family who respects you and love you. Do you know how lucky you are?" Brooke stared at him while stroking her chin as if admiring some classic work of art.

"I suppose, but I believe every human being can do what they need to do for themselves when the time comes. It's there. They just have to summon up the courage to do it. For example, not only did you call out Steve last night at the bar but you also humiliated him in front of everyone. Where did that come from?"

Brooke waved her hand at him. "Steve's a blowhard. He's afraid of me because of Max."

"Still, it took courage. I admire that."

"Thanks," she said off-handedly. "I just don't have the strength to suffer that fool anymore."

IT WAS ALREADY noon when they returned to the Austropa. Brooke peeled off her hat and jacket as soon as they entered the lobby. Parker rushed over to the antique hutch centered on the back wall. "I'll call Honey."

"Can you please ask her to be ready in half an hour?" Brooke started down the hallway.

Snatching up the curved handset of the retro rotary phone, Parker dialed Honey's room. She answered the call lazily. "Hello."

"It's Parker. We just got back. Brooke is running up to change so she asked if you'd meet her in the lobby in about thirty minutes?"

Honey agreed. After hanging up, Parker realized that Brooke had forgotten to grab her room key. "Crap." Securing the key fob from Günter, he hurried down the hall and called out to Brooke, who was still waiting for the elevator. "You forgot your key."

Cradling her jacket in her arms, Brooke turned around. The top few buttons of her shirt were unbuttoned, exposing a white camisole T-shirt beneath. It wasn't the sight of the smooth skin below her neck that held Parker's stare. It was the unique object that dangling from a delicate silver chain that rested there. "What's that?" he asked.

Her eyes followed his, and she grabbed hold of the necklace, twisting the chain in her fingers. "Oh, this is my stamp."

"Your what?"

"My stamp. Max gave it to me. It's from my birth year. Take a look."

Parker leaned in close enough for her delicious fragrance to cloud his thoughts. When his head cleared, he inspected the pendant: two circles of thin glass pressed tightly together, held by a band of silver edging. Set between the panes of glass was an old, dull stamp boasting an image of a pink-stemmed rose with soft green leaves.

The stamp itself was meaningless to Parker. The foreign words, however, imprinted elegantly across the bottom, sent shivers down his spine. One word was in Dutch and the other in French. They read like a rhyme, like a cherished, childhood poem long ago forgotten and just now remembered:

België-Belgique

"It's a Belgium issue from nineteen eighty-eight," Brooke explained.

Parker didn't say another word, but his hand trembled when handing her the key fob.

TEN

Salzburg

ZAFRINA'S once-promising prophecy had become perilous, and it gnawed at Parker like a beast on a bone. Scheduled to escort the Salzburg day trip on Monday morning, he could only cringe after reading Brooke's name on the list of passengers. Still, he didn't know the exact course of Brooke's heart despite the promise of time spent, the personal conversations they shared, the intriguing glances and flashes of flirtation. Even if Brooke did have a genuine romantic interest in Parker, there was every reason to believe that she'd never act on them. So he resolved to treat her like every other customer on that excursion, or better still, avoid her.

It should've been easy. SojournSports' tourists filled up the entire transport coach. Parker strolled down the aisle to greet each of them while the scruffy-bearded Lutz Travel guide stood in front, patiently eyeing his wristwatch. Coming back, Parker shuffled past Brooke, Honey, Ronni and the Donovans. Honey urged as he went by, "There's an open seat next to me?"

"Thanks, but I've got to sit up front with the guide, behind the driver." He made it sound as if he'd be involved in running the excursion. It wasn't true. The locals - a personable young man named Hans and a sour-faced, middle-aged female driver named Nadine - would do all of the heavy lifting. Careful not to make eye contact with Brooke, Parker continued to the front. As soon as he slipped into the window seat next to Hans' backpack, they were off.

Hans grabbed the microphone and stood in the aisle next to Parker, facing the tourists. "Hello everyone, and welcome to today's tour of historic Salzburg." The young man's full face was animated, eyes flashing and head swiveling to connect visually with as many passengers as possible. "You have before you a very committed person to make your travels today educational and pleasant. So please feel free to ask me anything at any time. Of course, the person working most hard for your comfort and safety will be our wonderful driver Nadine. We can please now give her applause to thank her."

Everyone clapped. Parker peered over his shoulder to see bright, smiling faces. He also noticed Honey waving her hand emphatically. Hans saw her too. He smiled pleasantly. "Yes, you have a question?"

Honey lowered her arm. "How long is the drive to Salzburg?"

"I will be reviewing our agenda for the day just now, but this is a fine question. So I will tell you that it is a little more than an hour to when we will make our first stop for sightseeing. Then continuing further, we will enjoy a beautiful drive through the alps for another hour or so to get to Salzburg."

"So it's about two and a half hours?"

"Correct, yes, it will be about two and a half hours total, but we will be making a sightseeing stop along the way. Meanwhile, you can just sit back and relax to enjoy the amazing scenery. I will fill some of that time with interesting information about the surrounding area and share with you the details of our Salzburg sightseeing tour."

The vehicle ambled on. Parker closed his eyes and leaned

his head back. Trying to block out Brooke, he focused on the groan of the engine and the shift of the transmission. But then she'd speak, and he'd be drawn to the voice, isolating each word as it floated out of her mouth. Every distinct utterance thrilled him until Honey's booming voice invaded his subconscious. "Franklin wouldn't let me rent a beamer. Otherwise, we'd be driving ourselves instead of being stuck on this bus."

Brooke's reply sweetened his ear. "I prefer to take the tour. We don't have to worry about how to get anywhere, and we have a local guide who knows everything. Of course, we also have Parker."

Tickled to hear her speak his name, Parker hid his delight from Hans who grabbed the mic, glanced at his watch, and addressed the group. "I see we are right on schedule, so I will like to tell you about our itinerary for the day and then share some interesting anecdotes about Salzburg and the surrounding communities."

Hans was an excellent storyteller, engaging everyone with his insights. After he finished, the whole vehicle buzzed with a myriad of conversations. Again, Parker was caught up in Brooke's vibe. It pulled him to her like some emotional undertow. Soon he was groping for the sound of her voice. Catching her laugh, he even manipulated the seat lever to lean further back and get a few inches closer to her.

THE TOUR COACH rolled into Salzburg right on schedule. They visited a few of the "Sound of Music" sites before arriving in Old Town. Hans retook center stage. "We are now in the heart of the historic city of Salzburg, and we will let you off just a short walk away from Getreidgasse, which is the main shopping street here. There is so much to see, stores to visit, and restaurants where you can have lunch. However, I will first lead everyone down to the birthplace home of Salzburg's most famous citizen, Johannes Chrysostomus Wolfgangus Theophilus Mozart."

Proud of his precise pronunciation, Hans grinned before continuing. "Yes, this is correct, the official baptismal name of our famous Wolfgang Amadeus Mozart. Admission to the birthplace museum is included with our tour today, and it is self-guided. As I said, I will lead you there, but after that you will be free to have lunch and wander the area on your own, knowing where the most intriguing sites are located by using the small guidebook and map that I will be passing out just now."

Looking at Parker, Hans winked and leaned over to set the mic in its clip. Parker reached for Hans' backpack. Accepting the bag, Hans pulled out a stack of thick pamphlets and then toddled down the aisle stopping to share the guidebooks, and some small talk, with each pair of passengers.

The lumbering vehicle settled at a convenient spot near the core of the historic city where it could unload its passengers. Hans reiterated his instructions and asked the group to gather at the corner so they could walk down the street to Mozart's birthplace together.

Parker stood on the cold concrete next to the door to help each passenger disembark. Honey came down the steps like a bear after a long hibernation. "How cold is it?" she growled.

"It's chilly, but not that cold," Parker replied.

Honey glanced up at the dark clouds gathering in the sky before giving Parker an angry eye. "I just hope we don't get stuck in a blizzard on the way back." Shaking her head, she stepped away just as Brooke stepped in the doorway.

Her face brightened beneath that tight beanie cap. Pausing atop the step to gaze at the old buildings, she smiled. "It's lovely here."

Parker's spine tightened and his nerves shuddered as

Brooke's vibe swarmed over him. He fought it off, though, exchanging only a polite smile while holding out a hand to help her down. She walked away, and he assisted the next passenger. Once everyone had exited the coach, Parker spied Brooke's cap in the center of the crowd. He decided to use it as a marker, like a lighthouse warning him not to stray too close to disaster. When Hans waved everyone to follow, Parker stayed in the back of the group and soon they were parading down Getreidgasse.

After inspecting a few storefront windows, Parker peered up to marvel at the finely crafted wrought iron signs that dangled like elaborate, age-old neon above the crowd. Ronni too, appeared to be mesmerized by the myriad of scrolling signage, walking only a few feet ahead of Parker in a pink down coat.

"There are courtyards behind these buildings that are supposed to be amazing," he said, stepping up to walk beside her.

Ronni took his word for it. "I'd love to see every one of them. This city is full of architectural gems, and it stinks that we only have time to see a few of the sites. Everyone seems to think that Salzburg Cathedral is a must-see, but the place I want to visit is Kollegienkirche."

"Collegiate Church?"

"Yes. Have you been there?"

"No, I took this tour last week but never made it there."

Ronni's eyes flashed beneath her slouchy knit hat. "Well, you just have to see Collegiate Church. If not this trip, then get there the next time you visit. I've read all about it. It's magnificent, one of a kind." A deliberate grin crossed her face. "You know I'm an architect by trade?"

"No, I didn't know that."

"Not many people do."

Parker understood, seeing her always take the back seat to

Steve. Intrigued to learn something personal about her, Parker pressed for more. "So are you a big fan of Mozart?"

The diminutive woman shook her head. "Not a big fan. I don't know his music, to be honest. I just know that I like what I hear when I hear it. It's not something we listen to very much."

"On Sunday mornings when I'm home from tour," Parker explained, "I like to kick back and listen to classical music. It helps me unwind."

"Hmm." Ronni seemed to be imagining his routine. "That sounds pleasant."

Parker smiled. "That's a great way to describe it."

There were a couple of excellent reasons for Parker to hang out with Ronni. First of all, she'd help him keep his mind off Brooke. Secondly, a good rapport with her could positively influence his relationship with Steve. It helped too that she seemed to be a fascinating person.

Parker gestured to Mozart's birthplace just ahead. "You know, some folks don't find exhibits like this interesting. It's just a curiosity for them. Unless they're really into classical music or history, well, it just can't compete with the shops and the beautiful old buildings."

"I know you want to check out Collegiate Church and some of the other architectural sites, so if you just want to cruise through this museum, I completely understand. But if you are willing to go through it with me, I'll do my best to make it interesting. I'm not saying that it'll be the highlight of your trip or anything, but I'll make it worth your while for sure."

Ronni's dark eyes brightened. There was an "aw shucks" quality in her voice. "Okay. That sounds good to me."

THE GLOCKENSPIEL CHIMED a quaint Mozart melody as

the group gathered around Hans outside of the mustard-colored row house. They listened intently as puffs of warm air belched from his mouth when he spoke. "This was the Mozart family home for twenty-six years - not the whole house, just the third floor. A family friend, Johann Hagenauer, owned the building. It was only a simple apartment consisting of a kitchen, a living room, one bedroom and a study."

The modern museum had expanded to three full floors with each floor dedicated to a particular aspect of Mozart's life. Hans detailed the museum's key points of interest and then sent them on their way. "So I am leaving you here but will meet back with you in just about two hours at the precise location where we left you off. Please have fun, enjoy visiting some of the sites, get a good bite to eat, and meet me back at the transport coach promptly."

Tipped off by Brooke's cap, Parker watched her jockey through the museum entryway with a crowd of other Tourcey Travel tourists. When she disappeared inside, Parker led Ronni to the queue by the door, and they began their tour. The pair traipsed to the third floor to peek at the tiny kitchen and Mozart's birth room. Ignoring the friendly conversations of others and the creaking floorboards, they also admired the original portraits of Mozart and his family members. Then they moved down to the second floor to view the stage sets and learn about some of the musician's most famous operas.

While perusing the exhibits, Parker engaged Ronni with historical insights into the culture of Mozart's time, the social structure and the dominance of the church in everyday life. Ronni responded with thoughtful questions, and it seemed to Parker that she was enjoying herself.

When the tour ended, Parker followed Ronni out onto the street. Immediately she was confronted by Honey. "What took you so long? You were in there forever. Remember we made lunch reservations on the ride over here? Now we're going to have to hurry, or we'll be late." Huddled nearby, Alice and Bill Donovans looked disconcerted by Honey's admonishment.

Brooke stood alongside Alice, also looking forlorn. Parker assumed that she was upset with Honey's outburst. She could have been worried about missing their lunch reservation. Then again, Parker couldn't help but wonder if perhaps she was jealous that Ronni had been hanging out with him?

Either way, Ronni tried to diffuse the situation with a bogus apology. "Sorry, but I got stuck behind some slow walkers, and a few exhibit rooms were jammed. I bumped into Parker though, and he showed me a couple of interesting things in there."

"That's surprising," Honey said. "I was bored to tears in there." Light snow began to fall, so Honey turned up her coat collar and walked away. Ronni followed, with the Donovans close behind.

Only Brooke remained, standing alone, chilled by the breeze. "If you'd like to join us for lunch, Parker, I can add you to our reservations."

Her invitation was genuine and sweet, but all Parker heard was the Siren's song. "Thanks, but I'll have to pass." A rush of air swirled the snow around her. She bristled and then snugged her cap down over her ears. Parker fought off the urge to hug her warm. "I ah, I have to scout out some sites. Otherwise, I'd go." Firming her lips, Brooke nodded and left, but Parker knew that she recognized the lie.

DESPONDENT AND TORMENTED by feelings for Brooke, Parker wandered the streets alone. After stopping for a light lunch and a warm cup of tea, he walked out into the lightly falling snow and onto University Square. Before him was the white façade of Collegiate Church. Parker stood in reverence of the place while examined every architectural detail of its exterior: the freestanding belfries, squared towers, and wrought-iron window coverings.

Caught up in despair, Parker wasn't interested in sightseeing. And although a world famous church would be an ideal place for his brooding, religious rituals seldom satiated Parker's spirit. He preferred an audience with the Almighty out in nature; ideally up in the great Northwoods, where the serene silence would soothe his soul: hiking, fishing, and canoeing. He found his way up north, his path to fulfillment and enlightenment. He discovered his power up there too, the dynamic capacity of his being. Up north was his spiritual center. It was where his father went to die.

The magnificent edifice that rose before him, however, was giving off an intense spiritual energy. This church felt different, not at all the foreboding house of worship that he'd been forced to go to as a child, but rather, a welcoming source of spirituality, a peaceful place of respite. Pedestrians walked by wrapped snugly in winter coats and hats, but not one of them had entered the church. No one else seemed to feel its unworldly allure.

Parker noticed that a thin layer of snow had settled atop the frozen ground. He looked back to see his wandering shoe prints faintly outlined in it. Facing forward, he viewed the church again. It was lying directly in his path. Sensing that he was meant to walk inside, Parker stepped up, tugged the door open and entered.

A blast of warm air greeted him. Unzipping his ski coat, Parker allowed the heat to penetrate his light blue flannel shirt and warm his skin. He continued further on, becoming more and more enthralled by its vast, steep and stunningly white interior. After taking in its splendor for half a minute, Parker felt comfortably alone. He sauntered down the wide nave as if strolling through a meadow, moving toward the central cross-section of the church. Parker stepped through shafts of light that filtered from the windows of the intimate dome, brightening the circular-patterned, brown and white square tile floor.

There were no pews; no other furnishings at all except for four benches, one in each corner, and a cluster of chairs shoved off to the side. Parker slipped into one of the chairs to savor the silence. It was spectacular. He pulled off his gray ski jacket and tweed edged cap and rested them on the seat beside him. Then he relaxed, closed his eyes, and began to meditate, allowing the sanctity of the building to envelope him. He was alone with his thoughts, and with the one being he defined as his Creator.

Parker was always comfortable talking to God, but the enormity of that church made him self-conscious. The stark central walls, adorned with only a few sculptures, made him feel a bit unworthy of an audience. He bowed his head again, though, and got right to the point:

Usually, I just say thanks. You know how much I respect the gifts you've given me. You also know I've been looking for someone like Brooke to come into my life for quite a while now. While I appreciate the opportunity, I have to push back a bit on the circumstances. Still, if it's time for me to decide between what I have and what I want, please give me the guidance to make the right choice.

A voice suddenly echoed from behind, shaking him alert. "Are you praying?"

It was Ronni, sounding as if she just exited his head. Parker struggled to reply. "I am, sort of, I suppose."

Ronni lit up. "It's amazing, isn't it?" her question was rhetorical. "I'm glad you were able to find your way here, too." She peeled off her cap and coat, laid them on a chair, and took the seat next to him. "I love the Baroque period, don't you?"

Parker was still wondering how he didn't hear her come in but answered her question anyway. "I don't know that much about it, but I am intrigued by this church. It's elaborate, in a minimalist sort of way."

Ronni smiled cordially. "This is the work of Johann Bern-hard Fisher von Erlach. He was the famous architect of the Imperial court in Vienna who studied under the great Bernini in Rome. What he did was create one of the most unusually impressive Baroque-style churches in the world. Some say that this is his masterpiece, and I would agree."

The unassuming brunette had become an enraptured orator. Her dark eyes glimmered, and Parker followed her gestures back and forth as she pointed out various aspects of the expansive interior.

"Now take a good look up at the spandrels. That's the space between the columns on the ceiling. There you'll find the Passion of Christ, the stations of the cross." She lectured with all the proficiency of an experienced professor, and her lone student remained engaged, bending his head back to peer straight up, then lowering his vision to spy her again, to confirm that it was indeed Ronni speaking.

Her depth of knowledge was impressive. "And notice how the architect has manipulated the natural light to create a visual illusion, a perception of immense space," Ronni smirked, and then pointed up, rotating around to view the interior in its entirety. "That's the genius. The genius of Baroque architecture lies not just in its elemental beauty, as seen in the innovative use of curves to please the eye, but how it uses illusion to create a sense of grandeur and magnificence."

Parker's private guide stood up and waved for him to follow. "Come on, let's take a closer look at the space." They strolled toward the ornate marble altar. "There are four chapels inside the church, each dedicated to the saint who represents the four faculties of the university: Thomas von Aquin, that's Thomas Aquinas, for theology, Ivo for law, Lukas for medicine and Katharina for philosophy. Notice, too, the seven, beautiful, red marble columns that represent the seven wisdoms."

Parker followed the shuffle of Ronni's soft-soled boots

across the marble floor. He focused on her detailed description of each artifact: the four statues of the archangels; the figurine of the Saint Maria Immaculata; the high altar, with its marble cherubs and sparkling gold leaf friezes, that reminded him of the Court Church in Innsbruck, and the tomb of Emperor Maximilian.

Occasionally the rear door would creak open, and a few tourists would wander in. They'd walk up and listen in on her lecture for a few seconds then slowly slip away. Alone again, Ronni led Parker to a secluded section of the church. "This is the confessional area," she explained in a whisper and then stepped back to allow him access. "Take a look at the exquisite detail here."

Following Ronni's gesture, Parker walked over to the confessional doors. While he was drawn to examine the excellent craftsmanship of the woodworking, Ronni said something peculiar. "So now's a good time to chat about what's really going on here."

Parker looked up while his hand smoothed across the etched, aged wood. "What do you mean?"

"I mean that you and I have a lot in common with Baroque architecture." Stepping next to him by the door, Ronni had a mysterious look in her eye. "We're both masters of illusion. You're the dutiful tour guide, and I'm Steve's fiancée."

Then she moved over him like a dark cloud, lips first: hungry, reaching, wet, wriggling lips. He tried to resist, but before he could even think, she had forced him through the confessional door and into the tight, square wooden booth.

"Whoa, hold on a second," he protested. "You've got the wrong idea."

"It's only wrong if we get caught." The narrow door creaked as she closed it behind them. Then she covered his mouth with her hand. "Quiet," she murmured. "All I want to hear from you is the sound of satisfaction."

Parker felt the delicate, wooden mesh screen against his back and his mind reeled. He thought about all of the poor souls who had dropped to their knees in that tiny space. How many repentant sinners, he wondered, had bent down onto the wooden kneeler at his feet, their hands crossed to pray on the worn wooden ledge where his rump now rested? Parker could almost hear their voices whispering through that square mesh screen, seeking forgiveness from the somber priest in the adjoining space.

There was no priest, of course, but it didn't matter. There would be no forgiveness. No penance could cover this deed. Even when Ronni removed her hand from his mouth, Parker didn't say a word. He didn't stop her from unbuttoning his shirt and kissing his chest. There was no protest when her fingers yanked the flannel shirttail from the back of his black corduroys, and then stroked the skin along his sides. Parker did take hold of her arms, though, but only to brace himself. That's when she looked up and smiled.

It had to be the heresy of the act. How could anyone justify the lust? But the devilish grin on Ronni's face, that Huck Finn grin, was meant to seal the deal. It was the kind of smile that spoke to the rebelliousness of human nature, one that was no stranger to the exhibitionist side of lust. That look said it all: how deliciously depraved it would be to go down on someone in the confessional of one of the most treasured of all Baroque Catholic churches?

Eagerly she unbuckled his belt. Parker searched for the courage and the strength to say no to her, but all he could do was whimper an excuse. "Ronni, this is not good. We'll get caught."

The words came and went in the close, stale air of that confessional. Ronni never flinched. She must have known that the opportunity would be lost if she gave him a chance. So she leaned into his chest and ravaged his left nipple. Again, her hands slipped inside his shirt and moved up his chest to tightly grip his pecs.

Parker couldn't move. The exhilaration that rushed through his body was overwhelming. A second or two passed before he again realized the audacity of their actions, the wrongfulness of the deed to be done. But those seconds did pass, and it was far too long before the next moment of guilt came by, because Ronni had returned to his pants. She unfastened them and lowered his fly while her wet tongue probed his tummy. A second later her busy mouth was going south.

Parker finally pulled her head away seconds before the sound of approaching footsteps was heard. A confused voice followed. "Ja, hello?"

Parker froze. His mind whirled. Gripping Ronni tightly by the shoulders, he thought of a response. "Hello there."

Buttoning his shirt in an instant, Parker slipped the door open just enough to poke his head out. He saw two priests dressed in black shirts and slacks, standing about twenty yards away. Parker strained to convey a calm tone. "I'm just waiting here … waiting for confession."

They both looked at each other, bewildered. Then the elder priest, a bald, tubby little fellow, shook his head. "Nien, no confession today. See de schedule."

The skinny, dark-skinned priest nodded, smiled awkwardly, and then shrugged as if it were an everyday occurrence. "This happens sometimes," he said. Then they both walked away.

Parker heard them step through a doorway somewhere and close it behind them. "We've got to go." He clenched his teeth. "Now!"

Ronni was too startled to object. He yanked up his cords, cinched his belt, and hustled her out of the confessional. Grabbing their outerwear as he passed, Parker dragged Ronni to the exit just as a handful of senior citizens entered the vestibule. Outside, they ran out onto the cobblestone square and into a blowing snow. Finally stopping, they tugged on their coats while catching their breath.

Ronni let out a wicked laugh. "Do you believe we almost got busted?"

"Yes, I believe it. That was absolutely the craziest thing I almost did."

"I know me too. Wasn't it great?"

"No, not at all," Parker raged. Then he glanced around and lowered his voice to make sure no one could hear. "Ronni, we almost had sex in the confessional of a church. That's just completely outta control."

"Didn't it turn you on?"

"No, it didn't. You turned me on, but that's not going to happen again. I can't let that happen again."

Looking hurt, Ronni lashed out. "It doesn't matter that we didn't do it. And it doesn't matter if we don't ever do it. I can always say we did."

Parker was more angry than worried. "You wouldn't?"

Ronni crossed her arms. "I would."

There was courage in her words but fear in her eyes, so Parker tried to speak to the reason that lies in between. "Ronni, if I led you on in any way, I'm sorry. I didn't mean it. I'll be honest with you though. You are a beautiful woman and a very interesting architect. Seeing you in there, in your element was awesome. Still, I wasn't sexually attracted to you."

"Anyway, you're Steve's fiancée, and I have to respect that commitment. I hope you can understand that. I hope you won't lie to Steve and betray that honesty. But I can't do my job in fear. I have a ton of tourists to take care of and to tell you the truth; I can't worry about what you do." Ronni shrank away like a wounded animal caught in a trap. Parker concluded with some sense of compassion. "Besides, I don't believe you're the kind of person who'd do something like that."

Puddles formed in Ronni's eyes; clear pools of despair that seemed to have no bottom. Parker thought that at any second she'd break down, but she didn't. "You *should* be afraid of me, Parker," Ronni replied coldly. Trembling, she pulled on her hat, turned, and walked away. Parker bit his lip nervously. Then her head swiveled back. Her voice was bleak. "I don't know who I am anymore."

ELEVEN

The Toboggan Run

FIFTY-FOUR TOURISTS SIGNED up for Reinhold's free excursion Tuesday night including Brooke, who jammed into the hotel lobby with everyone else waiting for the transfer coach. Parker nonchalantly walked past her, noticing that, while she wasn't with Max, she wasn't alone either. The Donovan's had taken her under their wing. Continuing outside, Parker strolled over to Mako who waited by the curb, the falling snow dotting his bristly black hair.

"I see that trouble's along for the ride," Mako said.

Parker didn't hide his anxiety. "Yes, she is. And I'm sweating it."

"Not to worry pal," Mako replied confidently, "you just do your best to stay away from her. I'll be there to cock block for you if need be."

Thus reassured, Parker tugged on his black winter cap. Seconds later, the coach pulled up. It was seven o'clock sharp. Stepping on board as soon as the door opened, Parker met an eclectic woman dressed in a knee-length, silver and black faux fur coat.

"You must be Mako?"

A bush of copper-colored hair sat atop her head, squeezed into shape by a white silk scarf wound tightly around her forehead. Before Parker could reply, Mako's voice boomed out from behind him. "You'd be genuinely disappointed."

The woman pushed Parker aside like a shower curtain to wrap Mako up in a bear hug. Raising the back of her leg, she almost jabbed Parker with her stiletto boot heel. Then she cooed in a husky voice, "I'm Viktoria. We spoke on the phone earlier today."

Mako leered. "It is *so* nice to meet you." Passengers were starting to stack up behind them, so Parker broke up their embrace. "Hey guys, we've got people who want to board."

They squeezed tightly into the empty spot by the bus driver's seat and let the tourist pass. Parker joined the line, heading for the back. A heavy hand on his shoulder, however, forced him into the second row.

"We'll sit here," Mako edged Parker into the window seat then sat down next to him and admired the view. "Check her out."

Parker did. Viktoria's open coat exposed tight, white, yoga pants that covered her legs from the top of her boots to the bottom of a short, black, A-line skater skirt. A black sweater covered her torso tightly, from shoulders to hips. A shiny, black belt straddled her waist. Hanging onto the metal brace behind the driver's seat as if it was a stripper pole, Viktoria nodded at each passenger, mouthing a head count as they squeezed past.

One of the last to board was Brooke. Following the Donovan's, she scooted down the aisle. Mako ignored her smile and friendly wave. Parker grinned nervously, and a polite hello squeaked through his lips. She disappeared somewhere behind them.

Viktoria looked over the group to confirm a final count.

Then the driver hopped onboard. She nodded, so he dimmed the lights and shifted into gear. Once they rolled out of town, Mako coerced Viktoria over with a wag of his finger. She crouched down in the aisle beside him. "So are you going sledding tonight or slaying?" Mako asked.

"Sleighing?"

"Slaying," Mako said, then he spelled the word, "S-l-a-y-i-n-g because, with that outfit, you are deadly."

Raising an eyebrow, Viktoria puckered her mouth. "Trust me, darling, what's under the outfit is worth living for."

The motor coach bounced out of town and into the countryside. Soon they drove passed an old barn - colorless in the dark - sitting at the base of a long, broad, hill of snow. Traversing an incline, the motor coach ascended a narrow mountain road. The vehicle negotiated a few switchbacks, edging past ice-covered tree limbs to emerge onto a semi-barren hilltop. Parker peered out the front window to spot a log cabin, its roof buried in deep snow. The tourists chattered with excitement as they exited the coach and gathered in clusters nearby.

Parker and Mako trudged behind Viktoria towards the cabin, but she entered it alone. Seconds later she emerged with a lanky fellow who was wearing a lime green, reflective safety vest over a black powder coat. The man stopped by a row of squat toboggans resting along a wooden rail. Parker picked one up. The seat consisted of multi-colored vinyl strips laced tightly and secured around two wooden poles. The poles rested on metal braces that bridged thick wooden rails. Although lightweight, Parker confirmed it was sturdy, examining the front rails that curled up like long candy canes and fastened to the front of the bed.

Viktoria introduced the man in the vest as the "toboggan coach." His voice bellowed loudly, asking for everyone's attention. The group gathered quickly, his thick accent forcing them to pay attention. "Simply board the toboggan like so," he demonstrated by lifting one leg over a prone sled. Settling his bottom onto the bed, he grasped a single braided rope tied to each curled wooden runner, then leaned to one side and pulled. "And use the rope to steer. Just like skiing, lean into the turns. We encourage two people per toboggan, but there are enough sleds for single riders. We have free helmets for you to borrow if you choose, available in the cabin."

Tourists swarmed up and down the line of toboggans as soon as he finished. Planning to be last, Parker walked around to the other side of the building to examine the toboggan run. It was a panoramic vista. An orange safety fence on one side and a raised ski lift on the other bordered the gently sloping hill. Ground lights illuminated each lift stanchion, casting a faint glow across the slope. A formidable mountainside loomed off to the right, shrouded with dusty-white evergreens. They were huge trees too, hugging the snow as far as the eye could focus.

"Parker?" It was Alice Donovan. She was standing right behind him with Bill and Brooke. "Can you help find a sledding partner for Brooke?"

Her inflection was pleasant, her words harmless in their appeal. Could he? Of course, he could. After all, Parker was their tour guide. It was his responsibility to make sure that every tourist was accommodated. "It's okay to sled on your own," he reminded Alice. "She doesn't need a partner." The demure woman fixed an eye on him until he concluded, "But I'll ask around."

Parker tramped on the snowpack, asking every other tourist if they needed a partner. Circling back, he stepped to the edge of the hill where a large group had formed, ready to take off. Cupping his gloved hands, Parker called out. "Anyone need a partner?" There was no response. He took another look around, this time trying to spot Mako. His alleged guardian, however, was nowhere to be found. So Parker turned back to Alice, Bill, and Brooke. "Well," he said, lowering the earband on his cap, "I guess she can go down with me."

Brooke cast an embarrassed grin as Alice nodded happily. Parker stepped over and grabbed a toboggan from another worker in a safety vest. He slid it over to the Donovans. Bill fumbled for the rope, then tugged it, and pulled it away. Alice followed him. Once out of sight, Brooke turned to look at Parker. Ruddy-cheeked, she spoke philosophically. "Pretty weird, isn't it?"

Puzzled, Parker asked. "What's that?"

"This. You know. I mean, here we are."

Yes indeed, and to say that Parker felt weird about it was an understatement. A mélange of feelings tortured him: guilt for being so spineless in his lack of resolve to avoid her, shame for being so foolish to think that he *could* do that, and relief in finally accepting what seemed to be his fate. But as he stood there relishing her beauty - her cute, crooked nose and narrow, pouting mouth, the warm hue of her eyes that wrenched his heart - Parker realized that there was nothing weird about it at all.

"Yeah," Parker finally replied. "Here we are, just where we're supposed to be."

Brooke smiled as if she understood.

"Come on." He gestured at the few remaining sleds. "The pickin's are getting slim."

The last few toboggan riders had already taken off. Parker dragged their toboggan over to the soft edge of the hill. A raspy groan, then a perverse giggle stopped him cold.

"Oh, no."

"What is it?" Brooke asked. Mako and Viktoria suddenly appeared from behind the bus, answering Brooke's question. "Where's your toboggan?" she asked them.

"Mako's so slick," Viktoria quipped, "he doesn't need one."

After faking a laugh, Mako walked over to the railing to grab a sled. Parker followed, and the two guides were soon locked in a glare.

"I left you alone for half-a-second," Mako said in disbelief. "And now you're sledding with her?"

"Just sledding. I've got no choice so please spare me the skepticism."

Viktoria interrupted with a shout. "Come on. Let's go already."

After a quick glance back at her, Mako conceded. "She owns me, man."

"What about your promise?"

Mako stared at his friend impotently. "You're on your own."

Viktoria's boot heels were staked in the snow like picks, forcing her to twist around awkwardly. "When you have a full load," she yelled to the drivers, "shuttle back up here. We'll run shuttles as long as there are people to sled. Please make sure the boys have a good fire going and that they are ready to serve drinks at the barn."

Parker stepped up to query the voluptuous guide. "What happened to Reinhold? He was supposed to evaluate the trip this evening."

She waved at him. "He always does this. He's too busy all the time. So he says, Viktoria, you be my eyes and ears for the trip."

Mako snuck up behind and slipped an arm around the waist of her long, furry coat. "He can have your eyes and ears, but I'm staking claim to the rest of this body."

Viktoria appeared perplexed as he nuzzled her neck. "That's not what I meant." She reached back for his cheek and giggled anyway.

"Come on," Parker said, "save that stuff for the after sled party." He turned toward the departure point.

"Wait, wait, wait." Mako ordered. "Not there. Follow me."

They did. Mako led them about thirty yards into the darkness. The couples stepped past a strand of scraggly brush and stopped at the top of a berm. Mako pointed down the snow hill that grooved along the other side of the orange fence. It continued through a slight ridge before spreading out onto a gully, rolling alongside the tree line. At their feet were a series of old sled ruts etched in the snow.

"The sledding guy told me to head out on this side," Mako replied. "Even though it parallels the main run, it flows into a ravine. He said it's the balls."

"It's out of bounds," Parker protested.

"Tonight it is," Mako explained, "but the guy told me that they move that fence all the time." Allowing for no more objections, Mako pushed his sled to the edge and leaped onto the bed. The wooden rails creaked as Viktoria hiked up her coat and laboriously fixed herself on back. She clung to his thighs with a squeeze of her boots, and in seconds they were swooshing away.

Parker looked at Brooke for approval. She shrugged, so he rested their sled on the rim of the berm and hopped on. Brooke did the same and pressed her belly into his lower back. Parker dug his heels into the snow to shove off. Brooke squeezed his ribs. "Go baby go," he shouted. She let out a scream, and they lurched down the slope.

The ride was fast and bumpy. Parker noticed that Mako and Viktoria had veered off to the right and disappeared. He and Brooke flew through a ravine and did not slow down until the sled skidded up to the top of the rise. Parker tugged the rope and dug in his heels to stop on a flat spot.

"This is crazy fun," he declared. "Did you enjoy it?" He

looked over his shoulder to see an enthused expression on Brooke's face.

"It's great."

Mako and Viktoria came back into view, careening over a ridge to the right. Mako wailed loudly, like a rodeo rider on the back of a Brahma bull. Their sled smashed into a mound of snow and tipped over nearby. Viktoria struggled to free herself from a thick pillow of snow. Mako rose up from the whiteness like the living dead. He was ecstatic.

"Whoa boy," he hollered, half out of breath. Then, cupping his gloved hands to direct his voice, Mako shared some advice. "Hang to the right," he pointed, "it has a nice, solid surface that flows over a couple of short hills." Parker peered off in that direction, using the moonlight to make out the contour of the run. However, he also noticed that it skirted the edge of the woods, paralleling the mountainside.

"No thanks," he said, "those look like killer trees."

Mako snarled. "They're a lot farther away than they look." He and his brake woman got up and pointed their sled into the teeth of the slope.

"It's safe," Viktoria yelled out, her furry coat pelted with puffs of snow. "There's plenty of room between the run and the trees."

Brooke frowned at Parker, shaking her head no. Quickly nestling into the "go" position, Mako and Viktoria took off again. They were screaming and slashing down the slope in seconds. Swirls of fluffy white snow flew in their wake.

Directing their sled away from the trees, Parker and Brooke raked the snow with their hands and heels until gravity kicked in. Pouring down the mountain slope, they flowed over a series of small humps and into a narrow gully. Their sled careened from side-to-side like a float tube in a wave pool. The natural contour of the hill, however, kept pulling them closer to the trees.

The gully opened up to a flat spot, so Parker tugged the sled to the left. It was slick, and as their speed intensified, the momentum hurled them into another ravine. This one dipped low, and when their tiny wooden sled shot out of the other end, it went airborne. Landing off balance, Parker felt the front rails teetering over.

The rest of the ride was a tumble: snow and sled, Parker and Brooke. Landing face first into some powder, Parker struggled to get up. Then he shook off the crystals. "Damn," he said while gasping for air.

Brooke had landed flat on her back. She was almost swallowed whole by the snow. Parker squirmed over and dug her out. "Are you hurt?" he asked seriously.

"I'm fine," she replied.

Parker smiled. "That was fun, eh?"

She nodded slowly. "Oh yeah. Real fun."

On his knees, Parker held his waist to catch his breath. Then he fell back to recline against the snow slope as if it were a comfy chair. Protected from the wind in that shallow bowl, Parker could see a thicket of trees to the right, less than fifty yards away. To the left, a single rider skirted the orange fence, his sled flowing along the rolling contour of the run. They watched the sled level off and slow to a stop by the barn further below.

Brooke smirked. "They groomed the perfect sled hill, and here we are, out of bounds."

Parker winced, and then pulled off his gloves. "If we get down in one piece we can sled that side of the hill." He reached back to dig some snow from the inside of his collar.

"I don't want to sled anymore." Brooke squirmed back to nestle herself between Parker's legs. Parker wrapped his arms around her waist, yanked her close and leaned back into the firm, snow-covered earth.

The only sounds they heard were a breeze through the

trees and the muffled laughs from the tourists far down the hill. Wisps of chilled breath spewed from their nostrils and lingered like steam from a teacup. They sat peacefully, enjoying the tranquility of their surroundings, the night and the winter.

"I wonder if Mako and Viktoria made it down okay?" she asked.

Parker looked among the hemlocks and pine off to their right and saw nothing. His eyes wandered further down the tree line until noticing the dark outline of a sled tossed on its side in the snow. He then saw something rustle behind a clump of bushes. Brooke saw it too. "They must be all right," she said with a laugh.

"They're not all right," Parker opined. "They are all the way wrong."

Brooke took hold of his cold, bare hands and hugged them close to her chest to keep them warm. "Are they?" she asked.

Parker said nothing. He just admired the side of her face; glowing skin profiled against the starry sky. His thoughts, however, turned to Max. That stupid man, he should've been there. If he truly loved her he would've wanted to be there; to sled through the snow and hear her laugh; to see her happily breathing out wisps of warm air, her rosy cheeks creased with a smile.

Why wasn't he there? Why would he miss those moments? It could be that Max was just too old, or Brooke was too familiar to him. Maybe he just took her for granted or perhaps, the thrill was gone. But that was unimaginable to Parker. He could never tire of looking at rainbows or be bored watching fireworks burst in the sky. Autumn would never be just another season to him. Thinking about that only made him feel sorry for Max. To lose that sense of wonder was a terribly sad thing.

"I want to kiss you," Parker said as if the taste of her lips was all he'd been thinking about since the moment they met. Brooke didn't respond. She just twisted back to accept him.

Parker leaned down and kissed her gently, longingly. After a minute or so they parted, and Brooke turned away. Her scent filled the void, but that was enough for Parker. Drawn to the supple flesh on her neck, he ran soft kisses up to her ear and then lingered there to nibble on it.

Brooke moaned, unleashing her passion. Parker's lips lurched anxiously for her while Brooke's mouth reached awkwardly behind for him. Her ski jacket zipped open easily, and Parker fumbled for a handful of flannel, then a button, then cotton, latex, and lace. He tripped the front snap and cupped her breast. She squeezed his hand as he squeezed her skin. They caressed and kissed until her crossed legs began to separate.

It wasn't a reaction. It was an invitation. Parker's hand tugged at the snap of her black ski pants, then slipped inside, creeping down her body slowly, yet determined, spurred on by her short, fervid breaths, and her left palm that came up to press against the back of his head. The excitement caused her arm to quiver. She strained it back to cradle his skull, while his hand struggled between the tight folds of her clothing.

There was no stopping, no hesitation. Parker pressed her thigh, and her legs parted further, allowing his bare fingers their freedom. Mad kisses sparked his aggression, but Parker was also thrilled to have the power to satisfy her; the sheer joy you get when giving someone a special present.

She squirmed with every delicate touch. She shuddered when Parker caressed her, his tender, slowly paced motions building in momentum to pleasure. Her hips began to rotate to the rhythm. Again she quivered, and then again and again, while her left arm flailed behind his head.

The fever pitch finally peaked, and her thighs clamped down on his hand. Her body clenched together like a tight fist that she held for a white-hot, breathless second. That's when the happiness came. Parker could feel it extend to every inch of her body, tingling every nerve, spreading across her skin and penetrating every pore like a now gentle wave, breaking across the beach.

They both exhaled from exhaustion. Parker's head slumped on her shoulder, and his hands fell limp across her lap. After a minute's respite, Parker found the strength to kiss her tenderly on the cheek.

"We'd better be going," was all she said, pulling herself together.

The ride down was uneventful. Clinging to the sled like hapless passengers, Parker and Brooke raced down the hill. After stashing the toboggan away they joined the après sled party, taking great pains to avoid one another. Mingling with the rest of the tourists, they were only pretending to be social and to have a good time. They had already gone well beyond that kind of fun.

Stepping away from the party, Parker walked off to a quiet spot overlooking the slope. Alone, he gazed off into the night to wrestle with his feelings. The passion that Brooke evoked stirred inside of him. It was incredible, much more than he'd imagined. It was as if together they had formed a life force all its own.

What would happen, he wondered, if they took the chance to develop those feelings? What if they did share something special? Wondering that, though, led him to worry. What if Brooke didn't feel it? What if it was just like Mako said, a vacation romance for her, the making of a memory and nothing more?

Then he heard Brooke's voice call out, wrapping around him like a handmade quilt. "Parker?" He turned to see her standing in front of the dying fire. "I think it's time to go."

Parker didn't notice the other tourists milling around behind her, trying to board the coach. He was too transfixed on Brooke. A bright smile covered her face, but it was her aura, he felt, that beamed most brilliantly, just as Zafrina had envisioned. It was as if she'd swallowed the sun.

Parker nodded and quietly followed her to the vehicle. The only thing left for him to wonder about was what the two of them would do next. All he had to worry about now was how to avoid being consumed by Brooke's resplendent star.

TWELVE

The Castles Tour

SALLY WAS in turmoil Wednesday morning. Parker could see it on her face the moment he stepped into the breakfast room. "Why so glum?" he asked.

"I just found out it's Max's birthday on Friday."

"That sucks," Parker said sarcastically.

Mako doubled down on the remark. "That's what I said." He waved his coffee mug in the air. "But now Little Miss Perfect wants us to do something special for him."

Parker glanced at Sally. "Like what?"

Her cheeks were sallow. "I don't know, but we have to do something. Max and Steve are having lunch with Dante today."

"How do you know that?" Parker asked.

"He told me."

"Max told you that?"

"No." Embarrassed, Sally finally admitted, "Dante did."

Mako glared at Parker. "And you were worried about me messing with her?"

Ignoring the remark, Parker warned Sally. "That guy's dangerous. You have no idea who you're dealing with."

"I know," she said defensively. "Dante's full of crap. He's full of crap and full of himself." Sally's face splintered with concern. "But he's working our group leader. He's trying to take the account. He doesn't think I care. He thinks that I'm not happy at Tourcey. He's even offered me a job with Euro Journey." Sally gathered her self-assurance. "I'm the only one of us who can get any information from him."

Parker was more concerned about Dante and Euro Journey than either Sally or Mako could know. By building a relationship with Max, they would be well positioned to gain if Tourcey Travel messed something up with the tours. If Max were to find out about him and Brooke, Parker figured, that would certainly qualify. "Okay Sal, I assume you have a plan?" he asked.

Sally firmed her jaw. "I do. There's this popular music show featuring Austrian folk music. They play traditional instruments, with singing and dancing, even cowbells."

"But no cow?" Mako joked.

Parker tossed him a dirty look before replying to her. "Can we get tickets?"

"Friday is sold out, but Günter said there's space open for tomorrow night. I'll check back with him right now. We have enough in emergency funds to cover the cost, but you have to approve that since you're in charge."

Parker concurred. "Let's do it. Secure tickets for you and Mako, Max, Brooke, Doctor Frank, Honey, Steve, and Ronni."

"What about you?"

Although the situation called for serious schmoozing, Parker just couldn't bear the thought of sitting through a dinner show with Max and Brooke together. Besides, it appeared that Sally was getting her confidence back. It would serve her well to lead the excursion. "I already have plans," Parker lied.

Mako sat up. "A date?"

"Sort of."

"Interesting," Mako replied looking for some scoop. "So who is this future heartbreaker?"

"Stick it, Mako," Parker growled. "I'm just catching up with one of the ski school girls I met last week."

"Sounds boring," Mako said.

"It probably will be, but I'm going anyway."

"Whatever," Sally said, impatient to finalize the plans, "I'll go right now and check with Günter."

Sally left. Parker noticed Ollie Hauptmann hovering over a table full of Euro Journey tourists. The three couples were badgering him for information.

Mako interrupted. "Hey, pal. I need a favor."

"What?"

"I need to switch with you."

"Switch what?"

"I need to swap day trips with you. I'll take your trip tomorrow if you do the Castles Tour for me today."

"Today?"

"Yeah, today."

"You're high."

"Seriously, man. Do me this favor, and I will owe you my life."

Arms crossed, Parker stared at Mako. "Let me guess, Viktoria?"

Clutching his face in his hands, Mako tried to hide his glee. "Yes, yes. But believe me, you don't want to know the details."

Parker saw Ollie walk over to the Austropa bar and an idea sprang into his head. "You're right. I don't," he said to Mako. "But hold it right there for a second. First I've got to go talk to Ollie."

He rushed to the bar where Ollie stood, sipping of coffee.

"Are those all of the Euro Journey tourists?" Parker asked.

"They have our last three rooms."

"You know, it's okay to direct them to Sally or me if they have any questions?"

"They already have a tour guide," Ollie quipped. "He's just never around."

"Well, he sure finds enough time to schmooze *my* group leader." Ollie raised an eyebrow. Parker continued. "He's taking Max and Steve to lunch today. I have to believe that Max will see through him, but you never know."

"Yes, and he and Steve could be best friends. I wouldn't underestimate Dante."

"We're not. Sally's making plans to take Max and his entourage out to a dinner show for Max's birthday. While I'm good with that, I figure if we were to organize a ski excursion to St. Anton, Max would be over the top. He's got to be sick of Steve talking about that place."

Ollie understood. "I'm sick of Steve too. He's been whining about skiing the Arlberg area since the day he got here. He's just too cheap to go by himself."

"We'd have to go Friday. Do you have a contact over there? Someone who can plan the trip for us?"

Ollie took another sip of coffee while contemplating the question. His reply surprised Parker. "Marc will do it."

"Marc? Are you sure?"

He shook his head. "Marc can set it all up. He probably should go along too. I'm sure he's free on Friday."

"That would be amazing, but I'll also need a ballpark cost right away so I can get approval from Lorrie."

"I'll call Marc this morning and have him email you pricing later today."

"Outstanding. I'll get approval for the extra expense, and if one of us can reconcile our weekly billing with Reinhold before then, I can go too."

Ollie set his mug on the bar. "I'm also going, but paying my own way."

Parker was surprised. "Are you sure?"

Ollie's reply was short on emotion. "It's good for business. My partners and I are working to secure another property. We expect to double our space at least next year, and I'd prefer to have SojournSports fill it, contracting though Tourcey Travel of course. So you see, I have a vested interest in keeping Max happy too." Ollie gestured toward the dining room where Max had just entered. "Just make sure they still want to ski St. Anton am Arlberg."

Parker nodded. "I will."

Before he could head back to the dining room, Sally came rushing down the hall and stopped him at one of the bar tables. "I got eight tickets for tomorrow night," she said.

Parker grinned. "If that's the cake, I've got the icing." Sally was thrilled to hear about the ski trip, but growing angst tempered her enthusiasm. "Okay, okay, that's awesome," she said while shoving a folded tour manifest in his face. "Max is here now, so I'll tell him right away. I'll get everything lined up, but you have to get going."

"What? Where?"

"The Castles Tour. It leaves in five minutes."

"The Castles Tour?"

"You agreed to switch with Mako."

"I didn't agree," he protested.

"He says you did." A grin slowly grew across Sally's face. "Got three new signups just this morning. I wrote them down on the back of the paper."

Parker took the manifest and flipped it over. Printed neatly in black ink were the names of the tourists who Sally had signed up: Alice Donovan, Bill Donovan, and Brooke McCaslin. Peeking toward the dining room, Parker saw Brooke slipping on her ski jacket and saying goodbye to Max. Keeping his giddiness in check, Parker conceded with a shrug. "I suppose I'll just have to take it then."

PARKER WAS the perfect host on tour. Sharing his enthusiasm with the group, he paced up and down the moving vehicle, chatting it up and pausing only to gasp in amazement at the majestic views of the passing Ammergau Mountains. While touring the famous Neuschwanstein Castle, Parker stayed back, stepping up close to hear every word of the guide's lecture. Then he'd hurry to the front of the group as soon as the guide was finished to assist his tourists up a step or through a doorway to the next exhibit room.

Somehow he was also able to keep his desire for Brooke in check. He treated her like any other customer, even on those occasions when he got close enough to be buzzed by her scintillating vibe. After the tour, as they rolled into the nearby village of Füssen, Parker churned with anticipation. The midday lunch and shopping stop might allow them some private time. He devised a plan too, just in case.

By then the sky was dark and threatening snow. The coach pulled up to the curb on a broad street just outside of the central tourist area. Parker overheard Alice Donovan talking about lunch choices, and Parker felt sure that Brooke would be eating with her and Bill.

The local guide, an earnest woman named Sophie, stood up front to make an announcement. The words flew from her mouth like sparks from a weld. "We are leaving you off here, close to the Altstadt where you will have precisely ninety minutes for lunch, shopping and to visit the sites. I suggest a visit to the beautiful Benedictine Monastery of St. Mang where it is just a short walk from here. There is also the Basilika St. Mang that is just a bit farther to go. Be aware that we have a tight timeline to get to the Castle Hohenschwangau this afternoon. So please stick closely to our schedule. As you step off the coach,

I will give you a list of restaurants and shops in the immediate area, and also a map." She took a short pause to brush back her long dark hair and then waved a stack of trifold brochures in the air. "Please enjoy your visit to Füssen and return here on time."

One by one the tourists rose, scuffled down the aisle and out of the vehicle. Parker waited in his seat. Peering through the broad, tinted window, he watched Brooke, Alice and Bill step onto the cold sidewalk edged with crusted, dirty snow and huddle up by the side of the coach. Then he exited.

"We didn't forget you," Alice said with endearment. Parker nodded, and she continued. "Brooke has to find a birthday gift for Max so Bill and I were wondering if you can recommend a nice place for us to have lunch?"

"That I can do." Parker took her brochure. Like a magician, he reached under his ski jacket and pulled out a pen. After a quick look, he circled a few names. "These restaurants are highly recommended and close by."

"Wonderful." Alice slipped a gloved hand through her husband's arm before turning to Brooke. "So dear, are you sure you'll be all right?"

"I'll be okay," Brooke said. "I just hope I can find something."

"This is our only shopping stop today," Parker said. "If you'd like, I can note a few stores for you to check out."

"Great, thanks." She handed him the brochure. "So, what are your plans?"

"I'd like to relax on the motor coach and grab a nap," he said while wielding the pen tip across the thick paper. "But I promised the boss I'd scout out the area for future trips."

Alice accepted Parker's fib with a warm grin. "Maybe you can do both? You deserve a break, dear. It's a tough job minding the herd."

They all chuckled, and Parker gave Brooke the brochure

back. She turned to Alice. "I'm glad you two are finally taking some time for yourselves. Enjoy your lunch."

Alice eyed Brooke warmly. It was only then that the four-some noticed thick snowflakes falling from the sky. They all looked up at the vexing batch of clouds that moved overhead, darkening the brightly colored buildings. Alice dug a cream-colored woolen beret from her floral print handbag, and after putting it on, she squeezed Bill's hand, and they walked away.

Aware that their local guide was still lingering in the open door of the motor coach, Parker carefully sidled up next to Brooke. As they watched the couple stroll down the quaint street, he half-whispered from the side of his mouth, "Meet me at Steakhaus Füssen. I circled it on your brochure. It's across the river, far enough out of town so it should be safe. Grab a taxi at the hotel across the street. I'll head in the other direction and get a separate cab." Walking away, Parker caught a glimpse of Brooke's grin in his peripheral vision.

THE SMALL BLACK cab puttered across a bridge over the emerald green water of the Lech River. Not fully confident in his plan, Parker tried to relax as the taxi meandered through a stretch of snow-coated evergreen trees that canvassed the surrounding hills. Tall ridges buttressed the rolling terrain, where an occasional pine tree would spiral above the frosty green vegetation to look out over the valley. Soon the cab swung off the asphalt two-lane and up an incline. It stopped abruptly at the foot of a short staircase that led to the restaurant.

After paying the fare, Parker hopped out and blindly hustled up the handful of stairs. On the top step, he looked up to see Brooke. She stood waiting for him, protected from the snow by a clapboard roof that covered the restaurant's entrance. He hurried through the blowing snow to join her there.

Brooke's eyes sparkled. She snickered mischievously before being consumed by a brilliant smile. Shifting her jean-covered legs back and forth, Brooke wrestled her hands from her coat pockets and bounded into Parker's arms. "I couldn't wait another second for you."

They kissed gently. "I hope it's worth the wait," Parker joked.

She kissed him again. "Oh, you are."

A shapely girl in a traditional, Tyrolean Dirndl dress greeted them at the reception stand. She grabbed two menus and swung around so quickly that her braided ponytail twirled in the air. Marching across the wide-board wooden floors, she led Brooke and Parker into a quaint back room. They sat down at a table for two. Parker took the seat facing the entrance so he could spot any of his tourists who might wander in.

The room was half-filled with diners. Brooke widened her eyes at Parker suggestively when she heard the other guests speaking only German. Parker leaned forward to whisper. "It doesn't mean they don't understand English."

The same girl who seated them returned. Parker ordered a club soda with a hunk of lime. Brooke had a glass of the house Grüner. Parker glanced around the room. "This should be the perfect place for us. I can't imagine any of my people coming this far out for lunch, especially with the snow." He peeked out toward the doorway before explaining. "I snuck away from the tourists last week too, and had a great lunch here."

Brooke nestled into the wooden chair back. "You must get sick of spending so much time with your clients."

Parker shrugged. "I enjoy it most of the time, but I do appreciate a break now and then. Everyone wants to spend time with the guide. It's part of the experience I suppose."

Brooke gazed at him softly and then lowered her voice to a

murmur. "I'm sorry to tell you this Parker, but I want to spend time with you too." Her lips remained in a pout after speaking, as if stuck on the desire those words conveyed.

The server arrived with their drinks, took their food order and departed. Brooke picked up the conversation right where she had left it. "What I meant to say was that I *really* want to be with you." This time she didn't whisper, and her soft gaze was now a glare. "And I don't care if anyone hears me say it." She consoled herself with a long sip of wine.

Parker looked embarrassed as he squeezed the lime into his fizzy beverage. "You are with me," he finally stated. "And honestly, I couldn't be happier."

Brooke wasn't entirely satisfied with his answer. Cradling the round bottom of her long-stemmed glass, she spoke as if wondering out loud. "How are we ever going to find time to be alone?"

"Today worked out pretty well."

Brooke wanted more. "I'll be skiing with Max tomorrow, but I can probably get free Friday. How do you look on Friday?"

"Not good. Steve's been itching to ski the Arlberg area, so we're hooking up with Marc and Ollie to take him to ski St. Anton."

"Max is going too?"

Parker nodded. "And I can't get out of it." Brooke's head began to sink, but his next sentence quickly raised her spirits. "Tomorrow night could work though."

"What's tomorrow night?"

"Sally has eight tickets for an evening musical show to celebrate Max's birthday. She told him right after we left this morning. I was thinking ahead and got myself out of it."

"You did?" Brooke was excited.

"I told them I already have a date," Parker explained, and then he used his fingers to count each guest. "So it's Sally and

Mako, Frank and Honey, Steve and Ronni and then Max and you, unless—"

"I can get out of it," Brooke said confidently.

"Are you sure?"

"I should be able to anyway. But if something does go wrong, I'll message you."

"Okay," Parker said, "you've got my number right?"

"Sure, it's in with our tour info, yours and Sally's."

Parker grimaced. "Please don't mix those numbers up."

"Like I would do that? I'll even be discreet, just in case. All business," She shook her head to reassure him. "Nothing mushy."

"Yeah save the mushy stuff for a letter or something."

"A letter?" Brooke wasn't asking a question. She was contemplating the subject, and when finished, she spoke wistfully. "I can't remember the last time I wrote anyone a letter. But you, you like letters don't you?"

Again, Parker was embarrassed. "Well, I do appreciate the effort a letter requires. There's something extraordinary about the act of putting pen to paper and your feelings into words."

"I never thought about it like that before." Honest admiration shown in Brooke's eyes as they narrowed. "What else don't I know about you?"

Parker shrugged. "You know a lot about me because I'm all we've talked about so far. I'd like to know more about you."

"I'm crazy about you. What more is there to know?"

Parker shook his head. "I just wonder what you like to do for fun, you know, when you're not on vacation. Besides collecting stamps."

Brooke grasped her necklace and gently slid it back and forth along the chain. "I don't collect stamps. Max does."

Parker saw an opening. "Well, I would like to know more about you ... and Max."

Brooke dropped her eyes. "I don't want to talk about Max."

"But he's good to you, right?"

"Our relationship is very complicated, Parker." Brooke grew somber. "Let's just say that Max is very good to me. He's just not very good *for* me."

Parker sighed. "I don't think he'd be very good to me if he found out about us."

Brooke pursed her lips. "Well, he wouldn't be happy, that's for sure." After a quick sip of wine, she changed the subject. "So you want to know more about me, right? Well, I'm a numbers girl at heart, a complete geek who derives great pleasure from anything to do with data science."

"That's cool," he said. "We've got that in common."

"What?"

"The numbers thing. I count stuff all the time, like the number of tiles on the bathroom floor or the number of cars in a passing freight train. I'm always counting stuff in my head."

She toyed with him. "Have you been tested for OCD?"

"Nah, it's just how I occupy my mind when doing mundane tasks. I consider it a quirk."

"I have one of those." Leaning forward, Brooke hastily smoothed back a few sand-colored strands of hair that hung over her forehead. Then she lowered her head to show off a small, jagged scar that disfigured her hairline.

Parker examined the old wound. "Wow, that was one nasty gash."

"I got it in Aspen, from an Aspen."

"You hit a tree?"

"Just a branch. I was going too fast to duck."

"So you're a daredevil huh?"

"Yeah, well, look at you, sitting here in public, with me." Proud of that remark, Brooke reclined, smirked, and slipped her fingers around the wine glass.

Pointing to her head wound, Parker continued with their playful joust. "It's interesting, but I don't think that's a quirk." He took a sip of sparkling water.

"Sure it is. It's an attribute."

Parker shook his head. "Not so much. It's a scar, what they'd call a distinguishing mark. You know, something they'd use to ID you if you were wanted."

"Are you calling me a criminal?"

Parker returned the quip. "Well, you are trying to steal my heart aren't you?"

Brooke grinned, at first. Then she squinted and shook her head. "No, I don't think so. That was too easy. I can't give you that one."

Sheepishly, Parker agreed. "Sorry, it was there, so I just went for it." He pointed at the scar again. "So when did that happen?"

"Back in high school."

"Were you popular in high school?"

Brooke wore humility like an old shoe. "I was a mess in high school, but it was high school. You can be a mess and still be popular."

Parker mugged. "I wish I knew you back then."

A naughty grin precluded her reply. "If you were in my high school I never would have made it to college."

"That would make me a bad influence." That crack made her snicker. She then finished her wine with one last sip before lowering the empty goblet to the table. Parker saw the dimples set firmly in the corners of her mouth and he gestured to her empty glass. "Would you like another wine?"

Her eyes flitted around the room again before re-focusing on him. "All I want is to make love to you."

Her loud, public declaration made Parker uncomfortable. He shook his drink glass, popped a chunk of ice in his mouth, and crunched it up just as the server waltzed to the side of their table. "We'll have another round, please." When she departed, Parker leaned back in his seat and raised his tone. "Now what were we talking discussing? Oh, yes, your prowess with numbers and your scheme to embezzle millions of dollars from Max."

Brooke screeched. Her mouth flopped open and her wide eyes beamed at him. "You're crazy." Exploding with laughter, Brooke squeezed her hands together and hugged them to her chest. "You make me happy," Brooke said longingly. "You make me feel so free, like the independent person that I always dreamed of being."

"Being happy is a choice, Brooke. You get to make it every day."

She shook her head. "Not when you are dependent on someone for every little need. Not without being free to be yourself, to have a life you can call your own. That's the kind of happy I want to be."

The second glass of wine arrived and with it, more of Brooke's frustration. "I want to make love to you," she cooed softly between sips. "I want to be with you so badly." The words seemed to float from her mouth and linger in the air. "I want to be with you tonight."

Parker was equally frustrated but kept it to himself. If only he could grab hold of her words just as they came out of her mouth, he thought. He'd put them away somewhere safe so he could take them out to listen to later, at a more private, a more comfortable time.

"I want to make love in your bed," she continued, "and wake up with you."

Imagining them waking up together in his bed at the Austropa frightened Parker, and it showed on his face. Brooke dismissed it, continuing with her delicious whispers. "I thought of something you didn't know about me, so listen. I love to take a hot bath."

Parker grinned. "We have that in common."

She peered as if astonished. "So why don't we do that? Let's take a bath together? We'll go back to the hotel and crawl into a nice hot tub."

"I've only got a shower in my room," he said insipidly. "And to be honest, I'm just glad that we can sneak in another meal together."

"I'm just so frustrated," Brooke said while twisting the stem of her wineglass. "All we're ever going to do together is eat."

Parker stared resolutely at her, his voice firm, his words slipping out slowly, sincerely. "Brooke, I feel the same way you do. It's just a weird coincidence that most of our quality time together so far has involved food, but don't think that's a trivial thing." Her head tilted as she grew more and more attentive to his words. "In my family, sharing a meal with people you care about is very special. It's that shared sustenance, the combined nourishment of food, conversation, remembrances, and sentiments. Those are the times that make the fondest of memories."

Brooke nearly swooned, her eyes flaring like embers in a breeze. "Oh Parker, when you say things like that, I just want to take you in my arms and never let go."

Overwhelmed by his passion, Parker leaned over and grasped for her hand. Then murmured low but with a firm voice. "And all I want to do is wipe every dish off of this table, lay you down on it and–"

From the corner of his eye, Parker saw the server approaching again. Reining in his frustration, Parker sat back quietly. He and Brooke had ordered the same meal: a thick bison burger on a pretzel bun, with large-cut steak fries and German potato salad.

"Please be careful. The plates are hot," the server said, placing the food in front of them.

With a smile and a genuine "thank you," Parker ushered

her away. Then he shared his emotions in less provocative terms. "Just to be sure, Brooke, you have to know that I'm frustrated too. It's maddening, knowing the way we feel about each other and the challenges we face trying to get together," he glanced at his plate. "It does seem like such a waste of time just to sit here and eat."

Brooke's eyes swelled with understanding, but a peaceful, satiated expression covered her face. "It's not just a meal, Parker. It's a memory."

BETWEEN BITES, Parker and Brooke talked about the morning's tour through Neuschwanstein Castle. Parker reflected on the timeless beauty of the palace. He pointed out of the restaurant window, using the wild scenery to explain how the massive structure was designed to fit in its natural surroundings as if formed from the earth itself.

All of the elaborate craftwork on display intrigued Brooke the most: the furnishings, the mural paintings, the tapestries, and the woodwork. She was obsessed too, with the chandeliers. The luxurious, elegant metal fixtures were twisted deftly into figures and circles and ovals. She spoke about the ornate candleholders that hovered overhead and dangled from solid wood ceilings and squared beams or supported by slender, delicate metal chains.

"I kept wondering as I walked around, how long did it take to light all those candles?" Brooke's confession made Parker laugh. Amazed at his reaction, Brooke laughed too, but only at his attitude. "What? Didn't you ever think of that?"

"Did you ever think of asking the guide?" he replied.

"Oh no, I didn't." Incredulous at her missed opportunity, Brooke finally said, "I was just so mesmerized by the place I guess."

Another highlight for her was the king's bedroom, with its

richly textured draperies and elaborately carved wooden canopy bed. "Just think about the labor it took to create all of that? Fourteen woodcarvers worked for over four years in that one room alone."

Swinging a long-handled fork through the air, she twirled it as she spoke, and then stabbed at the potato salad as if wielding a spear. "I think Singer's Hall was the most magnificent room I've ever seen anywhere." While she described in painstaking detail, the colorful murals that graced the walls, her voice resonated with child-like delight.

Parker realized that Neuschwanstein Castle wasn't a whimsical, dream castle to Brooke. It was all too beautifully real to her: the incredible artwork, the amazing architecture, and the furniture, the wood and stone construction. Brooke's Neuschwanstein Castle - and every excessive aspect of it – was a genuine labor of love. That's what spoke to the hopeful person inside of her. To Brooke, love wasn't the pursuit of some fantastically romantic, fairytale life. Brooke McCaslin was just like every other ordinary human being; filled with the earnest desire to be someone special to her special someone, someday.

Time was intruding on their adventure. Before the server cleared their plates, Parker asked her to call for two cabs. Brooke stood to slip on her coat while he squared the bill. She followed him to the front door, but before he grasped the doorknob to go outside, she swung him around, slipped into his arms, and fastened onto him with a long, lingering kiss. Then her lips moved to his ear. She hugged him tightly and whispered a revelation. "I think I've fallen in love with you, Parker Moon."

Flustered by the public display of affection. Parker nervously misspoke. "I'm not sure this is such a good idea."

Upset, Brooke ran outside. He hurried after, stopping her under the entrance roof, just short of swirling snow.

"It's not an idea," she cried.

Frustrated at his gaffe, Parker tried to explain. "That's not what I meant, Brooke."

She wasn't listening. "It's not something I thought about, Parker. It's something that has happened to me. It's just the way I feel, and it is out of my control."

He sighed. "Brooke, I just meant that I wasn't comfortable kissing you right then and there. I felt like we were on stage or something, that's all."

He pulled her close, but she moved away. Tears welled up in her eyes. "Someday this tour will be over," she said. "Do you think you can be in love with me then?"

The query seemed comical. Being near Brooke or just hearing the sound of her voice gave him such an unreal thrill. There was nothing funny, however, about the ardent look on her face or the wrinkles of hope that cornered her eyes. Her unanswered question dangled over an emotional precipice and Brooke clung onto it for dear life.

Parker hugged her again. Feeling her chest pound anxiously, he was spurred to speak from his heart, without any concern for the consequences. "Brooke, I've already fallen in love with you."

THIRTEEN

The Austropa Hotel

THE DING of an incoming message reverberated through Parker's quiet bedroom early Thursday morning, nudging him awake. Twisting over to the nightstand, he grabbed his phone and lay back down. It was a text from Don Tourcey.

> *"I'm giving you the go-ahead for the ski trip on Friday. Lorrie priced out at 6 pax - w/Marc guiding and Ollie on own. Lunch also approved but try to keep at 150 US. Call/text with questions/concerns"*

Parker rubbed his eyes and checked the time on the end table clock, "6:00 a.m." That meant it was eleven o'clock at night back in Chicago. Don was working late. It was something the big boss often did, if nothing more it seemed than to enjoy the perverse pleasure of complaining about it. Despite the time, Parker couldn't pass up the opportunity to trifle with him, texting a reply and setting off a steady stream of messages:

> *"Thanks, Don - stuck working late again, huh?"*
> *"It's the only time I can get any real work done"*
> *"The price of ownership"*

"The price of babysitting my staff all day"
"Well I hope you get everything finished soon"
"Hope in reality is the worst of all evils because it
*   prolongs the torments of man - Nietzsche"*
"We must accept finite disappointment, but never lose
*   infinite hope - MLK"*
"How did you look that up so fast?"
"Didn't"
"Right"
"Go to sleep"
"Go to work"
"Good night"
"Good day"

Relieved that everything was set for Friday's ski trip, Parker rolled over, snuggled his pillow and closed his eyes to catch a bit more sleep. Then Brooke popped into his head, stimulating his libido and staying his slumber. Still, he refused to spend any more time and energy fantasizing about an evening with Brooke. He wasn't too confident that she could get out of the dinner show later that night. After all, it was Max's birthday celebration. All he could do was hope that she'd pull it off.

Hope - there was that word again. Recalling Don's dour quote from their text messages, Parker felt pity for the man. No doubt the boss' history with women had been a drag on his optimism. Between two ex-wives and a variety of similarly shallow and needy mistresses and girlfriends, Don's love life seemed hopeless.

If only Don were lucky enough to meet someone like Brooke, Parker thought. Maybe he'd find some satisfaction in life. Perhaps Don would be happy with himself and more pleasant to everyone else. If the big boss felt for someone the same way Parker and Brooke felt for each other, then maybe he would be more optimistic about the future.

All Parker ever wanted was a simple, satisfying and fulfilling life with someone he loved. That was hoping for too much. But he wasn't a fool, either. Parker knew first hand that life is hard, full of ups and downs. That's why love was so essential. Love can sustain you through it all.

Love is the food that nourishes your life, and happiness is it's ever-present nutrient, pulsing through your veins. Love is the life force, and happiness is its energy. Love can sustain you through the most challenging times, and happiness can help ease your pain. Happiness lies dormant in us all, ready to be awakened by the love in your life: an old, pleasant memory, a kindness extended, a touch, a smile or a gentle kiss. When you have love, you can always find a moment of happiness. That's what makes love the greatest gift of all.

Brooke brought the promise of such a love, so Parker's hope was well placed. Somehow he and Brooke would figure out a way to be together. Finally trusting in that, Parker got out of bed and took a long, steamy shower.

Leaving the bathroom clad in a towel, Parker noticed an envelope lying on the floor. Someone had slipped it beneath his door. Firming the towel around his waist, Parker scooped it up. The envelope was addressed only to his room number, and it ripped open easily. Parker read it with growing excitement.

"Good morning, you had to know that I'd write you a letter! Anyway, I've devised a plan to get out of that dinner show tonight, the one you were clever enough to get out of ahead of time. Smart man! Certainly, you can figure out a way we can be together - alone! - for a few hours tonight while they're gone? I suggest the best room at the nicest hotel far away from here but close enough, so we don't waste too much time getting there. I'll pay for it. Just please, do whatever needs to be done. Love, Brooke"

Brooke had been scheming, and it appeared that hope was

no longer necessary. A feeling of inevitability took hold of Parker. The goal was about to be achieved. He couldn't have plotted it any better; that little lie that popped into his head to avoid suffering through the dinner show with Max and Brooke together would be the catalyst for a romantic rendezvous. An endless stream of ideas and conflicting concerns filled Parker's head in one fleeting moment. Eventually, the mind-rush subsided, and he realized that getting that hotel room was the first thing to do. Sinking into the patio chair, Parker opened up his iPad.

The breaking dawn brought streaks of light into the sky outside. While the tablet unlocked, Parker watched the pink hues lighten into morning. He thought about how fabulous it would be to lie in bed and watch the sky with Brooke. Spurred by that thought, Parker opened his favorite travel app to search for a hotel where they could live out that fantasy. The Grand Imperial Hotel, about a mile away, had availability, so Parker immediately typed in his credit card number to secure a reservation.

THE LUTZ TRAVEL office was a beehive of activity. When Reinhold zoomed into the stylish lobby to greet Parker, he looked like an ad in some fancy fashion magazine: immaculately groomed and impeccably attired in a skinny, blue suit and a red, paisley print tie.

He accepted Parker's compliment with aplomb. "I like to make a statement with my appearance every day." Gesturing to follow, he led Parker through the office. "Viktoria said the toboggan trip was met with much enthusiasm."

"Loved it. Everyone did. It went well."

"Good. Unfortunately, I won't be able to include that as an option for your incoming group because we're still working out pricing. Certainly, we'll be offering it next year."

They maneuvered through the bright, open office space, passing comfortable work pods, sleek, meshed-back chairs, and glass, half-wall dividers. Reinhold continued to converse as they walked, twisting his slender face toward Parker as he spoke. "So I understand your last group this Saturday is another sell-out? I'm correct to assume that SojournSports is a big account for Tourcey Travel?"

"Certainly could be. It's only the second year that they've contracted with us, but we've doubled our headcount from last year."

Continuing down a hardwood-floored hallway, Reinhold stepped through the glass door of his corner office. A teakwood desk sat facing a large window that looked directly at the adjacent building. Despite the lack of a vista, Parker was still intrigued by the old exposed brick.

Reinhold settled in at the desk. Ergonomically positioned, the business owner tightened the knot of his tie and then squared off in front of an open laptop. He began to type with rapid precision and then, after clearing his throat, Reinhold forced Parker to pay attention with a simple, curt pronouncement. "Let's look at the account."

Tourcey Travel passenger counts and charter bills were pulled up on the screen. Parker took out his iPad and reviewed the numbers that Lorrie had confirmed. Then he ran them through his calculator to compare with Reinhold's. All of the numbers jived, so Reinhold populated an invoice and emailed it to Tourcey the Travel accounting department, cc'ing Don, Lorrie, and Parker.

Viktoria suddenly appeared, straddling the doorway like some racy apparition in a body-hugging, red mini-dress. "Can I get you some tea?" Her short, brazen red hair looked to be iridescent under the fluorescent lighting. Parker found it hard to take her offer seriously.

"Uh, no, not now, but thanks."

Reinhold shrugged, annoyed by her interruption. Viktoria whipped around to leave forcing her chunky, black metal earrings to swing wildly, like stones tethered to a bungee cord.

"So where were we?" Reinhold asked.

After finishing all of their business, the two men engaged in a detailed discussion on the local tourism industry. Parker learned about Lutz Travel's diverse product line, from ground transportation to outbound tours, event planning, and weddings. Eventually, Parker remembered the dinner show that evening. "I need to book a quality ride for tonight. We're taking Max and about seven others to the Tyrolean Evenings show."

"The Gundolf family?" Reinhold replied excitedly.

"Yep, that's it."

"Oh, they will love the show. I can have a limousine do the transfers."

"Excellent. I'll ask Sally to confirm the time with you."

Reinhold nodded. "I'll give you a discounted rate as long as you tip the driver well."

"Are you sure?"

"Yes, very sure."

"All right, it's a deal."

With business concluded, the pair traversed back through the office to the lobby. "So where are you off to next?" Reinhold asked.

"Ski school. I've got a quick meeting with Marc."

Reinhold's gaze was piercing. "Marc is a good asset. I'm confident he'll be very helpful in your endeavor."

"My endeavor?"

"Your ski trip tomorrow to St. Anton am Arlberg."

Parker was confounded. "Yeah, that's it, my endeavor."

Reinhold spoke matter-of-factly. "It's a great opportunity for Tourcey Travel to secure that relationship and limit the chances of Euro Journey stealing the account."

"So you and Ollie have already spoken about it?"

"Self-interest brings people together every day, Mr. Moon. Much more than holding hands and singing Kumbayah could ever do."

"I agree, but you, Marc and Ollie all contract with the other tour companies. Isn't it a little risky to play favorites?"

Reinhold cast a rakish smile. "We appreciate all of our customers, of course. We just prefer the ones who pay their bills promptly, without complaint."

Viktoria flew around the corner to ambush them again. "Going so soon?"

"I've got one more meeting to go," he said, "but plan to tag along on the half-day trip this afternoon."

"I'll be staging those departures." Her earrings began to twirl again as she nodded. "So what are your plans for next Tuesday?"

Mesmerized by the jewelry's hypnotic effect, Parker hesitated. "Next Tuesday?"

"Yes, it's our Fasching celebration, the last Tuesday before Lent. You know, Carnival? Big parties? Lots of fun?"

Before Parker could reply, Reinhold leaned in carefully and spoke as if guarding a secret. "I always have a party to celebrate." Straightening up, he peeked around the office, smoothed his neck with his right hand, and then concluded. "It will be at our future office in the Altstadt. It's informal and great fun, and I would like to invite you and your associates."

"That sounds awesome."

"You may bring a guest if you'd like, but I'd prefer not to have Max or any of your customers attend." The entrepreneur snickered.

"Might get a little wild, eh?"

"It's just Fasching. Sometimes things can easily get out of control."

THAT EVENING a new night manager was fronting the desk at the Austropa Hotel. She had Ollie's unflappable demeanor and an impeccable appearance, sporting a black suit over her gold tie and flaxen vest uniform. Standing behind the desk with arms folded across her waist, she watched everything and everybody with a maudlin stare. She offered only a curt nod to whoever caught her eye. Her scrutiny made Parker nervous.

He was patrolling the lobby too, greeting a few tourists as they came and went while waiting for the group to gather for the dinner show. Nerves tingling with anticipation, Parker was confident that he'd done all he could to ensure a romantic evening with Brooke. He'd reserved a room at the exquisite hotel nearby and chilled the champagne, leaving it out earlier on the windowsill of his balcony. He also put on a clean pair of jeans, along with a crisp dress shirt and a brown, full zip sweater.

Sally was first to arrive. She sparkled in a knee-length, black lace dress.

"Whoa," Parker explained. "Did you look in the mirror?"

She panicked. "Why? What's wrong?"

"Nothing. I'm just not used to you looking so gorge."

Sally blushed. "Oh stop it. Is the limo here? Where's everyone else?"

"All I know is that the limo's on its way."

Just then Mako wandered in followed by Steve and Ronni.

"Ready to do this?" Mako asked Steve. The big man put his finger to his temple and wiggled his thumb. Mako laughed, but Sally's stern gaze stopped him from saying anything. The insipid front desk manager slipped over to announce that the limo had arrived. Impatiently, Sally peeked down the vacant hallway. "We're still short a few. Can you please let the driver know that we'll be out soon?"

The girl did as asked. Parker rushed over to the hutch and grabbed the old-fashioned phone. "I'll give Max a call."

Before hoisting the delicate handle, Parker felt his back pocket vibrate. Pulling out his phone, he noticed a text from Brooke. He quickly read it.

"There's been a change of plans. Please reschedule."

"Is that from Max?" Sally asked, walked toward him.

Trying not to panic, Parker lowered his phone. "No, It's nothing." The sound of approaching footsteps stopped Sally from coming any closer to him. Both guides looked over just as Max and Brooke sauntered in.

"Sorry we're late," Max said, an apologetic frown clashing with his classic, navy blue overcoat.

Sally dismissed the apology. "It's all right. There's plenty of time."

Parker had yet to move away from the antique hutch, but it was just as well. From that distance, no one could sense the sharp pain that text had inflicted on him or the fierce pleasure that Brooke's physical presence had bestowed. Fresh, flawless cosmetic touches had deftly concealed any hurt that Brooke was feeling: slight rouge to the cheeks, extended lashes, and a hint of shadow to highlight her eyes.

Winsome in a tan, pullover knit sweater, matching knit skirt and brown leather knee-high boots, Brooke accepted a compliment from Sally. Then she slipped on her coat. "Any chance either of you have an extra charge cord?" She asked the guides and winced. "I just found out the hard way that mine isn't working."

Sally replied, "We always carry spares."

"Oh yeah, always," Parker added, re-engaging with the group.

Doctor Frank walked into the lobby, alone, and immediately attended to Sally. "It looks like you'll have to be my date this evening." He offered his arm. She smiled and gracefully took hold of it.

"What's, ah, where's Honey?" Parker asked.

"She's tapped out," Frank replied.

"Frank will be the one tapped out," Max joked, "if she sneaks off to the casino while we're gone."

Polite laughter ensued. Max glanced back and forth at Mako and Parker. "So are you two ready to tackle St. Anton tomorrow?"

After playing with his collar to make it lay just right, Mako answered. "I've been out on the slopes here only once so far, but I skied for three days straight last month in Colorado, so I'm dialed in."

Parker wasn't in the mood for idle chitchat. "I'm good."

Max turned to Sally next. "I am so sorry that you're stuck with an unused ticket for the show now. Too late to get a refund I suppose?"

"Don't worry about it," she replied.

Max turned to Parker. "If we can secure one more ticket, perhaps you and your date will join us?"

Parker shook his head. "I have firm reservations."

"Too bad. Well, thank you so much for the evening out," Max said as he fixed a white silk scarf around his neck. "I hope you enjoy your date."

The front desk manager held the door open, prompting Max to turn and leave. Parker took the opportunity to share a sad, passing glance with Brooke before offering his reply. "There's always hope, I suppose."

FOURTEEN

St. Anton am Arlberg

PARKER HAD GONE to sleep frustrated and no longer clinging to hope. He couldn't expect that things would just work out for them. So when he awoke Friday morning, it was with a completely different mindset. Determination now took hold. After dressing for the ski trip, Parker had breakfast at the Austropa Bistro, away from Sally and the early morning risers gathered in the dining hall. Settling into the first table, he was close enough to the lobby to hear when the other skiers strolled in. Parker smacked on some strudel, sipped his tea, and focused his thoughts on Brooke.

Private time for intimacy was the goal. Parker scoured the tour schedule in his mind and quickly dismissed an evening rendezvous. It would have to be a daytime affair; a day when they could both sneak away from whatever it was that they were supposed to be doing. Sunday could work. Sunday might be their best chance. He'd be busy at the Austropa that morning, helping the new arrivals get off to their destinations and handling any trip changes or rental equipment issues. As long as he was accessible, the afternoon was free.

Parker began to imagine a wonderfully romantic afternoon

with Brooke at the swank Grand Imperial Hotel, the same property they had planned to enjoy the previous night. Last night's champagne would, of course, be put to good use while the romantic playlist he created, streaming from his ultra-portable wireless speaker, would set the mood. There would be snuggling and plenty of passion. Most importantly, there would be beautiful, harmonious lovemaking, the melding that only two souls in love can experience.

Firm, quick steps entering the lobby and a slight cough announced Ollie's arrival. In a blink, though, the hotelier marched back down the hall. There was still no sound of Marc. There was no transportation queuing out on the street either, so Parker stayed in his daydream, thinking of Brooke. Daring to think beyond the ski trip, he imagined how the couple could make the relationship work after the tour ended.

There was no question that Brooke would have to move to Chicago. She'd have to get far away from Max, and although he would certainly lose his job at Tourcey Travel, Chicago was still the best place for Parker's career. He had contacts in Chicago and a good reputation with the other travel companies headquartered there. He could freelance too, and work for them all. Heck, Don might even want him back next winter. Lord knows he'd be needed to manage the ski weeks out west.

If Brooke were to move to Chicago, she'd have to get a place of her own. Moving in together, Parker believed, was just too risky for the relationship: too much, too soon and perhaps too indulgent. Besides, Brooke needed her independence. That was the key to any long-term relationship with her. He was thrilled to imagine how happy Brooke would be when she became the individual she so badly wanted to be. Knowing that he would be by her side, providing love and support on her journey, made him feel proud.

The sound of nylon ski pants rubbing together forced him to focus on the present. Seconds later, Marc's booming voice shook loose the morning stillness. "All aboard for St. Anton am Arlberg."

Parker walked in to see everyone already gathered in the center of the lobby, encircling Marc. Most were touting their ski gear. "Before we leave, everyone must sign a waiver. They're at the front desk." Marc pointed at Günter, who hid behind a mug of coffee raised to his lips.

The men did as instructed and Parker slipped through the crowd to retrieve his rented ski gear in the storage locker. Bending back to avoid a hoisted ski bag that swung past him, Parker noticed something amiss. "Steve, what about a helmet?"

"What?" Steve gaped. "I don't have a brain bucket."

Marc intervened. "You know from before; if you want to ski with me, you have to wear a helmet. We all wear helmets, except for Ollie."

Steve relented, following Ollie back to the storage room to borrow some headgear. Steve's typically surly attitude didn't bother Parker though. He could bitch and moan all day as long as Max was happy, and Max *was* happy, grinning like a jack-o-lantern. "Thank you. This may be my best birthday present ever, " he said to Parker before ducking into the van's side door.

"It's overcast in St. Anton," Marc announced. "But it will be sunny by mid-morning. Great skiing weather."

That report was enough to keep spirits high during the long ride to St. Anton. The crowded van teemed with excitement. Parker's delight, however, was tinged with apprehension and he admitted as much to Ralph. "I'm not good enough to ski with guys like Marc, Ollie, and Steve."

"I'd rather not go rogue either," Ralph replied. "Can you pull out a trail map so we know what we were getting into?"

Parker unfolded a "piste" map, showing an expansive view of every ski trail on the mountain, including the various chairlifts and cable cars. He and Ralph reconnoitered it like Navy

Seals. Marc turned back from the front passenger seat. "There's no need to attack these runs. I don't expect everyone to follow the three of us," he gestured to Ollie and Steve. "Go your own way and set your own pace. Just stay safe. Let's decide on a place for lunch, and rendezvous there at noon."

THE SLEEK, silver and black-glass sided aerial tram moved up the snow-packed mountain face, dangling like a sinker on a fishing line. Parker imagined that the barren mountain ahead, crowned with sheer rock peaks, was like some CGI movie monster about to swallow him up. A sleek, modern building jutted out from the vast whiteness like a bird on a perch. Parker shuttered when the cable car jostled to a halt.

After exiting the tram, the group gathered and slammed into their skis. Marc took control, pointing to a path cut through knee-deep snow that disappeared in the haze. "Stay close and follow me."

They shuffled single file through the narrow rut and into some fog. Emerging back into the open, Parker saw Marc stopped at the edge of a sheer drop off. All around them, scraggly, snow-topped peaks pointed like rows of teeth through patches of clouds. Mako skied up next to Parker and they marveled at the incredible view.

"Amazing!" Parker shouted.

Mako echoed his excitement. "Top of the world, Ma!"

Marc gestured to the exact spot where he stood. "We'll all start here. Stay with me if you want to go off-piste. Everyone else should just stick to the trail. It's a great run."

"Who's first?" Steve asked.

Marc barked out the order. "I'll lead, then Ollie. Steve, you go third."

Steve didn't acknowledge Marc. Bent over, he was busy fidgeting with his boots. Parker was too focused on reigning in his fear to even think about his gear. Fixing his vision on the tips of his skis and the grooves in the snow, he tried to pretend that the frightful precipice didn't exist.

"Take your time and enjoy the run," Marc hollered. After securing his goggles in place, he pushed off. Ollie waited a few seconds before jamming his poles in the snow and shoving off next. Struggling forward to get in position, Steve got his skis crossed with Ralph, almost sending his friend down the mountain prematurely.

Parker grabbed Ralph's arm. "Hang on. I've got you."

Max went after Steve with Doctor Frank close behind. Parker was next to shuffle to the edge. A moment of fear materialized when he glanced down at the vast, white expanse ahead.

"Need a push?" Mako yelled.

"That's not a bad idea," Parker shouted back.

"Hold it," Ralph called out, "who's gonna push me?"

A few skiers were gliding up the path behind them. Parker had no time to waste. After firming his poles in the snow, he leaned his weight against them. "All right, follow me. Mako's last, agreed?" Their heads shook in accord. Without another second of hesitation, Parker came around and heaved himself down the slope.

The first few hundred yards were freaky-steep, but the snow was soft and easy to maneuver across. The trail cut through a narrow chute that wound past a smattering of rocks before opening into a steep bowl. Skiing too fast to focus on anything other than the path ahead, Parker got into a groove, weaving through the snow like a drop of rain running down a pane of glass.

Chest heaving from the exertion, Parker bore to the left and soon found a flat spot directly ahead where he could take a short break. Ralph shushed to an abrupt stop next to him and yanked down his blue-tinted goggles. Mako arrived a few seconds later. After catching their breath, the guys watched Ollie cut a pathway off to the right. "That's beautiful," Parker opined.

"Fuckin' master," Mako agreed.

Back on the trail, they were into fresh powder, slicing along like speedboats through the surf. Ralph broke out ahead, challenging Parker and Mako to keep up. They did. Flying over a ridge nearly in tandem, Parker and Mako fell onto another steep vertical. Then they funneled into a narrow section the forced them to tighten their turns.

The steady rush of air through Parker's helmet sounded like a turbine as he raced down the vertical. Coming out of every turn, Parker hurtled downhill. He was going so fast that his arms couldn't keep up with his body's momentum. Further down he saw the run even out. A group had gathered there, just about a hundred yards ahead. Soon he was on them. Recognizing his fellow skiers, Parker skidded sideways to stop. Mako was right behind him.

"That was a freakin' rough ass ride," Mako clamored, out of breath.

"I was out of control at times," Parker huffed, pulling down his goggles and emphatically sucking in oxygen.

Ollie smiled. "Come on, fellas. It's just getting fun. He pointed below where a steep, tree-lined run ran rife with moguls.

"No way," Parker said, "not for me."

"Me neither," Mako exclaimed. Ralph, Max and Doctor Frank were also no's.

"That's okay, guys," Marc said while motioning to a trail off to the left. "Take that piste. Ollie, Steve and I will meet you down the hill where the two runs intersect." He then popped out of his skis and knelt in the snow. "I've got to tighten this a bit."

Parker looked back at the rest of the group. "Who wants to lead?"

Mako spoke for everyone. "Go ahead. We'll follow."

Parker took off, cutting around a grove of trees and onto a much more comfortable track of snow. The five skiers flowed downhill smoothly for a while before the run took a quick turn to the right, rounding past a more significant stand of trees. That trail fell further right before broadening out onto a gentle slope where it crossed another trail, just as Marc had indicated. It gave them a perfect view of the mogul trail back up the mountain.

Stopping to look up just as the three men slammed into the moguls, Parker focused on Ollie leading the trail, his knees pounding like jackhammers through the snow. "Wow," Parker exclaimed. "That's amazing."

Ollie seemed to flow with the snow-packed moguls, bubbling over them like water over a rock-filled mountain stream. Max pointed to Steve, who was pressing Ollie from behind, pushing to catch up.

"If Steve goes down," Mako observed, "he'll cause a fucking avalanche."

Steve didn't go down, but he hadn't gained on Ollie, either. Parker led the gang over to the end of the mogul run where they waited for the mogul skiers. Ollie shushed to a stop a few yards away. He flipped off his goggles, lowered his gloved hands to his knees and hunched over, gasping for air.

"Those bumps can kill you," Ollie admitted, huffing for air between each word.

"No argument here," Steve declared, also short of breath. "But the chance to free ride up top was pure rad fun."

Marc led them off in a completely different direction on their next trip up the mountain. He led Steve and Ollie on a route that was out of bounds while Max took charge of the rest of the skiers. Halfway down, Max halted his group. "How about ten-minute break fellas? I can't feel my thighs."

Everyone agreed, and soon they were all bending, stretching and squatting to loosen up their hard-working muscles. After a few minutes' respite, they spotted Ollie, Steve and Marc merge onto the open trail above. Ollie was a mere streak, flying back and forth across the landscape like a weathervane on a windy day. Cutting his turns shorter, Steve was trying hard to catch up to the speedy Austrian.

Momentum shot Steve high over a hillcrest. He landed hard but kept his balance. Straightening out, Steve lowered into a tuck position to gain some speed. Parker couldn't help but admire the big man's prowess. "Wow, he's tearing it up."

"Yeah," Ralph stated, "Steve's giving it all he's got."

They peered on as Steve weaved ever closer to Ollie. He started to cut shorter, tighter turns, kicking up plumes of snow. Ollie went wide and then took a clean angle over a bulging rise. Cutting the same hump close, Steve almost lost it. Parker sensed trouble. "We'd better get going," he said.

They rushed over to where the two pistes converged. Looking up, Parker noticed Steve was tilting erratically on his turns. Finally, the big man flew off his skis like a blown tire. After a few cartwheels, Steve tumbled down the mountain like a massive, moving cloud of snow. It was a surreal scene, and when Parker accepted the frightening reality of it, he rushed to get to him. Although skiing ahead of Steve, Ollie somehow realized what had happened. He whirled around and accelerated toward the spot where Steve had finally stopped.

Parker hollered as loud as he could. "Is he all right?"

Bent over the prone skier, Ollie didn't respond. Marc was next to arrive. He held up his hand and waved for Parker to slow down. Steve was sitting up when Parker and the others got to his side.

"I'm fine," Steve barked. He tried to get up, but a streak of pain forced him to grab his right leg behind the knee. "Fuck!" Parker and Ralph bent down to stabilize him. "It's the ankle, just twisted. It'll be fine. Help me up."

"Don't move, Steve," Doctor Frank ordered. "I'm not a medical physician, but I'll have a look." Doctor Frank bent over and tenderly pressed his leg just above the boot. "Any pain here?"

"No."

"How about now?" He touched another area. "Can you try to put a tiny bit of pressure on it?"

Steve shrugged. "Sure." He eased the boot into the snow and then announced, "I don't feel any sharp pain, Doc."

Frank glanced over at Ollie. "I'd have to take the boot off to know for sure, but if I do, I may not get it back on."

Supporting each of his arms, Parker and Ralph eased Steve up. He rested heavily on the healthy leg while allowing the injured one to press gingerly on the snowpack. "Not too bad," Steve pronounced. He tried to make light of it. "Yeah, I do everything to the best of my ability, even wiping out." He winced again.

"Hurts, huh?" Parker observed.

"Yeah, a little bit." Steve firmed his jaw. "No big deal. It's just twisted." Despite his tough talk, Steve knew what the others had already assumed: their ski outing had come to an end. Max vocalized everyone's thoughts.

"You need to have someone look at that Steve. None of us will be disappointed to get off the mountain and head back to the hotel. You do need to ice that injury at the very least."

Ollie agreed. "Can you handle the ride back to Innsbruck?"

"Of course," Steve replied.

"Then we'll get some ice for the van. I'll phone Günter and have the house doctor waiting to look at it just to be sure."

Steve refused to ride down with ski patrol.

"You all finish the run," Marc said. "Ollie and I will take him down safe and slow. Meet us at the van."

ON THE RIDE back to Innsbruck, all indications were that Steve's injury was minor. That only made him more upset though, having to leave St. Anton before giving it a full day's effort. Ollie took some white tape from the van's emergency kit and taped up the tip of a ski pole so Steve could safely use it as a crutch.

They arrived at the Austropa before the doctor did, so Ollie hurried behind the front desk to ring him again.

"I don't think I need the doc," Steve said.

"It's just a precaution," Ollie stated. "Go get some lunch. He can see you in the dining room."

"Can you toss me my room key?" Steve asked. "I'm going to get a quick change."

Ollie handed over the key fob and Steve limped away, leveraging the ski pole for balance. Parker followed close behind him. At the elevator, Parker reached in and hit the second-floor button. "Are you sure you don't need any help?" he asked.

A stiff wave was Steve's only response as the elevator door closed. Marc cruised past Parker toward the bar.

"Pour me one?" Parker asked. "I'll be back in a few seconds."

Marc agreed with a nod and a smile. Hiking up the staircase and peeking around the corner, Parker watched Steve wobble the length of the hallway and step up to his door. Before Parker could head back down the stairs though, he was jolted by Steve's angry, hair-raising holler. "You fucker!"

Parker rushed down the hall and into the room through the open door, arriving just as Steve's cocked arm exploded a punch. Amid the sound of angry voices and fists hitting flesh,

Parker struggled to get between the fighters. Steve grabbed the other man by the throat and landed a second blow. That's when Parker finally realized it was Dante being pummeled.

"Stop it, Steve." Parker hollered. "Let Dante go!"

Steve had no intention of stopping, so Parker clung to his bicep, allowing Dante to weasel away and run out the door. Ollie came out of nowhere, pushing off of the doorjamb to catapult himself onto the enraged man from behind. Others swarmed into the room too, but Steve had already directed his anger at Ronni. "You twisted bitch!"

Quivering with shock, Ronni sat on the edge of the bed, her brown, striped flannel shirt unbuttoned and open, exposing bare breasts for all to see. "Nothing happened!" she screamed. "Nothing happened!"

Suddenly aware of his sore ankle, Steve yelped and staggered as Parker and Ollie wrestled him away and pinned him up against the wall. Scurrying into the room, Brooke ran to Ronni's side and wrapped her up in the white comforter that topped the bed.

"Dante?" Steve roared. "You've got Dante in here? Mother fucking Dante?"

Ronni clawed at the covers to pull them to her chin. Panting heavily, she finally gathered enough oxygen to shout back at him, aggressively. "That's right, Steve, Dante was with me. Dante. Think about that, Steve!" She laughed like a mad woman. "And before that it was Parker." Ronni pointed to the guide, whose shock was apparent, despite having his face smashed up against Steve's shoulder. "That's right, Parker. He tried to get me in a church of all places, in a church!"

"Shut up right now," Brooke demanded, grabbing Ronni by the shoulders and shaking her firmly. "That's a lie." Looking back at Steve, Brooke reiterated. "That's a damn lie, Steve. I was there and it didn't happen." Seemingly stunned by it all, Steve quit huffing and squirming. Brooke continued. "Parker was with us in Salzburg, but Ronni's making that up. I don't know why but she's making it up. It's a lie."

A wary gaze fell on Ronni's face and her eyes burned into Brooke. "You are the liar," she challenged.

But Brooke wouldn't have it. Again she grabbed Ronni's shoulders. This time she squeezed them tight and spoke calmly but firmly. "I know that nothing happened between you and Parker. I was there. I know nothing happened."

Bewildered by Brooke's resolve, Ronni stammered. "You were there?" Her eyes filled with tears and she broke down in uncontrollable sobs. "You were there."

"Get her out of here," Ollie yelled. Marc and Mako stood side by side near the door to allow Ronni safe passage. Brooke pushed the comforter away, wrapped an arm around the shaken woman, and hustled her out of the room.

PARKER AND OLLIE sat alone at the Austropa bar waiting for the day tours and ski shuttles to return.

"We've got a room for Ronni at the Hotel Franz Mair," Ollie said.

"Where's she at now?"

"In Max's room. My wife is with her."

"That's good. I'll make sure someone stays with Ronni all night. Sally will get her off on that first flight in the morning."

"We put Steve up at a hotel near the airport," Ollie confirmed.

Parker took his last sip of beer. "We've got him going on a later flight."

Günter snuck up behind them and said softly. "Shuttles are here."

Ollie stopped Parker from getting up. "I'll handle it." He nodded at the beer tap. "Pour yourself another one."

Parker did so, raising up on his haunches to top off his tall beer glass. Pleased by the sound of happy tourists flooding the hall, he quietly sipped his brew. A few minutes later Mako swooped in behind the bar to fill a mug for himself. "Have you said anything to Sally yet?"

Parker shrugged. "She just got back. Ollie's talking to her right now."

Peering closely at his friend, Mako wrinkled his brow. "Looks like you got tagged."

Rising again to peek at his reflection in the mirrored glass behind the bar, Parker saw a long red splotch along his forehead. "Just roughed up a bit."

Mako stepped around and sat next to Parker, clutching his pilsner glass. "That had to be some scary shit."

Parker shook his head. "Steve was out of his mind. He could've killed Dante."

"Did he get in a clean shot?"

"The first one was clean. It almost took Dante's head off."

"Damn, that son-of-a-bitch is lucky you came in when you did."

"Yeah. It happened so fast."

"He must've caught them in the act."

"Not quite."

"Was she naked?"

Parker shook his head. "Her shirt was unbuttoned and open but not all the way off."

"What a nasty scene to walk in on, right?" Mako asked rhetorically. "And you, seeing Steve wailing on Dante, Ronni half naked and completely freaked. Did you get a look? I mean, I bet she's got a great rack, huh?"

EVERYONE in the group was aware of the incident, and a somber mood permeated the dining hall. Parker was melancholy too, knowing that Brooke wasn't going to be around at all that evening. He and Mako sat alone at the rectangular table for eight - Max's usual table. Sally joined them right after the servers had delivered their pork tenderloin entrées.

"Sorry I'm late," Sally said. Parker had just taken a bite, so he only nodded. Mako shrugged as she explained. "At least those two are settled and out of our hair."

Parker swallowed. "Whose hair are they in?"

"Doctor Frank will be staying with Steve and Brooke's going to overnight with Ronni," Sally explained. "I'll run over to the Franz Mair first thing in the morning to get her on that flight." The server appeared with a hot plate of food for Sally and a side salad. After thanking the girl, Sally gazed at Parker quizzically. "So I heard she accused you of harassing her? What's with that?"

Parker wiped the tip of his nose. "It's nonsense. She made a move on me, cornering me in the church confessional of all places. It was just freaky, you know? That woman has problems I swear to God."

Sally didn't relax her stare. "Engaged to Steve? Ya think?" Looking down at her plate, Sally turned her fork backward properly and selected a piece of pork. "Thank goodness Brooke was there to witness it."

Parker stopped chewing. "Oh, yeah, glad for that."

Mako glared at Parker before adding, "Hallelujah."

Sally didn't catch the sarcasm, of course. "I don't know about you guys, but I'm glad this day is over."

"Almost done," Parker reminded. "Since we're all here let's run through our plans for tomorrow." Parker dug out the iPad so the trio could review the morning departure and arrival times. They perused the rooming list and agreed that Sally would stay behind again to help the staff get everything organized while Parker and Mako worked the airport turn around.

"Are you going to offer them a trip to the beer hall tomorrow night?" Sally asked.

"I don't see why not," Parker said.

"Is it okay if I pass? You guys know I don't even like beer."

Parker nodded. "No worries. I'll do it myself since you two are taking the tours out on Sunday."

"Hold on," Mako countered. "I got bit by the ski bug today. Can I hit the slopes on Sunday?"

Parker tapped the iPad open again to check on the day tour reservations. "We've got enough pre-paids on one of the day trips but no big numbers anywhere else. So, Sally, you can take that trip and Mako, you can lead a group to whatever ski area is the most popular with everyone. I'll stick around here and handle any crap that raises its ugly head. Now, let's take a look ahead at Monday's schedule."

Sally huffed with exhaustion. "Please, I don't want to hash out all of our work assignments tonight."

Parker didn't press any further. "That's fine. It's the last group, though, and I'd like to stay on top of it. Too bad that we won't have anyone at the Fasching celebration, not that I want to pay my own way. Don might cough up the extra expense, although we've squeezed him pretty good this week. Unless you want to give him a call, Sal?"

Sally raked up a forkful of mashed potatoes. "Whatever." All of the "cute" had drained from her face. "I just want to finish dinner and crawl into a warm bed."

Raising his cup of tea, Parker inhaled its soothing aroma. "I couldn't agree more."

THE FIRST THING Parker did was set his alarm for 5:00 a.m. That would allow him time to meditate, do some yoga, take a shower, shave and enjoy a good breakfast before the hectic airport turn-around. Sitting on the bed, he opened up the iPad to take one more glimpse at the tour documents. Once again, he perused the rooming list. Making sure that he could easily pronounce each of the passenger's names.

His tired mind began to wander. What was Brooke doing now? What were she and Ronni talking about? Did Ronni honestly believe that Brooke was there, in that church, to somehow witness what had happened?

Brooke could handle Ronni, Parker reassured himself. Then he heard a series of gentle raps on the door. They were soft and persistent, like the constant drip of a leaky faucet. Confident that Mako was messing with him, Parker jumped up and threw open the door. It was Brooke. Covered in her black down coat, she was also wearing a pair of tortoise-shell glasses.

Hurriedly, Parker pulled her inside and closed the door. "Who knocks like that?" Brooke only twisted her lips and shrugged, looking more and more adorable to Parker with each passing second. "Are you in disguise?"

"No," Brooke said. Then she yanked off her spectacles and reached out wildly as if she was blind. "I usually wear contacts."

He smiled but shifted back to a serious mood. "Did anyone see you come down here?"

"Uh-uh. Not a soul."

"What about Ronni?"

Brooke folded up her glasses, slipped them in a leather case and shoved them in her coat pocket. "She and Honey were both passed out when I left. Those two sure can drink their vodka." She noticed Parker's questioning gaze. "Honey staying with Ronni, too. I just had to come back for my contacts." She smiled broadly and then leaped at him. Parker caught her beneath the rib cage, squeezed her tight, and then lowered her to the floor.

Brooke laughed, slipped off her parka and tossed it on the bed. Parker grabbed her by the waist and quickly kissed her, releasing his pent-up passion. When they separated, Parker saw that Brooke's face flushed with pure happiness. He thought that she would never be more beautiful than at that very moment.

They remained locked in mutual admiration until Brooke pursed her lips and reached for another kiss, slowly, as if probing to make sure he was real. Parker mimicked her actions, pivoting his head slightly to the opposite side, puckering his lips and pressing them gently to hers. With eyes closed, he tried to concentrate every sense on her while his hands tenderly enveloped her torso.

Their kisses intensified despite the cackle of tourist voices echoing down the hallway. Brooke's mouth swarmed over his, wet, open and suddenly anxious as if he were made of something soft and sweet that would melt away before she finished. The only thing that melted, however, was the frustration that hardened him after the previous night's disappointment.

Easing his lips away, Parker focused on her face again to relish the view. Brooke returned the gaze, examining him with glistening blue eyes that shifted in minute increments, from his eyes to his nose, to his lips and over to his ears. "I'm so sorry about last night. It was horrible. When Honey backed out, I just had to go."

"I know, I know," he murmured. "It was tough for me too, but that's all in the past." All that mattered to Parker was that she was there. They finally had time to be together, and he was determined to make every second count. Despite being inflamed by her voracious kisses, he was not going to rush the thing. He had no intention of hurrying love for the sake of passion. Something so sweet must be savored.

"I'll pour some wine." Picking her coat off the bed, he hung it in the closet and then grabbed a bottle that was stashed on the shelf.

Brooke walked over to the small round table near the enclosed patio. Then she perused the room, nodded, and gave it her approval. "Not bad."

"I'd have gotten the suite if it wasn't already taken."

"Funny guy."

After retrieving two coffee mugs, Parker flicked on the bathroom light switch and dug a plastic corkscrew from his shaving kit. He left the bathroom door ajar so the soft light could filter into the rest of the room. Then he turned off the desk lamp and walked over to Brooke, guided by the dull luster of her red, V-neck, cashmere sweater.

She motioned to the cheap corkscrew. "That must get a workout."

"It does."

"Never know when a lady visitor will come by?" she teased.

"Never know when I'll be mired in chaos and in need of a drink," he replied, opening the wine. "I'm a tour guide, remember?"

Brooke smirked while he filled her cup. Then she hoisted her drink and made a toast. "Here's to chaos … and the opportunity it's presented us."

After a sip, Brooke turned to the window. She raised the taupe colored Austrian shade with her fingers to take a look outside. It was a serene view of cold brick buildings, surrounding a lovely, snow-covered courtyard. Every window dotting those structures was dark. Only the light of a full moon brightened the space.

Parker sidled up behind her, and they enjoyed the peaceful scene together in silence. Brooke gazed back over her shoulder at him, adoringly. Her hand smoothed the side of his face, and her lips moved up to kiss him gently on the cheek.

Moonlight cast a glow on Brooke's face. "You look like the prom date I wished I'd had," Parker said.

"That bad? Maybe you asked the wrong girl?"

He lifted her chin. "Oh, I asked the right girl, she just said no."

"That girl must've been on drugs."

"She was out of my league," Parker admitted. "But I've always believed that your reach should exceed your grasp." As if to demonstrate that conviction, Parker held up his hand. Brooke raised her hand too, mirroring his with the gentlest of touches, palm to palm. Taking her index finger, she traced an outline of his hand, moving slowly across each fingertip. After rubbing his open palm with her thumb, she pulled his hand to her lips, kissing it softly before nestling it to her cheek.

Parker caressed her face and then eased his lips to hers. Their kisses surged and waned with their passion: long, firm, and sensual; short, sweet and suggestive. Gently, Parker smoothed the side of his right hand along the plunging neckline of her sweater. The material was soft, but her skin was silky and inviting, so he edged a finger up her chest until it brushed against the dangling, glass-encased stamp.

Then his fingers slipped back down, moving beneath the loose fabric, searching for her left breast, which was only concealed by the downy, soft wool. Brooke's breath quickened. Tenderly, he aroused her nipple. Reaching over with his left hand, Parker moved her hair back to expose her right ear. He leaned in to taste its tenderness, offering soft kisses before tracing the inside edges of her ear with his tongue.

That was the path to her happiness. Parker knew because her chest began to pound and her neck muscles strained with the tension of arousal. Brooke closed her eyes. Her lips parted to gasp full breaths. She reached up, gathered all of his fingers, and forced his right hand to grab her left breast so he could squeeze her, fully and firmly.

Brooke pried open the buttons on Parker's shirt with desperate determination. Parker grabbed her hands when she fumbled the last button and finished the job himself. His shirt fell to the floor, and Brooke studied his chest, giving in to the urge to touch it, and smooth over his skin to better feel his firmness. Running her hands down his torso, Brooke followed her fingers with her eyes. When she finally looked up, Parker saw admiration in her gaze. It turned him on, and he pulled her close for a passionate kiss.

Parker sat her down on the bed and helped her slink out of her tight jeans. He knelt down and slowly pushed her legs apart, inserting himself into the vacant space. She lowered her head and kissed him softly, nibbling his lower lip. Enthralled by her kisses, Parker didn't open his eyes to adore her shapely legs. Instead, he felt them: caressing her thighs, running his fingers up and down those silky smooth limbs. The sensation was too much for Parker to bear. He slid his hands beneath the sweater, raised the hem and pressed his lips to her navel.

Parker kissed the sweet skin of her stomach while his hands reached for her hips. Brooke slipped the sweater over her head, and Parker responded by reaching his right hand behind her to feel the small of her back. He caressed along her spine and edged a finger beneath the sheer lace of her panties. Enjoying the feel of that texture, he brushed his fingers across the triangular patch of fabric that barely covered her backside and then squeezed the tender flesh that peeked out from its sparse covering.

His sense of sight offered another thrill: a bare hipbone, resting beyond the gentle slope of her belly. It sat flat and inviting, curving up above the embroidered waistband of her panties. His lips were drawn to it, kissing it gently a few times, at first. Then he pressed his lips firmly against it, grasping her hips fully to stroke her thighs with both of his thumbs. Brooke sighed as she exhaled. She pulled him up, so they were chest-to-chest and then secured them together with a firm hug and passionate kiss. Wrapped in each other's arms, they eased back onto the bed.

While their eyes were locked in a loving stare, Brooke took control. She slid her hands down his sides to find the belt loops of his corduroy pants. Slowly she began to cinch them down his waist. The belt-less trousers barely inched along, so Parker shifted from side to side to help hurry them down. Once past his rump, the couple shared a mischievous grin. Parker raised his torso, twisted aside to complete the task and then tossed the slacks on the floor. Turning back, he looked down to see Brooke lying flat on the bed, her pretty face flushed with promise. Then she angled her knees, raised her feet, lifted her hips and slipped off her panties.

Parker focused on Brooke's pleasure. All that defined him was tuned into her: passion, enthusiasm, sensitivity, and sincerity But he wasn't guided only by those intuitions. There was also the teachings of Taoist sexuality, a progress of plea-sure that Parker had once learned. He would be the instrument of that process, responding to her desires as he moved her slowly, purposefully, to the next level of excitement.

Following his gesture, she laid on her back in the healing position. He moved between her legs, grasped a bent knee and softly kissed the inside of her right thigh, slowly working down to the sweet flesh underneath. His lips energized her heart. Releasing her pleasure through moans of satisfaction, Brooke weaved her fingers through his tousled hair and then guided his head back up, squaring his face with hers.

Parker and Brooke shared an intense stare. Pausing as if at the peak of a thrill ride - the weight of their pleasure balanced on that very moment - the couple braced for release. In one slow, simple motion, Parker pressed himself on top of her and moved inside of her. Bending her neck and closing her eyes, Brooke released a soft moan.

Reckless kissing ensued. Brooke's tongue seemed to be an extension of her happiness as it strained to taste Parker. She held onto him tightly. Captive, yet in control, Parker's thrusts jolted her with pleasant spasms and short peaks of fulfillment. He felt that Brooke was afraid to let go and yet eager to do so.

She slipped her hands around his head, pressing them together, cheek-to-cheek, while her body quivered.

But that was just the half of it. The holdbacks made it so. Parker rolled onto his back so she could be on top and have control as well as freedom of movement. They began to writhe in unison, slowly again, rebuilding to a further stage of satisfaction. Minutes later, Brooke was all but breathless, and she flopped down on him, her searching tongue giving away to a nibble and an open bite.

Brooke's face contorted from the sensations. It grew flushed. Their gyrations meshed so perfectly that he could feel her mounting pleasure deep in his stomach. He took hold of her hips for deeper penetration. She pulled back up, straight and tall before arching back to let out an exasperating moan.

Soon it was upon them. Tensing with all the strain of G-force on takeoff, Parker lost all sense of being. He was anguished by the pleasure, while Brooke surrendered herself to that little death. Overwhelmed, every inch of Brooke's shivering body strained to deal with the wave of sensations. When it was all over, when the tingling subsided, when her flesh grew clammy, she drooped down on Parker like a wilted flower.

He caught her face, cradled it in his hands, and rested it on his heaving chest. Slackened and spent, Brooke laid on top of him. The weight of her body comforted Parker. He closed his eyes and smiled, knowing that he had filled every bit of the emptiness inside of her. Just as he had imagined, they had been one in mind, one in soul, and finally, one in body.

That body generated a lot of heat and perspiration. The cool room chilled their damp skin, so Parker pulled the covers up from underneath. Brooke moaned when he moved, but settled quickly to snuggle when the comforter fell over her. There was a grin on her face as she rested on his shoulder, and he brushed back her hair to see it fully. She looked cozy, so cute, and Parker got that feeling you get when you look at something warm and soft, and you just want to hold it tightly to your chest.

They were both exhausted. Brooke's belly pressed against Parker's side with each breath she took. He felt the expanse, and her gentle tugs of inhaled air, and the warm breath flushing across his neck when she exhaled. Her rhythmic breathing had a tranquilizing effect that lulled Parker into a light sleep.

Soon he came out of that dream-like void refreshed, and with renewed vitality. When Brooke opened her eyes, she seemed to be re-energized, too. They kissed.

"It felt like I was inside of you," she said.

"You are."

She snickered and rolled onto her back. "Oh my, we have to do this again sometime soon."

Sliding onto his side, Parker dug his elbow into the bed and propped his head up to look down at her. "What about Sunday? I'm in town, busy in the morning but as long as I'm close to my phone, I'm free all afternoon."

"Sunday? I think I'm skiing Sunday." Brooke pondered her schedule. "Yeah, I'm supposed to be skiing with Max."

"I understand."

Brooke's eyes widened. "No, you're not supposed to understand." She reached out, pulled him down on top of her and scowled. "You're supposed to say, 'damn it, Brooke, I want to be with you and Sunday is our next best chance. Make it work.'"

Hovering over her, Parker repeated her words, only he spoke softly and sincerely. "Damn it, Brooke." He paused to kiss her. "I want to be with you." He pecked her lips again. "And Sunday is our next best chance." After one last kiss, he concluded. "So please, please, please, make it work."

She returned his last kiss firmly, passionately. When her lips pulled away, she whispered, "Trust me, I will."

A dreadful noise shattered the moment. It was Mako, talking to someone down the hall. Parker hurried to his feet, slipped on his shorts, then moved to the door. He followed the soft light from the bathroom like a path across the dark floor. Listening carefully, he motioned for Brooke to get up. Quietly she slipped on her sweater and inched up her jeans. Still guarding the door, Parker watched her pull herself together. Then he abruptly stepped over and grabbed her dangling hand so they could kiss with the recklessness of lovers afraid to part.

"You know it, bro," they finally heard Mako say.

Another indistinct male voice replied, "Good night."

Mako walked down the hall, heading for his next-door room. Parker snuck Brooke into the bathroom to hide. They heard the fat splat of Mako's key fob as it was slapped repeatedly in the palm of his hand. They listened to the metallic scratch of the key when he inserted it into the lock. The door squeaked open, and then it stopped. Parker and Brooke gasped as Mako called out. "Parks, you up?"

Holding Brooke frozen in his arms, Parker said nothing. Mako moved closer to Parker's door. "Hey pal, are you awake or do you have company?"

Brooke nearly squealed, but Parker covered her mouth and directed her into the shower. Undoubtedly, Mako would persist. Regardless, he would have some suspicions - that was his nature. So Parker acknowledged by flushing the toilet. "I'll be right out," he shouted. Seconds later Parker cracked open the door and offered Mako a terse suggestion. "Go to bed already."

Mako tossed Parker a look of disgust. Then he pushed the door ajar and gave the room a quick inspection. "Ha, alone as usual."

Parker easily explained the messed up bed. "I was already sacked out for the night."

"That's your problem. I'm just swinging by for a pit stop.

Headed back out after a quick change," Mako rubbed his hands together, "and you are not going to believe where I'm going."

"You're right. I won't believe it. Goodnight." Before Parker could slam the door shut, Mako stuck out a thick arm to stop it.

"I knew it. You weak fuck." Opening the door wide, Mako pointed to the bottle of wine and the mugs on the table. "You had Brooke down here tonight, didn't you?" Mako's eyes grew wild as his head shook with pity. "You are in real shit now."

Parker's mind scrambled for a name, a girl, one of the girls at Ski School, but he drew a blank. No matter, it was fruitless to deny. "She was here," he finally admitted.

Wagging his finger, Mako scolded his friend. "I got a whiff that you two were up to no good."

"Like I said, she was here, but nothing happened."

"Of course nothing happened. I know, I know. She's a nice girl." Mako eyed Parker with disdain. "But holy fuck, bro, your ass is on the line here."

"Relax," Parker said, "nothing happened, and nothing's going to."

Mako didn't reply. He just shook his head and left. Brooke emerged from hiding as soon as the door closed. She had a gleam in her eye, a scared, strange twinkle. "How could you tell him?" she clamored.

"It didn't matter, he knew. Mako has an instinct for this stuff." Brooke was still upset. Parker reassured her. "Don't worry. He'll keep the secret."

Brooke tugged on her coat and moved stiffly to the door. Parker kept a hand on the knob as they kissed goodbye, and then he opened it up just enough for her to slip out. Brooke stopped at the threshold and reached for him with her eyes.

"I love you," she said.

"I hope so," he replied. "Because I love you, and I hate to walk out on that ledge alone."

Brooke smiled, and then she was gone. Her light steps could barely be heard creeping down the hall. Even if someone had heard, it didn't matter to Parker just then. He was in a fatalistic mood. After a chug of wine, he pulled on his shirt and pants. Then he went to the closet to grab his gray ski jacket so he could go out for some air.

The deserted streets were welcoming. Confident that Mako wouldn't say a word, Parker was still well aware that trouble was coming, one way or another. It would be coming fast, too, with the last group arriving that next morning and Brooke and Max scheduled to leave the following Saturday. Maybe they would have Sunday together, but what then? The more they were together the more they wanted to be together. How would that play out?

Circling the block, Parker finally realized that his ears were numbed by the cold. Cursing that he'd forgotten his cap, he stepped quickly toward the street corner. Ahead, the Austropa stood like a sentinel in the dark.

As Parker approached, a light came on in one of the rooms above the Bistro. It shone softly behind the blinds. Wondering if it was Brooke's room, Parker stopped to see if anyone was in it. But it wasn't the honeymoon suite, he realized. It was one of the standard rooms on the second floor.

Peering up, Parker noticed a silhouette come into view. It was a woman. It looked like Sally. Parker recognized the familiar outline of her hair and face; more so when the shadow of her arms rose up with open palms as if praising the Lord. She wasn't praying though. It was a welcoming gesture. That's when he saw another shadow. This one was a man who slowly walked over to hug Sally. Parker couldn't discern who it was, but he watched intently as their embrace turned into a long and passionate kiss.

FIFTEEN

The Grand Imperial Hotel

IT WAS HALF past noon on Sunday when Parker stepped out the front door of the Austropa Hotel. Bursting with anticipation, he was still able to harness his emotions and stroll past the Bistro at a leisurely pace. Once around the corner though, he accelerated his stride so that the lugged soles of his hiking boots skimmed across the frosty sidewalk.

The front desk manager at the Grand Imperial Hotel greeted him respectfully. "I see you have an early check-in, Mr. Moon." Firming his square chin, the man was reassuring. "We have your room ready, of course."

Parker accepted the plastic room key and followed the attendant's direction to the elevators. He waited there patiently, as nonchalant as possible. Stepping into the elevator alone, he hit the fourth-floor button. As soon as the metal door clanged shut, Parker broke out into a giddy grin.

It was an elegant room with red and gold floral print carpeting and matching draperies. An oval, gold-framed mirror sat on the wall by the window, reflecting sunshine that gleamed off of a brass chandelier centered on the ceiling. Sitting on the king-size bed, Parker unfolded Brooke's latest note. He read it for the third time as if he'd never read it before:

Parker, I reserved a room at the Grand Imperial Hotel. They guaranteed an early check in so try to get there right after lunch. I'll be there as soon as I can. I miss you so bad it hurts! I'm so excited to see you, can't wait! Love, Brooke

The hell with text messages Parker thought, as he followed the graceful contour of her writing. Recognizing the gift of her very personal sentiments, he was able to feel Brooke in every written word. He swallowed each syllable of that last sentence as if consuming an excellent liqueur, warming his body from the inside out. One word above all else, however, settled in Parker's heart. A simple term that somehow summarizes everything that ever meant anything to any human being. That word, of course, was "love."

Brooke's peculiar knock announced her arrival. When Parker opened the door, he felt her aura illuminate the room. They embraced.

"Sorry it took so long for me to get here," she said.

"You're right on time. Did you ski?"

"I got one run in, but then I broke a binding."

"You did?"

Brooke grinned sardonically. "Weird, huh? That's never happened before."

AN OLD WILLIAM WORDSWORTH POEM, *The World Is Too Much With Us*, popped into Parker's head as he snuggled with Brooke in bed. Yes, indeed, all too often the world *was* too much with him: vigilant to his duties, a slave to the schedule - always a definitive schedule - and burdened by the enormous weight of his work. Even when Parker had free time on tour, he seldom took advantage of it. Sure, he'd take a minute or so to enjoy a sunset or a sunrise, and a morning meditation helped keep him balanced. But he was never able to check out and escape from his people. They were his all-consuming responsibility.

In Innsbruck, however, he had Sally and Mako, and Ollie for backup. Most importantly, he had Brooke. So he shut off his phone and became completely unavailable. Making Brooke happy was his only purpose. Relaxing in each other's arms, they talked and laughed while the sunlight drifted across the tightly woven carpeting. They reminisced about their precious moments of the past, sharing memories with a sense of longing: if only they had been together then.

"All right," Parker asked, "so where's the most beautiful sunrise you've ever seen?"

"That's easy," Brooke responded, "Stonehenge."

"Oh, that's good."

"So what about you? What's the number one sunrise on Parker's list?"

"It's hard to say. Somewhere in Greece or Scotland, I suppose."

Brooke leaned over and kissed his cheek. "Put either one of them on our list." Her inflection was definitive, and it warmed Parker's heart. "What about sunsets?" she asked.

Parker sighed. "That one's even tougher."

Brooke turned on her side to peek up at him impatiently. "Come on. There has to be one." Parker continued to ponder. Brooke lazily swiped a finger across her chest in the shape of a cross. "I promise not to tell anyone."

Parker's face grew serious. "Well, I've seen some beautiful sunsets in a bunch of amazing places, but I'd trade them all for any sunset on any clear summer night in the Northwoods, just before the mosquitoes start to bite."

Brooke's blue eyes twinkled above her broad grin. Turning

on her belly, she kept those eyes trained on Parker. Then she scooted up on her haunches, rested her forearms on his chest and posed like a cat about to strike its prey. Parker grasped her biceps to brace for the amorous assault.

To say they made love would be a travesty. What they did was slip across the edge of reality, into another world; a place that some people think exists only in the mind. The vehicle was their physiological capacity: touching, kissing, the pleasure of making love, but the emotions of love fueled the ride; two beings, united in passion, giving to each other to the fullest extent of their desire.

How long it lasted could only be guessed. Time lost its value. Their strained, muffled voices crying out, "Oh, God! Oh God!" weren't mere outlets of pleasure. They were cries sent out to the greatest of spirits, thankful for the opportunity to experience such incredible joy, grateful for the chance to share a rare moment of bliss. And in that place where love had driven them, Parker sensed an unmistakable presence. He knew they had been heard.

They should have conceived. That's what Parker thought, anyway. They would've conceived, too, had they not taken precautions. People are driven to make love for a lot of reasons, Parker's grandfather taught him: to prove their love, to release their physical need, for the nourishment of their souls, and sometimes just to shake their loneliness.

Conception, however, was its ultimate purpose. Grandpa said it was far too blessed of an event to take lightly. So they made love a second time to revel in their perfect harmony. Later, they made love again, but just for the fun of it. They kissed a lot too when they weren't making love, and every kiss counted. They took nothing for granted. Not one minute was wasted on worry.

"We have to leave," Brooke said eventually, blinking a few times to clear away her sadness.

Parker didn't move. He watched her get up and stroll into the bathroom. He heard the shower come on and waited in bed the whole time until it was turned off. His eyes followed her out of the bathroom, and he watched her get dressed. Finally, he rolled on his side so she could sit by him on the edge of the bed.

"I hate to leave," he said.

She smiled warmly while running her fingers through his hair. "Just don't be late for dinner."

"I have no desire to eat, either."

She leaned in to kiss him.

"You know the Austropa kitchen will be closed tomorrow night so they can prepare for their Fasching buffet," Parker reminded her. "Maybe we can figure a way to have dinner together somewhere?"

Brooke smiled. "Maybe we can come back here?"

Parker gently rubbed her chin and peered deep into her eyes. "I like the way you think."

They kissed again, slowly, gently, until Brooke eased away. "I've got to go," she whispered remorsefully, and then she did.

A CACOPHONY of voices spilled beyond the dining room Sunday night, as Parker walked down the hall. Turning the corner, he came face to face with Max.

"I'm starting to think that you're avoiding me," Max said.

A feeble grin wrinkled Parker's face. "No, I always make it a point to sit with every member of the tour at least once during the trip."

"Then it's my turn tonight," Max said before walking away. "I'll save you a seat."

Heading in the opposite direction, Parker bellied up to the bar. Mako came out of nowhere to tap him on the shoulder. "Hey, I need a beer."

Parker turned to face his friend. "Need or want?"

Mako sneered. "Makes no difference to me."

Two bartenders worked the busy bar, while Ollie manned the tap. He drew one beer each for Parker and Mako. "I hope Sally is feeling better," Ollie said to the guys before relinquishing his duties. He then scurried around the corner, heading for the front desk.

Parker looked at Mako curiously. "What's up with Sally?"

"Oh yeah, she called and said she had a headache," Mako answered. "I told her to lay low tonight."

"She didn't tell me."

"I told her I'd tell you."

"But you didn't."

Mako raised a brow. "I just did."

Exasperated, Parker grabbed his friend by the elbow. "Let's go."

"Go where?"

"To sit with Max. He invited me to join them for dinner."

Mako twisted his lips to form a smirk. "Oh, okay. I see. Boy, this should be good."

PARKER COULD FEEL Max's eyes on him the moment he entered the dining room. Seated at the head of the table, the owner of SojournSports waved for Parker, directing him to take the chair on his right, across from Brooke. Parker obeyed, suspicious of Max's affable countenance. Parker was determined to play it cool though. He wasn't going to avoid Brooke. Nor would he linger on her. After cordial hellos, Parker took in a series of long, full breaths. Then he leaned back and listened to the various conversations that crisscrossed the table.

Brooke, too, was reserved. Max made every effort to lure her into a pleasant discussion, but she remained aloof. Still, Max didn't ask any probing questions. He never cast a discerning glance at either Parker or Brooke. The only vigilant eye at the table belonged to Doctor Frank, and Honey was its focus. Whether it was wondering about her drink, "Too much ice?" or worrying about her meal, "Is your tenderloin seasoned the way you like it, dear?" the man doted over her.

Parker's paranoia eased with each minute of chitchat and every delicious bite of his meal. Halfway through dinner, however, Max abruptly pointed at him. "Something is bothering you," he said. "I can tell."

Max's confrontational command forced the blood to drain from Parker's face. He gritted his teeth to answer. "No, I'm okay, just a bit tired."

Max shook his head. "No, I can tell something's wrong."

Mako stopped speaking right in the middle of a sentence just to watch the exchange, forcing Doctor Frank and Honey to glance that way, too.

"I'm good, really," Parker replied with a shrug. Worried that he'd been conspicuously not himself, Parker reached for an excuse. "It's just been a long couple of weeks and with the last tour group in now, well, there's just a lot on my mind."

Max shook his head again and eyed Parker knowingly. "Oh, no, I know."

A server passed by and Max leaned over to glance at all of his guests. "Who needs another drink?" After placing his order, Max pressed further. "As I was saying, Parker, you're worried, and I know why."

Parker said nothing. Brooke ignored them both, intent on stabbing her fork into every last bit of salad at the bottom of her white porcelain bowl. As another server pulled their empty dinner plates away, Max eased back in his chair, folded his arms across his chest, and finally deduced, "you're worried about Sally, aren't you?"

Exhaling with relief, Parker jumped all over the excuse. "Sure I am. She's my right arm out here."

"Bad analogy," Mako added. Everyone looked at him, puzzled, so Mako explained. "Parker's left-handed."

Parker ignored Mako's remark. "She keeps it all together for us. And if it wasn't for her I swear," he gestured to Mako, "we'd be at each other's throats."

"Yeah," Mako acknowledged. "She's like our mom."

Max just grinned. "I'm sure she is. And after a bit of rest, I have no doubt she'll be just fine."

Max had ordered a brandy, and when the drink arrived, he wrapped his long fingers around the glass like tentacles. "I want you to know that Sally has been just wonderful to my folks. She has been amazing to every one of us here," he said to Parker.

Everyone but Brooke acknowledged Max's compliment. She had changed her focus from her empty salad bowl to a full glass of white wine. Max continued, "I respect what you do, Parker, you and Mako, and Sally. I can't imagine doing the work you all do."

"Yeah," Parker replied, "it's a tough job, but we love it."

Max countered, "I've never shied away from hard work either. I'd be troubled most by the commitment of time that your work requires."

"I don't give much thought to the amount of time I spend doing my job," Parker said.

"Of course you don't, that's the benefit of your age," Max concluded. "And the curse of my age is to have the time to look back and count the hours I've squandered."

"Listen, this is a great gig," Mako added. "I know a lot of people who'd kill for this job."

"They've never seen your paycheck," Parker countered.

Mako only grinned in agreement.

"I didn't mean to infer anything negative about your careers," Max explained. "All I was trying to say is that I couldn't do it." The usually ebullient man seemed to lose some of his luster as he continued. "When I was your age gentlemen, it was all about the money. I was fully engaged in the pursuit of wealth." Max stretched his hands far apart. "My life was over here," he glanced at his left hand before turning his head and nodding at the right one. "And I was over there, running along, watching it pass me by."

Aware of a shift in the mood, Max followed up with an apology. "I'm sorry. We just don't talk much at all about our personal lives." He reached for Brooke's hand, but she didn't respond to his gesture. Silence permeated the air around them all like a bad odor. Max fumbled for a conclusion. "The point is, we're all free to do what we want with our time, but when there's someone special in your life, someone you love, you have a commitment to them that must be honored."

Brooke broke her stillness with a vengeance. "You talk about love like it's an obligation; like it's just another business to run. Love has no algorithm. It's natural, instinctive. Your commitment to the people you love is something you should just *want* to do."

Max was stung by her sharp remarks. Parker tried to diffuse things. "I was raised to believe that freedom is the ultimate responsibility. You're free to make choices, but you have to be responsible for the consequences. Love is a choice of free will. Desire is what gets you there, so desire drives your commitment."

Parker was glad to see Brooke's glare soften to a wistful gaze. It was Doctor Frank, however, who ended the discussion with one of his patented pontifications. He spoke until dessert arrived - Austrian crepes filled with apricot jam and chocolate. A server also delivered the bar bill. Parker dug into his pocket. Max waved for him to stop. "It's on me."

"Sorry to run, but Mako and I have to make the rounds," Parker announced. "Since this is the last time we'll be together as a group until Wednesday night, we'll also be passing out dinner vouchers for tomorrow night's meal as well as your Fasching buffet tickets for Tuesday."

Max chimed in. "The food here has been excellent, but we are excited to try another local establishment."

Parker stood up and motioned to Mako. "Come on. Günter is keeping the vouchers and tickets at the front desk." Mako excused himself abruptly. Parker then nodded at Max. "Thanks for the drinks."

Max looked up and grinned. "Thanks for your company."

Relieved to survive his dinner with Max, Parker was still concerned about the obvious tension at the dinner table. "Has it always been so weird between them at dinner?" he asked Mako as they hiked down the hallway.

Mako shook his head. "Nope. Never."

"I understand why they don't talk about their personal lives."

Mako smirked. "Just be glad that your name didn't come up."

THE DINING ROOM was vacated soon after the guides had visited everyone and shared their information. Parker found Ollie still hanging out behind the bar, so he placed an order. "I'll have a club soda with a hunk of lime." Ollie dispensed the drink and then poured himself a beer.

"There's so much to do for our Fasching celebration," Ollie told Parker. "Tomorrow afternoon our chef's will take over the kitchen to prep for the Fasching buffet. Tuesday morning, after we serve our guests a light buffet breakfast of coffee and pastries, a team of carpenters will come in to re-work the entire dining room and lobby. They will build display tables all around the exterior walls."

Parker began to imagine an ideal Fasching night. He pictured himself dressed formally in a tuxedo, entering the room with Brooke by his side. She would be wearing a lavish evening gown. The couple would grab a glass of champagne from a server's tray and then leisurely peruse the mouth-watering dishes on display in the elegant room.

"The local people will dress in suits and evening dresses, but there is no formal dress code," Ollie explained. "The tourists are here on vacation, so we don't expect them to dress in festive attire."

"Everyone is already aware of that," Parker assured.

He then gulped down the drink, bid Ollie a goodnight, and walked to his room. Stepping through the door, Parker felt his phone buzz. He stopped to see that it was a text from Brooke, and read it with growing concern:

"Something's come up Parker, and I must see you! You need to meet me beneath the arch at 8:30 tonight - it's serious!"

It was already ten minutes after the hour. Parker took a deep breath and went into the bathroom. He turned on the taps and slowly washed his face and hands as if that would somehow clean away the sense of ill will that her note portended. Sneaking out of the hotel, Parker noticed that the air was warmer than usual. A light fog hovered around him, concealing the rooftops and obscuring the buildings. He hiked down the frost-covered sidewalk that twinkled under the street-lights. Crossing Maria-Theresien-Strasse, he arrived at the arch and waited. Soon he spotted Brooke's red jacket through the haze. Parker quickly snatched up her hand and led her under the small walkway arch.

Falling back against the old stone, Brooke clutched the back of Parker's neck and pulled him to her. She clamped onto his lips firmly, writhing her head as if trying to smother him with one long, passionate kiss.

Pulling away, Parker could see the angst in her eyes. "I'm so upset with Max," she huffed. "He's so selfish. He's acting like a child." Despair dulled her sharp words. It was worrisome.

"Do you think he suspects anything?"

"No, no. Max is just caught up in himself." Brooke reached to her exposed neck to find her stamp. Then she slid it nervously on the chain, back and forth. Parker saw her delicate face, tortured by conflicting emotions. "There's been a change of plans," she gasped. "I'm leaving for Vienna the first thing tomorrow morning."

"Tomorrow? Monday?" Parker replied, suddenly breathless.

"Yes. Max wants to make sure everything is arranged for the stamp show. I'll be back on Wednesday."

"So what's the problem?"

"Well, what if something happens and I can't come back?" Her face ached with concern.

The thought of that tormented him. "What do you mean? What could happen?"

"I don't know." She closed her mouth as if twisting a cap, bottling up so much more than needed to be said. Then she flung herself into his arms, pressing her head to his chest so firmly that his thumping heart could feel her anguish. "What are we going to do?" she implored.

Parker was reminded of his conversation with Jack just two weeks earlier. It was Jack who had summoned him then; Jack, who was in despair, laying his mangled emotions in Parker's hands. At least Brooke appeared much more put together than Jack had been: a luxurious designer sweater beneath her jacket, French manicured nails, and sandy blonde strands of fragrant hair contouring her lovely face. Still, her need was just as desperate as his. Once more, Parker was asked to shoulder a burden.

"What'll we to do?" she repeated, her words muffled by the pile fabric of his thick fleece pullover.

Jack's dilemma had placed a dear friend's heart in the balance. This time, it was Parker's heart on the scale, so he took a risk on reason, not bothering to weigh his words. "I've thought it out and came up with a plan."

"A plan?"

"Yep, and I believe it's the only way we can make things work for us." Parker gathered his courage to continue. "The thing is, you have to come to Chicago. You should come with me Saturday. You have to get away from Max, and I have to be in Chicago because I'm sure to lose my job and that's where I know I can get work."

Brooke's grip slackened. Her one eye, the one he could see, began to flit around as if trying to focus. Parker sensed her fear. "It's a big move, Parker, but, like you said, you've thought it all out."

"I've also thought about all those things you said you wanted, your independence, your freedom. If you come to Chicago, you can have that. You can get your own place near me. There are lots of great jobs in Chicago, and I'll give you as much space as you need to become the person you want to be, for yourself and for us. "

Brooke pondered the plan, her head still resting on his shoulder. "It's a big move, Parker. I just worry. I don't want anyone to get hurt."

"People do get hurt, Brooke," Parker replied sincerely, "but it's not fatal."

Brooke pulled away. There was a tear on her cheek. "No one ever really wants to hurt anyone, Parker. They're attracted to someone, and they believe it could be something more, something special. But what if it's just an infatuation? Or even if it is real, what if that person is just afraid to feel it? The fact is that people do get hurt and there's nothing that anyone can do about it."

Until that moment, Parker had been confident that he'd

thoroughly reasoned out his plan. He knew there would be anger and pain. Yes, Max would be hurt, and Don would feel betrayed. He was also prepared for Brooke to say no. What he hadn't considered was how it would feel if she came to Chicago and things didn't work out.

"There is a real risk that someone will get hurt. I won't minimize that. But there's always great risk in doing great things. And when two people share the kind of feelings we have for each other, believe me, it can be something great."

"I do feel wonderful when I'm with you," she confided. "You make me happy. You make me feel as if anything is possible. And it would be amazing for me to be free of Max, to get away, to be on my own, and be with you."

"Then come to Chicago to find your way. I don't want to make it sound easy or perfect, but life can be a wonderful thing if you're not afraid to live it."

She looked up, struggling to smile. "I'd be giving up a lot."

"That may be true, but there's great power in the giveaway. There's so much more to gain; happiness, fulfillment, independence, freedom."

"And love?"

"Oh yeah, love-a-plenty. It's a beautiful thing between us, Brooke. I can't explain it other than to say that it must be genuine. But for it to take hold and blossom, you'll have to do some things for yourself. I'm just afraid that you can't truly be happy in any relationship until you're happy with who you are."

Her gaze became penetrating. She was looking for something that had yet to be found; something that had to be there, like a cabinet-maker scanning for a mar in the wood. Parker interrupted her search with a kiss. Her arms squeezed him tightly. His hands held her shoulders then drifted up and down her back as if trying to hold onto all of her, so not an inch of her could be lost.

"When Max finds out," she said quietly, "it won't be so bad."

"I don't care what happens once this tour is over. I'm not going to worry about work. I'm only going to focus on what's best for me, and do the right thing for us."

Brooke was still flailing in a sea of fear, but her blue eyes stared up at him like life preservers, keeping hope afloat. "Right now I can't think about what's right for me or what's best for us. You'll have to do that Parker." Lowering her eyes, Brooke slowly voiced her despair. "All I know is that I'm happy being with you and I don't want to lose that feeling."

Heaving a sigh, Brooke laid her head on his chest again and sniffled in a tear. Parker combed her hair with his fingers. Steadily his resolve grew so that when he spoke, the words came out like steel, forged in his backbone and welded to her heart. "I'm not going back without you."

"What?"

"I mean it. I want you to come with me."

Slowly Brooke peeked up, her eyes filled with emotion. "You do? Are you sure? I mean, is that what you want?"

"I want that, yeah," he replied, "if that's what you want, too."

A smile sprawled across her face. "I do, Parker. I really want that. I mean it."

"Good, then go to Vienna and do what you have to do. I'll check availability on my flight and book your seat if it's tight. We'll wait until Friday night, right after dinner, to tell Max and everyone else. Then we're off to Chicago and on our way."

She squeezed him hard. "Off to Chicago," she reiterated, "and we'll be on our way."

SIXTEEN

Fasching

PREPARATION for the big celebration began in earnest Tuesday morning. A swarm of carpenters crowded into the lobby - closed to the public - to start building the displays. Meanwhile, the Austropa bar acted as the front desk, with the expansive board of dangling key fobs retro-fitted onto a side-wall. Still, it was just another workday for Parker, Mako, and Sally. Parker took a day trip, Mako led a ski group, and Sally stayed in town to lead a handful of folks on a historical city our. She also persuaded Don to pay for her Fasching buffet ticket so she could represent Tourcey Travel and mingle with their guests. That meant Parker and Mako were free to attend Rein-hold's bash.

Returning from his tour, Parker peered out of the coach window to view the steady stream of revelers heading toward Maria-Theresien-Strasse. After patiently following the last of his group through the side door, Parker hurried to his room to change. He then waited for Mako near the lobby so he could watch the room's final transformation. There were intricate ice sculptures to admire, flanked by elegant candelabras that were strategically positioned to maximize their serene glow. Sterling silver platters were arranged on lace-clad displays, ready to be filled with delicacies. A classic, coupe champagne glass tower centered the room. None of that mattered to Mako though. "Let's rip," he said, stepping up behind Parker and tugging at his sleeve to go.

JUST PAST DUSK, the street party was in full swing. Parker and Mako meandered through the crowd of celebrants who filled the wide mall. Near St. Anne's column, Parker recognized a large figure emerging from the masses. "There he is."

"He" was Antoine, a burly American tourist, not on the SojournSports trip, whom Parker and Mako had met at the Monday Night Ski Club meeting the evening before. Antoine was an entrepreneur from Texas, a camera guru who sold security systems, video surveillance and all of the latest technology.

Business, however, wasn't the primary topic of conversation between Antoine and Parker. Most of their discussion was philosophical, and Parker found the depth of their chat to be very stimulating. Parker knew that he'd made a friend. It was also apparent to Parker, because of Antoine's profession and proclaimed obsession, that he'd enjoy documenting the Fasching celebration, including Reinhold's party. So Antoine was invited to join the guides.

When they met on the street corner, the videographer's discerning eye did not disappoint. "I can get a great panoramic shot of the street party from the base of the statue" Antoine ambled over to the marble column. Panning the crowd, he steadied the lens to capture the masses: an eclectic mix of odd, costumed characters, suited business people, tourists and more than a few folks who looked as if they just stepped off the slopes.

Mako didn't like the idea of capturing what he believed

would be a record of excess, on video. "Just leave me out of it, okay?" he said, turning to hide when the camera swung past.

"Not a problem," Antoine replied, then he pointed to Parker. "Come on Parker; I could use a narrator." Parker agreed, so Antoine directed him to a spot by the column and re-positioned the camera in his eye socket. "Just be yourself. Be a tour guide, and say what you want. Do me a favor though, and start out with a 'hi' to my lady, Jocelyn. Ready? And rolling."

Parker comfortably settled into the role. "Hello, Jocelyn, my name is Parker Moon, and I'll be your host for Antoine's documentary of Innsbruck's annual Lenten festival known as Fasching. It's a little strange for me, I'm a tour guide by trade, so I'm usually doing my shtick in front of a captive audience, a motor coach full of tourists."

After milling around Maria-Theresien-Strasse for a while, the men made their way to Old Town, where the partiers clogged the narrow, cobblestone streets. Following the sound of Bavarian folk music, the guys wormed around a corner and came upon a swarm of people dancing and frolicking beneath a second story balcony.

That's where the music was coming from; a banner draped along the wall promoted the sponsoring radio station. Parker squeezed up to the entryway. He read the brass nameplate mounted on the wall - *Lutz Reisen* - and waved for Mako and Antoine. Reaching up he hit the buzzer, and a minute later Reinhold appeared. "Good, you made it." He ushered them in. "It's madness already."

Reinhold led the trio up to the second-floor space where the party was in full swing. "The wine and schnapps are here." He gestured to the middle of the room where two square wooden tables were pulled together and covered with a slew of bottles, some corkscrews, and various, long-stemmed glasses. Then he pointed to a small room behind them. "Our buffet is in there, great food. Bier is on tap in the back room. Be careful going back there. It's still under construction. Now go, help yourselves. Have fun."

Mako poured three glasses of wine, passed them over, and the men toasted Fasching. Juggling his wine glass deftly, Antoine scanned the room with his camera. Parker picked up the play-by-play. "We're in the heart of the original city, Old Town, the Altstadt, and at a party in the future home of Lutz Travel, a local provider that my US-based travel company has hired for transportation and tours." He gestured to the far wall were huge sheets of thick plastic hung loosely. "As you can see, it's still a work in progress."

Antoine focused on the newly refurbished hardwood floors; the freshly painted, eggshell walls; the broad, centered windows and the tables covered with bottles and glasses. Then he followed Parker toward a wall of dangling plastic that covered a metal studded wall from floor-to-ceiling.

Pulling aside a sheet of plastic that covered an entryway, Parker allowed Antoine and Mako to step through first, into the construction space. That room was twice the size of the main room, and it held the balcony that overlooked the busy, crowded street. The room was chilly, too, with loose insulation hanging from the ceiling.

There was a stainless steel portable beer tap in the corner to the left, beside a small table holding stacks of tall, clear plastic cups. Opposite the tapper, centered between two French doors that opened to the balcony, was a massive wooden desk. The only piece of furniture in the room, it supported all of the music equipment. A fortyish hipster, wearing a leather vest over a white shirt, grabbed a microphone, yanked open one of the glass doors, and stepped out onto the balcony. Leaning over the edge, he led the mass of partiers in song. "Ein Prosit, Ein Prosit, der Gemütlichkeit!"

Someone rushed from the room to hand the guy a cup of

beer. He swung it over the balcony edge, sloshing some brew on the people below. The crowd mimicked him, shouting a short countdown before drinking up: "Eins, Zwei, G'suffa!"

Parker looked at Antoine. "Did you get that?"

Antoine smiled. "Hell yay."

They enjoyed the DJs antics until Mako squeezed Parker's arm. "I need a refill." He dragged his associate back into the main room with Antoine close behind. Rushing to the table, Mako grabbed a flute glass and poured himself some schnapps, filling it to the brim. Looking all around the room, Mako slurped his drink to keep it from spilling. "Okay, so I'm going to check out the food." He then disappeared.

Enticed by the vast assortment of wine, Parker studied his choices and then grabbed an open bottle of red wine, still full. Refilling his glass, Parker swirling it enjoy a waft of its fragrance before taking a sip. Just as he began to peruse the label, a familiar voice spoke from over his shoulder.

"How do you like my wine?"

"Your wine?" he asked, turning around.

"Well," Jack said, "I didn't make it. I bought it."

Jack had cleaned up his act since they met last. Those soft curls were back, bouncy, flaxen spirals that sat atop his head like lamb's wool. He had begun to grow a beard too, and the stubble darkened his long face. It was the smile that gave away Jack's renaissance. A beacon of a grin, Parker soon learned why it shone so brilliantly.

"I'd like to introduce you to Franz," Jack stated.

A tall, lean man stepped up to shake Parker's hand. He had soft eyes that reflected a quiet self-assurance, and when he spoke, his accent was barely perceptible. "It is so nice to meet one of Jack's friends from back home."

Parker felt meaning in his every word. The two clasped hands. "The pleasure is all mine," Parker replied, and then he introduced them both to Antoine.

"I'm sorry to have to steal him away from you," Franz said to Parker. "But you have to believe me that our meeting was such a surprise to us both. We still look at each other and think my God, how did this happen?"

"But we're grateful that it happened," Jack interjected.

Franz's frame swayed as if to topple from embarrassment. "Oh, yes of course. I'm so delighted that it happened."

Parker tried not to laugh out loud from the relief he felt. Jack was happy and back on track, and that was all Parker needed to know. Still, he was worried about Mako. "Listen, Jack. You should know that I told Mako about you and your situation here. Not Sally or Lorrie, just Mako. He's been skiing a lot lately, and I thought there might be a chance that the two of you would cross paths."

Jack stopped Parker from any further explanation. "That's fine, Parker. It's okay. Where is he anyway?"

Parker looked to the back room. "He went for food."

As if on cue, Mako popped out of the crowd, holding the last bite of a ham sandwich on rye. "Well, look who's here," Mako said ominously. "If it isn't our old buddy Jack."

Grasping Jack's hand, Mako pulled him close as if hoisting a rope.

Jack yanked back just as firmly. "Good to see you, you son of a bitch," Jack said.

"Oh no," Mako replied. "You're the son of a bitch, blowing us off like that. And for what? You dumped us for this guy?"

Jack knew that Mako was just messing with him. Parker realized that as well. But Franz was unsure, gaping open-mouthed as Mako chewed up the last morsel of his food. He then grabbed Franz's fleece pullover and shook him playfully.

"I'm just shittin' ya. You're Franz, right?" The young man laughed uneasily as Mako continued. "You did us all a favor with this one." He gestured back at Jack. "He was a freakin' mess as a hetero."

Jack blushed, dropped his eyes with guilt then looked back up. "That I was," he confessed. "I really was."

Mako reached for a wine glass and explained. "I left my drink in the other room."

He poured another. Antoine set his empty glass down. "If you guys don't mind, I'm more of a beer man myself."

"It's in the other room," Jack replied as if he didn't know, "I'd like a beer too."

They all traipsed back through the hanging plastic and then waded through a small crowd to get to the tap. Reinhold was the only one in line, pouring himself a beer. He turned to face the guys with a smoldering joint squeezed tightly between the tips of his manicured fingers.

"Hey everyone," Reinhold's eyes glowed. "Let me please introduce you all to the DJ."

Anxiously stepping up beside Reinhold, the broadcaster smoothed back his long hair, tugged the bottom of his vest, and then shook everyone's hand. He didn't seem to pay attention when Reinhold barked out their names. His primary interest appeared to be the weed that Reinhold was offering up. After taking a huge hit, the DJ spoke in the middle of his exhale. "I bet you're all sick of this music?"

No one responded. The DJ took another long pull of the smoke, exhaled, laughed and handed the joint to Mako. Weaving quickly through the crowd, he hurried to the desk. Parker nodded at Antoine and the big man trained the camera on the DJ.

It was quite entertaining to watch the DJ at work. He'd scramble back and forth between songs, nonchalantly puffing a joint and then bolting to the desk, paranoid that something was forgotten. Occasionally he would grab the microphone and go out onto the balcony. A roar from the street partiers would erupt, and he'd rouse them with another raised beer and exhorted toast.

"He has a great following," was how Reinhold explained it.

The DJ started a raging dance rap and hurried back to socialize, grinning at his stealth. Mako sidled up and offered him another hit.

"I used to DJ myself," Mako stated.

"Really?"

"Yeah. So if you need a lounge break, I'll be happy to queue up some tunes for you." Mako pulled out his phone. "People beg for my playlists at parties."

Parker watched the DJ scroll through Mako's music. Then he felt a tap on his shoulder. It was Jack. "We've got to get going."

"So soon?" Parker asked

Jack nodded.

Franz shook Parker's hand. "We've got an early start tomorrow," he said.

Moving in for a hug goodbye Jack held Parker tightly to speak directly in his ear. "I phoned Sally earlier and apologized for everything. I believe that left her in a much better place. I also spoke with Lorrie about Franz. She's dealing with it well. I'm so sorry for dumping that responsibility on you. It wasn't right, asking you to talk to her for me. It was just that I was a bit out of my mind with all of this."

"Hey," Parker reassured Jack. "That's what friends are for."

THE ALCOHOL and second-hand smoke were getting to Parker as the party wore on. His peripheral vision was fuzzy, narrowing his focus. He was a bit slower to react, too, bumping through the raucous crowd while wandering alone. Occasionally, he'd stop and hold a serious conversation with a costumed reveler, or share a fun story with a buttoned-down businessperson. Noticing that Antoine had settled into a comfortable perch at a window in the main room, Parker squeezed over to him. "You're like a cop on a stakeout over here."

Hunched over, Antoine straightened up. "This locale is ideal. I can see everything out there." He shook his head happily. "Man, I could watch this stuff all night."

Parker took a quick peek out the window. An enthusiastic crowd covered the old, cobblestone square. There was a circle of dancers undulating to the DJ's music directly below them. A couple of spotlights shone through the darkness from the top of the building, casting an eerie glow on the faces below.

"I need some food," Parker said.

Antoine nodded. "Lead the way."

They walked into the buffet room. Parker was first to fix his plate, so he found a vacated café table to hover over while Antoine picked through the offerings. Munching on his food, Parker noticed a framed image hanging nearby. It was one of several drawings that ran the length of the wall. Intrigued by the caricature-like, black ink sketches, Parker thought they'd make good videos. "Check out these drawings," he said the moment Antoine sat down.

"What are they supposed to be?"

"I have no idea," Parker replied.

Viktoria stepped beside the table, drawing their attention with her black corset top, short leather skirt and tall black boots. "So where's Mako?" she asked.

"Probably hanging out with the DJ," Parker answered.

Viktoria nodded and then pointed to the image he'd been examining. "Do you like my artwork?"

"You did these?" Parker asked. "What are they?"

Viktoria leered at him smugly. "Take a closer look." She gestured to the nearest image.

Parker got up and went over to study the drawing. "This one looks like a lady," he said, perplexed. "She's standing, no, leaning back against something. There's a leash in her hand. Are those dogs?"

"They're optical illusions," Antoine stated.

Viktoria confirmed with a leer. "Ambiguous images."

Parker squinted like a snake to get another perspective. "They're kinky," he hollered, and then sporting a naughty grin, he walked down to view each erotic work of art up close.

"Enjoy them, now," she said. "Reinhold only allowed me to hang them up for the party."

No one saw Mako slip into the room. He snuck up behind Viktoria and clamped his arms around her waist. "There you are," he said, nuzzling her neck. She moaned. He squeezed hard, forcing her cleavage to bulge from its confinement.

Immediately Mako and Viktoria were lip locked, holding each other in a passionate embrace. Despite the lack of privacy, Mako snuck his hand beneath Viktoria's skirt and gave her bottom a firm squeeze. Viktoria was busy too, digging down the front of Mako's pants as if her fingers were on fire.

Parker shook his head and motioned for Antoine to leave. He stood up, but before they could go, Reinhold came around the corner. "What the hell?" he yelled.

Confused, Parker and Antoine just stared at each other. Rushing up to Mako and Viktoria, Reinhold pried them apart. "What are you doing? She's my sister for heaven sake."

Wrenching Viktoria away from Mako, Reinhold captured her in a firm grip. "Come on you," he commanded. "You're going out of here." He tugged the bewildered beauty's arm and pulled her out of the room.

Mako staggered as if taking a blow. Then he stepped over to the buffet and began to peruse the sliced meat selection.

Parker stepped next to him. "Are you all right?"

"Sure."

"Sure you're sure?" Parker pressed him again.

"Yeah, I mean, what the fuck, Parks?" Mako asked. "I

didn't know she was Reinhold's sister. So what if she is anyway? Why should he care? She's an adult."

"Yeah, I don't get that either. Don't worry if Reinhold complains to Don, though. I'll vouch for you."

Mako snarled, "I'm not worried about Don. Fuck him." He then peered up, listening closely to the pulsating rhythm that seeped into the room. "And fuck these fucking tunes." He waved a slice of salami in the air and started to walk away.

"Where are you going? "Parker asked with worry.

Ignoring Parker's question, Mako headed out the door. Immediately afterward, the DJ burst into the room. Behind him came a large following of guys. They mobbed the buffet like half-starved animals. Parker and Antoine watched them tear into the spread, piling food high on their plates. Hunkering down at a few tables nearby, they were all wild-eyed and giggly. Their conversation was loud, too, and growing more and more obnoxious. Parker sensed that the evening's fun was beginning to deteriorate. He turned to Antoine. "We might want to call it a night pretty soon. I know I've had enough."

Antoine nodded, "Yeah, I think you're right. Just let me have a few more minutes filming the crowd outside."

Parker agreed, and the two men weaved their way back to Antoine's perch by the window. Outside, the revelers were still going strong. Surging beneath the balcony, they bounced frantically to the incessant beat. The scene below intrigued Parker. For quite awhile he watched people sway back and forth in various directions, mesmerized by the repetition of sound, that electronic buzz-beat.

Then all of a sudden, the music stopped. There was a short moment of silence. An audible murmur hummed through the crowd when the strum of a guitar echoed out from the speakers. Parker immediately recognized the song, but the anxious horde did not. It was *Disarm*, the haunting tune from Siamese Dream, the classic, Smashing Pumpkins album.

The mass of humanity below seemed stunned by the strange somberness of the melody. Heads swiveled to look up quizzically, intent upon the balcony where the DJ had been entertaining them for most of the night. No one was out there, however. The people in the main room were also miffed, glancing over at the plastic walls and left to wonder why the music had changed.

A negative vibe shook Parker. Pushing through the mob, he ducked beneath the plastic just as the lyrics began. Then he saw Mako step out onto the balcony. The folks outside were eerily silent as Mako raised the microphone to his lips and began to sing along. It wasn't his voice reverberating over the speakers, though. The mic was off. It was only his emotions that came out, mimicking the singer's gut-wrenching wail. It seemed to smother the crowd.

Parker was too stunned to move. Looking from behind, he watched Mako cradle the mic in both hands and pour out his emotions to the assembly below. But Parker knew his friend was only performing for one person. He was singing to someone in his mind, someone other than Viktoria. He was singing about someone else, too.

Lip-syncing as if his life hung on every syllable, Mako was a complete mystery to Parker just then; a stranger he had never met. Slowly Parker stepped closer, not knowing how to stop the madness or if he even could. Leaning over the balcony, Mako repeated the refrain, shouting into the mic. The words ran from his soul like blood from a wound.

He was desperate, and doomed. They ripped through the plastic walls like a SWAT team. Enraged shouts drowned out the music, and flailing arms engulfed Mako before Parker could stop them. Still, he was right behind.

"Antoine!" Parker screamed for help and then leaped onto an arm to hold back a punch aimed at Mako's face. A glancing blow or two landed on Parker, but he struggled through the fury to free Mako from another guy's angry grasp. Suddenly grabbed from behind, Parker was tossed aside like an old suitcase. He bounced off the desk.

Back on his feet, Parker saw Mako clamped in a headlock. He jumped in the middle of it and tried to pry his friend free, but someone grabbed him from behind and wrestled him away. Enraged, Parker turned around, ready to take a swing. Antoine's voice stopped him. "That's enough. Enough!"

Ripping through the studded wall, Antoine calmed the chaos. After a few angry shouts, Reinhold called out over somebody's shoulder. "I think you'd better leave."

Parker held up his hands. "We will. We will. No problem."

Mako was still staring down some dude, so Parker grabbed his arm. "Come on, let's go."

His friend didn't move until Antoine grabbed his shoulder and pulled him along. Reinhold followed them down the stairs to let them out. When the door opened, Mako leaned into Reinhold. His head rolled from side to side as if he had no neck. "Hey man, I'm sorry to cause this whole fuckin' pickle but why did you get all over your sister's shit? It's like I'm not good enough or what?"

Reinhold placed his hand flat on Mako's chest and gave him a few gentle pats. "She already has a boyfriend, a rather large fellow with a fairly bad disposition. He's supposed to be at the party tonight. I was very concerned that you would cause a fight."

"Wow," Mako said, as he contemplated Reinhold's explanation. "Well, I'm sorry that I caused a fight anyway."

"Not to worry," Reinhold replied. Then he turned to Parker. "As I told you, it's just Fasching. Sometimes things can easily get out of control."

BACK AT ANTOINE'S hotel room, the trio licked their wounds.

Parker flopped onto the second bed by the window. Mako stumbled past him. "Can I smoke?" he asked Antoine.

"Only if you blow it out the window."

Mako tugged the window open a crack and plopped on the floor. Antoine was busy connecting his camera to the TV.

"I need some freaking sleep," Parker moaned.

"I need someone to sleep with," Mako countered while lighting up the cig.

Antoine had finished tinkering with his technology, so he flipped on the camera and sat on the edge of the other bed to review the day's events. Parker didn't care to watch. He had already become physically attached to a pillow. "Antoine, I'm dozing. Is it cool if we crash here?"

"Why not? Make yourselves at home."

"You can have the blanket, Mako," Parker said, "and the floor."

"After this smoke," Mako replied, "I'll sleep standing up."

Parker pulled his phone out from a back pocket. "Better let Sally know." The call went right to voicemail, so he left a detailed message. "Hey, gal. Mako and I are staying at a friend's room tonight, at the Hotel Franz Mair. No worries, we'll be back for breakfast, ready to go. Call if you need me, goodnight."

Antoine was deep into the video. The TV sound was turned down so low that silence prevailed when Parker hung up. Mako was lying on his back blowing streams of smoke toward the narrow opening in the window. He was deep in thought. Parker rolled onto the edge of the bed and looked at his friend. "So who was she?"

Mako rolled the cigarette between his fingers and glanced up at Parker. "She was going to be my wife."

"I didn't know."

"You can't know everything, pal."

Mako's eyes returned to the drab ceiling above. Parker

thought he'd heard the last of it, but his friend was full of surprises that night. "She was the whole fucking package, too. The real deal."

"Was being the takeaway there."

"She didn't care too much for my choice of careers, not that our relationship was rock solid before I took this job. Anyway, that next tour came and, you know how it is. I went. So she went too."

Parker couldn't think of anything to say to console his pal. It was just as well, he knew. Some pain is just inconsolable. Darkness covered the room like a comforting blanket, tucking them in. Antoine's bed creaked when he got up. He came over and stuffed a pillow under Mako's head. Parker took a deep breath, let it out, and entered the "Land of Nod."

DAYLIGHT HAD YET to brighten the sky when Parker awoke. Only two colors shone in the room. One was the white-lit "6:15 a.m." on the digital clock. The other was a tiny red light glowing on Antoine's camera. Peeking out of the window, Parker could see ominous storm clouds gathering in the gloom.

Antoine and Mako were sound asleep, so Parker decided to slip into the shower quietly. Passing the camera that rested on the desk, he felt for the shut-off switch. Rather than turn it off though, he must have hit play because the machine started to whirl. The TV also flickered quietly to life. Before Parker could shut it off, a vivid image caught his attention.

It was a view of the Old Town party in front of Reinhold's, shot from above. Antoine had scanned the street and zoomed in on various folks, some in unusual costumes. A close up of three old men with nicely trimmed white beards and wearing lederhosen filled the screen. The plumes on their hats wiggled as they bounced along in dance. The camera panned left through the crowd and then started to pull away.

That's when Parker felt the jolt: a sudden, nauseating spasm deep in the recesses of his gut. He stopped the camera and fumbled to find the "rewind" switch. Then he hit "play." Again, the Austrian men were dancing about jovially. Then, just as the camera pulled away, he hit "pause." Parker's eyes saw something that his mind wasn't prepared to grasp. The still frame focused clearly on a couple in the background. It was Sally and Max! They stood together in the crowd. Parker hit the button again and let the scene play out. He saw them laugh. Then Max hugged Sally close to his chest. They kissed. Parker swallowed hard.

THE AUSTROPA LOBBY was quiet when Parker came storming through the door. Except for the bare-wooden display tables, there was nothing left of the Fasching buffet. Parker scurried down the hall and into the breakfast room. Sally wasn't there, so he ran upstairs and knocked on her door.

"Sally, it's me, Parker. We need to talk."

Silence stifled the air like thick humidity. "Come in." Sally slowly opened the door.

Parker noticed a vein throbbing in her forehead as he barged into the room. "You were with Max yesterday," he charged. "I saw you."

Seeing the anger and confusion contorting Parker's face, Sally sat down nervously on the bed. There, she was able to gather her resolution and confess. "Parker, I'm so sorry that things have happened this way. I feel terrible. Max was going to tell you at dinner Sunday night, but it just didn't work out that way. That's why I wasn't there. I just couldn't be there. I was afraid to disappoint you, and I just can't do that, not after all you've done for me, all you have ever done."

The emotion in her voice drew Parker closer, and he sat next to her on the bed. Looking him in the eye, Sally continued. "The truth is I've been with Max a lot. We've fallen in love. I'm going to be with him Parker, once the tour is over. I won't leave you guys hanging like Jack left me. Oh, Parker, please say something. I feel so bad."

All he could think about was Brooke. Where was she in all of this? Parker tried to process it all, but thoughts of Brooke and Max and Sally became tangled in his mind like a spider's web. He couldn't pull anything free, so he just grabbed for a loose end. "What about work?"

"It's going to be all right. Max is going to talk to Don. I wouldn't have even considered it if I thought I was leaving you and Mako out on a limb, but I'm going to finish the job here. You guys can handle the flights back home. I won't be missed."

Sally would be missed, of course. Maybe not this week, not on this trip, but she'd be missed, eventually. "Sally," Parker asked. "Are you sure?"

She smiled. "Oh sweetie, don't worry about me. I'll be fine. Yes, I am sure. Besides, I'm taking your advice. You said to give someone a chance sometime."

"Yeah but Sal, I meant ..." Parker cringed, unable to come up with a good reason to give her.

She tilted her head like a dog confused by an odd sound, but then smiled wide and spoke softly, calmly, and entirely self-assured. "It's not like that, Parker. I've been in love before, you know. I'm not the kind of person who can date around for fun. I know that with me, it's all or nothing. I never wanted to live without love, but I was prepared to do that. Then this wonderful man came into my life. I knew it the moment we met."

Although heartfelt, her words sounded corny to Parker's ear. But there was nothing old-fashioned about the sentiment behind her words. Sally wasn't speaking just for herself. She was echoing the voices of anyone who had ever longed for true love and somehow, someway, kept a fire burning in their souls for it. Sally was just another ordinary person of good heart and good faith who was about to get everything she ever dreamed of. How it affected Parker's happy ending, however, had yet to be determined. He anxiously asked about what he cared for the most. "What about Brooke?"

The question altered Sally's mood. "She's been difficult, to be honest. That's why she left on Monday. She needs some time to sort things out. Doctor Frank says it was the best thing for her to do right now."

"Doctor Frank? What does he know?"

"Everything, of course. He knew Brooke would be jealous."

It was evident to Parker that no one, not Sally, not Max, not even the omnipotent Doctor Frank, knew about him and Brooke. "Sally," Parker readied to explain, "Brooke will not be jealous."

"Oh no, Doctor Frank says it's a natural reaction," Sally spoke with a know-it-all smirk on her face.

"You don't understand."

"Please, Parker, I do. There's a unique bond between father and daughter, and considering Brooke's circumstances—"

"What?"

"I said that there is a unique bond between father and daughter ..."

Some moments in life are just snapshots, poignant seconds when all of your being is captured and frozen in time. All of your feelings are exposed, too. Those who see you, see you in your raw, emotional entirety, but you can only *feel* it: sick, sad, and utterly embarrassed at being the person who, for a brief yet seemingly infinite moment, you have become. It was one of those moments for Parker; a terrible moment for him to live through.

"... Oh, Parker," Sally concluded with half-a-laugh, "it's not like they're lovers or anything."

SEVENTEEN

Vienna

———————————

IT WAS a scene right out of some old black and white film: a European flick, something that the great Ingmar Bergman would've spent hours and plenty of takes to get just right. Parker had that kind of time, but not the inclination. It was all too damn real to him; the loud, rattling train, the stark, lifeless views out of the window, the cold, and hard hurt that settled in his stomach. It ached like an abscessed tooth.

Doctor Frank and Honey sat opposite Parker, facing him. The couple had decided to leave earlier than planned so Honey could have more time to shop in Vienna. Honey's head gently jostled in rhythm with the locomotive, having nodded off minutes after departure.

Doctor Frank's motive for the trip, Parker sensed, was more paternal. He fit the part anyway, wearing a gray, herringbone tweed sports coat with leather patches on the elbows, and a white shirt that seemed to be missing its tie. The psychologist glanced up at Parker every so often while reading his hardcover book. Sensing the clinician's gaze, Parker would also look up, and their eyes would meet, and Doctor Frank would grin pathetically. Then he'd return to his tome and the occasional gum chewing, startling his jowls with a sudden droop and grind. While Doctor Frank's dispassionate eyes slid back and forth across the page, Parker sighed. Certainly Doctor Frank understood anguish. He just had no idea how it felt.

Securing his earbuds, Parker tweaked the volume on his iPhone. Every word of the conversation he'd had with Max and Sally earlier that morning, back at the Austropa Bistro, weighed on him like a deathbed confession. He squirmed in his seat uneasily, knowing that the long train ride to Vienna would force him to relive that conversation over and over again.

THE AUSTROPA BISTRO had never looked so uninviting. Breakfast plates sat scattered across the tabletops and coffee mugs littered the counter. Max, too, appeared disheveled, but he brightened up a bit when Sally sat down next to him. She slipped her fingers into his open palm, and they squeezed hands as if never planning to let go.

Parker grabbed the wrought-iron chair next to Doctor Frank and pulled it from the table. Planting himself down, he straightened his spine. "Sally says that Brooke may not be coming back today." Parker wasn't making a statement. He was asking for confirmation.

Max was startled, and he answered Parker's question with a question of his own. "We thought you could confirm that for us?"

"I've got nothing."

Max looked bewildered. "I had no idea about you and Brooke. We were too busy with ourselves." He smiled awkwardly at Sally before continuing. "We don't know what Brooke's going to do. All we know is that she has yet to check out of the Vienna hotel."

Parker was steadfast. "The last time I spoke with her was

Sunday night. She said she was coming back here today and then going to Chicago with me on Saturday."

Sally gaped and turned her haunted face toward Max. Doctor Frank, however, was the one to respond. "She's confronting old demons right now. Certainly, she's dealing with rejection and probably some feelings of jealousy."

"It seems that I've mucked things up really well," Max said as if peering through a death mask. "Sally and I planned on telling everyone at dinner Sunday night. We sat Brooke down beforehand and told her first. Her reaction, well, I just couldn't do it after that."

Sally shook her head and added, "It didn't go well."

"Certainly not," Max agreed.

"I was just sick about it," Sally confirmed.

Max pointed at Sally and then back at himself. "We had to keep it a secret until we were sure about our feelings, and our plans, about what lay ahead."

Parker contemplated his words for a few seconds before asking, "What are your plans?"

"Like I told you, Parker, I'm going to finish this tour," Sally said.

"And then what?"

"Then I'm going to Vienna with Max. After that, I'll be moving out to California." She tugged at Max's arm, and they shared a sweet smile.

"Just like that?" Parker questioned.

Max firmed his jaw and answered for her. "Just like that. I already put a call into Don this morning. I expect to hear back from him very soon."

Grinning wide, Sally squeezed Max's hand. "We're going to be happy, Parker. Things are going to be good for us."

Parker didn't doubt that this was the beginning of their happy ending. His way was to seek the good in people. Watching Max and Sally, holding hands like high school sweethearts, was proof enough for him. Sally was a saint. That was a fact. Chances were that she and Max hadn't even had sex yet. They didn't need to. They were having too much fun sneaking in a kiss or a midnight stroll, feeling a tinge of good guilt in their bellies while they laid awake half the night, wondering, waiting for their Fourth of July.

Those fireworks would come soon enough. Max would do it right, too, and afterward, rather than a smoke or a good night's sleep, they'd get dressed up and walk over to some remarkably romantic café for a hot cup of coffee and a thick slice of Black Forest cake à la mode.

"I've made a lot of mistakes in my life, Parker," Max confirmed. Then he drew his mouth in tight and spoke firmly, like a fist ready to strike. "Sally is not going to be one of them."

If only Max had shown that kind of determination for Brooke when she was a child, Parker thought. They wouldn't be in the mess that they're in now. He didn't say anything of course. He didn't need to bring up the past. All that mattered was the genuine concern Max felt for his daughter at that very moment. It was etched all over his face. "I knew my feelings for Sally would be a problem for Brooke, initially." He glanced at Doctor Frank before turning a hopeful gaze at Parker. "I expect that she'll adjust much more easily now. Now that I know about the two of you."

Doctor Frank was non-committal, looking cool despite the hot air that blew over them from the overhead vent. The heat was an additional burden on Parker, however. Raking his hair to keep from sweating, he tried to explain. "It was the same thing for us, I mean, we had to keep it a secret, too." He swallowed hard. "The thing is that, somehow, I got this crazy misconception about you and Brooke. But I want you to know that there are no misconceptions about how I feel about her."

Max gazed empathetically at Parker. "No, I don't suppose there are. And please know that there will be no negative repercussions from this. Your job is safe no matter what happens." Max slowly twisted his empty coffee cup in its saucer. "Parker, I love my daughter. I truly want what's best for her. Did she tell you about her past?"

"Just a bit of the bad stuff."

"There was plenty of that, I'm afraid. It was my negligence at first, and then Brooke married a very selfish and very abusive man. I've done everything I can since then to give her a good life. But I can't give her all of the things she needs. And I can't undo the damage that Brooke's mother has done to her."

Parker hadn't heard anything about Brooke's mom. Max began to fill him in. "We were divorced when Brooke was two. Even if I had a chance at gaining custody, I was too damn busy to take her. Brooke has always held that against me. But I did want custody. Her mother was a vicious, manipulative and hateful woman−"

"Who's not here to defend herself," Parker reminded him.

"Don't be mistaken," Max countered. "I'll shoulder much of the blame. I was young and ignorant, an absent father, and I allowed things to happen that should not have happened. It's a sorry history for anyone to have."

Doctor Frank concurred. "I can verify all of that, Mr. Moon. You see, Max used to be my patient."

Listening to Max's past was painful for Sally. So she focused, instead, on his redemption. "Max did as much as he could to make up for his mistakes, Parker, perhaps too much. But that's because he loves Brooke with all his heart. He's so worried about her. He's called several times, but she doesn't answer. You need to reach out to her, Parker." She extended her arm across the table toward him.

Parker pulled out his phone and typed out a text. Sally came around to stand next to him. "I've got a nine o'clock tour to see off, and then I'll check in with Ollie. Just so you know,

Parker, everything is under control. You're free to do whatever you need to do."

Parker said nothing until she leaned down to hug him goodbye. It was a long, sincere hug. Parker peeked over at Max. "You better take care of my girl," he threatened.

"I promise I will."

"It should be easy," Parker said. "All she needs is all of your love."

He smiled warmly. "That she has, and for always."

Parker held onto Sally's arm as she released her embrace. "So what is it that Brooke needs?" Parker asked Max.

Doctor Frank readied to speak, but Brooke's father stopped him with a wave. "What's best for Brooke is for Brooke to decide."

THE WHITE COLUMNS and arched entryways of the Vienna hotel lobby reminded Parker of that glorious church in Salzburg. It was a comforting memory, but a fleeting one as he noticed Brooke seated on one of the white sofas positioned in the middle of the vast public space. It was an odd location for a private conversation, he thought. Nonetheless, Parker followed her wave, negotiating through the maze of elegant furnishings. Turning aside a white, barrel-backed, armless chair, Parker sat down to face her. A server appeared. He set a pilsner glass full of beer on the table beside them.

"I ordered for you," Brooke said, leaning back against the sofa. "I hope you don't mind."

"No, great. I'm glad," Parker answered honestly.

Sliding off her black heels, Brooke dropped them to the floor and tucked her legs beneath her. Her black, scoop neck dress contrasted sharply against the sofa's stark white fabric. Although radiant and poised, Parker sensed that at any moment she could come apart at the seams.

"I'm so sorry, Parker," she said, perusing the quiet lobby to make sure no one could hear. "Everything happened so fast. I just had to leave."

"Leaving didn't bother me," he said. "It was the not coming back part that had me concerned."

A tremor shook her calm. "I wasn't not coming back, not for sure." Brooke looked at her champagne cocktail that sat on the table next to Parker's beer. He handed it over to her and then grabbed his beer and gulped down a mouthful.

After a healthy sip, Brooke tried to explain. "I just can't get over this thing with Max and Sally. I mean, it's all going so fast. They say they're in love and planning to be together, but they've only known each other for such a short time."

Parker was stunned. Seeing his reaction, Brooke realized the irony of her words and she dropped her eyes to her lap. Parker smirked and pondered his beer before speaking. "You know, a lot can happen in just a few days. I still can't believe that all this time, I thought you and Max were a couple."

"But that's my fault." Brooke clasped her forehead with one hand as if to keep her head from falling off. "Oh Parker, I had no idea. I was just trying to protect you, hiding from my overly protective father." A couple passed, walking nearby, forcing her stillness.

Parker invaded the silence, groping to explain. "It's just the way things were perceived." He set down the beer. "Mako got it all started, showing me that you and Max were roommates, different last names, first name basis. It was all so suggestive."

"Max wanted to accommodate as many customers as he could," Brooke explained, clinging to her drink. "So we decided to share the suite and free up another room."

Parker shook his head in disbelief. "Still, I mean, I should have figured it out."

Brooke looked anguished. "No Parker, it's my fault, and I'm truly sorry for the misunderstanding." She sounded despondent. "Yes, Max is my dad. Max the entrepreneur, the philatelist. Max, the owner of SojournSports. He was my roommate on this trip, but you know, I've never even thought of him as a friend."

"But he'll always be there when you need him."

"That's the problem, Parker. I've always needed him."

Her conclusion, spoken in the past tense, gave Parker a glimmer of hope. "I spoke with Max this morning," he said. "My job isn't in jeopardy. Weird thing, it probably never was. The point is that he's good with it all. He's ready to focus on himself now, on Sally, and the both of them."

The lump in Parker's throat felt like a tumor. "He only wants what's best for you. So do I. That's why I need to know. Are you coming back ... to Innsbruck with me?"

Brooke's clear complexion hardened like plastic. She held out her champagne glass, and Parker took it away. Then she reached down beside her for a small handbag wedged between the couch cushions. Yanking it out, Brooke grabbed a tissue and shoved the bag back. When she looked up, Parker saw that her face had cracked. "It sounded so easy the other night when we were together in Innsbruck. Just run away to Chicago with you." She held up the tissue to dab an eye. Her lower lip trembled. "It should be that easy, though, shouldn't it?"

Parker got the feeling that Brooke hadn't nestled herself on that couch. She had confined herself there. Secured in that public lobby - centered in that maze of elegant chairs, end tables, and sofas - she looked like a bird in a cage.

"Maybe not easy, but certainly simple," Parker said somberly, "but I never thought about you running away. I only thought about us going away, to be together."

Brooke's eyes continued to falter. Parker flitted around her doubts and fears. "If you come back to Innsbruck with me, we can meet with Max and Sally. It might be best for all of us to talk it through, clear the air. That could help you figure out what's best for you."

Brooke took a few seconds to compose herself. "I've had a lot of time since coming here to think about what's best for me."

"That's good."

She shook her head in agreement. "Seeing you here, knowing what it took for you to come here ... Parker, what I have to decide has nothing to do with Max or Sally. It's about you and me."

"It is. You're right."

Brooke lowered her feet to the floor and sat up straight. A solemn, sense of self-confidence slowly grew on her face. "I can't remember ever being as happy as I've been since I met you." Brooke's mind seemed to turn like a tumbler, feeling for the right way to say what she needed to say. She continued confidently when all of the right words clicked into place. "You've given me a glimpse into who I can be. You've helped me understand what it feels like to be in love. But I can't go to Chicago to be with you only to be alone the next time you go away."

Brooke held onto her courage long enough for Parker to realize that he'd been wrong. The couch in the middle of the lobby wasn't her cage. It was her keep. Pained by rejection, he leaned over, cradling his belly.

Brooke crumbled and turned away. "Oh, Parker, I'm so sorry." Her head began to sway from side to side. "It's just that your world is so huge." She glanced over, and her eyes froze on him. Then they began to melt, dripping tears down her cheeks. "I'm afraid I'll only be lost in it."

Parker's heart ached. Brooke wiped her tears and then raised the tissue to her nose. Parker wanted to come over and comfort her, to hold her and tell her that everything would be all right. He didn't need to do that, though. Brooke's fortitude had reappeared, and he knew that she knew, that everything *would* be all right.

"It doesn't matter where I live or whose life I move into, it won't be mine," Brooke said through a sniffle. "So I'm going to take your advice and find my center. California's my sanctuary." Brooke's will grew stronger with each word she spoke. "I'm going back there Saturday, alone. I'm going to learn how to make a life for myself. It's what I have to do. It's what I need to do, for me."

Parker put on a brave face and nodded, while all of the love he felt for Brooke - that brilliant, all-consuming vibe - dripped from the hole in his heart. Soon the only feeling he had left for her was respect.

"There's strength in your words," Parker said. "But it's your courage that'll give you the power to succeed. Trust in that. Stick with your convictions, and someday soon, you'll be who you want to be."

"I'll do that, Parker," she said as if making a promise. "And then I can come to Chicago. I'll make my way back to you."

A lesser man would've believed her. They both got up and she fell into his arms. They hugged for a long moment. Parker was overcome by the sudden urge to kiss her, so he took hold of her face and moved his lips to hers. Although he savored that kiss, it wasn't sweet or sensuous. It wasn't a kiss of contentment or a kiss of little consequence. Sadly, it was just a kiss goodbye.

"I'd better leave, I guess," was how he put it, using all of the strength a scorned man could muster.

Brooke tried to be sympathetic to his angst. "Once I get settled out there, I'm going to forward you my new address and contact info." Then she took out her phone and dialed up Doctor Frank. "Can you please meet us at the hotel entrance? Good, and make sure there's a cab available. Oh, and you'll ride back to the train station with Parker? Okay, thank you."

The last time Parker saw Brooke she was standing on the

hotel steps waving goodbye. There was beauty in her resolve, a timeless, classic splendor like a stone frieze etched high above a historic building. As the cab pulled away, a sad sense of desolation washed over Parker, so he kept Brooke fixed in his vision, every last second until they drove out of sight.

Searching his mind for something positive, Parker immediately thought of Sally and Max. At least they would be happy. That was a lock. He remembered how they looked that morning, the first and last time he'd seen them together. They were the couple they had always been meant to be. Sally's aura had been shining so bright, shining as if she'd been reborn again.

Like Brooke, Sally's horrible history had stopped her from living. Somehow, though, she got over the fear, and slowly, assuredly, she went from cold to cautious to complete. She knew who she was and whom she wanted to be. Then Max came along. She gave him a chance because she got the vibe, and when Sally knew Max was the one, she let it happen and let everything else go.

The only thing happening for Parker, unfortunately, was that long journey back to Innsbruck. Despondent, he sunk into the back seat. Doctor Frank hadn't said a word until the cab came to a stop just outside of the Vienna train station. Sitting up front, the demure doctor twisted around to turn his statured head toward Parker. "I know this is a hard thing to deal with, but you can't let your mind become gripped by this relationship. The only sound advice I can give you is to make a concerted effort to let her go."

It was a good try, and Parker was polite enough to say, "Thanks." But how could he let Brooke go? She was never really his.

Epilogue

The Duck Inn

THE FLIGHT back to Chicago seemed endless, but at least he was home; exhausted, disheartened and disillusioned. Only once before had Parker come back from a tour feeling that way. It was early in his career, after working with Mako on a series of college spring break trips. Every check-in had been maddening: collecting stacks of cash deposits, handing out keys to swarms of greedy hands. Every party was a potential calamity: overpriced liquor in hollow-bottomed cups, frenzied mobs at the wet T-shirt contests. Almost everyone he came in contact with was pathetic: hustlers and degenerates, wasted, would-be women and drunken, college-boy bums.

Then, after weeks of insanity, there was that harried departure, he and Mako hustling rented rollaway beds down A1A Boulevard. They were sweat-soaked and nerve-racked, like ex-cons risking parole. Nothing would stop them although it seemed like everyone would try, and eventually, they made the mad dash to the airport and *got out.* They were frazzled but alive; safe, but a little less sound than before. And all they came home with was the shock and dismay that only hindsight could afford. "Did we really do that?"

Yes, working spring break was the ultimate degradation. Parker had been tainted by that experience, by everyone who took from him but gave nothing back in return. Now he had Austria, and every fond memory of Innsbruck, of the majestic scenery, the places, and the people, would be burdened forever by the weight of what might have been.

Arriving home late the night before, Parker slept most of the day Sunday. He didn't crawl out of bed until early that evening, and that was just to draw a hot bath. Slipping into the deep, porcelain tub, Parker sought solace in the flickering light of a single candle. It gave off a peaceful sense of serenity. Beads of sweat grew on his forehead. Gathering momentum, they ran down his face, down his neck, and into the Epsom-salted bath. A chilled can of sparkling water kept his insides cool while reflections of his latest adventure rose like the steam, vaporizing into the darkness.

He should've known better than to fall for Brooke, despite the strong attraction, that incredible desire. If nothing else, he shouldn't have fallen so hard, so fast. It was sad to think that he could be so reckless with his heart. No doubt Zafrina's vision had skewed his senses.

Sitting on the tile floor nearby was Parker's phone. The consummate professional, he'd trained himself to avoid every personal call or text that he received while on tour: he just wouldn't allow for the distraction. Everyone he knew, family and friends, understood. They also knew he'd get back to them when the trip was over. That was his ritual, and so it began.

Snatching up the phone, Parker saw the white number thirteen resting atop the phone icon in a little red square. After balancing the drink can on the porcelain soap dish, he tapped the image, and then "voicemail." It opened to a list of familiar names, but Parker didn't swipe up to read them all. He was stuck on the very first name. It was a call from Lorrie, from her personal phone. Her message was only a few hours old.

"Shit." Parker said out loud. The last thing he wanted to do was to talk to Lorrie. He wasn't ready to comfort a friend in need. Reaching for his cool can, Parker took a quick pull, allowing the fizz to tickle his throat. Then he set it down and slanted the phone in front of his face to listen to her message.

"Hey, it's Lorrie. I was hoping we could meet before the debriefing tomorrow. I'm heading over to the Duck Inn tonight, and thought maybe you could join me, about eight?"

She paused as if they were actually speaking and waiting for his reply.

"So I thought maybe we could, you know, talk about stuff. There's just a lot going on, right? Call or text me if you can make it, okay?"

Parker set the phone on the floor and slid it across the tile a safe distance from any drips or splashes. It was already six forty-five. He thought, the hell with it, just blow Lorrie off until tomorrow. They could go out after the debriefing. Leaning forward to turn on the spigot, he let some more hot water trickle into the tub.

Parker's mind shifted back to Brooke, and he sunk lower in the bath. Where was she, and what was she doing out there in California? But those thoughts made the room feel gloomy. Parker's wounded heart thumped so hard it seemed as if, any second, tiny waves would ripple to the far end of the tub. But there were no waves, only woe. The Duck Inn, the old, neighborhood pub nearby, suddenly seemed like a much better place to be, even with Lorrie's problems.

THE SQUAT TAVERN was sparsely crowded. Lorrie sat at a tall table for two facing an old stone fireplace filled with charred wood and glowing embers. When he stepped into view her hazel eyes beamed behind those nerdy black specs; eyes that Parker always found inviting, like puddles of rain begging to be splashed through.

"I'm so glad you came," she said in a subdued tone. "That was one heck of a tour, huh?"

Shunning the stool, Parker stood opposite her and tossed out his signature line. "Could've been better, but it could've been a whole lot worse."

She waved a half-filled glass of beer at him. "I suppose you've had enough of these in Austria?"

"Enough is such a subjective term." As if on cue, a young server appeared. "I'll have what she has," Parker said. After wiping her hands on her short white apron, the girl nodded and left.

"I had a long talk with Jack," Lorrie confessed.

"That's good," Parker replied with all honesty. "I'm glad for that. And I'm happy for him but still worried about you."

"I'll be okay, Parker," Lorrie replied. "It'll be all right. I'm happy for Jack too. He finally has someone he can truly love." She took a drink of beer and then set it down, holding the pint glass delicately. "I can't say that I don't feel a little foolish for not knowing."

"How could you know? Jack didn't even know, not really."

"Well, I did know that something wasn't right with our relationship." Lorrie took another sip. "Let's just say that the bedroom wasn't our favorite space."

"Okay, we'll just leave it at that then. Besides, that's all in the past. Jack has finally found himself, and I met his new man. He seems like a great guy. Hopefully, they'll do all right and make something of it. I really appreciate that he was able to talk to you, to tell you everything himself. That's a good sign. It was the right thing to do."

"Yes, he stepped up and did right by me that way, at least." She pursed her lips to delve deeper. "You know as much as it hurts, I have to admit that I settled for Jack. He was easy because he was crazy about me, and he fit right into my life at the time. He was good to me in so many ways. I know he loved me, but still, there was always that missing piece. I just never knew what it was until now. I never understood why he couldn't love me completely, you know?"

Pleased to share in her soul-searching, Parker opined, "Sometimes life is just like going to the grocery store. You walk down the aisle, grab things that look good and throw them in your cart. It's not until after you check out and get home that you realize you never got the one thing you came in for."

Lorrie smiled. "You're making me hungry."

He peered into her diffident eyes. "And you're making me feel pretty good right now."

She furrowed her brow. "My wallowing in rejection pleases you?"

Parker was embarrassed. "I'm just relieved that's all." The server delivered his pint. When she left, Parker finished with his explanation. "You just seem to be handling it so well."

"I surprised you." She stated, sounding cocky.

"I just didn't think—"

"Concerned about my frailty?" Lorrie interrupted. Parker tightened his jaw to prepare for her chastisement. "Jack said you agreed to tell me about him and Franz and everything when you got home. He said he was too afraid to tell me himself, at first. Why would you do that?"

It was a leading question, but Parker attempted to answer anyway. "I just figured it would be better for you if it came from me. It seemed like the best thing to do for you."

"How do you know what's best for everyone else?"

His face flushed under her interrogation. "I just thought it would be easier that way. I figure it's difficult for anyone to get that kind of news long distance. News like that should be delivered in person, personally."

"So what if it's hard?" she asked curtly. "That doesn't mean it wasn't what's best for me." Lorrie batted her eyes. "It certainly wasn't the right thing to do for Jack. Telling me was his responsibility."

Lifting her glass, Lorrie readied to take a drink. Then she set the beer back down, deciding, instead, to finish her thoughts. "Maybe it's better for me to feel that pain, all of it, all at once. If a person doesn't experience things like that," she continued, "then they may never truly understand what's best for them, what they want and what they need. Without that, how can anyone grow as a person?" She balanced her reprimand by reaching out to gently rub his hand. "My point is that you shouldn't assume you know what's best for everyone."

Her caring gesture moved Parker. "I just know what you deserve."

Lorrie blushed. "Thank you." She lowered her eyes. "I do deserve better."

Parker felt compelled to make a revelation of his own. "I know how you feel, too, at least to some degree. I had a painful experience on this past trip. So yeah, I met someone. Someone I thought could be special. We had serious feelings for each other, but it's not going to work out. It didn't work out anyway. I learned that it wasn't right for her."

"But you thought she was right for you?"

Parker sighed. "That's the weird part. Getting home and taking some time to think, I realized that she wasn't right for me. I think I just got caught up in what I believed was meant to be." He shook his head. "The feelings were real though. The feelings we shared were the only real thing between us, and I guess that's not enough."

Lorrie tried to console him. "I'm so sorry for you. I'm truly sorry because I know that it hurts."

"Sure, it hurts, but I'll get over it. And I'm not sorry, either. I have no regrets. It's a part of life. I know that there's a process for healing, but you don't have to wallow in the hurt. I'm not going to wallow anyway. I won't allow for it."

Lorrie bucked up, too. "You're right. It's just too easy to feel sorry for yourself. After speaking with Jack, I decided that I'm done settling. I'm through with just accepting things. From now on, I'm going to decide what I want, and go after it."

Her declaration roused Parker to offer a toast. "So here's to getting what you want."

They clinked glasses and drank. Setting the beer down, Parker noticed that Lorrie wasn't really in a celebratory mood.

"All right, what is it?" he asked.

After drawing in her emotions with one deep breath, Lorrie replied. "I gave Don my notice on Friday."

"You what?"

"I quit. I gave Don my two weeks."

"You quit?" Parker squeezed out that last word with such genuine surprise and dismay that it left a high-pitched squeal hanging in the air.

She pretended not to hear him. Instead, she focused on the business implications. "Don agreed to move Daniella up to take over as Tour Ops Manager. I've been grooming her for the job just in case."

Parker bit at her admission like a distracted dog. "I thought you were grooming Jack for that?"

"So did everyone else."

Parker sighed loudly. "First Jack, then Sally and now you. How depressing. I'm being deserted." He grasped his skull in his hands. "Okay, so I'm back to wallowing."

Lorrie let out a sly grin. "Oh, Parker, you'll never be alone."

"Yeah, right. I still have Mako."

"Now that's depressing."

He took a long swig of beer, set it down carefully, and

shook his head like a horse shaking its mane. "All right, I'm ready. Give me the details."

Lorrie sat back and smirked. "For starters, I'm moving back to my parent's place in Wisconsin. I'm going to get my nursing degree. You know, something secure, with a solid future."

It was an excellent career choice for her, Parker thought. She was an assiduous professional and skilled communicator who could solve a problem in an instant all while leveraging her naturally empathetic disposition. He summed it up by saying, "You'll be exceptional in that role."

Lorrie cocked her chin and eyed him curiously. "But?"

"But?" Parker challenged. "Why do you think there's a 'but' in there?"

"Oh, there's a 'but' in there."

"No, there's not." He spoke adamantly at first. "There is a caveat, however."

Lorrie was all over his equivocation. "Hmm, a caveat, as in, 'but there's a caveat?'"

"Listen, it's a big move. I just hope you put some serious thought into it, that's all. It seems like a rather quick decision. I won't say rash, but sudden. I just hope it's not a reaction."

Lorrie's face glowed with endearment. She tilted forward, crossed her arms, and rested her elbows on the tabletop. "I know it might seem like a reaction, but honestly, I've always wanted to be in healthcare." She spoke with clarity, like someone who'd had a good looks-within and liked what she saw. "When I was a young girl I used to dream of being a doctor or a nurse. It wasn't because of the uniform or the stethoscope either. I've just always wanted to take care of people."

Parker found Lorrie's benevolent desire comforting. "You've done a great job taking care of me, anyway. Don, too, and the rest of our team."

Lorrie remained pensive. "I don't know how, but somewhere along the way, I just got sidetracked. Then came the opportunity to work at Tourcey Travel." She shook her head. "It's so easy to be seduced by the travel business." Parker shrugged in acknowledgment. Then Lorrie cocked her head as another revelation came to her. "You're gonna miss me, huh?"

Parker wasn't startled by her words but rather by the sentiment that they stoked inside of him. "Sure I'll miss you." That reply didn't fully explain how he felt. It couldn't because he only realized just how much he'd miss her after he spoke. "I'm just worried that things won't be the same," he said fumbling for the right thing to say, "with you so far away."

His sentimental words made Lorrie's aura glow. "I'll still be close, just north of Milwaukee." Lorrie reached for Parker's hand again. The anticipation of her touch this time, made his whole body tingle. "As long as we've been friends," she said warmly, "no one has been farther away than you. But you always come back, and we make it work."

Lorrie rubbed Parker's forearm. Something in her touch was healing. "I think you've found your calling," Parker said.

She only snickered, and Parker was left to wonder if she understood all that he meant. "Let's have a shot," she said. Without demur, Parker waved for the server and placed an order. Delving into more details, Lorrie spoke of her plans, of her family and the course she was about to chart.

The fire behind Parker crackled and flared to life, flashing in Lorrie's glasses and casting a mysterious orange hue across her face. It provided the perfect cover for the next change in her disposition. Raising a finger to her temple, she eyed him furtively. "Do you understand everything I said about my relationship with Jack?"

Parker was smug. "Well, the gist of it seemed to be that the intimacy wasn't very intimate."

"Not intimate, not at all. And that's not the only relationship I've had like that."

Parker felt pity for Lorrie's bad luck, but sympathy was the last thing on her mind. "What I'm saying Parker, is that I am a twenty-eight-year-old virgin."

Of all the recent surprises, this one startled Parker most. He wanted to say something witty, but all he could do was strike a contemplative pose and mumble, "I can't imagine how that could be."

"It's a choice Parker," she said. "People make choices."

"Sure," he said, "I understand that. I just wonder, well, why?"

She grinned as if expecting the question. "I guess I just never got that vibe." A cute laugh followed her playful jab. Parker only returned the grin and shrugged. Then Lorrie's serious demeanor returned. "Honestly though, no matter how intimate the relationships have been, I just never felt deep down inside that making love to that person was, you know, right."

She couldn't possibly have explained it better than that. She wasn't suffering from some repressed, abusive childhood experience. It was just her will; her desire not to share the most personal, vital aspect of her being with anyone until she felt it was the right thing to do for herself. Parker was quick to share that understanding. "When the right situation and the right person comes along," he said, "you'll know it."

The server delivered a pair of tiny glasses brimming with clear liquor. Lorrie slid one to Parker, and they raised the drink to their lips simultaneously. Slamming the goods, Parker savored the gentle burn that eased down his throat and settled like a hot ember in the pit of his stomach. Lorrie drank more slowly, appearing unaffected by the harsh taste. Easing the shot glass to the tabletop, she re-centered her specs on her nose, wiped her lips with a cocktail napkin, and then finally responded to his last statement. "I know, Parker. I do know."

Her long overdue response was strange, but not as unusual

as the gleam that settled in her eyes. It was the glare of a mutineer. Something had taken possession of his dear friend Lorrie, Parker realized. And although the following words he heard weren't something he ever expected Lorrie to say, they were her words, firmed by resolve and tempered by heartfelt desire. "I know that I want you to be the one."

Parker gasped. "To be the what?"

"The one. I want you to make love to me ... tonight." Parker struggled for air as if sucking on a vacuum. Lorrie continued, "I've put a great deal of thought into this decision, Parker, and I am certain about it. I just have to know what it feels like to make love to someone. I need to feel that closeness right now, and I can't do it with just anyone. You're the only one, Parker. You're the only one who cares enough for me." She fixed her mellow eyes on him. "I deserve you."

No longer reeling from her request, Parker now wrestled with her loving vibe. It came over him like a tsunami. Rather than blowing him away, though, it wrapped around him, coaxing out his true feelings for her. That vibe bound his wounded heart, allowing it swell once more.

Still, Parker was reticent, knowing how easy hearts can break. "Lorrie, you have no idea how flattered I am. But we have to consider the risks. There are real emotions on the line and a great friendship. What if it ruins what we have?"

"What if it only makes it better?" He had no response to that, so Lorrie continued. "I remember when we first met," she chuckled. "I had such a crush on you."

"You did?" He tried not to sound too thrilled.

"Oh yeah."

Lorrie's honesty was infectious. "Of course I was attracted to you too."

"You were?" She only sounded surprised.

"Sure I was. How could I not be? You're so amazing, and beautiful. Everyone is attracted to you, even gay guys for crying out loud." After they both laughed, Parker spoke seriously, bubbling over with emotion. "You're the most genuine person I've ever known. You stick with a guy, too. Every time I go away, it's like you're always there with me. And that goofy wordplay you do with me, parsing every syllable I say. I love that about you. I mean, it drives me crazy sometimes, but I love that."

Realizing all that he had said, Parker retreated. "Lorrie, you're precious to me, and what you're talking about is a big step. It's a real leap. I mean dang, what if it's a miss? What if it goes bad?"

"I'm not afraid of that Parker because I love you. I've always loved you and I always will. I've only been able to love you as a friend, a dear, sweet friend. And that's never going to change. That's the kind of foundation you want to build a relationship on, isn't it?"

Her words were punctuated by the passion in her voice and the twinkle in her eye. Parker also recognized the spark in her, too. It was the same one that burnished whenever they got together after a tour. Convinced that she had come for the fun of it, to listen to his stories, Parker now realized that she had also come for the storyteller.

"I care so much about you, though," she concluded. "If you don't feel comfortable, I understand. If it's just not the right thing to do."

The right thing? Parker thought. It was a beautiful thing, the most treasured gift that anyone could give away. He moved beside her, close enough so she could see the acceptance on his face. Lorrie's compliance came from the whole of her being, shimmering out in waves of a brilliant aura.

Basking in its glow, Parker stared into her eyes, and into her heart. "My place?"

Grinning happily, Lorrie just nodded.

"How early do you have to be at work tomorrow?"

She shrugged. "I already told Don I wouldn't be in 'til noon."

LORRIE REMOVED her long quilted coat and shook off a chill. Parker slipped off his fleece pullover and then hung their outerwear in the nearby closet. Lorrie remained stiff, planted in the entryway of Parker's apartment like a flowerpot.

"Do you want a drink?" he asked.

She refused the offer with a shake of her head.

"How about a cup of coffee or tea?"

Again she refused. That's when Parker noticed a tiny white-gray down feather stuck in her hair. Carefully, he plucked it off and held it up for her to see. She smiled and reached out. Parker thought she wanted the feather, but instead, she grasped his hand.

That touch crossed the last barrier that kept them apart. Caressing her cheek with his fingers, Parker kissed her. Lorrie kissed him back. It was a fragile kiss, one they lingered over; not to savor the sensation, but to relish the realization that something long dormant had finally been allowed to blossom. Slowly parting, they opened their eyes to gaze at each other like first time lovers do. Lorrie bit her lip. "Do you have pajamas for me?"

"Sure," he replied, and they walked into the bedroom. Reaching behind the door, Parker pulled a cream-colored, thermal Henley off the hook. "Try my winter jams."

"Don't you have bottoms?"

"I just wear boxers."

She frowned. "Kinda cold for boxers?"

"I could light a fire?"

Lorrie glanced around, perplexed. "You don't have a fireplace?"

"I know."

He smiled adorably, and she laughed. Then they just stood there, gazing at each other in sheer bliss. Parker broke the silence suddenly. "Well, I've got a down comforter?"

Lorrie snagged the Henley from his hands. "That'll do."

THEY LOUNGED IN BED, cozy beneath the billowy, red plaid comforter. Resting on their sides, face to face, the couple talked and talked. There was so much more to Lorrie, more than Parker had ever known, and those intimate insights were like a fishing line to his heart. He had taken the hook, and now she was reeling him in, profoundly endearing him until he leaned over and kissed her gently, right in the middle of a sentence. She breathed quickly and smiled.

Never mind the details, the fact was that Parker had never made love with anyone so happy with it all. Between every pleasurable moan and passionate kiss, a grin would cross her lips. More than a few times it seemed like she'd laugh right out loud. Perhaps she was just relieved, he thought, to finally have the experience. Maybe she felt the same way he did during that drunken, late-night swim back in Mexico: devoid of fear, perfectly centered, and positively ecstatic.

Parker's bedroom had blackout blinds so he could sleep at odd hours, whenever the demands of travel required it. He and Lorrie took advantage of that, waking just after nine the next morning. Resting on his chest, Lorrie felt his whiskers as if testing whether it was safe or not to kiss him.

"The beard's safe but not the breath," Parker stated.

She kissed him anyway. "Not so bad." Lorrie reached beneath the covers for the Henley. "Now I need a shower."

"No, no, a little lower," he joked, "and to the right."

She smacked him playfully and then sat up to slip the just-discovered jersey over her shoulders. Her head popped through the opening like a jack-in-the-box, but she came out all-smiles, and Parker could barely hold back the urge to grab her hips and move her on top of him.

Fortunately, it was an urge he didn't have to suppress. Lorrie initiated the maneuver. Shaking her hair back, she swung a leg over his prone torso. Parker felt pressure from her arms when Lorrie placed her hands on his chest and leaned forward. Then he felt her weight shift as she eased herself on top of him.

Neither Parker or Lorrie responded vocally to the pleasure, at first. They were content just to focus on the feel, the comfortable, consuming sensation of making love to someone you loved. They didn't even kiss, but he did reach under the loose fitted shirt to feel the tender flesh of her back. It was an incredible softness, and it urged his hands to caress the whole contour of her torso, from slender waist to broad hips. Lorrie slowly swayed up and down with the gentlest of movements. She stared at Parker with a look of wonder, giving into the temptation, once in a while, to close her eyes, ease her head back, and allow their harmony to possess her.

Parker practiced a holdback so the couple could share the peak of orgasm together. It was difficult, but he succeeded, and immediately afterward she collapsed in his arms.

"So now what?" he asked kissing her cheek.

"Now I take a shower." Her eyes opened wide. "Oh wait, your tub. I've always wanted to soak in that big tub of yours."

"No, I mean, what's the plan?" Parker was asking about the big picture, the two of them together, but Lorrie seemed unaware. He tried to change course. "So, when's the move?"

"Oh, that's mostly done. I made a run up there yesterday morning."

"I guess it's just off to Wisconsin, huh?"

Lorrie appeared to ignore his question, easing herself off the bed. Suddenly she turned back and pounced, wriggling onto his prone body once again. Parker locked hold of her hands. Surprised by her strength, he laughed as she wrestled his arms down over his head and pinned them tight to the bed. Her face dropped so low that her hair tickled his forehead.

"Listen to me, Mr. Moon. Two weeks from today, when you go on your California Coastal Tour, I'll go up to my parent's house in Wisconsin. And when you come home, I'll be waiting right here with a family size Villa Nova pizza, sausage and mushrooms, extra crispy. I'll bring a really good bottle of cheap wine, and you can tell me all about your trip. And I'll feel your excitement through those stories. I'll see the fun you had, shining from your eyes. And then when I feel like taking your whole, sweet-self into my arms and kissing you, I will."

He cocked an eyebrow. "Why don't 'cha kiss me now?"

A grin eased out of the corner of her mouth, and she reached for his lips. They came together slowly, softly pressing. They held that kiss while gazing deeply into one another's eyes. Finally pulling away, Lorrie sat up. Parker was still a bit insecure.

"So you're sure this can work?"

Lorrie smirked. "The drive will take about two hours, although maybe longer if traffic sucks which it always does. It doesn't make any sense to fly, but I did run the train schedules. That's an option when the weather is bad, and I'm in school and have my own place in Milwaukee." She hopped up and strutted away. "Now I'm getting in your tub." Instead of the bathroom, though, Lorrie veered off into the living room. "But first, some tunes."

"My phones in here," Parker called.

Lorrie didn't respond, and seconds later, she could be heard rummaging through his collection of records. "I want to listen to your mom's vinyl," she giggled.

"How 'bout some Sarah Vaughn?" Parker mused.

"Ah. Nope."

He heard the scrape of needle on album and quickly recognized the obscure Bruce Springsteen ballad. The singer's strained, somber voice greeted Parker like an old friend. He voiced his approval. "Nice selection."

Stepping back into the entryway, Lorrie leaned against the doorframe and crossed her arms. "Why don't you get up and make breakfast?"

Parker slipped his hands behind his head, propping himself up to better admire her beauty. "Remember the first time I made breakfast for you?" he asked.

"Yeah, basted eggs," she said with a cringe, "who has basted eggs?"

"Everyone should. Hard whites, soft yolks, it's the perfect egg."

Lorrie grinned. "Well, everyone can't have *you*."

She turned away. Parker called out as she disappeared into the bathroom. "Too bad we didn't make love back then."

Lorrie yelled back. "Then we wouldn't have this."

He heard the bath water come on. Next, the Henley flew out of the bathroom door and slid across the hardwood floor. It stopped just short of the bedroom threshold, but Parker was too comfortable to give in to its temptation. He rolled onto his side and closed his eyes, but then Lorrie hurried into the room wrapped in one of his fancy, souvenir hotel towels. "I better do this right now." She strolled to the nightstand and scooped up her phone.

"Do what?" he asked.

She was too busy tapping away on her keypad to reply. A second later, Parker's phone dinged. Lorrie grabbed it and tossed it on the plaid comforter beside him. "I just forwarded you my new address. I know how you are, so please save it right away?"

Grinning sheepishly, Parker picked up the phone and rolled onto his back. Lorrie sauntered off to the bathroom as if satisfied. The funky melody, however, re-focused in Parker's ears, distracting him from the given task. The serenity of that soft, sweet rhythm revived his contemplative mood.

Every detail of his recent ordeal flashed through Parker's mind, from Zafrina to Brooke to Lorrie, all the people, places, and problems in between. Suddenly remembering Lorrie's admonishment, he forwarded her text, and a new contact window opened up. Parker's jaw dropped when he read the address:

> *home*
> *4613 Silver Lake Lane*
> *Belgium, Wisconsin 53004*
> *United States*

Parker couldn't hold back the laugh. It would've busted his gut. Beyond the soothing melody, he heard Lorrie splashing in the tub. Then all of Zafrina's prophetic words came rushing back to him. These were the ones though, that got him out of bed:

"The fear you have is not with the water itself, but what lies beneath it. You fear having to face those emotions hidden deep inside of you. But the water ... the water is where you belong."

The End

CPSIA information can be obtained
at www.ICGtesting.com
Printed in the USA
FFOW03n0910310318
46112397-47137FF

9 780999 748220